Some Mother's Child

Also by Amanda Rayner

An Accidental Daughter

√s

Some Mother's Child

a novel by

AMANDA RAYNER

For Barbara
Who knows what it is really like!!
Love
Amanda Rayner xx
17th March 1997.

RICHARD COHEN BOOKS · London

The characters and events in this story are fictional
and any resemblance to individuals, living or dead,
is coincidental.

British Library Cataloguing in Publication Data:
A catalogue record for this book is available from the British Library

ISBN 1 86066 093 2

First published in Great Britain in 1997 by
Richard Cohen Books
7 Manchester Square
London W1M 5RE

1 3 5 7 9 8 6 4 2

Typeset by Palimpsest Book Production Limited,
Polmont, Stirlingshire
Printed in Great Britain by
Mackays of Chatham plc

For my parents 'Diz' and 'Ada'
for giving me a love of words

Acknowledgements

The author extends her thanks to the following:

Ivan Allen of Global Events Ltd for a solid grounding in the exhibition world; Jan Boxshall for her sympathetic editing; David Broadhead, General Manager, Claridge's Hotel; Michael Franks, Jenny Roman and the DMG Exhibitions mob; Clemency Firth for her knowledge of matters 'U' and 'Non-U'; Dr David Lewin and Jason Payne-James for forensic information; Colin Maitland for period matters musical; Stuart McInnes, Pritchard, Engelfield for matters legal; Phil McKenna, Defense Attaché's Office, US Embassy; the Metropolitan Police; Ray Simpson at Earls Court Exhibition Centre for guided tours of the building; Ros Skinner at Pitman's; Vickie Taylor, Marketing Manager at Ragdale Hall Health Hydro; Yvonne Walker at J. Lyons and other sources to numerous to mention.

PART ONE

Build-Up

Jo Edwardes was about to say 'Cut' to Tony, her cameraman, when they found the body sprawled face down in the grime. At first it was difficult to tell exactly what it was as the dust stirred up by the contractors' pickaxes was still swirling around the huge concrete cavern. The yellow arc lights didn't help as they cast odd shadows, brightly illuminating some of the squat stone pillars while throwing others into darkness. These patches of light and shade looked peculiar on the TV monitor and Jo had seen that to shoot much more of the old pool area would simply be a waste of tape. Then one of the workmen had yelled and all fourteen people in the vast basement responded to the urgent tone in his voice, rushing over to where he stood.

'Keep going,' Jo hissed at Tony as he gazed incredulously through his lens. 'Get that.' She indicated the heap on the floor, feeling a thrill run through her. 'And everyone's reactions,' she added, trying to sound unruffled, even though her heart was pounding with excitement.

Christ, it's incredible! Jo thought to herself. *My first real directing job and I fall across something like this. Stay calm, just stay calm. Don't let them see you're twitchy. Remember it's* your *shout.* You're *in control. They'll do what you tell them. This is your film crew and you're their director.* If she said it to herself often enough she might believe it.

This was what Jo had been working towards ever since she decided when she was twelve years old that she wanted a career in television. It had taken years of hard grind, slogging her way from tea-girl to focus puller to location assistant. But at last Jo was doing what she wanted, directing a major television documentary, and she was determined it would be good.

She heaved a sigh of relief. She had so nearly not been in the basement of the Pimlico Centre. She and her crew had only just started filming in Britain's leading exhibition centre, an old thirties building which sat majestically alongside the Thames, and they had a huge amount to get through. On a preliminary visit she'd been told about the vast empty water tanks in the basement, operated by ancient hydraulic machinery. They had once been used to supply water to the exhibition halls above but had been redundant for many years, and now they were being dismantled to make way for a new cinema complex. Shooting in the basement wasn't on her original schedule but yesterday, when she'd been informed that this was her last chance to see it before the machinery was taken away to the Museum of London, she'd followed a gut instinct to capture it on film. So she'd dragged her crew away from the three vast halls where they were shooting the build-up of the Home Maker Exhibition, which was just beginning its annual three-month tenancy – and almost instantly regretted it.

As soon as she'd left the sunshine of the Embankment and descended into the gloom of the basement Jo had kicked herself. This was going to be a waste of time – she should have stuck to the original plan and left the crew upstairs. Especially as the programme she was making for the *Women in Focus* series was about Suzanne Prescott, the exhibition's chief executive, and she was only filming the exhibition itself as background material. It looked as if this morning's work would end up on the cutting-room floor – and put her over budget in the process. That was the moment when she'd been about to say 'Cut' – and when the workman's discovery showed she'd been right to follow her instinct.

Jo felt exultant. Finding a decaying body in a basement when she happened to have a full film crew with her was a massive bonus. It was the stuff romantic novels were made of, not reality.

Tony obediently adjusted his focus and started with a close-up of the body before pulling back to pan round the group. The man who had made the discovery was crouched on his haunches. His mask was still up over his nose and mouth, keeping the dust out, and his hard hat was pulled forward. In between his eyes stared out, wide with shock, at the foreman who stood over him, by the body's head, his fists shoved deep in his pockets. Behind him the other six members of the demolition team clustered uncertainly. Facing the crouching man was Tony with the camera, the attached microphone picking up the sound of everyone's deep breathing; Bill stood beside him with the hand-held arc light which threw the figure on the floor into sharp relief. Jo and her assistant Laura hovered at the back. At the body's feet were the representatives of Exhibitions International plc.

Gordon Mayfield, the administration director, was there to check that the contractors did nothing to disrupt the work going on overhead in the main halls of the Pimlico Centre as the preparation for the Home Maker Exhibition got underway. Alan Waterman, the marketing director, was overseeing the TV crew, making sure they didn't get in the way.

'Don't fancy being in your shoes when you tell Suzanne. She'll go ape-shit!' hissed Gordon in Alan's ear.

'What makes you think *I'm* going to be the one to tell her? You're the admin guy,' Alan growled back, in equally subdued tones.

'And you're in charge of PR and *this* isn't what I would call good PR, would you? Sorry, mate, it's your baby!' Gordon's relief at having passed the buck was evident.

'Some baby!' murmured Alan, looking with distaste at the crumpled form at his feet, accepting that it would be down to him to tell their Chief Executive about the find.

The body lay on its front close to one of the stone pillars that supported the props under the enormous tanks. It was at right angles to the large pipe which had carried the water into the hydraulic system. Its right hand was raised above its head; what was left of its right cheek rested on the floor. The other limbs were bent and contorted. Its position was typical of every body ever seen in a TV murder film. All that was needed to complete the picture was a white line round it. Where it differed from the TV images was in its actual appearance.

The skin looked like a cross between thick parchment and well-tanned leather. Unlike the faces of the onlookers, shiny with sweat from the heat of the lights, it was dry and very wrinkled. Over the years as the body's moisture had disappeared its skin had shrunk around its skeleton so its rib cage jutted out and the line of the bones beneath could clearly be seen. In some places, such as the bent elbow and knee, the skin was stretched so tightly that the bones strained against it, almost breaking through. The head was bald and the skin on the face had all but disappeared, revealing the hollow cheeks of the skull. There was also a deep gash across what had once been its forehead. The eyes had long gone but its exposed teeth made it look as if it were grinning at some huge personal joke. Across what had once been the body's buttocks was a bit of thin cloth. Other than that it was bare.

'No, don't do that!' said the foreman sharply as one of the men stepped forward and bent down as if to turn it over. 'We'll have to get the police in. Better leave it until they get here.'

'I'll go and call them. For crying out loud, will you turn that bloody camera off!' The conversation jolted them all back to reality and Alan had suddenly realised that they were still filming.

'OK. Cut,' Jo said unwillingly. 'And don't you dare tell me there was a hair in the gate.' She knew it was a feeble attempt at humour but being flippant maintained her authority with the crew and protected her from the sight on the floor.

'No, it's fine,' confirmed Tony, as he peered into the camera.

The workmen were getting agitated and had moved away to huddle in a corner with the foreman, who was insisting that they touched nothing. They were paid by the hour so if they didn't work they didn't get paid. As their voices rose one of them stepped away from the others.

'Soddin' company. It ain't our fault that some fuckin' idiot gets himself holed up in here, is it? Why should we have to suffer 'cos of 'im?' He pulled a cigarette packet out of his jeans and lit a match. As the flame flared he saw a glimmer out of the corner of his eye.

''Ere, you with the light,' he called over to Bill, who looked at Jo for approval.

She nodded and, checking that Alan had actually left the area to go and call the police, quietly said to Tony, 'Follow him and see what he's found, but don't let him know you're filming. I'll stay here so I don't give the game away. Go *on*!' she urged in a loud whisper.

Oh God, I love filming! Jo thought to herself, again aware of the excitement she was feeling about the material they were getting on camera.

The little group made their way across the basement and round the other side of one of the six large hydraulic hoists. 'No, round 'ere, mate. I'm sure I saw somethin', yeah, look there. What's that?'

Bill raised the light and then stepped the rest of the way round the large black pipe. The light glinted on its paintwork and as he moved the beam slowly down its length a long green-tinged shadow spread across the floor. Carefully propped between two of the huge bolts that anchored the hoist to the concrete floor was an old, very dusty, empty champagne bottle. The camera played over its surface.

The workman erupted. 'Jesus Christ! Do you mean to tell me that we're losing pay 'cos some old geezer got himself so pissed he couldn't get out of this place? Fuckin' idiot. I'm going for a coffee. You coming?' he asked the rest of the work crew as he stomped off in disgust.

'Cut'.

If anyone had looked through Suzanne Prescott's office door that morning they would have sworn that the chief executive of Exhibitions International plc was hard at work on that year's show. Although the days were getting longer there was still a chill in the air and Suzanne reached over the back of her chair to pull an old cardigan round her shoulders. Work was the last thing on her mind as she sat staring at, without seeing, the papers on her desk.

She glanced at the clock. Ten-fifteen. *Ten o'clock*, she thought. *At ten o'clock they were due to start on that basement.* Maybe she should have gone after all? She swallowed hard and shut her eyes, remembering how she had battled with the board to stop them doing this work. If they had only listened. 'God I tried, I really tried,' she said to herself, opening her eyes again to fix them on the clock.

She could still remember how she had felt when Jonathan had given her the news. 'They want to do *what*?' She recalled how noticeably her voice had risen as she leaned across her desk all those months ago to stare at her financial director. Jonathan had jumped slightly at the intensity of her question and she had made a mental note not to take her feelings out on him. After all, it wasn't his fault. Jonathan repeated what he had just said, this time expanding the information he had given her.

'The Board of the Pimlico Centre have decided to convert the basement of the building into a multi-cinema complex. They've applied for planning permission which has been approved, and because of the age of the building they've also got a bloody great grant from the council. They're going to rip out all the old pool stuff that was sealed under the floor back in the sixties. Everything – the tanks, props, pillars and the hydraulic mechanisms. The only time they reckon it can be done is during our build-up period in the first two weeks in April.

'It's going to be a bloody nightmare,' he continued. 'Bad enough trying to get the show houses built in Pimlico Three and those huge stands in Pim One without the added disruption of major building works going on beneath our feet. It means that all the cabling, water and waste pipes that we usually drop into the space between the floor and the top of the sealed tank are going to have to be channelled in properly which will take time – and cost us. Unfortunately there's nothing we can do about it.'

'Why not?' She'd demanded. 'It's during our tenancy period and, bearing in mind that they screwed us for even more money when we renewed the year before last, I'm buggered if I'm going to let 'em start swinging pickaxes while we're there.'

'It's not as simple as that.' He had walked round the desk to stand beside Suzanne. 'I've gone through the tenancy contract and if you look here,' in her mind's eye she could still see his pointing finger indicating the paragraph half way down the page, 'it stipulates exactly what we get under the terms of the contract. It clearly identifies all three halls, Pimlico One, Two and Three; the offices we're allocated under the contract, the hospitality suites, loading areas, the twelve parking bays in the front car park. It also says what's not included: the public catering sites, their own management offices and hospitality rooms, the public car parks – and I think this is where they've got us: "any other area with its designated contents not specifically stipulated shall be deemed for the purpose of this Agreement to be retained under the control and jurisdiction of the Pimlico Centre Ltd." In other words the basement.'

She recalled how he had tried to show her he was in control of the situation. 'I've already got the lawyers on to it just in case, but I don't hold out much hope. I gather all the original thirties equipment is still down there but the tank was sealed in 1966 and no one has used it since. If we had used it just once in the last thirty odd years then we might be able to argue the toss. But as we've always found it easier to bring in our own tanks when we've needed water it's going to be difficult to stop them. I've asked Gordon to give me an estimate on what it's going to cost us to reroute all the cabling because if we can't stop it then I fully intend to make the bastards pay us a hefty compensation figure.'

'Jonathan, compensation won't come into it.' Suzanne had looked up from the document in front of her. 'They are *not* renovating the basement and that's final. My God, can you imagine the fuss the exhibitors will make if that lot is going on as they move in? Jesus! We'll have everyone of our 1,200 exhibitors in the office moaning at us, probably led by Old Man Malloy, demanding a discount. And knowing that lot they'll move so damn fast it'll make Concorde look slow. Hesketh, Dinglefield had better find a way out of this,' she had slapped the contract with the palm of her hand, 'or else.' Or else what she hadn't said. How could she – she already knew that they wouldn't win, but she had to fight.

Jonathan got the message and had quickly left Suzanne's office. What she didn't know then was that the solicitors had already told Jonathan they couldn't stop the plans going ahead. However, she had to admit he had stuck to his guns about the compensation.

He timed it well and the tactics he used had won her respect. When he finally told her that there really was nothing they could to stop the work, the building contractors had already been in touch with Gordon to discuss the reorganisation of the creation of this year's Home Maker Exhibition. They had co-operated with him to ensure that, on paper at least, their work would interfere as little as possible with the build-up of the exhibition going on five feet above their heads in the main halls. Jonathan had established that in truth the disruption was going to be minimal and had assured her that with a bit of luck most of the exhibitors wouldn't notice a thing. That aside, Jonathan had had several meetings with the Pimlico Centre's solicitors to agree a compensation package worth close on quarter of a million pounds.

Suzanne sighed. He *had* got a very good deal indeed out of the Pimlico Centre but it still didn't change anything. Of course, from a business view what they were doing made total sense. With over 30,000 square feet going begging beneath the exhibition halls putting in a cinema complex was logical, but sense didn't have anything to do with her feelings. The whole development would disrupt the exhibition – *her* exhibition – the one she had worked so hard for. The one to which she had devoted her life, making her so wealthy it had bought her total financial and emotional independence. She was so close to her final goal – and any disturbance might prevent her from achieving the one thing she had worked towards all these years.

'I know the hairdresser isn't due until Wednesday, but my hair needs washing and setting *today*. You seem to forget that I pay a lot of money to live here so I can still have a bit of freedom. Freedom! It's more like a bloody prison camp. Now get me a hairdresser!' Maggie hit the control unit on her wheelchair and propelled herself rapidly out of the door and into her living room. It was the closest she could get to flouncing out of the room. June trailed unhappily after her.

'Please, Maggie, don't be difficult. You know what happens when you get upset, your blood pressure goes up and you find it even harder than usual to get about, don't you?' June hovered in the hallway, not daring to follow her charge. Her voice had a wheedling tone which made Maggie even snappier.

'Don't patronise me. I've got bloody arthritis, not Alzheimer's – I do know what's going on and how I react which is why I try to keep calm. *You're* the one who's upsetting me, *you're* the one who's making me ill, arguing with me.'

'I'm not arguing, just pointing out . . .'

Maggie didn't bother to turn her chair round as she shouted angrily from the living room, 'Yes you are, and if I get worse because of what you're doing you'll be in such trouble . . .'

The threat hung in the air. June stood and played nervously with the frill on her apron as she tried to work out what to do. Maggie Edwardes was easily The Warren's most difficult inmate and her ability to wind herself up into a high rage over nothing was well known amongst the carers who came in each day to look after the residents.

June gave a sigh. 'I'm going to talk to Stella and see what she says.'

'God, you're useless. Can't you do anything without referring to that busybody?' Maggie muttered sullenly from the other room knowing that unwittingly, by referring the problem to the warden, June had beaten her. It was not that Stella was a battleaxe – far from it. It was more that once she was brought into something it was difficult to get rid of her. Some people bemoaned the way she would just breeze in and out of their homes, but the relatives of the residents of The Warren agreed that a nosey warden was really what was needed in sheltered accommodation.

Maggie heard the front door click shut behind June as she hurried away. She didn't really want her hair done. It could have easily have waited the two days until Wednesday, but she was bored, and when she got bored she got fractious.

Slowly she turned her chair round and the engine whirred as she went down the corridor to the kitchen. Despite the fact that her fingers were knotted and bent with arthritis she was able to move around the kitchen and fend for herself. It was the combination of independence and care that had finally persuaded Maggie to sell the mansion flat in Little Venice, Maida Vale and move to The Warren. The other factor had been Joanne's insistence at finding her own place.

When Joanne had first said she was moving out twelve years ago

Maggie had done all she could to talk her out of it. Not because she particularly liked having her daughter around – she reminded her too much of Howard – but because selfishly she knew that in the long term she could not cope with the large flat by herself. She needed Joanne to look after both it and her. Her daughter leaving home made Maggie aware of her own approaching years and for how long she had been alone.

She hated it.

But Joanne had shown a quiet determination her mother had not recognised. She had made it quite clear she was going, waiting until she had exchanged contracts on her own maisonette in Hampstead before telling Maggie about it.

If Joanne had been had been moving in with a man then maybe Maggie would have accepted it more easily. It was the fact that she was moving out to be by herself that had really offended her. Though she would never admit it Maggie admired Joanne for being so determined to go after what she wanted. It had reminded her of herself as a young woman, hell bent on achieving her own goals, but those memories were upsetting. They reminded her of what she had lost. So instead Maggie channelled her feelings into anger at what she saw as her daughter's desertion, and resentment of her youthful vitality.

Maggie knew that Joanne had felt guilty for leaving her but she wasn't going to let her off the hook. She hated herself for making her daughter feel miserable but, after everything that she felt the last time someone walked out on her, why not? She exploited Jo's guilt at every opportunity and when, a few years later, Maggie had been forced to swallow her pride and finally admit that she could no longer cope in the big Maida Vale flat by herself, it had been Joanne who had scoured London to find The Warren. And as much as Maggie was loath to admit it, it was perfect.

The block had been specially built with easy access for wheelchairs. All the flats had carefully adapted kitchens and bathrooms so the residents could look after themselves as much as possible. The warden lived in her own house alongside the flats and, as each room had an alarm button, she could be with a resident almost immediately if they buzzed for help, or if any other problems came up – such as Maggie Edwardes' tantrums.

Stella listened thoughtfully, a slight frown on her face, as June filled her in. 'There, there. It's not your fault. It's just Maggie being difficult again. Come with me and let's sort it out together, shall we?' Stella bustled out of the door as June scurried after her. Stella's lips were pursed as she found Maggie's key on the large bunch in her hand. She rang the bell as a courtesy but didn't wait for a response before inserting it in the lock and pushing open the door.

'Only me, Maggie. Now, what's all this I hear from June about you making trouble again, hmm?'

'*I'm* not making trouble. It's that lazy good-for-nothing. I make a simple request to get my hair done and you would think I had asked her to fly me to the moon. Now Stella, am I being unreasonable?'

Stella looked down at the woman in the wheelchair, noticing the way she had slumped into her seat. *Funny how she manages to look particularly frail whenever she wants anything* she thought to herself as she caught sight of the Zimmer frame in the corner of the room. When she had popped in earlier that morning it had been in the bedroom and as no-one had been in to clean it was obvious that Maggie had used it herself. Once again she was crying wolf.

'Maggie, don't you think you're being just a teensy, weensy bit unaccommodating? The hairdresser is due on Wednesday and I know we can get you an appointment at any time you like then.' Stella was using her special voice, the sing-song one that she felt was soothing and comforting.

To Maggie it was simply infuriating. 'I don't want an appointment on Wednesday. I want one now. But of course a pair of frumps like you wouldn't understand how important it is to a woman like me always to look nice.' Maggie's tone made it clear that she thought herself superior to Stella. The insult struck home.

'Maggie, this has got to stop. We can't expect everyone to drop everything just because you want them to. Now we've told you. The hairdresser is due on Wednesday and that's an end to it.'

Maggie had other ideas and the row continued, going round and round in circles while she grew increasingly agitated. June stood and watched in silence until, at last, Stella threw her hands dramatically in the air. 'Enough. June, stay here and watch her.' She made her way down the corridor to the phone in the kitchen.

'Hello, is that Laura? Laura, I'm sorry to bother you. It's Stella. Is Joanne available please?'

'I'm sorry, Stella, but she's in an important meeting and definitely can *not* be disturbed. I can get her to call you as soon as she comes out.'

'Well, if you could, Maggie's playing up again and we're at our wits' end.'

'I'll make sure she calls you. She shouldn't be more than half an hour.'

Jo sat stony faced opposite Dinah Deadman, her executive producer on *Women in Focus*. When Dinah had approached her, offering a package that included not only the role of assistant director on the whole series but also gave her the chance to produce and direct the programme featuring Suzanne Prescott, she had leapt at the chance.

Jo knew that giving her this double role meant Boadicea Productions would save money, but she didn't care.

Suzanne Prescott had spent her entire working life hiding behind the Home Maker Exhibition, so much so that very little was known about this enigmatic, aloof, but extremely wealthy and powerful woman, and as a result she was on everyone's 'want to interview' list. That they had got her to agree to take part in the programme and that Jo was going to be the one to make it was a great start to her career as a director. She was determined to get to know the real Suzanne Prescott, however much work it took.

Over the years Jo had begun to think that her turn would never come and even though during that time she had been privy to the various rows and disputes that accompanied every production, this was the first time she had had to face Dinah herself. The anticipation of the meeting on top of that morning's discovery at the Pimlico Centre had sent adrenaline pumping through her.

'I'm sorry, Dinah. The budget is set. And I am not going to let you steamroller me into redoing the figures, cutting it or curtailing the location stuff. I still maintain it's important to have the full crew down at the Pimlico Centre for both the build-up and break-down of the exhibition once it's all over, as well as for the exhibition itself. I mean, it's not as if we're going to be able to say "Oops, sorry, missed a bit can we pop down again?". If we miss it then that's it.' Jo had placed a couple of files on the table in front of her with another open on her lap which she prodded with her forefinger as she spoke, emphasising the points she was making.

'Also,' she continued, 'it's not as if I've got the luxury of working on just the Prescott episode, is it? Come on, Dinah, I know this is an expensive series to make but you're saving a packet with me doubling up. Don't forget, I'm still battling with the other programmes as well. I'm not going to let you make me into the fall guy on the budget. It's not my fault that we've got to run off copies of the body footage for the police, but we discussed costs when you first offered me *Women in Focus* and you promised me then that once the budget had been agreed it would *not* be cut. You also agreed that my costings were sound, so not only can't I, but I also categorically refuse to compromise the quality of the production, or its professionalism, because I'm forced either to use a smaller crew or less experienced people.'

Jo closed her file and tossed it on to the empty chair beside her. She pushed herself to her feet and began pacing up and down the room, trying hard not to let a note of hysteria enter her voice, but still wanting Dinah to know how angry she was. 'I could understand this if I had come in from outside but I've been with Boadicea Productions long enough to know how we work. For Christ's sake, one way or another over the last eight years I've done virtually every job in the place, including making the tea, so I should be able to stick to a bloody budget.'

Jo stopped in front of Dinah, who during her outburst had sat and listened in silence while she grew more and more heated.

'Of course, we've got the release forms so we could always sell the footage to the news networks,' Dinah mused.

'Like hell! And give away what's likely to be the best part of the whole programme, never mind the whole bloody series? Come on, Dinah, with footage like this, enough pre-publicity and people's bloodlust, we should be guaranteed good ratings.'

'So what do you suggest we do?'

'I don't suggest *we* do anything. As far as I'm concerned *Women in Focus* is now in production on an agreed budget. You always taught me that once a production got underway then the budget was set. It is my responsibility as the *producer*,' she emphasised the word, 'to spend that budget as carefully as I can, which I will do, provided you don't pull it away from me. You take one penny back and I swear I'll take this thing so far into the red you won't know what's hit you!'

Dinah frowned as she crossed her arms and rested them on her desk. She looked up at Jo standing at the other side of the desk, leaning on her turned-out hands, eyes blazing. Very quietly and calmly, she sat back in her chair again. 'OK. Keep the budget as it is. But if it goes over . . .' She didn't bother to finish the sentence.

Jo gave her a tight smile, gathered up her files, left Dinah's office and dived into the ladies on her way back to her own. She put the files on the shelf above the sinks and looked at herself shaking in the mirror. 'Watch it, Edwardes,' she said out loud to her reflection as she ran cold water and splashed it on her face. She knew she had come very close to overstepping the mark, but *Women in Focus* was too important to her to let even the executive producer walk all over her.

You were lucky to get away with it, she told herself as she headed back to her own office. *Rubbish*, said another voice, unbidden, at the back of her mind. *You got away with it because Dinah respects you as a professional.* It was a startling thought and Jo stopped for a moment to consider it before, smiling and shaking her head, she carried on.

But it had been an accurate one. At that moment Dinah Deadman was talking to Boadicea Productions' financial manager.

'I'm sorry, Jack, but there's no way Jo is going to budge. We're going to have to look at cutting something else or trying for another co-production. I must admit she surprised me. I really thought she'd agree but she wouldn't be persuaded. Actually I admire her for it. I think if she had just said "yes" I would have worried that I'd given it to the wrong person. As it is I reckon with the body footage already in the can and some decent editing, we should get some very interesting stuff out of her. Now let me have a look at the *All in Good Time* proposals and see what we can do there.'

The moment Jo got back to her desk she saw Laura's note.

'Oh shit! Not today, please,' she mumbled wearily to herself as she dialled The Warren's number. As she waited for the phone to be answered at the other end she switched it on to hands-free mode so she could begin putting her files back in the filing cabinet next to her desk. Stella picked up the phone sooner than she'd expected making her turn round quickly, catching her thigh on the corner of the open drawer. Jo swore to herself as she lifted the receiver to her ear. The pain was out of all proportion to the injury but it made her sound terse.

'Stella, Jo. What's up now?' She didn't bother with any formal greeting. 'Stella, please,' she interrupted the woman's flow of conversation. 'I don't need a blow-by-blow account, just tell me what's happened.' Jo listened as Stella explained the problem.

'Well get her a hairdresser, then.'

Stella rattled on at the other end of the phone.

'OK, OK.' Jo sighed. 'I'll come down but you'll have to wait. It'll take me half an hour to finish here so depending on the traffic I should be with you by six-thirty. Try to calm her down before then, or at least don't get her any more upset. Tell her I'm on my way.'

Jo hung up the phone. Laura put her head round the door. 'Problems?'

'Just my bloody mother again. Honestly, Laura, what am I going to do with her? She's like a spoilt child. Why, oh why am I the only one who can calm her?'

It was clearly a rhetorical question and out loud Laura left it unanswered. To herself she remarked, *Because you're prepared to go running the whole time*. It was an astute observation.

Unfortunately the traffic was very heavy and she hit a slow-moving jam as soon as she eased her car out on to the Bishops Bridge Road. It stayed like that all the way across Vauxhall Bridge through Peckham and New Cross to Blackheath.

As she made her way slowly through the traffic Jo found herself wondering for the hundredth time why she let herself be dragged into sorting out her mother's tantrums. Without knowing it her thoughts echoed Laura's as she ruefully admitted to herself that it was because she was prepared to respond to Maggie's every beck and call. She knew she was motivated primarily by guilt for although The Warren was safe and comfortable it wasn't, and never would be, Maggie's home in the way the large Maida Vale flat had been. But moving out had been the only way to ensure her own emotional survival. It was either that or be ground down by Maggie's constant criticisms – that she was useless; that her friends were worthless; that she would never get (and keep) a boyfriend if she took her work so seriously; that generally her life was drab and dull. If she had stayed she would have become the dreary person her mother had, in her own mind, already made her. Jo knew she had done the right thing but she still felt guilty. So here she was, stuck in rush-hour traffic once again, on her way to sort out yet another petty, probably non-existent, problem.

Although she had left the office at five-thirty it was close to seven-thirty by the time she made her way round the small one-way system and into the courtyard in front of the flats. At the front door she didn't bother buzzing Maggie's number but instead pushed the button marked 'Warden'. As she expected, Stella was back in her own place, probably leaving one of the youngsters from the social services with Maggie. *That's not going to help*, she thought ruefully as Stella's voice brightly informed her she was coming.

Stella wittered at Jo as they made their way down the wide hallway, telling her she didn't know what to do and apologising for having to call her out and hoping she wasn't busy and asking how her work in Television (*Trust her to give it a capital 'T'*, thought Jo) was going. As usual Stella simultaneously let herself in as she rang the bell.

'Maggie? Look who's here,' she said brightly, stepping to one side as if she were a magician's assistant unveiling some sleight-of-hand.

Mother and daughter looked at each other.

Despite her protests about needing her hair done Maggie looked neat and tidy. She seemed delicate and birdlike, with sharp features. Her eyes were bright behind a pair of fashionable glasses and her short grey hair was arranged in regimented waves across her head. Jo had known that opening up the basement would be a dirty job so, like the rest of the crew, she had worn her oldest jeans and a jumper. The unscheduled meeting with Dinah hadn't given her a chance to change and she both felt and looked grubby. Seeing her fastidious mother and sensing the unspoken criticism of her own appearance made Jo feel even grimier.

Involuntarily she ran her hand over her light brown hair, tucking the stray bits behind her ears. At five foot five she was taller than her mother but had inherited her neat, curvaceous figure and hazel eyes. Although they did not strongly resemble each other there was something in their general look that said they were related. Jo knew she got her fair share of wolf whistles and honked horns but Maggie always made her feel ungainly. Jo didn't know which were worse, the spoken criticisms or the silent ones. The comments she hated most, however, were the ones Maggie made about Jo inheriting her build from her father. It condemned them both. It was Jo who broke the silence.

'Well, what's all this about, Maggie?' Her mother had made it clear to her years ago that she would not tolerate being called mother, mum or any other derivation of the word, because it made her feel old.

'They're bullying me again, Joanne.' Maggie always used her daughter's full name. 'Take me away from here. If you don't I'm going to die.' If Maggie had thought this comment would gain her daughter's sympathy she couldn't have been more mistaken. Jo laughed.

'Oh, don't be so damn stupid! Of course you won't. From what I gather you're just being bloody-minded. The hairdresser will be here on Wednesday and you'll just have to wait until then.'

Maggie stared back at Joanne, trying to work out how far she could push her. She decided she could get a bit more out of this before stepping down. It really didn't matter now anyway. She'd got what she wanted – a bit of excitement to alleviate the boredom. That was the trouble, if you had fun when you were younger. Being old was just so dull.

Gradually she stopped being petulant, letting her daughter appear to talk her round. By the time Maggie was in what for her passed as good humour again, Jo had been there for about an hour. She had more or less managed to ignore her mother's barbs but before she could leave there was a genuine problem to sort out. June had been right about one thing; getting worked up had sent Maggie's blood pressure soaring. It was clear she would need someone to stay with her overnight to help her in the bathroom and bedroom. That took another half hour to arrange and it was close to nine o'clock when Jo finally pulled out of the courtyard.

As she drove down Shooters Hill towards Greenwich she reached for her mobile phone and called her own home number. 'Hello, it's me.'

'Where the fuck are you?' Simon sounded really cross. Jo began to explain to her fiancé that she'd been called out to Maggie, but even though Simon knew how difficult her mother could be he wasn't in the mood to be sympathetic. 'I'm starving. I thought we were going out to dinner tonight.'

'We are, sweetheart. That's why I'm calling. Look, why don't I meet you in Archie's in half an hour. I can easily make it by then.' Simon was hesitating at the other end of the phone.

'Si, please don't be cross with me. I couldn't help it, could I?' For the second time that day she found herself cajoling and pleading. 'Tell you what, as I've got the car why don't you get a cab or jump on the Tube then you can have a drink without having to worry about driving.'

'I suppose so,' he said, slightly mollified. As she drove Jo raised her eyebrows, uttering a silent vote of thanks. Finding a place to park in Covent Garden was difficult and it was ten-fifteen before she walked down the stone stairs into the restaurant.

Jo stood looking along the cellar of arches that made up Archie's

Place. It had been converted from an old warehouse but rather than trying to hide its origins the owners had worked with the architecture to create a cosy atmosphere. A long bar made from huge beaten wooden barrels stretched down one wall, and opposite this large worn wooden tables and discarded church pews had been tucked into the arches to give customers privacy. The floor was covered with straw and sawdust, while the pale painted walls were decorated with a hotch-potch of old wooden and tin signs and faded photographs which changed constantly as they were all for sale. Hanging from the vaulted ceiling on laundry racks was an equally diverse assortment of kitchenware and other odd items which could also be bought. Lighting came from wall sconces and candles in bottles so thick with wax they had become a permanent part of the furniture. The place was cool in the summer and warm in the winter. She and Simon often went there, so the gay couple who ran Archie's greeted her warmly. Everyone knew them as Bill and Ben mainly because of a large plant, affectionately known as Weed, that grew on the corner of the bar and thrived on the dregs of wine that people emptied into its pot. No one knew the boys' real names but it didn't matter. They always made everyone feel as if they had walked into a comfortable get-together with old friends.

The stairs gave a clear view of all the arches and Jo quickly scanned each one trying to spot Simon. Bill saw her and made his way along the length of the bar. 'Hello, gorgeous.' He leaned over the barrel and she walked towards him to receive the usual kiss on either cheek.

'Don't tell me, he's been here ages. I know I'm late. The traffic was horrible,' she said as she straightened up.

'The day you get here first is the day I really worry.' He gave her a huge grin and went to face the relevant arch to yell across at Simon, 'Here she is, darlin'.'

As soon as Jo bent across the table to kiss Simon she knew he had taken her at her word and been drinking. There was an almost empty tumbler of scotch which Simon put his hand on to stop the waiter removing it as he brought a bottle of beer to the table and took away the four empties already standing there. He asked Jo what she would like but, aware of her own tiredness and the fact that she would be driving home, she decided to settle for a mineral water.

Simon was still in a mood with her, making it clear he had not enjoyed sitting at the table by himself for half an hour as he waited for her. As they ordered and ate their meal Jo eased him out of his sulk by asking him about his day. He was a senior broker with a large insurance company. Although it was not a subject Jo really knew much about she had learned enough during their four years together to ask key questions in the right language. They were drinking their coffee before Simon finally asked her about her day.

She lit up as she told him about the discovery of the body in the basement. 'Si, it's the sort of thing any director, let alone a new one, dreams about. Being in the right place at the right time. It's one hell of a break. OK, I admit that maybe I should show a bit more respect towards whoever he was but I can't help it! And what's even better is that when I stood up to Dinah she actually backed down. Not even Di Deadman dared pull it away from me.'

Simon reached across the table and gave her hand a squeeze. 'Good on you.' From the way he said it Jo knew he hadn't really been listening to her and that he was much drunker than he appeared. She pushed down her enthusiasm for her work and suppressed a sigh. She had been about to continue and tell him more about Maggie's tantrum, but knowing her fiancé's feelings about his future mother-in-law (although how long in the future she did not know as they had yet to set a date for the wedding) she decided not to mention it again. Anyway Si was saying something to her about the coincidence of his company having a large stand at that year's Home Maker.

'Yes, Si, I know. You told me last week that you'd be there. Remember?' Clearly he didn't and Jo decided it was time they left. She called for the bill and after the usual elaborate goodnights to Bill and Ben she managed to steer Simon towards St Catherine's Street where she had finally parked the car.

On the way home to Hampstead Simon draped his arm across the back of the driver's seat, letting it rest on Jo's shoulder. She could feel the heat of his hand through her jumper. Despite the fact that she didn't like him touching her when she was driving (which he knew only too well) she said nothing, sensing it wouldn't take much to upset him again.

With a sigh she carefully locked the car and followed Simon up the steps. They had barely got indoors; she was just putting her keys in the bowl by the phone when he reached around her waist from behind and she felt his lips kiss the nape of her neck. Automatically Jo turned in the circle of his arms and put her own around him. They stood in the hall, kissing. Jo could taste the beer he had been drinking; at the last count it had been nine bottles before she gently suggested he'd had enough.

'Come on, let's go to bed.' He ran his hand over her buttocks as he spoke and Jo could feel that he was aroused. After her day's work and the dash over to Blackheath to soothe her mother, not to mention coping with Simon's mood, the last thing Jo felt like was sex. All she wanted to do was have a hot bath to wash the grime away, go to bed and cuddle up to him as he held her. But in his drunken state Simon wouldn't understand, he would see it as a rejection and it would lead to another row. *We seem to have an awful lot of those lately*, Jo thought as she untangled herself from Simon's embrace.

'Mmm . . . lovely idea, but I need a bath first. You go ahead and I'll see you in there.' Giving her a kiss on the forehead Simon took off his jacket and slung it over his shoulder as he went upstairs. Jo followed him a few minutes later and ran herself a bubble bath which she sank into, luxuriating in the hot water and lavender-scented steam. Simon called out asking if she would be long and even though she replied she was just coming she stayed where she was for another ten minutes, letting her thoughts drift around.

Part of her still marvelled at the fact that Si found her attractive, given that appearances were so important to him. He was such a classically handsome blond he could have had anyone. She never had worked out why he had talked to her at Katie's party that night, or why he had called up her friend the next day to get Jo's number to ask her out. But he had, and they had been a couple ever since.

So how come they rowed so often now? Maybe it was because things had changed so much since their early days together. Then she had been around more, more available to cook him dinner every night and generally look after him. Taking on more responsibility at work meant that she was increasingly home after him, and now with *Women in Focus* she often worked weekends too.

Maybe it's not Si's fault? I'm the one whose work pattern has changed, not him . . . I wonder if we would still be together if he hadn't moved in?

At that thought Jo smiled to herself. Simon's moving in nearly three years ago had always been a joke. It was only meant to be for a couple of weeks while he tried to find somewhere else after the owners of his previous flat came back from overseas, but somehow they had both tacitly understood he wasn't really looking. It was like their engagement. He had never actually gone down on one knee. They had been walking through Hampstead one Saturday afternoon and stopped to look at chronograph watches in a jeweller's window. They went inside to have a closer look and by the time they came out Simon had bought Jo a huge solitaire diamond ring. It rather summed up their relationship. No definite decisions, no discussions, just a drifting from one stage to the next. But what was next? Jo wriggled further down in the water.

It's crazy. We never really talk about things. I can tell my boss where to get off but I can't even tell my own fiancé I'm not in the mood . . . he can't even read my feelings any more. What's happening to us? We never used to be like this. I do love Si, but just once it'd be nice if he were the one to compromise instead of me. I wish I could make him understand about Maggie . . . I hate it when I get hauled over there but what can I do? It might help if I actually liked her a bit . . . oh, come on Jo, that's not fair . . . you know you don't mean that. If you didn't like her you wouldn't care. But why do you care? If she wasn't like she was maybe Howard would still be around . . .

That's enough! Thinking about her father was dangerous. It made her start wondering about his relationship with Maggie and what had really happened between them. Maggie abruptly curtailed any attempts Jo ever made to discuss her father, and over the years she had given up trying to get her to talk about him. She knew virtually nothing about him – what sort of man he'd been, what his work involved, or how he disappeared. All she had were the vague impressions of a small child. But that Maggie still felt great bitterness towards the man after thirty-odd years was obvious.

It was a path Jo didn't want to start going down again, not tonight anyway. She dried herself off and sprinkled talcum on to her damp skin. Quietly she crept into their bedroom and with relief saw that, as she had hoped, Simon had fallen asleep waiting for her. He was snoring a little and gratefully she sidled into bed next to him. He stirred, automatically pulling her towards him. She turned out the light and settled herself in the crook of his arm. Within a few minutes she too was asleep.

While Jo was battling with Maggie Suzanne Prescott was again sitting at her desk. She had not done as Gordon had predicted and gone 'ape-shit' when Alan told her about the body, which had rather surprised him. Suzanne in a temper was no one's idea of fun, but somehow her quiet 'I see' sounded more menacing. Calmly she'd asked Alan what it would do for the show and he had repeated what the police had told him about starting an investigation, adding his own analysis of the situation from a PR point of view.

So it begins, she thought. It was getting dark and she switched on the Anglepoise lamp over her desk before bending down to find her handbag. She took out her keys, turning each one round on the ring until she found the smallest. Opening her bottom drawer she removed a battered old cash box and inserted the key, hesitating for a moment, as if she were uncertain about what she was doing. Then, making up her mind, she carefully lifted the top layer of papers to remove a small bundle tied in blue ribbon from the very bottom of the box.

Pushing the box to one side she made a space in the middle of her desk and delicately began removing the ribbon, wrapping it round her fingers into a coil. Slowly she began to go through the slim pile of papers in front of her.

There were three old, faded photographs. The first was of a man in his mid twenties, in a pilot's uniform with the Canadian insignia on his shoulder. His left hand was bunched into a fist at his waist and his head was at a jaunty angle, matching his cap. He grinned cheekily at the camera as if he were winking at it. The black scrawl across the corner read, 'To a Great British Lady. Yours, Chuck.' The word lady had been underlined and a few X's added after the signature. Suzanne sighed as she put it to one side, face down.

The next photograph was smaller than the first and showed a couple of people on a beach. A serious little girl in a baggy knitted swimming costume was standing next to a sand-castle, holding a spade and squinting into the sun which was somewhere behind the camera. Kneeling next to her in the sand was a pretty woman in her mid twenties. The wind was blowing her hair and she was laughing widely so you could see her even teeth as she threw her head back, lifting her chin to the sun. The shadow of the photographer, clearly a woman, fell across the corner of the picture.

Suzanne turned the photograph over. On the back someone had written lightly in now faded pencil, 'Us lot, Dorset, August 1947'. She put the image with the first picture. Next came a letter in an envelope with a 1958 London postmark. Someone had written on it 'Not known at this address'. When the letter had been returned to her Suzanne had known that it was a lie. She knew it had been opened and resealed. That it had been read.

She looked at the last bits of the bundle all at once. Another photograph – a portrait of a good-looking man. Glossily retouched, his skin looked so smooth he could have been anything between forty-five and sixty. He oozed confidence and seemed to say to the viewer, 'You know you can trust me.' His suit was clearly of expensive cloth and cut; his tie matched the handkerchief carefully folded and sticking out of his breast pocket. Suzanne propped the photograph against her phone.

Then there were the two letters, her original proposal and the reply giving her the permission she'd needed. Both dated 1967, and both impersonal as they had been written and despatched by solicitors. Nevertheless they were important letters, the ones that mattered. The next envelope she pushed aside without reading it. She knew its contents only too well. She had lived with them for the last thirty years. No, she didn't need to reread that. Finally, there was the note that had accompanied the photographs.

Suzanne jumped as the overhead lights flashed on suddenly. The cleaner was standing in the doorway looking just as startled as Suzanne. 'Gawd, Mrs Prescott, you didn't half make me jump! I thought you'd all gone so I wanted to get a bit ahead of meself. There's a party down at the club so I hope you don't mind?'

'No, Milly, of course not. I was just catching up on a few bits and pieces.' She quickly covered the photographs and letters with a folder snatched from a pile beside her. 'Just give me five minutes to tidy up and then it's all yours. I promise I won't be longer than that.'

'OK, I'll start out here than shall I?' It was clear that Milly intended to get to her party and nothing, least of all Suzanne Prescott, was going to stop her.

As soon as Milly had left the room Suzanne quickly reassembled her bundle, making sure it was locked away securely in the cash box again. She didn't open it often, though she always made sure she had it with her, whether she was based at Exhibitions International's headquarters or here at the Pimlico Centre. In fact it was probably several years since she had last done so, knowing its contents as she did off by heart. But after the discovery in the basement that morning she had needed to look at them properly again; to remind herself what it was all about. Why she was doing what she was and to reassure herself that taking part in *Women in Focus* was a good idea.

'*It is going to be all right.*' She pushed her momentary feelings of panic to one side as she began packing her briefcase. *It's got to be*. She concentrated on what she was doing, ignoring the fact that her hands were shaking and a slight sweat had appeared on her top lip. 'There you go, Milly, less than five minutes as promised. It's all yours,' she said to the cleaner with a false brightness as she hitched her briefcase under her arm and swung her handbag over her shoulder. 'Hope it's a good party.' The lift doors closed on her taking her down to the car park.

'I'm sorry, but I have nothing further to add to the statement issued this morning. If you have any questions I suggest you put them to the police press officer.' Alan Waterman was sitting at his desk, shirt sleeves rolled up, his head propped in his right hand as he mechanically spouted the words that he had already said at least a dozen times that day. 'Yes, yes, I know you're trying to do your job but all the facts we have were in this morning's release. I'm not holding out on you. There just isn't anything more to add at this time.' He was battling to keep his temper in check. The first journalist had turned up at the Pimlico Centre within forty minutes of the announcement of the body being found. The phones and fax machines had started going wild shortly after that.

Usually the press office wasn't set up at the Centre until three days before the opening of the Home Maker Exhibition. However, it had quickly been agreed to move Alan there as fast as possible. Although nothing had been said officially someone had obviously got wind that something unusual was happening at the Pimlico Centre and, afraid that they would miss out on a big story as it broke, the press had begun to gather. Not knowing what they were waiting for they were content just to hang around, enjoying the ribald banter that flew back and forth when they weren't falling over each other for a 'scoop'. It was quite a friendly atmosphere at that point. Us against them – 'them' being everyone inside the building. The tension began when Alan and his staff of four elbowed their way through the cluster of journalists to move into a corner of the suite that the police had commandeered as a temporary incident room. When the police finally released their statement, it became every man (and woman) for himself.

The police had finished their on-site forensic work in the small hours of the morning so the ambulance that pulled up at one of the back loading doors was virtually unseen. The body bag was quickly and efficiently moved from the basement into the waiting vehicle which whisked it away to the mortuary for further investigation. The few people who were working overnight watched it go with mild curiosity, then went back to their various jobs. Only one person had any real interest in what was going on and he oversaw it all with a knowing smile.

This midnight activity meant there was a lack of any hard information, which was what had successfully kept the story out of the main news the night before, although it had merited a couple of lines in a late-night local news round-up. A small paragraph had appeared in one of the tabloids, but by nine a.m. it had become apparent that some sort of statement had to be issued. Alan agreed one together with the police. It simply gave the facts without over-sensationalising the find.

'I want to play the whole thing down if we can,' Alan had explained to the Detective Sergeant. 'It's this period that's key for us as far as ticket sales are concerned. We're already down on last year and this could really balls it up.'

'Do me a favour.' The policeman had laughed at him. 'Something like this will have 'em screaming out for tickets. Trust me, mate, the public love a bit of blood an' guts and a rotting walled-up body is even better. I guarantee that far from losing you ticket sales it'll give them a boost.' Alan looked doubtful. 'In fact I'm so sure I'd bet you twenty quid that your figures will take a hike.' And he had dug in his wallet to take out a crumpled twenty pound note which he slapped on the desk.

Alan had reluctantly accepted the bet. Not because he thought he would win – after all it, would be better for the show if he lost, as they genuinely needed to sell more advance tickets – but because he instinctively felt that it would be a wise move. Having a member of the investigating team on his side could be useful.

By ten-thirty the release had been approved and handed out to the now large group of pressmen outside, and simultaneously issued by fax. The *Evening Standard* made it the lead story in its lunch-time edition and the TV and radio news programmes that had units on stand-by quickly got them down to the Pimlico Centre to do live links back to the various studios. Alan had gone down with Detective Chief Inspector Thomas to face the cameras and assure the public that it would be business as usual at this year's show. Of course they had been so busy worrying about visitors to the show that no one at Exhibitions International had stopped to think about the effect the news would have on the exhibitors. It was left to Gordon Mayfield to answer their queries – a situation about which he was not happy.

'That bloody cow gets on my wick. I'm the floor manager – not the bloody sales director. It's Ian who should be dealing with this lot, not me. Christ, the sooner I can get me pension sorted and out of here the better.' He marched from the office leaving chaos behind him. But not for long. When it became apparent that a number of key companies were threatening to pull out – even if they did have to forfeit the money they had paid for their stands – Ian Browne and his sales team were quickly brought down to the Pimlico Centre to look after disgruntled clients, ensuring they didn't withdraw.

It was early afternoon when Jo finally caught up with Alan. She had not been in a good mood all morning, but had battled to keep it hidden. It began as soon as she got up, when she and Simon had another row. He accused her of waiting until he was asleep before getting into bed the night before. Jo apologised, saying she had dozed off in the bath, but Simon hadn't believed her and the fact that he was right made her snipe at him. They ate breakfast in stroppy silence and Simon had flung himself out of the front door and into his car to go roaring up the road.

Jo had continued getting ready, making a duty phone call to see how Maggie was before leaving for work herself. Maggie had continued complaining about how awful everyone was to her until Jo had finally cut her off mid-stream as she was going to be late.

So what should at least have been an interesting day work-wise got off to a bad start personally. *Thank God for work*, she thought as she headed to the Pimlico Centre. *At least there* I'm *in control without any one pulling my strings.* She chose to forget about Dinah even though the memory of the previous day's meeting was still running round in her head like a looped film. She had scanned the papers for news of the body but had seen nothing; missing even the one paragraph, which was tucked away at the bottom of a page. On her way in she listened to the radio, again surprised that there were no reports but also pleased because it meant Dinah had taken her comments on board and had not sold the footage to the networks.

As she pulled up in front of security she became aware of the crowd being held back by the police cordon. 'Morning, Miss Edwardes.' The security man came out of his hut to talk to her, anxious to gossip about the excitement. Although she had not spent that much time at the centre she had already made a point of befriending the security guards and the traffic office staff, knowing from past experience what useful allies they could be.

'Morning, Cyril. I didn't expect all this.'

'Well it's not every day you turns up a body in yer basement, is it? Mind you, beats me 'ow they 'ears about it. Not a dicky bird anywhere. I've looked at the papers. Had me radio on all morning and there's nothin' nowhere. Ah well, if you take space six, Miss, it's away from the crowd. OK, OK . . .' he finished, standing up and yelling at the driver of the car behind Jo as he began using his horn.

She parked the car and went into the Portacabin that had been parked in the forecourt of the Pimlico Centre and was Boadicea Productions' office for the duration of the show. The crew sat around, slumped in chairs or perched on the edge of desks, drinking the first cup of thick coffee of the morning. However, as soon as she walked in they roused themselves and began whooping and applauding her.

Startled, Jo gave a mock bow and then laughed. 'I'm delighted my genius has finally been recognised, but what's this in aid of?'

'We heard how you stood up to DD – the old boot – and anyone who can do that deserves their fifteen seconds of glory.'

Jo gave a wry smile. 'Oh, that.' She dismissed the incident but was secretly pleased that word had got back to the crew. She didn't bother to wonder how (she had worked in the industry too long to question the speed of gossip and rumour). She just knew that her victory over Dinah would help win her the crew's respect, and that would make things easier.

'Well, I must be mad but I like working with you lot and if there's anyone being kicked off the production then I'm the one who's going to do it . . . and for my own reasons! So watch it!' Jo joked and they all grinned back at her. She might be a rookie director but at this stage of her career they regarded her as one of their own. Becoming more serious she continued, 'Now come on, there's masses to get through. We got some terrific footage in the can yesterday and even though we can't expect Exhibitions International to unearth a body for us every day there's still more great material out there and I want to get it done, and done fast. There's no room in the budget for an over-run. If we get this right,' she continued, eyes sparkling with eagerness, 'and we'd bloody better, we'll be up there at the next BAFTAs with the rest of them. So let's get some solid atmospheric stuff while we can. I warn you all now that with this going on we'll have to rewrite the schedule. I know, I know – it's a pain.' This was directed at Bill who had groaned at the thought of replotting the shooting schedule. 'But I want to get an interview with Suzanne Prescott as soon as possible and see if we can get feedback from some of the people on the floor. However, until that's done we'll stick to the original plan. You go and set up. Tony's in charge. I need to talk to the lovely Alan to rearrange things'.

She crossed to the main building, flashing her pass at security, and made her way to Alan's desk in the press office but he waved his hand at her, signalling her away. That went on all morning until she finally ignored his gestures and hovered while he finished his conversation. 'Look, I know that when the show is running we do what we can to get you here but this is different. It's out of my hands. It's up to the police. I can't do anything. If I could I would.' He pulled the handset away from his face. 'Miserable sod hung up on me. Do you have to talk to me today?' he asked Jo brusquely.

'Sorry, but I do,' Jo replied brightly with her most engaging smile. 'I would like to talk to Suzanne, on camera, to get her reactions to all of this.' Jo indicated the small team of police working in the corner, and the hastily assembled press office, encompassing it in a wide sweep of her clipboard.

'You'll be lucky!'

She was about to give him a suitable reply when she saw how genuinely tired he looked. She knew that feeling of exhaustion only too well, and locking horns with Alan would do nothing to help her get a meeting with Suzanne. The support of the marketing director was important; he could make her job difficult if he chose to. 'Let's not talk about it here. Come and have a coffee, you look as if you could do with a break.'

Alan had to admit Jo was right. He had been in public relations all his working life but had never had to deal with anything like this. The Exhibitions International team were looking to him for direction, advice and support, which he usually had no problem in giving. But this time he was as lost as they were, the only difference being that he wasn't allowed to show it. Suzanne had also made it clear that the police were Alan's domain and that they were to treat him as their main company contact. Alan, therefore, was trying to direct them to the relevant Exhibitions International staff to help them with their enquiries, as well as try to keep the day-to-day work of an exceptionally busy press office going. All this – and a TV documentary crew wandering around the place. A break and a cup of coffee was definitely what he needed. He pushed his chair back and bent down to collect a walkie-talkie radio from the rack as he went. 'I'm on channel one if needed,' he said as he switched the radio on.

They picked their way through the various cables and crates of equipment, the inevitable debris from building the exhibition which spilled across the halls' floors. Only two other people were in the downstairs café and after the hubbub upstairs the comparative silence seemed strange. Jo got them both large mugs of cappuccino with a doughnut and tried to eat hers without getting in too much of a mess. Alan dropped a lump of sugar in his mug, watching it sink below the surface of the froth, enjoying the absence of a ringing phone. The radio stood on the table and he automatically kept an ear on the conversations crackling back and forth between his colleagues in case a call went out for him. It was Jo who broke the silence, determined to get what she needed.

'I know this can't be much fun for you. You're trying to keep press people out but as I'm already here filming you could actually turn it to your advantage. I mean, if you say that you've done an exclusive deal with Boadicea Productions you won't be able to let anyone else in, will you? I appreciate that what is going on right now isn't what usually happens' ('You can say that again,' Alan mumbled) 'but it has happened and I can't ignore it.'

'No, I suppose not,' he sighed, and was about to continue when he heard his name being called on his radio. 'Press office to Alan; Alan, come in please. Over.'

'Oh Christ, now what?' He picked up his walkie-talkie and depressed the button. 'Alan to press office. What's up? Over.'

'Don't worry. It's good news. Thought you'd like to know we've just had a call from advance booking. Since the news broke the phones haven't stopped. In the last three hours nearly fifty thousand quid has been taken. Over.'

'Bloody hell, that's over six thousand people off the back of the lunchtime news. I'm coming back to the office. See you soon. Out. Sorry Jo, but it looks as if I'll have to get back to you. We're obviously going to do good business so I need to get extra phone lines in and staff set up. We'll have to talk about this some other time when things are a bit quieter – say the end of the week maybe?' And before Jo could reply he had grabbed his jacket and left her sitting there hurriedly trying to swallow a mouthful of doughnut.

You bastard! Jo thought. *I need to talk to her now. Leave it to the end of the week and the impetus will have gone. Well, screw you.* She also sped out of the café, but instead of following Alan she went straight to the management suite and knocked firmly on Suzanne's office door. Her secretary was sitting in the outer office and Jo pushed her anger down to greet her warmly. 'Hi Julia, you coping with this bedlam?'

The girl smiled. 'Well, it's a bit hairy as you can imagine.'

'Look, I know I should really go through Alan for this but the poor man is up to his neck so under the circumstances I hope you don't mind me coming direct to you. With everything that happened yesterday I was hoping Suzanne might be persuaded to give me an unscheduled interview. I know we've agreed a timetable but obviously when that was drawn up no one expected to find a body. It would help so much if we could get her *immediate* feelings on the subject. Do you think she might agree?'

Jo knew that she was being her most charming and ingratiating but it was vitally important that she got some reaction from Suzanne on tape. So far she had only talked to the woman on the phone and she knew herself well enough to know that her questions would be sharper if she could ask them now, before she became too familiar as a personality. Julia was uncertain, knowing how adamant Suzanne had been about allocating only a certain amount of time to the interviews. She was about to say something when the door to the office next to hers opened and Suzanne herself came into the room.

'Oh, hello. Is there a problem, Julia?' She looked quizzically at her secretary and for a split second Jo felt like a naughty schoolgirl visiting the headmistress. She swallowed nervously and then jumped in, holding out her hand to the well dressed older woman.

'We haven't actually met, although we have talked on the phone. I'm Joanne Edwardes. I was just talking to Julia about the excellent footage we're getting. It really is quite something, isn't it? And obviously what we got yesterday was a bit –' she hesitated, thinking of the right word '– unusual, so I was hoping that you might be willing to let us squeeze in an extra session with you. I know we've got an agreed schedule but as I was just saying to Julia, it would be great to get some comments from you on record while it's all fresh.'

Suzanne's expression didn't flicker as she looked at Jo. After all this time of building up a relationship on the phone it felt odd seeing her face to face. The younger woman wasn't what she had expected. There was a softness about her that she found surprising. *Though why I should have assumed she'd be like . . . Mustn't think like that. Stop it.* Suzanne told herself off.

To Jo it seemed that Suzanne stood there deep in thought for ages before she finally asked Julia, 'How's it looking for tomorrow?' Julia appeared surprised but checked the diary and between them they agreed that Jo would be there at eleven a.m. She was delighted.

Alan, however, was not so pleased when he found out that Jo had gone behind his back.

'How dare you? You know our agreement stipulates that any contact with Suzanne will be made through me. You're way out of line.'

'Now just a minute,' she blazed back at him. 'I tried to go through you but you side-stepped me all morning and when I did get you you dashed off burbling something about talking to me at the end of the week. If this is going to work then I need reaction and I need it *now*. I know things are difficult but they're not easy for me either and I haven't got time to sit around waiting for you to deign to see me!'

Alan hit back angrily. 'Listen, I admit your documentary is going to be useful to us, but not until next year, so right now it's not vital. Another move like that and I'll seriously consider pulling out, and don't think I can't because I can, and I will!' Before Jo had a chance to argue he walked out of the Portacabin leaving Jo staring at an empty space, her cheeks aflame with embarrassment.

* * *

Checking that no one was around he opened the outer office door as quietly as he could and made his way quickly across to Suzanne's door. He listened carefully for a moment before silently turning the door knob. It had just gone nine o'clock and the only light in the room came from the lamp on Suzanne's desk. He watched her for a moment, her head bent over a pile of paperwork as she scanned lists of figures with a pen in her hand. 'You make a real pretty picture sitting there like that.'

Suzanne jumped at the sound of his voice. 'I didn't hear you come in,' she said flatly.

'You never heard me anywhere, did you, love? It's the basis of our friendship after all, isn't it?' He gave the word 'friendship' special emphasis and stepped further into the room, shutting the door quietly behind him.

'You and I aren't friends. Now it's already late and I've still got a lot to get through, so tell me what you want and go.'

'Aw, come on. That's the not the way to speak to someone who's virtually a partner now, is it? Can't I at least sit down and have a fag?' Without waiting to be asked he lowered himself into the chair opposite her desk and slouched in his seat. Slowly he took a packet of cigarettes and box of matches from his top pocket and tapped the base of the pack to dislodge one. With equal slowness he put it in his mouth and lit it, flicking the spent match at the bin beside her desk.

Suzanne said nothing. She could feel her heart thumping and a knot of panic gathering in the pit of her stomach. She thought about calling for help but dismissed the idea as soon as it entered her head. 'I haven't got time for this. What do you want?' she asked again, more insistently.

'A friendly chat, but I can see you're busy looking after our future so I'll come straight to the point. You must have felt sick as a pig when they found 'im down there like that. But you see, it's given me a right problem. A dilemma if you like. All these years you've been tipping me a few readies . . .'

'A few readies!' Suzanne exclaimed. 'You've had a fortune out of me.'

'Maybe love, maybe, but look what you've had in return.'

'Let's not go into that. Get to the point.'

'Where was I? Ah yes, me dilemma. It's like this. I'm due to retire next year and the pension ain't great. Add the "few readies"' – he enjoyed repeating the phrase – 'and I'll get by. But I was thinking it's about time we renegotiated; 'specially since they found *him* downstairs. Now by my reckoning that's got to be worth a few extra quid a week. What do you think?'

Suzanne finally got to her feet and walked round the desk to the main light switch. They both blinked as the room was flooded with light. She stood in front of him and in an effort to make herself seem in control of the situation sat against the edge of her desk, ankles crossed, arms folded across her chest. 'I think you're on a hiding to nothing. When you first approached me I panicked and, like a fool, agreed. But so did you by signing our agreement. I was young then. Now I'm more secure, with a better idea of how business works. Besides, who would believe you after all this time? If it came to taking your word against mine you wouldn't stand a chance. Consider yourself lucky that you've had a job here long enough to merit a pension. The answer is *no*. Now get out of my office.' All of this was said in a voice that belied her feelings. Her tone was firm and brooked no argument. She pushed herself away from the edge of the desk, knocking her radio to the floor. She ignored it, and walked to the door, opening it to show him the way out.

He stood up with a scowl. It wasn't worth arguing with her. As he reached the doorway he stopped and for the first time during the interview they were standing facing each other. 'Think about my offer, 'cos it's for a limited period only. After that you might find a few expensive "accidents" happening and we wouldn't want anyone to get hurt, would we?' Without waiting for an answer he slunk past her, checked no one was outside in the corridor and crept back out of the office.

Just as a warning he decided to prove his point the following day.

'Keith to Gordon, come in please, over.' The radio crackled through the noise of the organisers' office as another day began to swing into action. Gordon picked up the radio and depressed the button to answer one of their newest sales executives.

'Morning, Keith, it's Gordon. What can I do for you, mate? Over.'

'I'm in Pim Two and we've got a problem. A *big* problem. I think you'd better get down here, and make it sooner rather than later. Over.'

'What sort of problem? Over.'

'Stands 443 to 473 have gone. Over.'

'What do you mean, gone?'

'Just get down here, will you?' The tone of the man's voice stopped Gordon asking any more questions, and he immediately got up. He heard Suzanne contacting Keith. 'Suzanne to Keith. Come in, please.' Even over the radio her anger was apparent. Keith responded to her call. 'When you've finished with Gordon I want you up here please.' Despite the radio's static it was easy to hear that Keith was not looking forward to that meeting when he gave his affirmative response.

'Stuck up bitch,' Gordon thought to himself as he entered hall two of the Pimlico Centre and looked at the space ahead of him. Where yesterday there had been a number of stands newly erected and ready to be dressed by exhibitors, was now a huge gap. The poles and boards that had made them up were stacked in a neat pile, together with fascia boards and cables. In the middle of it all stood one confused sales executive and some very irate exhibitors. Gordon quickly went to join the puzzled young man who walked rapidly to meet him. Keith's face was pinched and he began speaking rapidly before he reached Gordon.

'I came in this morning, did the usual walk round to check everyone was happy and found it like this. It was all fine yesterday evening when I left. I just don't understand it. I mean it's not as if it's fallen down, is it? Look, the whole thing has actually been dismantled. It's crazy.' He ran his fingers through his hair and looked unhappily at Gordon who put a reassuring arm on his shoulder.

'Calm down, mate. Let's see if we can get to the bottom of this.' The next half hour was spent in total confusion as word of what had happened gradually spread round the exhibition halls and more people made their way to Pimlico Two to see for themselves. No one had any answers. Security confirmed that the night before the stands had been ready to be dressed. PimEx Services, the company responsible for building the exhibition stands, also agreed that they had finished their part of the job, on schedule, the day before. Electricians and carpenters, sales staff and Exhibitions International personnel, no one but no one could explain how, when or why the large block of stands had been taken to pieces again.

Gordon knew that an investigation would ensue but his immediate priority was to get the stands rebuilt, and fast. Before he could get things moving Suzanne also joined the crowd in the middle of the hall. Quickly she took control, authorising the expenditure needed to get extra staff in to rebuild the section. This extra cost was increased when one of the exhibitors complained that as his lorries would have to be kept waiting his delivery charges would be higher. Other exhibitors jumped on the bandwagon and Suzanne agreed that Exhibitions International would cover these bills provided delivery dockets could be presented to Gordon. *Shit*, he thought, *more fuckin' paperwork. Mind you, s'pose it's worth it if it means Madam has to shell out a bit more!* An hour after they'd first been alerted to the problem in Pimlico Two the rebuilding work was underway.

After checking his clients were happy once again Keith, looking even more miserable, followed Suzanne into the organisers' office where she proceeded to tell him off for broadcasting his distress on an open radio channel that everyone could hear. 'Jesus Christ!' she exploded. 'We have enough trouble keeping things on an even keel as it is without you rocking the boat. Yes, we had a problem. Yes, it needed sorting but in a situation like that you find a land line and ring across to the organisers' office or switch to a secure radio channel. You don't know who's standing next to whom around the hall and everyone is already twitchy about that bloody body without you adding to it. Now get back out there and make sure those stands are up and ready by lunchtime.' Gratefully Keith escaped while everyone else in the office concentrated on keeping their heads firmly down.

'Gordon, get on to Roger Dudley and find out the full security rota for last night, and I don't want any of his excuses about delegating it to someone else. He's head of security and I want to know what the bloody hell his team are being paid for. I cannot believe that whoever took that lot down did so unseen. It must have taken all night. I'll be in my office.'

'Boy, is she pissed off!' exclaimed Liza, Gordon's assistant.

'Well it *is* odd, and it totally buggers build-up.'

'Yes, I know,' she replied, 'but don't you think she over-reacted just a touch?' Gordon shrugged. The last thing he had the time, or desire, for was a discussion about Suzanne's behaviour. As far as he was concerned she was bad enough at the best of times.

Suzanne took a few deep breaths to calm herself. When Julia eventually knocked on the door twenty minutes later to tell her that Gordon and Roger Dudley were outside with the night security list she was once again in control. Calmly she cast her eye down the names. 'I want full statements from everyone about what they saw and where they were last night, including both of you.' They scowled at her tone; she was so bloody condescending. One of these days she'd get her come-uppance. 'In particular this group.' She indicated the names that had been assigned to Pimlico Two. 'You can leave this with me.' The door shut with a click as the men let themselves out, moaning to each other about what Suzanne needed to make her more human.

Suzanne sat at her desk looking at the list of names in front of her. She could hear Julia working on her computer just outside the door and beyond that the banging, sawing and yelling of the exhibitors as they prepared their stands for the exhibition. Capital Radio competed with Radio One and the tannoy outdid them all. It didn't matter how many times she went through the build-up period, she still managed to get the same thrill from it as she had done the first time she saw it. Each time it represented another year under her belt with the company, another year more entrenched, another year's security. *And I am secure*, she told herself emphatically. *I'm also in charge and I'm not going to let anyone take that away from me*. She checked the time and saw that Jo would be with her shortly.

Having agreed to the interview she had taken even more care than usual over her appearance that morning. Now she got up and crossed to the mirror to replenish her lipstick. She had gone to the hairdresser's on her way to the Centre and her short brown hair was carefully styled to look neat but not too regimented, with no attempt to hide the salt and pepper streaks that were beginning to appear. Lazlo had tried many times to persuade her to have it coloured but she refused. 'I want to look good but I've no illusions about my age, so let's keep it under control but not totally camouflage it,' was her standard response. And as with most things, she'd had her way. Her red woollen dress and black jacket flattered her slightly rounded figure and the black scarf with the expensive gold brooch at her neck completed the sleek, sophisticated look. An expert eye could tell from the deceptively simple cut of her clothes that it was an expensive outfit. The overall impression was that of a confident woman.

But as she stood in front of the mirror the questions she was asking herself belied her look. *Why on earth did I agree to do this damned programme?* She re-applied her lipstick to her top lip. *Is it really worth it after all these years?* She blotted her bottom lip knowing the answer was an emphatic 'yes'. She had waited so long for the right moment. When she received the letter from Jo Edwardes inviting her to be featured in *Women in Focus* it took her a little while to realise that after all this time the opportunity she had been waiting for had finally presented itself.

Alan had been more than a little surprised by her acceptance of the invitation. When he had taken on the job of marketing director he had quickly appreciated the publicity value of having a female chief executive, especially in a business that was so male dominated at the top level – and there was no doubt that Exhibitions International plc *was* the top level. Suzanne, however, had other ideas and flatly refused to do anything that involved self-promotion. Alan had almost given up trying to persuade her to do interviews, and simply put requests before her as they regularly came in. He was so delighted that she had finally consented that it didn't occur to him to ask why.

If he only knew. A flicker of a frown crossed her brow. *But he won't know, no-one will know except me and her and that's all I want. That she knows. And thanks to Jo she will.* Her thoughts flipped to her brief meeting with the young woman the previous day but before she could get a firm hold on them they were interrupted by a tap on the door.

'You asked me to call you at five to eleven.'

'Yes. Thank you, Julia. Please can you make sure there's plenty of coffee for everyone.' The calm exterior was back in place and by the time Jo was shown into her office Suzanne looked her usual controlled self.

The finished programme would use linking shots of its subject speaking to camera, with a dubbed narrative over the other images.

It was still necessary for questions to be asked to trigger that information, and years of working on this type of documentary had made Jo skilled at asking those questions. The answers seemed spontaneous, not like responses at all, so they could be used, without editing, as voice-over material. She started gently by asking Suzanne about her background and what had attracted her to a career in exhibitions. Her researcher had done her job well so the questions Jo asked provided the expected answers.

'The Home Maker Exhibition has always been a good barometer of the ecomony. Fashion may come and go. You can do without the latest frock if you have to, but we all need a roof over our heads so people's homes and the lives they create in them are what matter. Despite what happens to the country's economy there will always be a need for home-making, as long as people want to live in pleasing environments.

'Think of the number of businesses that went to the wall in the late eighties and early nineties. Well, the Home Maker Exhibition carried on regardless, because people didn't move home but redecorated where they were. It is because of that constant nesting instinct that the show has existed in some shape or form since the late nineteenth century and I know we'll still be here into the twenty-first. We represent stability throughout it all.'

Jo responded. 'I can see that, but in the sixties you were unique, the only exhibition of its kind. Now there are several major competitors, not to mention the fact that people no longer have to trail up and down the high street but can visit just one superstore to get everything they need. With that sort of opposition how do you keep attracting visitors to Pimlico?'

Suzanne began to relax a little as the interview got into its stride and she realised that the questions weren't designed to catch her out. 'By staying one step ahead, by making the Home Maker fun and entertaining as well as informative and by presenting new ideas and attractions each year,' she answered, virtually quoting from their own sales brochure.

Great! thought Jo, what a beautiful cue. Out loud she carried on in the same tone, knowing that she had gained Suzanne's confidence. 'So what about the discovery of that body in the basement here at the Pimlico Centre? What sort of attraction do you think that will prove to be?'

Suzanne's pupils widened a little but no one except Tony, who had Suzanne in close-up at that moment, actually saw her blue eyes darken and he was so busy concentrating he didn't really notice. 'The discovery of the body was a huge shock to everyone, and very unfortunate. However, as Exhibitions International don't actually own the Pimlico Centre but just lease it, thus becoming tenants for three months, it really has nothing to do with us. Especially as our tenancy agreement specifically excludes the basement areas.

'Having said that, there has obviously been a lot of publicity about the discovery and as we're the current show in the Centre it has, in some way, unfortunately been associated with the Home Maker Exhibition. But our advance bookings show that far from damaging our appeal our ticket sales have taken a huge leap so I suppose in the public's mind yes, it is an extra attraction, albeit one we didn't intend.'

She gave a wry smile before continuing: 'Now I appreciate that the body is of enormous interest but as it is in the hands of the police and it's the responsibility of the Pimlico Centre's management to sort it all out I'm really not in a position to say anything more.'

Shit! Jo thought, knowing that the subject was closed, but as she couldn't end the interview there she let it continue for another five minutes before glancing at her questions and winding it up. Tony lowered the camera from his shoulder, checked the counter and gate and turned off the light.

'Thank you, Suzanne. I really am grateful to you for fitting us in.' Jo stood up, getting ready to leave. 'Especially today, as I know the dismantled stands must have created more work for all of you. But it was useful to be able to get some background at this stage. I hope that from here on we should be able to keep to the agreed schedule.'

'Oh, I don't mind. It was good to meet you at last and I must admit I quite enjoyed it. Maybe Alan was right and I should have agreed to be interviewed a long time ago,' Suzanne said jocularly, genuinely surprised at how easy it had been.

'I'm delighted you didn't. If you had where would the real interest be for me?' Jo slapped her hand over her mouth and for the second time in as many days found herself red-faced in front of a senior member of the Exhibitions International team. 'Oh, Suzanne, I'm so sorry. I didn't mean it like that. Of course you're interesting. I wouldn't be here now if you weren't. What I mean is because you're such a recluse it's better for the programme. It adds greater curiosity value. I mean . . .' Jo trailed off helplessly, knowing she was digging an even deeper hole for herself, but Suzanne just threw back her head and gave a surprisingly robust, and vaguely familiar, laugh. It made Jo blush an even deeper shade of crimson. She tucked her hair behind her ears. 'I'm really putting my foot in it, aren't I? What I'm trying to say is . . .'

'Don't worry. I know exactly what you're trying to say. And to show there are no hard feelings why don't you come back up here at the end of the day for a drink? I'd like to have more of a chat with you about the series anyway, just you and me, woman to woman.'

Frantic to make amends Jo jumped at the invitation. 'That would be lovely. Thank you.' It would mean making excuses to Simon again but after the gaffe she had just made she knew she couldn't refuse. He would just have to like it or lump it. Besides, despite everyone else's warnings about how cold and superior Suzanne could be, she had found herself oddly warming to the woman. Quickly she shooed the crew out of the office and as they waited for the lift Tony gave her a sideways look.

'I don't believe you said that.'

'Neither do I, but it looks as if I got away with it. Actually it'll be great to have a proper chat with her, might give me more of an idea about what makes her tick. After all, no one seems to know anything about her private life. Just for God's sake please don't anyone say anything to Dinah.'

Suzanne was also pleased that Jo had accepted the invitation. It was equally important to her to have an opportunity just to sit and chat with the younger woman. She wanted to get to know her a bit better, especially as the schedule agreed with Alan meant that at times Jo was virtually to be her shadow.

The standard office furniture was picked out by the beam of the torch as it swung round the room. As a facility office used by different people throughout the year it lacked any personal touches. It made his job much easier. No awkward piles of old papers to go through. Whatever he was looking for had to be in the desk. That was part of the trouble, he actually didn't know what it was he was trying to find. She might not have brought it with her. But he'd know it when he saw it, whatever it was.

He knew there had to be something, something that would keep his hold over her. He only hoped it was here and not back at the Hammersmith office where it would be harder to unearth. Finding that body had done him no favours.

He put the heavy torch on the desk and sat down in the comfortable director's chair. The light was pointed at the stack of filing trays and even though he thought it unlikely he would find anything there still he went through the slim piles in each tray, making sure he replaced things exactly as he found them. As he expected, nothing.

He picked up the torch again and directed it down the three drawers that made up the base of the desk. He tried the top drawer and then the others. Unsurprisingly they were locked. He laughed to himself as he took out a set of skeleton keys, picked one of the smaller ones and inserted it delicately into the small keyhole. His eyes screwed up as he concentrated, sensitive to the feeling of the mechanisim. After only a few seconds it opened, releasing all three locks simultaneously.

The top two drawers revealed nothing, but as he felt around the bottom of the lowest one his hand hit a solid object pushed to the back. He pulled it out. It was an old cash box. Again it was locked but his heart began to beat a bit faster as he picked another key on his bunch and quickly lifted the lid. He noted the way the blue ribbon was tied round its contents and carefully eased it off. He looked at the photographs and read the letters until he came across a hand-written note. A slow smile spread across his face.

'So, me darlin', that's who you are, is it? Well, well, well. Interestin' and useful.' He re-read the note before folding it up and reassembling the pile. He locked the box, returning it to the back of the drawer, and made sure all three were secure before he left. No one would have known he had ever been there.

'In retrospect it seems silly to think I was so nervous about having a drink with her. It's just that everyone painted this picture of a real tough nut, but I found her very easy to get on with. Not cosy exactly, just . . . oh, you know, nice.' Jo took a sip of wine and put the glass back on the carpet next to her. Simon was sprawled on the sofa, his arm draped round her shoulder as she sat leaning against it. He had been as cross as she'd expected when she had called to explain why she was going to be late home. To make it up to him she had suggested that they cancel all their plans for the weekend and spend the time together by themselves.

Simon had willingly agreed. To have Jo to himself for two days would be bliss and so that Friday evening, instead of meeting up with his old university friends in the pub, he had come straight home. Jo insisted that the usual viewing of the material shot that day – the rushes – be over by six and she also made it back to Hampstead early. And when Katie, Jo's oldest college friend who was coincidentally married to Simon's oldest friend Stuart, called for a friendly chat Jo also cut her short.

'I'm sorry, Katie, but Si and I are spending a romantic weekend together and, much as I'd love to gossip, if I do it'll mean he has every right to leg it off to the pub. I'll call you Monday, how's that?'

Katie had laughed. 'Randy pair. What can I say but yes? Have fun and don't do anything I wouldn't!' she quipped as she rang off. 'Thank God for that,' she murmured to herself. Out of all their friends she knew better than most that Jo and Simon had been going through a rough patch lately and since she had introduced them she always felt vaguely responsible.

Dinner that Friday night was leisurely and comfortable and they found themselves enjoying just being with each other in a way that neither of them had for a very long time. Jo was so relaxed that she actually felt she could discuss her work with Simon without him reacting badly. He was relaxed enough to allow her to do it. 'What was so special about her, then?' he asked lazily, curling a lock of her hair round his finger.

'I don't really know,' she mused. 'She was surprisingly interested in what *Women in Focus* was all about. Not just her programme but the whole thing. The idea of looking at high-flying women who just get on with their job but whose work has parallels with all women. She loved the analogy of the Speaker of the House controlling the rabble in the Commons in the same way a mum controls the rabble round her dinner table. She laughed when I told her about the cartoons and sketches we're commissioning to go with each programme. Come to think of it, I actually made her laugh quite a lot. I don't know what I said that was so funny but she obviously found me amusing.'

Simon ruffled her hair affectionately. 'She was also asking me about myself. Who I was, how I got to be involved in TV. She really seemed interested and I found myself telling her all sorts of things.' She trailed off a little as she remembered how easy it had been to talk to Suzanne. With Suzanne's encouragement she had surprisingly found herself explaining a lot about what she went through with Maggie. She felt Simon tense behind her which quickly brought her back to reality and she scrabbled to her knees to put her arms round his neck. 'No, silly, I didn't tell her anything about us – except that you're wonderful. I mainly told her about Maggie and what a pain she can be. I know, I know. We agreed not to talk about her so I'm not. I'm just telling you what it was like to talk to another woman who seemed to be on my side.' She was careful to stress the word 'woman', not wanting to make Simon feel excluded. It wasn't easy trying to be the traditional woman he wanted while also trying to run her own life and career. Once again she was making an effort not to offend. Suppressing a sigh, she got to her feet.

'I'm going to bed. You coming?' Simon stretched and looked at the half empty bottle of wine beside him on the floor.

'In a minute. I'll just finish this first. You go ahead.'

Saturday was a perfect early April day. The sun was shining brightly and a stiff breeze tossed the burgeoning trees from side to side. It was too nice a day to spend cooped up indoors so after a lazy breakfast of fresh squeezed orange juice with coffee and croissants they put on jeans and jumpers and set off for a long walk over Hampstead Heath. Within five minutes Simon reached for her hand and the cosiness that had been rekindled between them the night before carried on throughout the day. Happily Jo squeezed his hand in return and as they walked she felt increasingly optimistic about their relationship. The breeze proved to be deceptive in its chilliness and by the time they stopped at the Coffee Cup in Hampstead High Street their cheeks were rosy and stinging with its freshness. Jo wrapped her hands round a cup of hot chocolate and smiled as she realised how easy it had been to reassure Simon that despite appearances she still needed him.

Less than twenty-four hours of making him feel wanted was all it had taken to put things back on an even keel. OK, so she'd had to compromise again, but maybe she was being unfair to Simon. After all, it wasn't his fault that she wasn't home every night to cook for him was it?

By the time they walked back home again the sun had set. The lack of cloud meant they could see stars beginning to appear in the sky. The temperature had dropped rapidly, promising a frost the next morning. They had barely got through the door when Simon took her in his arms and kissed her. For the first time in ages there was genuine love, rather than lust, in his kisses and she responded eagerly. In the deepening twilight they made love on the living-room floor. Jo revelled in his touch, knowing she would remember this afternoon for a long time. For months she'd felt as if she and Si had been going through the motions – just having sex – but right now all the old passion was there again. They dozed off, arms and legs wrapped round each other, waking with a start as the chill finally got to them.

That evening they decided to go out for a quiet dinner. Jo put on her favourite lambs' wool dress, which hugged her figure in all the right places. Its soft deep raspberry shade set off her colouring perfectly. Simon wore his best jeans with a crisp white shirt and dark blue wool blazer. His blue eyes seemed deeper than ever as she sat opposite him at dinner, loving the way his thick blonde hair flopped in his eyes so that she wanted to reach across to smooth it out of the way. Instead she used the cover of the tablecloth carefully to slip her foot out of her shoe and run a toe playfully and lingeringly up and down his leg. In return he held her hand across the table, only reluctantly letting it go when their food arrived. That night they again made love, this time with a tender gentleness that Jo had forgotten Simon possessed.

The next day their mood continued. The weather had changed completely and they awoke to the sound of rain rattling against the window. They snuggled down again and stayed in bed all morning. When they finally got up they lit a rare open fire and spent the afternoon lazily reading the papers and watching an old documentary about New Orleans jazz on Channel Four. Jo sat at one end of the sofa propped up on cushions with her feet curled up underneath her. Simon plonked another on her hip, using it as a pillow as he curled up beside her. An overwhelming sense of love surged through her. He tried so hard to please her, really he did. Gently she ran a finger across his cheek and smoothed his hair as he began to snore quietly.

Jo gazed at the fire, mesmerised by its flames and the glowing hollows among the logs and coal, until eventually she too nodded off, not stirring until Simon woke up with a jolt an hour later. He stretched and eased his way off the sofa to give the now dying fire a prod. Without being asked he went on into the kitchen to make them a cup of tea. Jo stayed where she was, not quite awake, enjoying the sense of serenity she was feeling, listening to the noises from the kitchen as Simon poured the water into the teapot and toasted crumpets.

Simon brought the tray into the room and kissed her forehead lightly. 'Tea up,' he said tenderly. Jo took the offered mug and rearranged herself to sit with her feet tucked under him. She couldn't bear not to be in some sort of physical contact with him. Simon was obviously feeling the same and the sense of togetherness was powerful. Jo was about to tell him how much she had enjoyed the weekend, and how pleased she was that things were better between them, when the phone rang.

Its shrill, insistent tone cut through the air like a knife, making them both jump. Jo was going to ignore it but Simon was already on his feet, padding his way in his socks to the hall to answer it. He came back quickly.

'Who was it?'

'Just a lot of heavy breathing and then a clatter before the line went dead. Probably a wrong number.' As he finished speaking it rang again. He retraced his steps and Jo took the opportunity to get up and turn the lights on around the room. As before Simon came back quickly. He shrugged. 'Same again.'

The phone rang for a third time. 'This is getting silly.' Jo followed Simon into the hall and watched as this time he snatched the receiver from the cradle and snapped, 'Listen, mate, I don't know who you are or what you want but you really ought to do something about that asthma because the heavy breathing routine went out with the ark. Now stop wasting your money and go and bother someone else.' He hung up sharply. 'That ought to do it!' Jo was going to suggest he dialled call-back but Simon had already returned to the fire. She didn't want to take the initiative and risk upsetting him. She left the receiver in the cradle and followed Simon back into the warmth, but the mood had been broken and the calls had made Simon withdraw a little. Jo felt as if the barrier they had been trying hard all weekend to destroy had been re-erected between them.

Later that evening the phone rang again and this time it was Jo who went to answer it. 'Joanne?' queried a tremulous voice after a couple of seconds' silence. Jo's heart sank as she heard Maggie's voice. *Don't do this to me. Not now*, she thought to herself. Swallowing a sigh she kept her voice as level as possible, not wanting to let her irritation show.

'Hello, Maggie . . .' But before she could say anything else Maggie interrupted her, words tumbling breathlessly over each other.

'Thank - goodness - I - tried - to - get - you - earlier - but - I - was - too-upset-I-couldn't-talk-please-come-over-you've-got-to-come-over-and-help-me-I-don't-know-what-to-do.'

'Maggie, you haven't told me what's wrong. Now take a deep breath and start again from the beginning nice and slowly. What's happened?' For once Jo was concerned. Her mother sounded genuinely upset, and the fact that she had called Jo herself rather than leaving it to Stella to summon her was also unusual. It added to Jo's feeling that something was really wrong. She heard Maggie gulp before she began to talk again. After a few false starts she eventually began to speak. Her voice was still shaky but she sounded more in control. 'Phone calls, I'm getting nasty phone calls. They're frightening and . . .' Maggie's resolve gave way and she began to whimper.

'Is anyone with you?'

'No. I told June she could go after lunch.'

'Have you contacted Stella?'

'Joanne, please. I couldn't cope with Stella. Please.' She began to get worked up again. Quickly Jo jumped in, understanding only too well what her mother meant about Stella.

'I'm on my way. I'll be with you as soon as I can. Now, I'm going to call Mary and ask her to come and sit with you until I get there. If the phone rings again just *don't* answer it.' She rang off and yelled over her shoulder to Simon as she looked up Mary's number. Mary was an amiable girl from a large Irish family who lived in Blackheath village. She went in three times a week to clean Maggie's flat and was one of the few people who let Maggie's moaning wash over her with no effect. Bearing in mind it was a Sunday and difficult to get hold of anyone she seemed the best bet to keep Maggie quiet until Jo got there.

'It's Maggie and something's upset her. I'm going to have to go down there,' Jo called as she dialled Mary's number.

Simon came to the living-room door. 'Typical. We try to have one lousy weekend together by ourselves and the moment your bloody mother snaps her fingers you go running.'

'Si, that's not fair. She is very upset and . . .' She held a hand up to Simon as someone answered the phone at the other end. 'Hello, Mary? Jo Edwardes. I'm so sorry about this but I have a favour to beg. Maggie's just called and she seems really distressed. Something to do with dirty phone calls. Yes, I know, horrid. Anyway, I'm about to jump in the car. I should be there in an hour at the most so would you be able to go and sit with her until I arrive? You're an angel. See you soon.' She turned to Simon but he had gone back into the living room. She followed him but he ignored her.

'Si, I agree she's a bloody pest but this time she really does sound wound up about something. You tell me what else I can do but go over there?'

Simon finally looked at her. 'Oh, I don't know, Jo. It's just knowing she annoys you almost as much as she does me and the fact that you can't stand her that I find so galling. It's so damn hypocritical!' He was clearly trying to be understanding but his tone gave him away. He also spoke quietly, which made him sound even angrier than usual. A shouting Simon she could cope with, but this controlled version scared her, making her sound hysterical in comparison.

'I don't like it any more than you do but you're not helping the situation. You know I'd rather stay here with you. We've been having such a lovely cosy weekend but . . . Well, who else is there? Between the pair of you I feel pulled in all directions at once. You know I don't *want* to go but I can't just ignore her, can I? Look, why don't you come with me? I'd like that and at least we'd still be together.'

'Oh p-leee-se! I've got better things to do on a miserable Sunday night than baby-sit your bloody mother.'

Jo could have kicked herself. Simon had made it obvious a few months after they started going out that he found Maggie a pain and that he had no intention of going with Jo when she was hauled across town to visit her. For Jo, unintentionally, to call his bluff by suggesting he went with her was a mistake. His flash of trying to be understanding had been just that, a flash. The look on his face told her that any chance she'd had of winning him round had now gone. '*Damn!*' She swore under her breath.

'You're in the way. I want to watch the football.' He bent sideways round her to flick the remote control at the TV. Jo knew it wasn't worth continuing the argument. Besides, she didn't have time for it now. She ran upstairs to change into her boots and get her coat. Five minutes later she was in the car with the wipers going at maximum speed as she made her way towards Regent's Park.

Progress was slow as the rain continued to beat down, making visibility difficult, but because it was Sunday the roads were at least fairly empty. After less than an hour she parked in front of the flats and ran to the door. For once she didn't buzz Stella's flat but pressed Maggie's bell straight away. Mary answered and let her in. As Jo pushed her way through the double doors leading to Maggie's bit of the hall she met Mary coming towards her. 'Oh, it's that glad I am to see you. I don't know what's wrong but something's got her worried. She kept looking at the phone, scared like, but she wouldn't say nothing 'cept "Where's Joanne?"' Jo undid her coat and shook her head, showering raindrops around the hall.

'That's fine, Mary. Thank you for coming out on a night like this. She sounded so upset I didn't want to leave her by herself.' She rummaged in her bag and got out her purse. 'Here, take this for your trouble,' and she handed the girl a crumpled five pound note.

'Thank you, Jo, although I wasn't here for a full hour.'

'Maybe not, but it probably felt like it,' and Jo smiled as Mary replied, 'It did at that.'

Squaring her shoulders she walked purposefully into the living room where Maggie was sitting huddled in her wheelchair. Jo was quietly pleased to see she had last year's Christmas present, a burgundy cashmere shawl, round her shoulders. At the time Maggie had made some derogatory remark about the gift even though Jo knew she really appreciated its luxury. If Maggie had been completely well she would never have let Jo see her wearing anything she had given her. The fact she was doing so now reinforced Jo's opinion that, for once, Maggie was not putting on an act.

That and the way in which she was sitting. Even when she was feigning illness Maggie always sat upright in her chair, somehow projecting frailty from the angle of her head and the position of her bent hands. Now her shoulders had fallen forwards slightly and her head had dropped a little towards her chest. The twisted fingers were as they always were, on her lap, but instead of resting on each other Maggie had somehow managed to interweave them and the knuckles were shiny and white from the tension this created.

'Maggie?' Jo asked softly. 'What is it, what's happened?'

Slowly she raised her eyes to look at her daughter. They were as bright as ever behind the glasses but this was due to a misting of tears that threatened to spill over. 'Phone calls,' she whispered. 'Nasty phone calls.'

'What about them? What do they say?' Jo was concerned. Bored and with nothing to do, the local youngsters had recently got into the habit of throwing things at The Warren's windows, or rattling the ornate grilles outside the public rooms. The police had been called in and caught them, a group of five young teenagers, but Jo hoped that they weren't now starting up again in a different way.

'They said "Make her co-operate",' Maggie said in a small voice.

'Make who co-operate with what?' Jo was puzzled.

'I don't know.' June had been there preparing lunch when the phone rang for the first time so she had answered it. She told Maggie what had been said but as it meant nothing to either of them they had both ignored it. It was after June had left and Maggie was quietly watching TV that the phone had gone again. This time Maggie had heard the man for herself. It still meant nothing. The phone had rung another six times that afternoon. Every time she considered letting it ring but just in case it was someone else she'd answered it, only to hear the same message repeated. Soon it stopped being a nuisance and became frightening, which was when she called Jo.

Now that Jo was here she began to feel safe again, but she didn't want her daughter to know that. If Jo had been paying more attention to Maggie's appearance and not been so bothered about trying to work out what the message meant, she might have noticed Maggie sitting a little bit straighter in her chair, her eyes looking less watery and her fingers gradually returning to their normal colour. But she was puzzling over the words and missed the signs. Which was also how Maggie persuaded her to stay the night.

Jo tried to explain to Simon what had happened, that Maggie really did need company, but he didn't want to listen. He was furious.

'You were the one who declared we should spend the weekend together with no interruptions. You were the one who said it was to be a special time just for us. You were the one who made this whole fuss about "togetherness". If I didn't know before who was more important to you I do now. It's obvious that manipulative old crow means more to you than me or our relationship. At least I know now where I stand. I hope you sleep *really* well,' he finished sarcastically.

'Si, please, can't we talk about this like two sensible people?' But he had already hung up without saying goodbye.

The evening dragged by, broken only by June coming in to prepare dinner. At ten-thirty June got Maggie ready for, and into bed. Jo offered to help but Maggie refused to let her. She couldn't bear the indignity of her daughter seeing her twisted body, so Jo busied herself by rooting out spare blankets to make up a bed on the sofa. She set a borrowed alarm clock for five-thirty a.m. to allow herself time to get back to Hampstead and change for work the next morning. It was annoying, because to get home she would have to drive right past the Pimlico Centre only to turn round and go straight back again to meet the crew there at eight. *I should keep a change of clothes there*, she decided.

It wasn't until she was settled down on the sofa that a thought occurred that made her chuckle for the first time since Maggie had spoken to her on the phone. The calls that Simon took during the afternoon and so effectively got rid of hadn't been a heavy breather at all. They were Maggie trying to make herself understood as she panicked over the messages she had been getting. Without knowing it, Si had told her mother to get lost. Not naturally malicious, Jo did nonetheless find herself thinking, *Serve her right*! and *At least that'll make Si laugh*, as she dropped off to sleep.

The next day she was jolted awake by the alarm ringing in her ear. For a moment she couldn't remember where she was but as she woke up properly the events of the night before came back to her. Carefully Jo eased herself into a sitting position. Her head was thumping and she was stiff from sleeping on the sofa. The argument with Simon had obviously upset her more than she appreciated. Even though she had slept deeply, angry, violent images had chased through her dreams all night long, leaving her emotionally drained.

She dressed quickly before creeping down the hall to put her head round Maggie's bedroom door. Her mother lay propped against her pillows, snoring gently. Her neat hair was held in place by a soft hairnet. The pink of her scalp shone through her thinning curls and without her glasses she looked gentle and vulnerable. *If only*, Jo thought ruefully to herself as she scribbled a couple of quick notes, one for her mother and one for June who would be along at seven to get Maggie ready for the day.

As she eased the car on to the main road Jo caught sight of a woman standing at the communal lounge window. She waved excitedly as Jo drove past and automatically Jo waved back. Edna Brealy had been one of the first people to move into The Warren. Everyone had expected her to die shortly after she had taken up residence, but far from fading away she had physically thrived in the close community. Mentally she had slipped further and further into her own world. She had a simple childlike trust and happiness, so if anyone found her strolling round the hallways or grounds singing to herself they would gently turn her round and lead her back to her own flat. At ninety-two she was the archetypal dotty old lady, and residents and visitors alike knew her well. You couldn't help smiling or waving back at Edna and seeing her now, standing at the window with her cardigan misbuttoned over her nightgown, a scarf wrapped round her neck, Jo found herself wondering how much easier life would be if Maggie had slipped into an equally demented existence instead of becoming the bitter woman she now was. *Maggie's always been like this, though*, Jo said to herself as she shot through New Cross. But she knew that wasn't strictly true. *When Howard was around she did laugh and have fun.* Jo glanced left as she turned into Lewisham Way, checking nothing was coming.

Everyone had fun when he was around. The last time she saw her father she was six years old and she'd always thought of him as a big man. Admittedly this could have been because she was a little girl but the few photographs she had seen of him made her think she was right. He used to spoil her constantly, coming home with dolls and toys, or sometimes he would come to say goodnight bringing a large box with him. This was her cue to get out of bed again and help him open it, peeling back layers of tissue to reveal another pretty dress which she always had to try on immediately.

The adult Jo now knew that Maggie had felt left out, that the bond between father and daughter excluded her so that she always tried to come between them – to no avail. When Howard was with his 'Sparkie' no one else got a look in. The sudden memory of her father's nickname for her made her swerve and the driver of the car in the next lane hit his horn angrily. She felt a prickling up her arms and legs as she realised what a near miss she'd had and, pushing all thoughts of Howard out of her mind, she concentrated on getting home in one piece.

When she got there she was relieved to discover that Simon had not shot the bolt on the front door, so she could let herself in. He was already up and she could hear him clattering around in the kitchen. She took off her coat, leaving it at the bottom of the stairs, and made her way down the hall. Simon was waiting for the kettle to boil and was leaning on the counter reading the morning paper. He was wearing his robe and had yet to shave or comb his hair. Jo always found him particularly endearing when he looked like that and she quietly moved towards him, slipping her arms round his waist, rubbing her cheek on his broad towelling-covered back. The kettle boiled as she did so and he straightened up, unclasping her hands from around his middle. He made his tea and then, still without saying a word or even looking at her, he walked out, leaving her standing there feeling foolish.

'Si. I'm sorry.' She trailed after him.

'I don't want to talk about it. I'm bored by the whole subject and tired of your excuses. Now I would like to get dressed in peace and quiet if you don't mind.' He shut the bathroom door in her face.

Jo's pride reared its head and she joined Simon in a battle of silence as they both got ready for work. She had done her best to apologise but if he didn't want to try to understand or meet her half way, then tough. *I'm not grovelling, not this time*, she told herself determinedly as for the second time that morning she got into her car and headed for the centre of town.

Although it was only seven forty-five when she waved good morning to Cyril and parked her car, the rest of the crew were already there and work in the exhibition halls had been going on since six. 'What I need you lot to do today is set up time-lapse cameras for the show village. We'll probably only use a few seconds in the final thing but please make sure the angles include an overview to give the feeling of everything that's going on. Exhibitions International are very proud of what they're doing this year so let's try and capture some of that.

'Give me a yell when everything is in place so I can come and check it. I've got a meeting at the House with the Speaker's PPS to sort out some of the scheduling for *that* programme so you'll be pretty much on your own today.'

Tony and Bill set off with the equipment to the centre of the hall. The rest of the crew disappeared to their various tasks so Jo took advantage of the empty office to do yet more desk work on the House of Commons programme, trying to reschedule it with the others in the series. It looked as if there was going to be a nasty clash between a big debate in the House and the start of a major Old Bailey trial that she wanted to get for the Helena Kennedy programme.

She was deeply engrossed, with charts spread across her desk as she cross-referred from one to the other, a rubber and pencil gripped in her fingers. It was an automatic response to say 'Come in' when someone knocked on the door. She carried on with what she was doing, frantically scrubbing out some of the pencilled schedule, and didn't look up until she heard a polite cough.

'Sorry if I'm bothering you but I wanted to extend a peace offering.' To all intents and purposes she was being addressed by a large pot plant with a white flag stuck into the front of the pot.

Puzzled, she laughed. 'Who's behind that thing?' Her face fell and her temper began to rise as Alan Waterman lowered the plant to peer over it.

'Oh, don't be like that,' he said quickly, seeing her face. 'I've come to apologise for my behaviour last week. I was right out of order saying what I did to you and I'm sorry.' He seemed so sincere and genuinely apologetic that she couldn't help but smile again, the anger subsiding almost as quickly as it had appeared.

'Apology accepted, but this,' she indicated the plant, 'really wasn't necessary.'

'Yes it was. I needed it as camouflage so I could storm the enemy camp.'

'I'm not that bad, am I?' Jo gave him a coquettish look which covered her real thoughts. She hated to think that the image Alan had of her, either professionally or personally, was as an ogre, but she *was* meant to be in charge.

'No, of course not,' Alan reassured her. 'Don't forget I work for Suzanne, I'm used to tough women. In fact they're my favourite sort so I was hoping that I might be able to start again, if you'd let me? I was wondering about dinner tonight. I know it's short notice but once we're here and build-up gets going it's a question of grabbing time when you can. How about it?'

Jo thought for a moment. Given all the trouble with Simon over the weekend it might make more political sense to go home tonight and attempt to make things up with him. On the other hand Alan was making an effort and Simon had been such a pig he needed to be taught a lesson. It was more the idea that going out with Alan would upset Si than the actual appeal of a meal with him that made her finally accept. 'I'd like that,' she said. *To hell with Si, let him stew in his own juice for a while*, she thought petulantly, knowing she would probably only be making matters worse.

'Pick you up here at seven then.' And with a mock bow he went whistling his way down the Portacabin steps and across into the main building.

It turned into a very hectic day. The time-lapse equipment played up so it had to be returned to the hire company and more brought in. Jo was almost late for the Houses of Parliament. Her meeting there dragged on but at least it gave her a chance to absorb more of the atmosphere of the place. As she sat discussing timetables she was also mentally lining up shots and angles in her head. The short journey back to Pimlico was also unusually difficult and by the time she arrived there she was tired but surprisingly alert. It was a feeling that grew as the evening drew closer. She kept telling herself it was silly, that it was only a friendly meal between work associates, but somewhere deep inside she felt a small tremor. It reminded her of how she had felt about Simon when they first started going out with each other. She pushed the memory to one side. Nevertheless, at six forty-five she made an effort to tidy herself up. She rummaged under her desk to dig out a pair of high-heeled shoes from the assortment that always seemed to follow her around and from her bottom drawer pulled out a long scarf that she had unceremoniously dumped there a couple of days earlier after filming some reverses (when the camera had been turned on her as the interviewer so she could record some reaction shots to be edited in later) and not quite got round to taking home.

'What's all this in aid of, then?' queried Laura when she came to get her coat to go home.

'I'm going out for a friendly dinner with Alan.' Jo caught sight of her PA's expression reflected in the mirror and turned to face her. 'Don't go getting the wrong idea. He brought that this morning,' she pointed to the plant, still complete with its white flag, 'as an opener, and he wants to apologise properly by buying me dinner. That's all. And anyway, it's been a shitty day and I could do with a bit of spoiling.'

'If that's all then why . . .' Laura began, but was interrupted by Alan appearing at the door.

'All ready? Great, then let's go.' Alan hailed a taxi, explaining that parking would be difficult, and directed the driver to the Albery Theatre in St Martin's Lane. Jo was surprised by the instruction but Alan explained that even London cabbies had problems finding Goodwin's Court, the tiny passage where the restaurant was, so it was easier to be taken to the theatre at its bottom end. When they were dropped off Alan led the way up the narrow alleyway. It was lined with small doors and windows and they had walked almost its full length when Alan stopped, ushering her towards a door on the left-hand side. They went through a curtain and into a sizeable but cosy room. There was a bar in front of them and beyond that a restaurant with a big leaded curved window.

The tables gleamed with silverware and crisp white linen. The walls were lined with photographs of famous people, all signed with love to 'Giovanni', and as she looked round the clientèle already seated at their tables she recognised several faces. The dumb waiter rattled up from the floor below and she could see plates of steaming food being put on to the trolley. The smell of garlic, rich tomato sauce, fresh fish and meat mingled with the more general smells of polished wood and good wine. Jo's mouth began to water. *Thank God I tarted myself up a bit*, she thought as an elegant, distinguished man in glasses made his way towards them.

He greeted Alan warmly and was introduced to Jo. 'This,' said Alan, 'is Giovanni. He makes the best *fritto misto* in London and I'll let him tell you about the parma ham.' Giovanni grinned and politely showed them to their table. He asked Alan about his family before going to fetch the menus. 'I was first brought here by my parents when I was about twelve and I fell in love with it then. Nothing's really changed since and that's one of the things I love about it. My God!' he said suddenly, 'I never thought to ask. You do like Italian food, don't you?'

'I love it,' Jo replied with a grin, 'especially good Italian food, which is what this looks like.' Giovanni returned in time to hear her comment and swelled with pride, accepting the compliment as his natural right.

He talked them through the menu, explaining that the parma ham was flown in from his family in Italy where it was home cured, and after much deliberation Jo decided to start with the parma ham and melon followed by trout. Alan also chose parma ham but followed this with *fritto misto*. 'I always order the same thing,' he explained. 'The fish here is so fresh that I can never decide what to have so a bit of everything seems the best solution.' Antonio, the wine waiter, came over, discussed the wine with Alan and disappeared to return with a bottle of white so cold that the condensation dripped off it.

Alan tasted the wine and gave his approval. It was only when the bread sticks were open and their glasses were filled that they were finally left alone. Alan raised his glass. 'May I now formally say how sorry I am about the way I behaved last week. I have no excuses other than the fact it really was a bitch of a week. However, that doesn't excuse the fact that I was both unprofessional and ungentlemanly in the extreme.'

Jo lifted her glass to meet his. 'May I also apologise for my behaviour. You had – have – a difficult job to do and I shouldn't expect everything to stop because I need or want it to.' With the ceremonies out of the way they both settled down and began to chat.

The conversation was cautious at first, both of them very much on their best behaviour, but as the evening went by and they started their second bottle of wine the tension began to ease, as they relaxed in each other's company. Jo found it easy to talk to Alan and he was also pleasantly surprised to discover what good company she could be.

It was true that he did feel bad about his behaviour the week before but initially his invitation had had more to do with the fact that he'd heard about Jo's evening drink with Suzanne. This piece of information had made him realise that the programme was probably more important to his boss than he had first thought, so he had decided to push the boat out to make amends.

However, what had originally been intended as a good bit of personal PR was turning into a surprisingly enjoyable evening. Jo told tales about some of the things that could happen on a location shoot. Her stories ranged from the tale of a film crew wrapping a loo bowl tightly in cling film so it could not be seen, and what happened when some unsuspecting newcomer went to use it, to the incident of a director who, covering a new item for the first time, was so busy concentrating on his subject that he didn't realise – until he got back to the studio – that a flasher had availed himself of the cameras behind the interviewee. Alan retaliated with stories of exhibition life. Of the exhibitor at an alternative health show who had refused to work with the organisers because their auras were the wrong colour. And of the model at a wedding exhibition who had forgotten to mention she was six months pregnant when she was booked for the bridal fashion show. By the time their main courses arrived they looked like old friends chatting and laughing together.

Eventually the conversation began to turn to more personal topics. Alan made some comment about his background and soon Jo had found out that he was the black sheep of his family, having deviated from the traditional Waterman path of a career in the City for one in PR and marketing. Alan's impression of his father's reaction when he told him he wanted to work in public relations made Jo laugh and the mouthful of fish she was eating went down the wrong way. Alan jumped up to give her a thump on the back. Jo gasped as she cleared her throat. 'I'm OK,' she said without much conviction.

'Here, drink this.' Alan sat down again and gave her a glass of water. Gratefully she took it and sipped slowly, replacing it on the table when she had finished. Her left hand was still spread across the middle of the table cloth, her right held to her throat as she gradually began to breathe normally again.

'Are you sure you're all right?' Alan asked, putting his hand over hers on the table. Jo pulled it back quickly, as if it had been burned, catching Alan's palm with her ring as she did so, making him also draw his hand away to lick the skin where the diamond solitaire had caught it.

'Oh God, I'm sorry,' Jo apologised. 'You made me jump, that's all.' In fact the touch of Alan's hand had done more than make her jump.

His warm firm fingers had made her feel the same frisson of excitement she had felt that morning when he asked her out. Already concerned about Simon, these were emotions she certainly did not want even to consider at the moment.

'What was that?' Alan asked as he rubbed his thumb over his sore hand.

'My ring.' She held up her left hand and in the warm light the diamond sparkled particularly brightly. Alan felt a quiver of disappointment shoot through him as he acknowledged her engagement ring.

'Who's the lucky fellow?' he asked, trying to sound uninterested.

Jo hesitated for a moment. She had been about to give Alan the usual pat answer about her wonderful, gorgeous fiance but suddenly she wanted to tell someone about Simon, about the problems they were going through and her doubts about their relationship. Katie knew some of it but Jo had held back from moaning too much. Katie and Stuart were too close to her and Si for comfort. Other women might talk to their mother but with Maggie that was out of the question. The angst of the last twenty-four hours welled up inside her again. The pleasure she had been feeling ebbed away to be replaced with the nagging sense of unhappiness that her disagreements with Simon had lodged, it felt almost permanently, deep inside her. To her intense fury, and surprise, the resurgence of the knots in her stomach made tears catch at the back of her throat. She swallowed a couple of times, pushing them back down.

Seeing her discomfort Alan leaned forward across the table. 'Jo, I'm sorry, I didn't mean to pry.' She was clearly upset and it bothered him to think that such an innocent question could trigger such an intense reaction. 'Come on, I'll get the bill. If you want the loo it's downstairs,' he finished tactfully.

Thankfully Jo excused herself and made her way to the ladies. She was the only one in there and gratefully she leaned her head against the cool tiles, gazing mournfully at her reflection. The tears final spilled over to trickle down her cheeks. 'Oh shit,' she murmured, grabbing at the paper towels to scrub away angrily at her eyes. She took a few deep breaths and got herself under control before making her way back upstairs. Alan had settled the bill and was waiting by the bar with her coat. They made their farewells and Jo smiled at Giovanni, assuring him that she had had an excellent meal and that she would be back.

'Fancy a stroll before going home?' It was a light question but Jo agreed; she wanted to put off facing Simon for as long as possible. The cool night air ruffled their hair and as Alan steered them towards Leicester Square Jo took a sideways glance at him. He was not as stunningly drop-dead as Simon.

But, she asked herself, thinking of her fiance's solid, broad frame and classic blond-haired, blue-eyed looks, *who is?* Nevertheless, he was good-looking. She reckoned he was about six foot tall and, unlike a lot of men whose suits seemed to wear them, Alan looked comfortable in his. His brown hair was well cut and his brown eyes had genuine laughter lines at their outer edges. Jo also noted that when they crossed the road he automatically crossed to her outside. It made her remember how her father did that too, and how he made her feel very grown-up and safe, explaining that a gentleman always walked closest to the road to protect his lady.

The unbidden memory made her stop suddenly and Alan did likewise, his head on one side as he looked at her curiously. 'I've got something in my shoe,' she explained lamely as she went through the motions of taking it off and shaking it out. In truth what had made her stop was the awareness that with Alan she felt safe. From what or whom she did not know, but it was a feeling she had forgotten. It was one that Simon had not evoked in her for a very long time, not even, she told herself, at the weekend when they had been so close. Comfortable, yes, but safe? That was something different. It was all so confusing.

They had reached Leicester Square and as it was ten-thirty the cinemas were beginning to empty. People teemed across the pavement and a couple of street entertainers were trying to earn a final few meagre pence before packing up. They stopped by a fire eater and without thinking Jo slipped her arm into Alan's. For a moment he was surprised but then gave her an affectionate squeeze with his elbow. The little show finished and they carried on strolling round before eventually sitting down on a bench.

'I'm sorry for that silly display,' Jo began.

'Will you stop apologising? It happens. No problem.' Alan tried to soothe her but now she had started Jo wanted to carry on, and carry on she did.

'No, you don't understand. I was – *am* – having a lovely evening. I'll be honest, I didn't think I would. I thought you were doing this out of some sense of duty.' In the dark Alan felt himself redden a little as Jo correctly identified his original motive. 'And I only agreed to come out with you because I knew it would piss Simon off. We had the most terrible fight yesterday and even though I wanted to make up he's carried it on today. It's just been awful.' Alan could sense the misery she was feeling, it had wrapped itself round her like a blanket, and was all the more surprising because he'd had her down as a bright and cheerful person. In fact when he had first met her he had dismissed Jo as flippant. To discover this vulnerability and depth of feeling to her was a pleasant surprise.

He knew from personal experience how Jo was feeling. He had been married and divorced by the time he was twenty-seven and even now, ten years later, could remember all too clearly the anguish of the constant fights and bickering, and the way it dragged him down. The fact that he and his ex-wife were now good friends made their marriage even more laughable. It had been a classic case of two people who should never have got married in the first place. Maybe that was how it was with Jo and Simon? He said nothing, keeping his thoughts to himself, wanting her to continue. Slowly she began to talk again and over the next hour, as the crowds in the Square began to thin out, she poured her heart out to Alan. At some point he took her hand and this time she didn't pull away.

It was such a relief finally to be able to say what she was thinking, to voice her confusion about her relationship. Alan stayed silent as she told him about her mother and how she affected her relationship with Simon. About how she had worked to get where she was, the odd hours her job involved and how that had also changed things with her partner. How despite Si's assertions that he wanted a modern woman, Jo felt that underneath it all his traditional upbringing made it harder for him than he realised. Jo voiced her concerns about Simon's drinking and her feelings generally for him, and spoke about how grateful she was to him for loving her, for taking away the loneliness. She briefly talked about her father and his relationship with Maggie. She touched on how difficult it had been growing up without him. It was close to midnight when she finally ground to a halt.

Alan withdrew his hand and placed his arm round her. Emotionally drained, she put her head on his shoulder, feeling the warmth of his body next to hers and savouring again that same sense of security.

'Feeling better?' he asked. Jo nodded.

Trust me! he thought. *Trust me to find a woman I really fancy who is not only engaged to someone else but is so screwed up about him that if I had any sense I'd run in the opposite direction. Here's another lame duck for your collection!* His family often joked that since his marriage he had done nothing but go out with women with problems. It was his sister who had let slip over lunch one Sunday that his various girlfriends were referred to by the rest of the family as the LDC – Lame Duck Collection – which led to a hilarious hour as they took it in turn to dissect various partners he and his two sisters had had over the years. Alan thought about his family now about the closeness and comfortable friendship that existed amongst them all, and realised how lucky he was. He understood this was something Jo didn't have and it looked as if he might again be running to his usual form, adding to the LDC.

'It's late. We'd better get you home,' he said softly to his latest lame duck.

Reluctantly Jo raised her head. 'Yes. Staying out all night isn't going to solve anything, is it? I have to face Si at some point and sort this out.'

'If he matters that much to you then yes, you do.'

Slowly they stood up and made their way towards Piccadilly Circus. Alan hesitated for a moment and then took Jo's hand. Again she didn't pull away, enjoying the warmth the contact with him gave her. They agreed that neither of them should drive home and as Alan lived in Northwood they would share a taxi, detouring via Hampstead. They found a cab easily and sat, still holding hands in the back. Their driver tried to chat to them but, getting nothing but grunts from his passengers, gave up. As they drew close to Hampstead Station Jo told the driver to pull over. 'I'm just round the corner and it's probably better to drop me here.' Understanding that although it had been an innocent evening she didn't want to make matters worse with Simon by risking him seeing them together, Alan reluctantly let go of her hand.

'It's going to be all right. You'll see.' He leaned towards her and kissed her gently on the cheek. Jo got out of the taxi and stood under a street lamp, watching the cab until it disappeared round the curve in the road. She ran her fingers across her cheek where Alan had kissed her and began to walk slowly towards Church Row, her hands in her pockets and her head down. As she got to the corner she took a deep breath, raised her head and quickened her pace to bounce up the steps to the front door. The Chubb lock was on, so it was obvious that Simon was still out. She got inside and checked the answer machine to hear her own voice telling Simon she would be home late.

The next call was from Simon leaving a similar message for her. It was clear he didn't know she'd been out all night. Relieved that there would be no row that evening she cleared the machine. Although her original motive in accepting Alan's invitation had been to upset Simon, the last thing she now felt like was facing him. Wearily she got ready for bed and had just settled down and turned off the lamp when she heard his key in the lock. From the way he thumped his way upstairs she could tell he'd been drinking. She buried herself under the duvet and pretended to be asleep.

When the radio turned itself on the next morning Simon gave a grunt and rolled over. Jo had been awake for some time but had lain unmoving, watching the sun trickle through the gaps in the curtains, showing up the dust particles, as she thought about the night before and Alan. *How the hell am I going to face him? I'll tell him nothing happened.* Making sure she didn't wake Simon she carefully rolled over. *But nothing did happen did it, you stupid woman? Big deal, you told him your life story and snuggled up in the back of a taxi. So what?*

But you wanted more, said another little voice at the back of her head. Guiltily she ignored it, telling herself all she wanted was Simon, that he was the one that mattered. It made her aware of his sleeping form lying next to her and the need somehow to put things back on track again.

This silence can't go on. It's getting silly. One of us should try to start the ball rolling. Trouble is, if I leave it to Si his bloody pride will get in the way and we'll end up never speaking to each other again. So it's down to me again. Why does it always have to be me?

She listened to his gentle breathing and shifted to lie on her other side, facing his back. She could feel the warmth of his body and carefully moved closer, her own body taking on the curve of his. When he rolled over he bumped into her and opened his eyes sharply.

'Morning.' Had he forgotten that he was maintaining a barrage of silence? 'I feel bloody awful.' Clearly it wasn't so much that he had forgotten, more that he had a terrible hangover. 'Sorry I came in so late last night. I was being stupid. Am I forgiven?'

Whether he was apologising for his late night or his part in their argument Jo wasn't sure. She was just so relieved that for once he had been the first to breach the gap that she felt an overwhelming surge of affection inside her. The gratitude she always felt towards him simply for loving her raced to the surface. Jo ran her fingers lightly across his forehead then, seeing him wince, got out of bed and headed for the bathroom cabinet. She dropped a couple of soluble aspirin in a glass of water and made her way back to the bedroom. 'Here you go, drink that.' Cautiously Simon half sat up and took the glass.

'It wouldn't be so bad if I'd enjoyed it but I only did it to get my own back on you. And anyway, I was just being silly. I know you had to go to Maggie's. Trouble is, I just don't like sharing you. I want you here with me. I mean it's bad enough sharing you with your job.' He sprawled in bed, his hair flopping in his eyes, and for a moment Jo was reminded of a naughty schoolboy with his shirt tails hanging out and his cap on crooked.

'I know, but let's not discuss it now. Let's wait until you're feeling a bit better, hmm?'

What am I saying? Jo thought. *Yes, now, yes, let's talk about things, let's discuss it all properly. What are you scared of, Edwardes?* She gave Simon's hand a squeeze. 'I'll go and put the kettle on.'

Jo grabbed her dressing gown and made her way downstairs. As she waited for the water to boil she leaned against the counter sipping a glass of orange juice. *Why can't I just sit him down and talk to him? Tell him what I'm feeling? It's madness. I can sit in Leicester Square and say exactly what I want to a virtual stranger but to the one person who matters, the man I really care about, I can't say a thing. Maybe I just don't want to face up to the fact that Si and I have grown apart and really shouldn't be together any more.*

It was such an unexpected thought that it made her stand upright, slopping some of her juice on the counter. Before she could examine the idea any further the kettle turned itself off and she heard Simon making his way downstairs. Grateful that she could bury her thoughts by being busy she began to bustle around making the coffee.

The rest of their early morning passed by as usual and it wasn't until the taxi dropped Jo at the Pimlico Centre that she thought again about Simon or Alan. Laura gave her a cheeky grin as she walked into the office. 'Hiya, I noticed your car was here this morning and as there was no sign of you I assume it was here all night. Good dinner?' She raised her eyebrows slightly and bit her lower lip, amused.

'Mmm, it was, and it was also easier leaving the car here than coming by to pick it up,' Jo said defensively. 'Hey, why the hell am I explaining myself to you?' she asked, laughing to hide her confusion about the night before.

'Because like every good PA I'm the depository of your innermost thoughts. So if there really are no juicy details you wish to share with me I'd better tell you that Suzanne has asked to see you. Nine thirty upstairs.'

Jo glanced at the clock. Shit! It was already nine-twenty so she quickly grabbed a notepad and, clipping her security pass on to her lapel, made her way to the management offices. She knew she would have to face Alan at some point, apologise, yet again (*Why do I do nothing but apologise to that man?*) but she hadn't expected to see him sitting on the edge of Julia's desk. Jo faltered for a moment but quickly regained her composure. 'Thank you for a lovely meal,' she murmured as Julia showed them into Suzanne's office.

Suzanne left her desk to sit on one of the functional, if not stylish, armchairs with Jo and Alan sitting at either end of the matching sofa. Julia brought in a tray of coffee and put it on the low table between them. 'Julia, can you find somewhere for Kew Gardens please?' Suzanne picked up a heavy vase full of opulent oversized lilies that sat in the centre of the table. 'They provide these automatically. Every day I move them off the table and every night the cleaners put them back. It's just another of our sillier on-going battles,' she explained. 'Now, to work.

'As you have probably discovered during the week or so you've been with us, this place,' she indicated the Pimlico Centre, 'is exhausting. Build-up is bad enough but once we've opened and the hordes are with us it gets worse. On a bad day, that is a good day for visitor numbers, it's not unusual for it to take half an hour to get from here to the organisers' office in Pim Three. You need to be fit and healthy to get through it unscathed. After six weeks of air-conditioning, stuffy exhibition halls and other people's bugs and germs it's a rare person who hasn't gone down with something – so be warned!'

'One of these years we'll do a deal with someone for free supplies of tissues,' Alan quipped. Jo noticed he was sitting a bit stiffly in his seat and realised with surprise that he felt slightly ill at ease in his boss's presence. She pulled her attention back to Suzanne.

'We all prepare ourselves in our own way and mine is to leave everything to the rest of them for a short time while I disappear to a health farm. So come Thursday I'm off to Ragdale Hall for a weekend of primping, pampering and spoiling. I've thought carefully about this and I know it's short notice but if you would like to come with me I'd welcome your company.'

Alan's eyebrows shot up as he listened to Suzanne. Her trip to Ragdale was as much a part of their preparations for the exhibition as building the stands and selling tickets. Up until now it had always been sacrosanct. When she was there she refused to hold meetings, take phone calls or even respond to faxes. Every single exhibitor could walk out, the Pimlico Centre could burn down but still Suzanne would do nothing until the Monday morning when she was back in harness.

It was an amazing invitation. Alan held his breath, not knowing why it had been extended but hoping Jo would understand that she was being given the chance to see the truly private Suzanne Prescott.

Although unaware of the enormity of the invitation, Jo did appreciate that it meant she had won Suzanne's trust. It was a good feeling, and she knew that getting to knew Suzanne better would make the programme better too. Unlike Alan she wasn't in awe of Suzanne, feeling oddly at ease with her. She hesitated as fleeting concern about Simon's reaction when she told him she was going to be away over the weekend crossed her mind, but it was only a moment's hesitation. 'Suzanne, thank you. I'd be delighted to accept.'

'Good, I'll get Julia to make the booking. How do you feel it's all going?' she asked, changing the subject.

The question caught Jo slightly unawares and she found herself mumbling something about it being a much bigger operation than she had originally anticipated.

Suzanne laughed. 'Most people just don't realise exactly what's involved in putting on a show the size of Home Maker. And yes, I do include the exhibitors in that. The way some of them go on you'd think they were the only company showing here. Ah well, nature of the beast, I suppose.' She stood up, clearly indicating that the short interview was over.

As Jo and Alan headed for the door Suzanne called him back. *Damn!* thought Jo as she made her way to the lift. It wasn't, she told herself firmly, that she particularly wanted his company (though she did), but rather that she wanted an opportunity to apologise for her behaviour the previous night. Like everyone else who worked at the Pimlico Centre she had quickly learned that the lift took a long time coming, but today, of course, it arrived almost immediately. She let it go telling herself that if Alan hadn't emerged by the time it returned she would get that one. In fact Jo let the lift go three times before the office door opened and Alan appeared. She suddenly felt shy and gave him a tentative smile as he stabbed the down button again.

'Alan, about last night . . .' Jo began cautiously. 'I wanted to say I'm sorry about the way I behaved. I had a lovely evening but I don't want you to get the wrong idea. I mean . . .' At that moment the lift arrived and they both got in. Two other people were already there so Jo stopped speaking, not wanting to continue in front of them. When they got out at the ground floor she opened her mouth to continue but Alan put his hand out and stopped her.

'Let me make it easier for you, shall I? We'd both had a lot to drink. You're obviously having a bit of a shitty time personally at the moment and I would only complicate things further, so much as you enjoyed my company and had a good evening that's as far as it goes. How does that sound?' he asked without rancour.

Once again Jo found herself red with embarrassment as she talked to Alan. 'That's pretty well it,' she said feebly. 'No hard feelings?'

'No, of course not. But remember, any time you need to talk I'm here, OK?' *Bloody hell, Waterman, you sound like everyone's best buddy, you creep!* Alan thought to himself as, biting her lower lip, Jo nodded. Like a fool she suddenly found herself feeling choked and quickly turned away, letting her hair swing over her face to cover her emotions as she made her way back to her own office.

The build-up was not going well. The police were still snooping around and ever since part of the exhibition had been so carefully dismantled the carpenters, stand-fitters and electricians had become deeply mistrustful of each other. The security men had become even more surly and it seemed as if the usual rift between organisers and exhibitors had widened and deepened overnight. Gordon made a point of coming in even earlier than usual. For a few days the halls resounded with the usual mixture of noises; the tannoy messages, the blaring radios of the contractors, the banging and drilling on the stands all overlaid by people yelling and shouting to and at each other.

It was while Suzanne was away at Ragdale that someone carefully went into one of the newly decorated show houses and very precisely stripped the freshly applied wallpaper from the walls, leaving a soggy pile in the middle of each room. The mess was found just after the contractors came in at seven o'clock the next morning and once again the word spread round the exhibitors like wild fire. They all knew the contractors worked on a very tight schedule to get these full-sized show houses built in the exhibition halls in time for press day. If the work wasn't finished then Health and Safety would not allow the show to open and every exhibitor would have an insurance claim to file. No wonder they all held their breath waiting to see what would happen.

A lone figure on one of the electrical access walkways looked down on the confusion as nearby workers gathered to find out what was happening. Alan pushed his way through the crowd and disappeared inside the house to look at the damage.

The man standing high on the gantry walkway enjoyed the worried expression on the marketing director's face. From his overhead vantage point he watched Alan weave his way between the half-finished stands. The man kept his radio to his ear, listening to the exchange between the staff as they asked frantic questions and called instructions to one another from all areas of the vast halls. That was the joy of radios. You could be anywhere, still in touch and no one knew where you were.

'Alan to Gordon. Over.'

Gordon answered the call. 'Go ahead.'

'Gordon, I don't know where in God's name in the halls you are, or why you're not here, but could you please get a team over to house three to clean up. I'm going to talk to security to see if we can find out what the hell's going on.' Alan was livid that the floor manager wasn't around. This was Gordon's responsibility, not his. He was so angry he didn't care that Suzanne would bawl him out when she heard he had used an open radio frequency. Besides, with everything that was going on you would have thought that *this* year at least bloody Ragdale could have gone by the board. And why the hell did she have to drag Jo with her?

Furiously he began picking his way through the wood, cartons, tools and cables that criss-crossed the floor, but a sudden eruption of noise behind him made him turn round and quickly retrace his steps.

The contractor responsible for decorating and fitting up the houses had hurled abuse at the security guard about not doing his job. The guard in turn had responded with some equally fruity language. By the time Alan made it back to the men things had become very heated. The contractor had curled his hand into a fist ready to swing at the security man. Alan got there just in time to intercept the blow.

Boy, is he gonna 'ave a shiner and that will take some explaining to Madam, the watcher thought smugly to himself as he carefully tucked the scraper back into the carpenter's pouch he had found hanging on the gantry the night before. 'She'll soon come to her senses,' he murmured cheerfully as he made his way down the ladder. He brushed down his jacket, settled his radio in his hand and squared his shoulders before walking out of the side door and back to his work.

'So you never found out who dismantled those stands then?' Jo took another sip of her tea and looked at Suzanne over the rim of her cup.

'No, but I had a pretty good idea. Trouble was, with no real evidence there was nothing I could do. Want another one of those?' She indicated her head towards Jo's cup, changing the subject.

'Mmm, please. I'll get them.' Jo went to push herself out of the comfortable armchair but Suzanne was already on her feet so she sat back again and handed her the empty cup. Jo watched as Suzanne made her way over to the small bar. Like so many of the other guests at Ragdale Hall she was wearing little more than a long, warm dressing gown. Her usually immaculate hair still looked clean and shiny but as a result of hours spent in the pool, sauna and steam room it lay closer to her head. That, combined with her total lack of make-up, gave her a more vulnerable air. *Maybe that's why I'm finding it easy to forget who she is and why I'm here?* Jo mused as Suzanne made her way back to their corner of the peaceful, conservatory-like garden room.

As she sprinkled sweetener into her own cup Suzanne looked at Jo. Without realising it her thoughts were mirroring those of her guest. Jo was also wearing an over-sized robe (although Suzanne told her she could hire one from Ragdale Jo had preferred to borrow Simon's) and she kept having to roll the sleeves back when they flopped over her hands. She had curled her feet up under her and pulled the generous collar up round her face. She too had forgone make-up but in Jo's case this contrived to make her look much younger.

During the two days they had been together the women had got to know each other better. Jo had leaned that Suzanne was a much softer person than she had at first realised. There was a warmth about her that hovered quite close to the surface but which Suzanne chose to keep hidden. It made Jo feel surprisingly comfortable with her, so much so that she actually commented on it, making Suzanne chuckle.

'It's easy to understand. Show them you're a soft touch and you've had it. Especially in this business. There are some real characters in the exhibition game but most of them are men, and mostly they're a sexist lot. I'm not saying that out of some great feminist crusade. In the main they're a great bunch – a few crooks of course, but don't get me wrong. It's just a fact. This is very much a male-dominated industry. I discovered a long time ago that the trick is to flash 'em a bit of ankle now and again but play them at their own game. Make them think you can be as hard, if not harder than they are. Actually,' she continued with complete honesty, 'sometimes I wonder why I bother.

It's not always easy controlling everything and I think it would be nice to be one of the team again, but I guess I gave up that right years ago when I took over the company.' They fell into an easy contemplative silence, sipping their tea.

Jo suddenly found herself comparing the companionship she was experiencing with Suzanne with the relationship she didn't have with Maggie. It was probably because Suzanne was about twenty years her senior and therefore old enough to be her mother that Jo started thinking in that way. Once the thought had popped into her head she had problems dislodging it. while she was at Ragdale Jo came to realise that her relationship with Maggie lacked any sort of rapport. They just endured each other.

It was as if she and her mother were constantly facing each other from either side of a boxing ring, waiting for the bell to signal the start of round one. The trouble was it never did, and for years they had been squaring up to each other without ever reaching any conclusion. Initially she discussed none of this with Suzanne. Instead she watched the older woman when she wasn't looking, making the comparisons that led her to think it might be better if she and her mother actually yelled at each other. Then she recalled the rows that had gone on between Maggie and Howard and decided that maybe things were better as they were.

It was when she and Suzanne were feeling particularly relaxed, sitting by themselves in the steam room, that they drifted on to the subject of relationships. It was a cocooning, secure environment and Jo finally voiced some of the thoughts she had been mulling over about her feelings towards Maggie.

This is turn prompted Suzanne to talk more personally than she had before. For once, Jo didn't regret that she was not recording the conversation; she enjoyed just talking and listening to Suzanne as a person, not the subject of a documentary film.

'What my parents wanted didn't come into it. You must remember I was a Blitz baby and I was still very young when they both went. It was my aunt who brought me up and so long as I was happy then so was she. I don't think she ever felt that she was *allowed* to want anything for me as I wasn't really hers. It was almost as if she was scared to say she loved me in case someone came and said to her *She's not yours, give her to us*, but despite that I knew she really cared because everything she did showed she loved me.'

'Didn't that make you feel uncomfortable, though?'

'Why should it?' Suzanne asked with a puzzled smile, beginning to get het up as she continued to speak. 'I didn't know anything else, did I? I mean I knew that my aunt wasn't my mum, but I also knew that she cared. That was enough. My own mum had left me. Surely it's better for a child to be with someone who loves them even if they're not a parent, than with someone who doesn't give a *damn?*'

Suzanne became more insistent as she spoke and Jo was startled by the way she almost spat out the last word; involuntarily she drew back a little into the swirling steam.

'Sorry, I didn't mean to make you jump,' Suzanne said, lowering her voice. 'But I get so mad when people say a child's place is with its parents. Why, for goodness' sake? I know too many children who were brought up by people who didn't care about them. Kids aren't stupid, you know. They can tell what someone feels for them and respond accordingly. I mean look at how you feel about Maggie. From what you've told me your feelings stem from hers – or her lack of them.'

'Yes,' said Jo cautiously, 'you could be right. If I compare my feelings towards Maggie with those towards Howard – that's my father – they're totally different. He . . .' She paused for a moment. 'He left when I was small, so my memories of him are a bit hazy, but the one thing I still have from him is the feeling of being totally loved and admired. In as much as a child can know what it's like to be admired. Maggie always makes me feel so useless. I mean she's always picking on me. That sounds childish but it's amazing how someone constantly griping away at you can grind you down. It sort of overshadows the love issue. I suppose she does at least care about me in some way but she doesn't show it which, as you say, is probably why I can't show her any affection, even if it were there. But that's typical of Maggie. It's not "done" to show your feelings like that. Not between women, anyway. In her book men are what matter. There's no doubt that Maggie loved and worshipped Howard but because I'm female she doesn't waste that sort of emotion on me.'

Jo didn't know it but as she spoke about her father she was smiling. Even through the steam Suzanne could see the blatant look of adoration and the raw emotion on her face made her squirm a little. But Jo's expression clouded over as she continued. 'When he went I think Maggie stopped feeling anything for anyone but herself and her own loss. It just didn't occur to her that I might be feeling that loss too.

'I think all little girls are in love with their father when they're that age and I was no exception. So when he went it was a really confusing time for me as well as her, but it was as if suddenly I didn't matter. It took me a long time to realise that the only reason she had ever paid me any attention was because it pleased Howard. As I said, in her book it's men who are important. If she meets a new man, even if he's the chiropodist, she can't help but flirt with him. Women are only important if they make her look good or pose a threat to her relationship with a man. So you see, once Howard had gone I don't think she even knew I was there, all she wanted was for Howard to come home. You know, I think it's the only time she and I ever wanted the same thing.'

Jo trailed off as she considered what she had been saying. It was a long time since she had been able to talk in depth about Maggie without getting worked up. Being away from home and work like this was obviously a good thing as it had given her time to think. In a way being with Suzanne had also helped. There was something about her that Jo found oddly soothing.

She was about to expand the theme and bring Simon's name into the conversation when she had second thoughts. Instead she said, 'So in answer to your original question, yes. In certain cases maybe it is better for a child at least to be with someone who loves them.'

Listening to and watching her Suzanne found it easy to picture Jo's life as a child without her father. It was as much what she hadn't said as what she had that helped her to sense how Jo must have felt as she tried to understand where her cherished father had gone. With a pang Suzanne recognised the emotion and for a split second she wanted to give Jo a hug, to tell her that she knew exactly how she felt. That she understood what it was like to feel lost and confused and alone because someone you loved had gone. But common sense stopped her. She reached up and pushed the essence button above her head, pumping more pine-scented steam into the cabin. She was about to say something when Jo stirred. 'I've got a massage next so I'd better get along. See you at lunchtime?'

Suzanne just nodded and even though she knew that Jo didn't need to go down to the treatment rooms just yet she didn't say anything, allowing her the dignity of escape as air from the opening and closing door made the steam swirl around the small cabin.

The serene surroundings, good food and soothing treatments made Jo feel more rested than she had for a long time. A few massages eased the tension in her shoulders and the peaceful atmosphere gave her the opportunity she needed to be by herself. The series was still in her mind but in her new calmer state she found she was able to see an easy way through the scheduling problems and even save something of the budget. She was in bed by ten at night and slept like a log until the gentle knock on her door at eight told her that breakfast had arrived.

Suzanne, however, was not feeling quite so relaxed.

The period of peace and quiet that usually acted as a balm was not working. Her ability not even to think about what was happening at the Pimlico Centre had deserted her. She could do nothing *but* think about it. On a couple of occasions she had actually gone as far as lifting the receiver to call the office to check how things were going, but aware that this would break the habit of all her years in the job, had placed it back in the cradle.

She found herself thinking about things that had happened long ago. In many cases the images in her head were more vivid than the reality around her. If she tried to picture the Pimlico Centre she would see it as she had left it a couple of days before but then the memory of how it had been years ago would superimpose itself with such clarity that she found herself remembering corners of the building that she thought she had forgotten.

There was the cupboard in the corner of the office that had been built around the heating pipes where she used to put the teapot to warm; and the silly nook half way up the old fire stairs that someone had painted bright red. Things that she didn't even know she could recall were now so real she felt that if she reached out she could touch them.

She slept; but images danced with her through the night and when she woke up she was entangled in the sheets, drained and exhausted. She glanced at herself in the mirror, seeing the dark rings under her eyes. 'When did you age?' she asked her reflection. It didn't answer and beyond the tired eyes that looked back at her she could see the woman she had once been. She slipped off her dressing gown and stepped back, looking at her naked self, mentally comparing her figure with what it had been thirty years before.

What had then been high, full, rounded breasts now drooped slightly, the once smooth skin wrinkled. She raised her hands and lifted them, taking the weight off the skin making it even again. Her hands continued down over her stomach and she noticed the thickening flesh that covered her torso. Her stomach had never been flat but it was now rounded, with slight folds appearing at the tops of her thighs. Her legs were still in good shape but their sleekness had gone. Turning round she saw what had once been firm buttocks now dimpled and full. *Did he really think I was that much of a catch?* she asked her reflection.

Its eyes looked back at her with the same worried crease between them. *Yes*, it said. *You were a catch all right but only because he couldn't have you. It's not your fault.* With a sigh she wrapped herself in her dressing gown again and went into the bathroom for a shower, burying her turmoil below the surface before going down to meet Jo in the swimming pool.

The first meeting Suzanne had when she returned was with Alan and sure enough he was sporting a swollen eye. Now a couple of days old it was not as puffy as it had been but the lid was still a vivid red and the purplish-blue across his cheek was merging with the yellow and green spreading from under his brow. When she heard what had happened Suzanne exploded. She hauled Gordon in to see her to remind him of his responsibilities as floor manager. Both Alan and

Gordon were more than a little relieved when they left her office later that morning with instructions to double the security arrangements and ensure that none of the teams from any department patrolled by themselves. Everyone, but everyone was to be watched at all times.

Jo was also being brought up-to-date with what had been going on and whereas Suzanne had been appalled to hear about the stripped show house and the fight Jo, in the professional sense, had been delighted to learn that the crew had got a camera to the spot in time to catch it all on film.

'I knew it! I knew it!' she said happily. 'This programme is going to be so shit hot it'll . . . it'll . . . Oh, I don't know what it will do but it will certainly be remembered for a very long time!'

'So where, madam director, are you planning to use this incredible footage?' Laura asked her boss with a hint of sarcasm.

'You're so picky,' Jo laughed back. She knew she was being sent up but she didn't care – her gut feeling was telling her she was right. 'I don't actually know what we'll use it for but I'd hate to think of a good footage opportunity being missed. All right?'

'You're terrible,' Laura complained as Jo leaned back in her seat, her hands clasped behind her head as she grinned at her PA. 'It may be organised chaos but everyone's going through hell out there and all you can worry about is – *Did I get it on film?* There are moments when I think you've become a real hard-nosed cow – Dinah Deadman'd better look to her laurels!'

Jo let the front legs of the chair swing back to the floor and her face clouded over. 'Laura, you don't really mean that do you?' She was worried that there might be some truth in what her PA was saying, particularly when she recalled how keen she had been to record all she could when they found the body. *I wouldn't have been doing my job if I'd missed it*, she told herself, trying to justify her actions.

'Well, maybe not a total cow.' Laura began back-pedalling. 'It's just that most of the time you're so nice that when you say something I would expect Dinah Deadman to say it comes as a shock. That's all.' Inwardly Jo shuddered at the description of herself as 'nice'. *That's my problem,* she thought *I'm always trying to be 'nice' when maybe I'd be better off looking after myself for a change.*

Before either of them could say anything else there was a knock at the door and Alan came in. He was a bit pale, which made his bruises even more prominent. Something was clearly bothering him. 'Could I have a word?' he asked Jo hesitantly.

'Sure, pull up a pew.' Jo saw Laura's questioning look and threw her a warning glance before turning her attention to Alan.

'I actually meant alone if you don't mind?' He looked pointedly in Laura's direction. Surprised, Jo asked her to leave and with a knowing look and a wink, Laura picked up some files and did as she was asked.

The door had barely shut behind her when Jo addressed Alan in a very firm manner.

'Look, I told you that I enjoyed having dinner with you, and I meant it, but all that smoochy stuff was a mistake. I was wrong to tell you all I did and I'm sorry. You just happened to be in the wrong place at the wrong time. Just because Si and I are going through a rough patch at the moment doesn't mean you can muscle in. I made it sound worse than it is and I know we're going to sort it out. I mean, do you really think I'd stay with him if things were as bad as I made out? I'm still engaged to him, remember?' She held up her left hand to show him the ring again.

'This has nothing to do with Simon or me,' Alan said gently. 'I'm sorry but I've got some bad news. I thought it would be better if you heard it alone.'

Jo looked at his face and could now see that as well as looking pale his eyes were bloodshot, with dark rings under them. His usually neat hair was also looking a bit ruffled.

Oh God! He's going to tell me we can't film any more. That Suzanne's changed her mind. What did I say at Ragdale that I shouldn't have? She began to recap all the conversations they had had at the health farm and took a deep breath, fully expecting to hear the worst; that she had over-stepped the mark. That they were going to impound the footage of the fight.

Thank God the body stuff is already stored in the editing suite, she thought as she nervously tucked her hair behind her ear.

Alan saw the gesture and began cautiously, 'It's about the body.'

'Sorry?' Jo was confused. Why was he talking about the body?

'They know who it is. At least the forensic guys got enough information together and sent it out and eventually they got a match with dental records and . . . Oh Hell, Jo, I'm sorry, I don't know what to say. It's Howard. It's your father.'

Pressure had been applied to DCI Thomas from his superiors to get everything moving rapidly so the coroner's inquest had been opened, adjourned and the post-mortem begun as quickly as possible. When he had called the senior Exhibitions International staff together that morning they had all tried to get out of it. It was just three days before they opened. The last thing any of them needed was an unscheduled meeting but the police had insisted everyone from Exhibitions International, along with the management of the Pimlico Centre, attend.

DCI Thomas had made it quite clear at the meeting that he resented working for the benefit of the show and, even though the Home Maker Exhibition had been going so long that it was almost a national institution, he did not see why it should be allowed to get in the way of his investigation. It was only when he was told that a member of the

Royal Family would be opening the show that he had begrudgingly encouraged his team to work faster.

Everyone had been forced to sit in the meeting for nearly an hour, even though Suzanne tried to hurry the man up, but he had insisted on taking them through the whole procedure. 'The pathologist's report tells us that the corpse was male, Caucasian and somewhere in his fifties. Not much to go on, but combined with the results of the forensic reports we're pretty certain we can name our man. It was the X-ray of the jaws that really gave it to us. He had some nice wire work in there, I can tell you, quite advanced for 1966.'

'Get on with it,' Alan had murmured under his breath as he carried on doodling on his pad. Everyone round the table heard the remark and mouths twitched as Alan put into words what they were all thinking. The Detective Chief Inspector also heard, but ignored the comment to continue at the same steady pace until he felt he had built up the atmosphere enough to identify the man. Nobody noticed Suzanne go pale and her expression shift.

'Why are you telling us this?' she asked. 'Isn't it usual to inform the family first?'

'We're still trying to track them down. The records show a wife and kid, but we don't make a habit of keeping in touch with everyone who reports someone missing, and certainly not after three decades. We've got our own boys working on it but I've got better things for them to be doing than chasing up thirty-year-old cases. That's why we wanted to tell you lot. Howard Edwardes used to be involved in your game,' he managed to make the job of organising exhibitions sound dirty and almost illegal, 'and we thought you might have some ideas. If you have then you know where to find us.' He was standing by the large plate-glass windows that overlooked the exhibition halls. In the reflection he thought he saw the marketing man (*what was his name?*) stop doodling and his head jerk up. Quickly he turned round again but the man was again gazing blankly at the notepad in front of him. DCI Thomas looked expectantly from one person to another, hesitating for a moment as his eyes met Alan's.

As the meeting broke up Alan considered the situation carefully and then made his way over to Jo's office. He was sure someone else would work it out but he wanted to be the one to tell her before the gossip reached her. Alan had had no idea what he was going to say. Which was why he was now standing in front of Jo watching her reaction to the awful news.

Well done, Alan, he told himself sarcastically, as he realised how clumsily he had broken the news to Jo. She was staring at him across her desk, sitting perfectly still. Alan stood and watched, not knowing what else to do.

Jo couldn't move. She was having problems concentrating. She felt herself go cold and hot and then cold again and everything seemed to happen in slow motion. Alan was moving slowly towards her but even though she knew he was getting closer he looked as if he was disappearing down the wrong end of a telescope. The roar of the traffic outside and the whistles of the barges on the Thames faded away to be replaced by a loud rushing noise in her ears and she heard someone very close by screaming '*NO!*' over and over again at the top of their voice. There was the sound of flesh on flesh. A loud slap. Her cheek began to sting as she became aware of her feelings.

Alan had expected some sort of reaction from Jo but he had been totally unprepared for the primitive yell of raw pain that welled up out of her. Her anguished shouts felt as if someone had stuck a knife into him. He made his way round to her side of the desk as quickly as he could. That she was hysterical was obvious but the only thing he knew about treating hysteria came from watching TV. Not naturally a violent person, he had to muster all his emotions to give Jo the hard slap that brought her back to reality.

No sooner had he slapped her than he wrapped his arms round her and held the now sobbing woman against his chest. Gently he stroked the top of her head, crooning nonsense noises at her as he would a distressed child. He could smell her perfume and at that moment, if he had been offered the opportunity to take her to bed he would have done so. *How can I even think like this*? He was horrified by his own reaction and hoped that Jo wouldn't sense the effect her vulnerability was having on him. Slowly her sobs subsided.

This isn't happening, a steady voice said inside her head, but she knew it was. The sobs kept coming in huge gulping waves but a part of her was still detached, hovering high in the corner of the Porta-cabin watching the scene below. Jo sat holding on to Alan's jacket lapels, wishing she could stay like that for a long time. The same sense of safety and security she had felt when she was with him in Leicester Square swept over her. She knew she would have to move eventually but delayed the moment, waiting for the final part of her to slot back into place before pushing him away a little to raise a tear-stained face. He returned her gaze and with one finger released a stray strand of her hair that had plastered itself against her wet cheek.

'I'm over-reacting. Sorry,' she said in a quiet but quivering voice as she finally turned away from him to grab a handful of tissues from the box on top of the filing cabinet.

'Don't be silly. God, I don't know what I would do if someone gave me news like that. I hope I didn't hit you too hard? I've never done that before.'

'No, you didn't, and it worked. Thank you.' Jo went to help herself to a cup of coffee but Alan got to the hot-plate before she did and poured one for her, adding extra sugar. Gratefully she took it but her hands were shaking so much that she spilled a lot of it on the desk. Carefully she put it down again, using the wad of tissues to mop up the mess. *This is madness*, she told herself. *I've just been told that a withered shell of a human being is my father and I'm worried about some upset coffee!*

'I don't know what to do,' she said to Alan. He gave a shrug of his shoulders feeling equally useless. 'I suppose I should go and talk to the police, shouldn't I?'

'Well, they are trying to find you and your mother. Do you want me to come with you?' Alan offered. He felt dreadful on her behalf and it was the only way he could think of helping her. Like everyone else he had been morbidly fascinated by the body. He had joined in the office speculation about who it was and how it got there. He knew it was stupid to feel that because it now had an identity something had changed, but after listening to Jo describing her father he had a clear image of how Howard had appeared to his adoring little daughter. That image had nothing to do with the now dissected corpse lying on a mortuary slab somewhere.

The man Jo had described with such adoration that night in Leicester Square was a jovial man who had a style about him that was totally natural. Jo had smiled wistfully as she recalled how she used to sit on the kitchen table as he polished his shoes, swinging her legs while he told her stories. And how he would take his tie off at the end of the day and roll it carefully round his fingers to unfurl it again at her, hissing 'S-s-snakes-s-s'. How he would buy her gorgeous clothes and dress her up whenever he and Maggie had visitors so he could show her off. She had smiled as she explained that, unlike those parents who liked to see their little girls in frills and flounces, Howard had dressed her in brown velvet dresses decorated with thick crocheted lace or heavy, full-skirted corduroy skirts with soft polo-neck jumpers. She had talked about days at the seaside and picnics in the country, about picking bluebells in the spring and blackberries in the autumn. It was a blissful portrait of an idyllic childhood which had ended abruptly when Howard disappeared. All she had had of her father as she grew up were these happy memories and until a few minutes ago they were intact. Now they were overlaid with a gruesome image and it was all his fault.

Silently he walked with her out of the office and into the main building. When they got to the lifts she put a restraining hand on his arm and without saying anything he let her walk into the lift alone to go and find DCI Thomas. Jo walked purposefully towards the police office, ignoring anyone who greeted her. She pushed open the door and observed the hubbub. Now that they knew who the body was the police investigation as to how it got into the basement, and whether or not foul play could be considered, would move out of the Centre. The press office was in the process of being reclaimed and prepared for press day. People were hurrying about packing computers and folders into crates ready for that move.

'I'm looking for DCI Thomas,' she announced in a voice louder than she intended, but it was a voice that commanded attention. The woman nearest to her looked up.

'I'm sorry, he's busy. You'll have to come back some other time, but can I take a message?' It was a standard dismissive response.

'Before I go would you just tell him that Joanne Edwardes would like to see him?' The woman opened her mouth to reiterate what she had just said but before she could say anything Jo added, 'Howard Edwardes' daughter.' The woman shut her mouth like a trap and on hearing the name a number of people in the office turned to look at her. She pretended not to notice. The woman made her way to the far end of the room, returning a couple of minutes later to show Jo into her superior's office.

DCI Thomas stood and came round the desk to meet her. 'Miss Edwardes, I can't tell you how pleased I am to meet you. Mind you, I didn't think it would happen so fast. Not half an hour ago I was asking if anyone knew where you and your mother might be and here you are. I assume it was young Waterman who put two and two together?'

Jo nodded, a sense of incredulity sweeping through her. *My God! The man sounds as if he's talking about the coincidence of bumping into a neighbour on holiday in Spain!*

DCI Thomas suddenly seemed to remember who he was talking to and why. His amazement at having found one of the Edwardes women so quickly was rapidly disguised as once again he became the consummate professional. 'I'm so sorry. It must be a dreadful shock to you after all this time. Can I offer you a cup of coffee, or maybe something a little stronger?'

Jo shook her head. 'No thank you. I've just had one – a coffee,' she explained. 'Please could you confirm that you are absolutely certain that that . . . thing is my father?' Her eyes eagerly watched his face, hoping that he would say 'No'. That it had all been some horrible mistake.

For years after Howard disappeared she had thought he would come home, but as she got older she realised this wouldn't happen. Instead she had clung on to the belief that he was alive. That he had left them because he couldn't cope with the fights he kept having with Maggie, or her incessant nagging. And when he had been legally declared dead seven years after he vanished, in 1973, she hadn't believed it. Hadn't wanted to believe it to such an extent that even today as she walked down a busy street she would see the line of a man's back and quicken her step because it looked familiar, only to be disappointed when she looked at his face to discover it wasn't Howard after all.

By accepting that the body was definitely Howard's she would lose all that hope. She had lived with it for so long that it was a part of her and she didn't know if she could cope without it. It would finally leave her alone with Maggie and her recriminations. With a tenderness that no one who had been with him that morning would have recognised, DCI Thomas gently confirmed that they were sure the corpse was that of Howard Laurence Edwardes.

'Do you know what happened to him? How he got there?' They were obvious questions but Jo had to ask them.

'Not yet, but we're working on it. The coroner's inquest has established who and when, we know the where. The pathologist is still working on the how. Depending on what that report reveals we will decided whether or not foul play is to be considered, in which case we will have to investigate the why. But let's not jump the gun, Miss Edwardes. Once the path guys have finished with the . . . your father, we will be able to release his remains to you for burial.'

'Burial?' Jo repeated. It hadn't occurred to her that there would now be a funeral.

'However he got there he's still entitled to that. Now, I'm sorry to have to ask you this, but is your mother still alive?'

Jo nodded. 'Oh my God! How am I going to tell her about this?' For the first time since hearing the news she thought about Maggie and realised that she would have to be told.

'If you like we'll tell her.'

'*NO,*' Jo said, more sharply and loudly than she'd intended. 'I'm sorry, I didn't mean to shout. It's just that Maggie, my mother, is in a home and she can be a difficult woman so I'd rather tell her in my own way. Thank you.' She felt the interview was at an end and had got up to go when another thought occurred to her and she sat down again.

'What about the papers? I mean, they got really excited about the body when we found it. What are you going to tell them?'

'We'll have to tell them something but we do like to ensure that in cases such as this all relatives are aware of the facts first. Obviously if your mother is fragile' (despite how she was feeling Jo smiled wryly to herself at the thought of anyone describing Maggie as fragile) 'then you will know when is the best time to give her the news. Of course, from our point of view we would prefer this was sooner rather than later . . .' DCI Thomas let the implication hang in the air for a moment before he continued. 'However, despite what you might hear about the police we're not the brutes people would have you believe, and we do appreciate the delicacy of the situation.'

Jo heard his words but she got the feeling that he was not being as sincere as he might have been; that in truth he would prefer it if she immediately went to give Maggie the news so they could get on with other work and close the file on what was clearly a bothersome old case. Well, tough. It was going to be hard enough breaking the news to Maggie, and she was determined to do it her own way and in her own time. When she stood for the second time she succeeded in leaving the office, but promised she would let him know as soon as the news could be released.

Still feeling numb she made her way back to the Portacabin. The sudden blast of fresh air made her blink as she walked across from the main building and up the stairs. She was glad to see that the office was empty and rather than sit at her own desk sat down in the visitors' chair next to the window. She gazed out at the Thames glittering in the spring sunshine. The river bus was making its way down-river to Canary Wharf while other boats chugged up and down the waterway. Buses crossed Vauxhall Bridge. Looking up at the patch of sky just visible through the Portacabin's window she could see the clouds scudding rapidly across it, casting areas of bright light and shadow in turn as they covered the sun. It amazed her that everything seemed so normal. Didn't people know what had just happened? That everything she had accepted for all these years had suddenly been turned inside out and upside down?

Nothing made sense.

The questions began to tumble through her head. How did Howard get into the basement? What was he doing there? Why hadn't anyone found him? Why hadn't people gone to look for him? *What had happened?*

She had a picture of him lying there, dying quietly as thousands of people walked five feet above his head enjoying an exhibition. People who could have helped, people who worked there, who should have *known*. She shook her head to remove the thoughts but still they went round and round.

Her phone rang suddenly, making her jump. Automatically she reached out and answered it. 'Jo, it's Suzanne. Alan's just told me what's happened. My dear, I'm so sorry. If you're free and would like to come over then I'm here.' Suddenly there was nothing Jo wanted more than the companionship of the older woman. Having Alan hold her had helped but she had been appalled to find how much she didn't want him to let her go.

'Thank you, Suzanne. I'll come over now if I may?'

Wearily she made her way back to the main building and the lifts. Julia was ready for her when she arrived. She avoided looking at Jo in the way people do when they're too embarrassed to know how to commiserate. Keeping her eyes averted she ushered her into the inner office. When Jo walked in she found she had to adjust her thoughts to equate the once again elegant Suzanne with the comfortable woman in the dressing gown with whom she had spent the weekend. However, the moment Suzanne began to speak Jo felt they were back in the conservatory chatting over cups of herbal tea.

'It's not going to be easy telling Maggie, is it?' Suzanne asked with astute perception as she busied herself with the coffee pot.

'No. No, it's not. I – I haven't really thought about it but I suppose I'll have to work out what to tell her and how. Then there's the question of organising a funeral.' Jo took a sip of her coffee as Suzanne began talking. She was expressing the usual condolences and Jo found herself listening with only half an ear as the thoughts tumbled round in her head. *I can't go by myself. I can't. Oh God, Si, why did this have to happen now? Would you come with me? I doubt it . . . Alan would though, wouldn't he? Are you mad? Even asking him would finally end it all with Si. Oh God, but I feel so at ease with him . . . it might even help me keep everything under control . . . I won't want to make a fool of myself in front of him, will I? Oh shit! She felt another wave of emotion wash over her.*

Suzanne was drinking her coffee; her eyes sympathetically watching Jo. It was as if she understood that what Jo currently needed was companionship. She seemed to know that Jo had said all she was going to say and gently began to talk again, a bit about Howard, a bit about the show and a bit about the programme. If anyone had walked in on them they would have seemed like two old friends having a chat, but despite the outward appearance her mind was racing as much as Jo's.

Surreptitiously Suzanne looked over the rim of her coffee cup at Jo. The younger woman was still very pale but seemed to be in control. She had a glazed look on her face and it was clear from her conversation that she wasn't really listening to what Suzanne was saying. Suddenly Jo put the cup down and buried her face in her hands. From nowhere a wave of sheer pain and grief had welled up like a balloon, starting from the bottom of her stomach. She sat, with her shoulders shaking, gently rocking back and forth.

Quickly Suzanne moved across to crouch next to her, putting a protective arm across her shoulders, hugging her tightly. For the second time that day Jo found herself being comforted by someone who was little more than a stranger. Again she forced herself to calm down, not daring to give way completely as she was afraid that once she started she would never stop. Eventually she felt under control and, slightly embarrassed, made her excuses to Suzanne and left. But the thoughts going through Suzanne's mind meant it was some time before she got back to work.

The Home Maker Exhibition was due to open in two days' time.

Swopping over the cables in the cookery theatre display kitchen had been easy and he was pleased to note that this simple act had created the most disruption so far. It had been so simple to say he was going to the loo and to slip into the control room instead. The best bit was that it didn't actually blow the system immediately. The safety switch saw to that. All it had taken was one of the 'sparks' to add an extra plug and that was it. He wasn't anywhere near the junction box at the time so even if they had wanted to no one would be able to trace it back to him.

It had a greater effect than even he had anticipated, as it fused a much bigger slice of the building than he had foreseen. The large freezers already stocked with ingredients for the daily cookery demonstrations which were a central attraction at the show also went down. Even worse, in those freezers was a huge batch of luxury ice cream that had been shipped from America in preparation for the massive sampling exercise that was to launch the product in the UK. And in the panic to sort out the main electrical systems it was twelve hours before anyone realised the freezers had been affected by the power cut.

As soon as the fault had been identified the American importer was the first in the queue to see Gordon. He shouted at him as he made his point.

'Listen, buddy, I don't care whose fault it is. All I know is it ain't ours. In my book that means it's yours. Thanks to some idiot there's several thousand dollars' worth of top of the range product creaming its way across the storeroom floor. Now, you've advertised that the stuff's gonna be here and I guess you'll be in the shit if it ain't. I can get it replaced . . . but it'll cost. And my company ain't paying for it. I suggest you go to the big white chief and get her to sign the money over so we can replace it, because if you don't I swear you'll have a lawsuit for negligence slapped on your butts so damn hard it'll feel as if it's been nailed there!' The American stood up and without saying another word stormed out, leaving Gordon still sitting behind his desk.

Everyone else kept their heads down and carried on answering the phones or responding to calls on the radio, pretending not to have noticed the outburst.

'I don't need this,' Gordon said to no one in particular. 'If you want me I'll be on the floor talking to the sparks to see what they have to say and then I'll be up with Suzanne. Liza, get the mess cleared up as quickly as possible. It's beginning to seep out from under the door and fuck up the carpet tiles so you'll need to get PimEx to replace those as well.'

'. . . And another thing I am not happy about is that I had to find out from the focus puller that the body was your father. Jo, why on earth didn't you call me and let me know?'

Jo was back in Dinah's office, squaring up to her boss once again to fight for the right to keep the Suzanne Prescott programme on the rails.

'I'm sorry, Di, but yesterday is not going to be a day I mark in my diary as one of my particular favourites. It just didn't occur to me to let you know. I mean, the identity was personal to me and nothing to do with the programme. I'm sorry.'

What am I apologising for? she asked herself. *It's none of her bloody business.* She took another sip of coffee.

'That's just what I wanted to talk to you about. The personal thing. You see, as much as I'm sorry for you about what has happened, I do have the programme to think about. I wonder if maybe you aren't now a bit too closely involved to be able to maintain the objectivity that we originally agreed was so important to the series, hmm?' Dinah gave the younger woman a querying look.

Jo thought before she answered in as controlled a tone as she could muster. 'When you offered me the chance to direct this one you obviously thought I could do it. You've seen the rushes. You know the shooting schedule and the rest of the material I want to get. To date I've heard no complaints from you about the *quality* of the work so I can only assume that you're happy with it?' Dinah nodded. 'Well, nothing has changed on my side. When I started shooting I was Howard Edwardes' daughter, half way through I'm still his daughter. The only difference is you now know about it. Admittedly I was – am – very shaken to discover that the . . .' she hesitated and swallowed before continuing, '. . . that the body was my father but like you I am a professional and no matter what, I intend to finish this job. Dinah, please don't take me off it.' Her voice cracked as her composure disintegrated and her eyes eagerly searched her boss's face.

'I know I can carry on doing a good job. I know my way around now. More importantly everyone involved with the Home Maker knows me; Suzanne trusts me – look at how she took me to Ragdale with her. The crew's working well. Think of the disruption if you have to get someone else in at this stage. It'll also lack continuity. Please, Dinah, I promise it won't get in the way.'

God, I hate it when you plead like this, said a little voice in her head as she watched Dinah, trying to second guess what she would say.

'Oh, all right, but I warn you that I'll be watching you like a hawk. Any sign, and I mean ANY sign, that the personal connection is getting in the way of the filming and I'll stop threatening and start taking action, you understand?'

With a mental sigh of relief she was sure Dinah would hear Jo nodded and, not wanting to give her boss time to change her mind, quickly got up.

'One other thing, Jo.' Dinah's voice had softened. 'I *am* happy with what you're doing. Very happy indeed. You've got some really good footage and I'm sure the final edit will do it justice.'

It was clear that the crew had also heard the news. At the early morning meeting that day they'd been very subdued, not knowing what to say. Jo was in the process of double checking that they knew exactly what they would be doing during the afternoon when she finally caught Tony's eye. She had to say something to break the tension. 'I know this is difficult for you but it's not easy for me either. But as they say, "the show must go on", so let's get on with it.' The mood in the room lightened a little and she carried on with the briefing. After being called out to her unexpected meeting with Dinah she returned to the Portacabin and continued with her work, finally glancing at her watch when the sound of Big Ben striking two drifted down the river.

Two o'clock was the time she had set herself to drive over to Blackheath to see Maggie. She knew if she didn't go now she would keep putting it off. Besides, she had cleared her diary. With a sigh she rose and went to the mirror to tidy herself up. She had dressed with care that day and was wearing tailored trousers with a loose cut jacket. They were a soft reddish tweed and under the jacket a cashmere sweater picked out the gentler hues of the colour in the cloth. It made her feel that she could face her mother.

However, when she got down to the car park she realised just what it was she was about to do and a wave of nausea hit her – hard. She bent over, thinking she really was going to throw up, when a familiar voice spoke to her.

'Jo, are you feeling OK?' She straightened up a little and found herself looking at Suzanne, who was also more smartly dressed than usual as she'd had an important meeting with a sponsor. Her suit was a flattering mid grey marled wool and she wore it with an ochre cowl-neck silk blouse. The suit was well-cut with a straight mid-calf skirt that showed off her neat ankles, and the design of the jacket hid the parts of herself she liked the least while giving her the illusion of a trimmer waist than she actually possessed.

'Yes, I'm fine. I'm on my way to see Maggie and I suddenly felt a bit odd, that's all.' She gave a watery smile.

Suzanne glanced at her watch. 'Look, I've actually got back a bit earlier than I expected and this whole thing has obviously got you more stirred up than you would like to admit. You could probably do with a bit of moral support so why don't I come with you?'

Jo was surprised at the offer, and her expression showed it.

Damn! I shouldn't have seemed so eager! 'I won't come in with you, unless you want me to. I can just wait in the car. I just thought you could do with the company.'

Say yes. Please say yes! Suzanne was careful not to let her thoughts show, concentrating on holding a concerned look on her face.

'OK,' Jo decided, surprised to feel relief flooding through her that she didn't have to make the journey alone. 'You're right. I could do with a bit of support but I'll drive if you don't mind. It'll give me something to do and keep my mind off things a bit.' Suzanne nodded her agreement and together the two women climbed into Jo's car.

Cyril saluted as he saw the boss of Exhibitions International go by. Suzanne studiously ignored him, though Jo gave him a lacklustre smile as he raised the barrier for her. Her comment about driving taking her mind off things proved false when on their way to Blackheath she remembered an instruction for Tony she'd forgotten and used her mobile to call Laura.

'Are you always this conscientious?' Suzanne queried.

'Yes. I can be such a coward over some things, like seeing Maggie, but if I really want something then I'll go all-out to get it. Just quietly chipping away until I make it happen. It can take years, like waiting to be allowed to direct a programme, but I get there in the end.' It was a very matter-of-fact statement.

'Yes,' said Suzanne, half to herself as she glanced out of the side window. 'I can be a bit like that too.'

For most of the journey they didn't say much, each caught up in her own thoughts. Jo was trying not to worry about the impending meeting with Maggie, and also found herself thinking about her meeting with Dinah, especially her parting remarks. Dinah was not known to be very forthcoming in her praise so the comment had been, by her standards, fulsome.

Suzanne was wondering how far the attacks on the show would go and what it would cost her to pay the price asked. *But if I do that it won't end there. I've got to think. There must be a way of stopping him without giving in.*

As they drew closer to Blackheath Jo tried not to think about how Maggie would react to the news. Instead she began telling Suzanne a bit about The Warren. She explained how it gave Maggie enough freedom to maintain her dignity and a degree of independence while at the same time giving Jo peace of mind because she knew that Maggie was being taken care of. As they got nearer Jo found herself growing more nervous and by the time she manoeuvred the car into a parking space she was again feeling physically sick. Suzanne, sensing Jo's discomfort, put an arm round her shoulder and gave her a squeeze. 'Good luck.'

Jo gave her a feeble smile back and then blurted out, 'Suzanne, I know you said you'd wait in the car but I think I'd like you to come in with me. After all the . . . I mean, Howard was found as we were working on the Home Maker and although it's nothing to do with the show – or you,' she hastily added, 'it's all sort of tied together, isn't it?' Jo searched Suzanne's face, hoping she would understand that she really could not face her mother by herself.

For a second Suzanne looked taken aback, but she quickly regained her composure. 'Well, if you're sure that's what you want? I don't want to be in the way.'

'You won't be, I promise.' In truth Jo didn't quite know how Maggie would react to hearing the bad news with a stranger present, but she didn't really care – she just wanted someone with her.

Together they got out of the car and walked towards the door. The two women looked business-like and in control. Which, for different reasons, could not have been further from the truth. Suzanne's head was spinning. This wasn't how she'd intended it to happen. She hadn't had a chance to prepare herself. But now it was here she was going to make the most of it. *Thirty years it's been and finally, at last . . . It can't be this easy to finish this, can it? Surely it's not just going to be handed to me on a plate?*

She gave Jo another squeeze. 'Chin up. This sort of thing's never as bad as you think it's going to be.'

The buzzer released and let them in but before they reached Maggie's flat a slight figure came dancing towards them, singing gently to herself. She was clearly wearing a skirt over a dress as well as a misbuttoned cardigan over two, if not three, frilly blouses. She was draped in a shawl with long tassels that dragged on the floor. Numerous strings of beads and bracelets also dangled about her. Perched on her head was a large-brimmed hat with a sweeping pink feather that bobbed as she sang and danced. Jo put her hand to her face and despite herself began to laugh. 'Oh, Edna, why today of all days?'

The little woman stopped in front of them. Jo quickly filled Suzanne in as Edna danced happily, holding her shawl out as she dipped and swayed to the tune she was humming. 'Edna.' Jo caught her by the shoulders and stopped her as she twirled. 'This is a friend of mine. Her name is Suzanne.' Suzanne held out her hand and after hesitating for a moment, her fingers held to her lips as she considered this new person, Edna's hand darted out and shook it. She then bent her head and gave Suzanne a thoroughly flirtatious look from under her wide brim before prodding her in the chest with a bent finger and bursting into song again.

'Oh Suzanna, don't you cry for me
For I've come from Alabama
With my banjo on my knee.'

As she sang the last words she raised her knee to give it a little slap and at the same time rolled her eyes at her audience. She looked like a little girl who had dressed up in her mother's clothes and when she gave a final toss of her head the hat that had been so precariously balanced there finally worked its way loose to land on the floor. Edna looked so crestfallen that Jo and Suzanne couldn't help themselves but laugh out loud. Hearing the laughter she joined in and picked up her hat to flourish it at them.

'Come on, Edna, let's take you back to your flat, shall we?' Jo gently took the old woman by the hand and turned her round, propelling her towards her home. Suzanne followed behind but Edna kept turning to wink and sing the song that she had obviously dedicated to her. It took the little procession about ten minutes to get Edna safely back inside but by the time they returned to Maggie's front door both women found that their feelings of ill ease, while not totally gone, had at least lightened.

'Hello, Maggie, it's only me,' Jo called out as she opened the door using the special access code.

'What do you want? It's not like you to come and see me in the middle of the day for nothing.' Maggie's querulous disembodied voice called out from the living room. Although this accusation was not actually true Jo decided, as usual, to let it go. It wasn't worth stirring things up by correcting her. She led the way into the living room where Maggie was studiously facing the television, the back of her wheelchair to the door. Jo gave Suzanne a look that said, 'I told you so.'

She took a deep breath before she began to speak in a slower, louder voice than usual. 'Maggie, I needed to see you today. I've got some news. Please switch the set off and turn round.' Maggie ignored her. 'Please, Maggie.' Jo could hear the wheedling tone in her voice, not dissimilar to the one she had used that morning with Dinah.

With a tut Maggie finally did as she was asked, making it quite clear that she would rather not bother. With a bent finger she stabbed the button on her chair's control panel and slowly it turned round until she was facing the two other women. When she saw Suzanne she gave a gasp and quickly Jo jumped in.

'Maggie, this is Suzanne Prescott. She's the chief executive of Exhibitions International, remember, she's one of the women we're featuring in the series I'm doing? She's come with me today because I've got some news that sort of involves her and . . . Maggie? Maggie, what is it?'

Jo moved towards her mother who, on seeing the two younger women, had collapsed in on herself and now seemed to be trying to burrow her way backwards into the cushions that usually helped to support her. She had gone terribly pale and there was a slight sheen on her top lip. Her normally bright eyes looked huge and dark behind her glasses as her pupils dilated. She was plainly terrified.

'I'm sorry if I startled you,' Suzanne said kindly as she stepped across the room, her hand held out towards Maggie who was still cowering in her chair. Maggie stared wide-eyed at Suzanne who steadily returned her gaze. Slowly she took the hand extended towards her in her own knotted fingers to shake it feebly. After a few moments she seemed to pull herself together and began shifting in her chair until she was sitting in her normal erect position.

'I'm so sorry. I don't know what came over me. Please forgive me.' Her words said she was back in control but the tremor in her voice suggested otherwise. 'Do have a seat. Joanne, would you make a cup of tea for your guest?' Jo, who had crouched down beside Maggie's chair, got back to her feet and smoothed herself down again. Whatever it was that Maggie had seen, or thought she had seen, was clearly a passing thing but her reaction had made Jo's nervousness come flooding back.

Suzanne sat down on the overstuffed sofa and Maggie moved her chair round so she was facing her from across the other side of the room. Jo didn't move but stood awkwardly in the middle trying to pluck up the courage to tell Maggie about Howard. Again she swallowed and after a couple of false starts finally began to speak.

'Maggie, I'm afraid we've got – *I've* got – some bad news. Umm – you know that body they found in the basement of the Pimlico Centre?' She paused, waiting for Maggie to respond, but her mother said and did nothing, just stared straight ahead at Suzanne, her expression inscrutable. Jo tucked her hair behind her ears and carried on. This was going to be even harder than she had imagined. 'Well, the police have identified it.' She paused before continuing. 'It's Howard.' She looked at her mother waiting for the storm, for the violent outcry, but none came.

'I see,' Maggie replied after an interval that seemed interminable. 'That's where he ended up was it? Well, I suppose it's what he deserved. You didn't have to come all this way just to tell me that. A phone call would have done, you know.'

Jo suddenly felt a finger of rage shoot through her. 'Christ almighty! For years you made my life hell because he went. Because you thought he'd gone off with someone else and left us in the lurch. I come here to tell you that they've found him. That he *didn't* desert you. That he really did die, and you say I could have phoned you?'

'Joanne, I don't think we should be discussing this now. We have a guest,' said Maggie. By now she had fully regained her composure and her voice had a firm, admonitory tone. Jo ignored her and swept on. Having expected a storm from Maggie this calm response was an anticlimax. She was also furious that Maggie was showing no signs of grief for the man who had ostensibly meant so much to both of them.

'No, we *will* talk about this now.'

Then it was Maggie's turn to feel angry and as she replied the hatred in her voice made Jo draw back.

'Shall I tell you what upsets me about finding Howard after all this time? It's knowing that I had to wait seven years before I was allowed to be called his widow. That for seven lousy years I had to scrimp and save and do all I could to ensure you had a roof over your head. Oh I knew the money was there but until those seven years had gone and he could legally be declared dead I couldn't touch it. I had to stand by while other people looked after his affairs and in some cases took over completely. Do you know what those seven years cost me? They cost me *everything*. If your precious father had done the decent thing and died where he could have been found I would not be living like this. I flatly refuse to give that bastard the opportunity to have the final word by grieving for him now.'

During her outburst Maggie had finally deigned to look at her daughter, pausing only once to throw a glance towards Suzanne who was sitting quietly on the sofa trying to look as if the family row did not concern her. To Jo nothing seemed to matter but what her mother was saying and she was concentrating so hard on Maggie that she had forgotten Suzanne was even in the room.

'Is that all he meant to you? Money?' The anger had gone from Jo's voice to be replaced by disappointment.

'One day you'll find out what he was really like and you'll know what I had to put up with. Then, miss, you won't stand there in judgement over me.'

At last Suzanne rose to her feet and walked over to put a restraining hand on Jo's shoulder. 'What about that cup of tea your mother suggested? I think it might be a good idea, don't you?' She increased the pressure with her hand slightly. Jo had been about to reply to Maggie but she thought better of it and left the room. Suzanne sat down again.

'I bet you're enjoying this, aren't you?' hissed Maggie as soon as she knew Jo was out of earshot.

'Not much. Jo's a nice, caring girl who deserves better than you as a mother. In fact she deserved better than Howard as a father, but as I reckon the only good thing she got from her parents was decent memories of him I'm not going to let a bitter, self-centred old woman like you take them away from her.'

Maggie winced at the description of herself as old.

'Believe it or not Jo actually cares about you,' Suzanne continued smoothly. 'She doesn't *like* you much but she does care. Which is more than I do after close on forty years, but I've said nothing to dissuade her from that and I don't intend to. If you have any sense you won't either. Now, when she comes back you're going to apologise.' Seeing a stubborn look settle on Maggie's face Suzanne got up and walked towards her. She bent over until her face was level with the older woman's then, lowering her voice a fraction, added, 'Because if you don't I'll make sure that Jo will never want to speak to you again. You'll become just another lonely old lady whose family leave her rotting in a home until she dies.' Suzanne straightened up as she heard Jo come out of the kitchen. By the time she re-entered the room Suzanne was sitting on the sofa exactly as Jo had left her.

Maggie shot Suzanne a look of pure venom over Jo's head as she bent down to put the tea tray on the table. The thoughts whipped through her head. *If she thinks I'm grovelling to her now . . . After all she's put me through, then she's got another think coming. I beat her down last time and I'll do it again now*. She then rearranged her face and pulled her eyes to her daughter as she straightened up. 'Joanne, I'm sorry if I upset you. It's just that after all these years the knowledge that they've finally found him is difficult to take in. Of course I mind, but my pain happened when he went. It hurt a lot. I don't want to open those wounds again, and certainly not in public. Can you understand that?' Maggie put her gnarled hand on Jo's wrist as she placed the tea cup in front of her. Jo looked at her and seeing the pleading look in her eyes felt a sudden wave of compassion.

'I'm sorry too.'

The rest of the visit was uneventful and on the way back to the Pimlico Centre neither mentioned the comments Maggie had made.

'What did you and Maggie talk about when I was making the tea?'

'Nothing much. Just small talk. You know.'

Although Jo was meant to go back to the office that afternoon she couldn't face it and phoned Laura to say that if anyone called (especially Dinah) she should tell them that she was at the Old Bailey and couldn't be contacted.

Wearily she made her way home and took the opportunity to prepare a proper meal instead of bunging something in the microwave. Simon arrived home at about six-thirty and was thrilled to find her there.

'Mmm,' he said appreciatively, 'I don't know which is more welcome, the smell of home cooking or you.' Jo gave him a tired smile. 'How did you manage to get off early?'

Jo realised that, due to a combination of a late night at work the previous day and her confused feelings about discovering that the body was her father's (was it really only yesterday she had found it out?) she had yet to share the news with Simon. It was odd to think that her own fiance currently knew less than Suzanne, Alan and her own crew about what was probably one of the most important events in her life.

She served their meal and, as they ate, slowly she began to fill Simon in, explaining how the police forensic team had finally identified Howard and how she had, for once, actually had a row with her mother instead of just biting back her words and emotions as usual.

'Thinking about it, it was quite embarrassing, what with Suzanne sitting there. I've got so used to her that I just sort of forgot about her.'

Simon looked at her sharply. 'Sorry, you've lost me. Do you mean Suzanne Prescott?' Jo nodded. 'What the hell was she doing at your mother's?'

'It's silly really, but as I was leaving the Pim Centre to go to Blackheath I suddenly came over a bit peculiar. I think it was the idea of having to face Maggie that did it. Anyway, Suzanne was on her way back from a meeting, saw I was in a bit of a state and offered to come with me, so I accepted.'

'Hang on. You took a total stranger with you to tell Maggie that that rotten old body was Howard? Why the hell didn't you call me? If you needed a bit of moral support I would have come with you, despite the fact that I find your mother a total pain in the butt and the thought of her having hysterics leaves me cold. I would have still come with you.'

Jo looked shamefaced. 'It didn't occur to me,' she said weakly, suddenly realising how hurtful it must be to Simon that she chose to take a colleague (in fact worse than a colleague, the subject of the programme), with her than him. 'Si, I'm sorry. I was feeling sick, she was there, you weren't and I just reached for the first supportive person I could find. Christ, that sounds awful. I don't mean it like that . . . what I mean is . . .'

'Don't bother explaining,' Simon interrupted. 'For whatever reason you chose to ignore me. Again. Jo, I don't know what's happening to you. You used to call me at work twice a day. A meal like this was the rule, not the exception. Hell, what with you working on this sodding programme I never get to see you any more. If I'd known what directing this bloody thing was going to mean to us I would never have let you do it.'

Up until that moment Jo had been feeling contrite. She knew Si was right. If she had stopped to think she would have called him. Or better still waited until they were together to ask him face to face to go with her. Despite his protestations Simon would probably have said 'No' but at least she would have given him the chance to be involved. But his last comment wiped away the contrition. Angrily Jo responded.

'Simon, I didn't need to ask your permission to direct *Women in Focus*, any more than you ask my permission to go on your sales conferences. I worked bloody hard for the right to direct this and I'm sorry if that doesn't fit in with your antiquated ideas about the traditional roles of men and women. Suzanne was literally there and she came with me. Full stop. End of subject. Now,' she continued without appreciating the irony of what she was saying, 'do you want another helping of bread-and-butter pudding?'

As always, and despite the 'accidents' that had occurred during the build-up period, the Home Maker Exhibition opened on time with its usual fanfare and razzmatazz. Jo and the crew were at the Pimlico Centre at six on the day the show opened, shooting footage of exhibitors as they frantically tried to finish their stands, tweaking fake flowers and straightening fixtures as the last gas and electrical connections were made. At nine-thirty the crew took it in turns to go and change into smart suits and when at five minutes to ten Suzanne took over the public tannoy to have a final word with everyone they were standing by the red carpet, ready to film the Royal who was going to cut the ribbon and formally declare the show open.

'Ladies and gentleman, this is Suzanne Prescott. The doors will open in five minutes. At that time all stands must be dressed and tidy, with any build-up equipment put away. I am delighted to tell you that we will be opening our doors with ticket sales already twenty-three per cent ahead of last year's. Good luck, and I hope everyone has a very good show.'

A few minutes later Suzanne was also standing at the head of the carpet and Jo shared the general thrill of excitement as Gordon took over the microphone in the organisers' office. 'Ladies and gentlemen, the show is about to open.' Just for the hell of it he added a countdown: 'Five . . . Four . . . three . . . two . . . one. Ladies and gentlemen, we are now open.'

It was as if everyone in the building took a deep breath that wouldn't be exhaled until the show closed six weeks later.

As the sound of Big Ben striking the hour was broadcast round the halls the security guards swung open the heavy plate-glass doors and the preview day crowd burst through. 'Now the fun *really* begins!' hissed Alan as he walked behind Jo, giving her arm a gentle squeeze before taking his place next to Suzanne. Outside the central doors a large black car glided to a stop and before they knew it Suzanne was curtsying and handing over the special scissors to their Royal visitor. She ceremoniously cut the ribbon that was being held by two rather overwhelmed little girls.

From then onwards Jo and her crew seemed to be in at least three places at once: following Suzanne and Alan as they escorted the Royal group round the show; filming visitors as they arrived and (when the Health and Safety Executive wasn't berating them for leaving cables everywhere) getting comments from them; trailing after the various celebrities who had special invitations for Preview Day and generally getting an overview of the whole event as it opened its doors to the public for the first time.

It was bedlam so Jo decided to give the crew a chance to catch their breath by going to shoot in the press office. But if she had thought this would be a quiet haven she quickly had to revise her view. The mayhem continued in here. It was early afternoon and although over a hundred journalists had already registered and were out on the exhibition floors enjoying themselves (albeit they tried to convince colleagues back at their respective offices that they were really working) still more kept arriving to register. Alan was back at his desk and very much in control. He managed to juggle the phone and the radio calls for him with amazing dexterity and at the same time was able to answer the barrage of questions that his team of PR assistants constantly hurled at him. As a phone was replaced on its cradle it would immediately ring again but whoever answered it managed to sound cheerful and alert.

This applied equally to the three girls on the registration desk whose smiles stayed firmly in place as press passes and media packs were handed out.

'No,' said Annabel, one of the PR girls brightly, in response to a query from a tabloid journalist. 'I'm sorry, there really is nothing to add about the body but I'm sure you'll find plenty to interest you at the Home Maker without that. Now this will give you . . .' and once again she launched into her PR patter as a cameraman crept furtively behind the desk to catch a shot of her standing there in her stockinged feet, rubbing one aching foot against her other calf as she maintained her smile and carried on giving directions.

'Wanker!' she murmured as the foiled journalist left, only to turn on her smile again as a group of three women, clearly from a women's magazine, came gossiping into the office.

Jo instructed the sound man to try to pick up some of the exchanges on the radios that crackled from the various desks. Some of it she knew would be unusable – particularly the dialogue between Gordon and the organisers' office about what he would do with a metal rod if someone didn't save him some of the sandwiches that had been brought in for lunch. It was both descriptive and very graphic but delivered in such good humour (especially by Gordon's standards) that it was clear everyone involved in the Home Maker Exhibition was also being carried along by the buzz. The air of excitement and anticipation reminded Jo why she had wanted to get into the business in the first place and she spent the day being swept along on a tide of adrenaline.

By the time the show closed for the day at seven o'clock they were all exhausted but exhilarated. The entire crew had been caught up in the whirl and they all ended up in the press office. Using her seniority with her own crew to move Bill from a seat, Jo kicked off her shoes to nurse her acting feet. 'If that's what it's like on preview day, how busy will it be when it's a general public day?' she asked Alan.

'It's going to be hell!' he said happily. 'Sheer bloody hell!' As Suzanne had announced, their ticket sales had already outstripped last year's and, allowing for the people who would just buy tickets at the door, it was clearly going to be an incredible year.

'By the way, Suzanne's opening a few bottles of bubbly in her office in about fifteen minutes and she's asked me to invite you all.'

The crew looked hopefully at Jo who got the message. 'OK, OK,' she laughed, 'I guess we've all earned a drink. To hell with the rushes. If we haven't got it then it's too late now. Just don't tell Dinah I said so!' They didn't need telling twice. Hurriedly they packed away the cameras and rushed to join everyone else. By the time they walked into Suzanne's office there was already quite a party atmosphere.

Jo was surprised to find she was enjoying herself. Since promising Dinah that the discovery of the body's identity would not get in the way of her work she had thrown herself utterly into filming and planning the rest of the series to prove to her boss that she had meant what she said. Dinah had obviously thought further about the situation since their meeting and had phoned Jo at the Pimlico Centre to offer her some time off. Jo had politely turned it down, knowing that she needed to keep busy. She had tried her best to push the picture of the body out of her head but still it haunted her. She wasn't sleeping properly, she wasn't eating. As far as Simon was concerned, not only were they not making love any more but she was shying away from any signs of tenderness he tried to show her.

That she desperately wanted and needed Simon's affection didn't help. He had realised, too late, that although her father had stopped being a part of her life in 1966 it was only now – faced with the physical evidence that he would not be coming back – that she was able to mourn him properly. He bitterly regretted the row they'd had when she told him the body was Howard, and knew now that instead of moaning about Suzanne he would have done better to show more compassion for Jo. But the damage had been done. Jo had built a wall between them and nothing he said or did seemed to break it down. He didn't realise that if he had simply barged through the barrier of grief she had erected and wrapped his arms round her, everything would have been all right.

It would have been so simple – but he didn't do it. Instead the distance between them increased and Jo found herself thinking more and more about Alan and how he had instinctively known what to do. At times when the feelings of grief began to well up inside her she found she could control them by shutting her eyes and picturing herself holding on to him just after he had told her the awful news. She could feel the fabric of his jacket and, if she really concentrated, could almost smell the mixture of his aftershave and warm skin that she had found so soothing.

But she didn't dare to allow herself that luxury, especially not with Simon nearby, which added to her feelings of sadness. For the past three days she had pressed all her emotions as far down as she could. The moment they began to rise to the surface the tears came with them. Only the day before the show opened she realised that she hadn't been shopping and desperately needed to stock up. She darted into the supermarket and was standing in the middle of the aisle scanning her list when a little girl holding her father's hand came skipping towards her. Jo couldn't bear to watch and had almost hurled herself into the freezer cabinet, using the excuse of studying frozen chickens as a way of hiding the tears that were once again pouring down her face.

So to find that she was actually able to laugh at the silly jokes flying around Suzanne's office and even join in with them was an enormous relief. 'So,' she was saying to some of the Home Maker Exhibition sales team who had been moaning about an exhibitor's excessive political correctness. 'This poor director was having one hell of a time with this absolutely dreadful producer. When the gorilla came lumbering on to the set the director objected, pointing out that the script had called for a trained chimp. When the producer heard this he marched over and screamed at the top of his voice, *"That's Gorillaism and I don't suffer any isms on my set. You're fired!"*' Everyone hooted with laughter as Laura came up behind her. 'Jo, your mobile's ringing in your briefcase.' Jo excused herself from the group and went to dig her phone out from under the pile of coats and bags that had amassed in the corner of the room.

It was Simon, concerned because he hadn't heard from her all day. Normally she was emotionally a very steady woman but her behaviour had been so withdrawn lately that, even though he didn't know how to show it, he was genuinely worried. But just as Jo answered the phone someone in the room gave a very good impression of one of the higher-profile exhibitors which made her chuckle. That and the gale of raucous laughter which hit the air echoed down the line to Simon. Immediately his concern evaporated, to be replaced by cold anger.

'Here am I worried sick about you, how you're feeling, the fact that you're working late, but listening to the noise going on around you I can tell I needn't have bothered. You're clearly having a great time. I presume you save all the moping around just for me. Well, I've had enough. I'm bored with it, so don't bother coming home tonight.' Before she could explain he had hung up. She stared at the phone as the line went dead. Alan was walking past to refill his glass and, seeing her bewildered expression, stopped.

'You OK?'

She gave an awkward giggle. 'I think it's a hotel for me tonight. Si's kicked me out.' She sounded puzzled, tucking her hair behind her ears. Alan put his glass down on the table.

'I thought it was your place?'

'It is, but if he's going to lock me out what can I do?'

Alan saw the misery on her face. 'Come on. Let's get out of here. Wait for me by the lift. I'll get my stuff and say my Good nights.' Jo didn't need to be told twice. She picked up her coat and bags and without a word to anyone went to wait by the lift. It was a good five minutes before Alan joined her. 'Sorry, it took longer than I thought.' He led the way to his car and helped her in. The adrenaline that had buoyed her up all day had finally gone, leaving her drained and tired. Neither spoke and it wasn't until they were turning off the A40 that Jo thought to ask where they were going.

'You're staying with me tonight and tomorrow you can sort this mess out. No, don't worry, I have a spare room,' he added hastily, seeing a look of alarm cross her face.

Alan's flat was at the top of a road that led straight on to Northwood High Street. It looked small from the outside but its appearance was deceptive, as it went back a long way. 'Pop your stuff in there,' he said, pointing to a room half way down the hall as he made his way to the back of the flat. Jo did as she was told and, not knowing what else to do, followed the light down the corridor into the kitchen. It was surprisingly large and very modern, which she was not expecting. White glass-fronted wall units held heavy blue glass and bold blue and white crockery; gleaming white tiles covered the worktops and even though the floor was covered with large blue ceramic tiles it still managed to feel cosy. It was clearly a man's kitchen but as she looked around she saw a row of cookery books and shelves holding an assortment of blue and white pots. Alan followed her eyes to the pots. 'I love cooking and pottering around in the kitchen.'

Jo found herself trying to imagine Simon 'pottering around in the kitchen' but failed. Alan was busying himself with the kettle but Jo stopped him.

'Actually I think I've drunk enough coffee today to refloat Brazil. Any chance of something a bit stronger?' He hesitated and then opened the fridge to take out a cold bottle of white wine and a tub of olives.

'Will this do?' Jo nodded.

He took a couple of glasses from a cupboard and pulled out one of the bar stools. 'Sit down.' He patted the seat. Jo settled herself as he opened the bottle and the olives, putting them on the breakfast bar between them. 'Thank God Preview Day's over and done with. I always feel happier once we've got that under our belts. Anyway, here's to . . .' He hesitated, not knowing what to say. 'Whatever.' He lifted his glass and chinked it against the side of Jo's. She smiled weakly and, raising her glass to her lips, took a sip.

A silence descended between them, broken only by the sound of their chewed olive stones dropping into a saucer. For once Alan's PR skills deserted him. It was one thing to make people feel comfortable at work, but it felt odd here in his own home. Not knowing quite what to say to Jo Alan said nothing, filling the silence by getting up to put a CD on the player in the living room so the music filtered through. Jo was once again trying to sort out the muddled thoughts tumbling through her head.

Coming back from the living room Alan stood by the kitchen door and watched her as she stared into space. The recessed lighting gave a warm glow. He wanted to reach out and touch her, to hold her and reassure her that it would all work out, but what he couldn't decide was exactly what that meant.

Working out for Jo clearly meant going back to Simon and the close and loving relationship they had once had, but for him it meant her *not* going back. For Alan 'working out' meant Jo being free to be with him. Right now he wanted to pick her up and carry her into the bedroom. *Eat your heart out, Rhett Butler!* he laughingly said to himself as he went to sit down again beside her, eying her surreptitiously over the top of his glass. They had almost finished the bottle and she was twirling the stem slowly between her fingers, her hair as ever flopping forward. And that was another thing. Alan wanted to sweep that hair off her face, take away the screen that she hid behind.

Christ, I could kill the people who did this to you, he thought with a surge of anger directed at those in Jo's life who had so effectively dented her self-confidence and chipped away at her self-esteem. Suddenly Jo turned and looked straight into his eyes with such a direct gaze that Alan felt himself begin to blush.

'What am I going to do now, Alan?' The question was asked quietly and flatly, with little emotion.

'You mean about Simon?'

'I mean about all of it. About Si, about Maggie, about Howard. All of it. I think I could cope with just one bit, but the whole lot all at once is too much. It would be good if just one area of my personal life seemed right instead of this feeling of bone-deep weariness that I seem to be dragging with me all the time.'

'Maybe you shouldn't try to solve it all at once. I mean, try to separate it all out and resolve each bit one piece at a time. Surely the immediate problem is Simon?'

Go on, Jo, dump him and come to me. Alan made an effort not to move, afraid a gesture might give him away.

'Immediate, yes, but it's so interwoven with everything else. I get no emotional support from him with Maggie. OK, he said he'd have come with me when I went to tell her about Howard but a bit of me wonders if he would have done that if I had asked him *before* I went. I mean, did he offer because he knew I'd already been? You might ask why should I expect any support from him anyway? She's my mother, not his, but he doesn't even try to see it from my point of view. And the fact that I can, and do, understand why he gets so pissed off with her, because I do as well, doesn't help. Then there's his feelings about my work. Alan, I'm like you. I love what I do. I've worked bloody hard for the right to do it and I *know* I'm good at it but I still get the feeling that Si resents it. That he thinks I'm playing; that I'll give it all up to be wife, and ultimately mother, when we get married – whenever *that's* going to be,' she added sarcastically. 'And the one time when I could really do with him being there for me, when they find my father dead and rotting after thirty odd years, he can't see why I'm upset. It's all knotted together and the middle of the knot seems to be Si himself.'

Alan reached out and took Jo's hand, uncurling it from the glass's stem. He held her fingers and with his thumb gently stroked the back of her hand. 'Jo, tell me to mind my own business but I'm going to ask you a question and I want an honest answer. Do you love Simon?'

Jo snatched her hand away. 'Of course I do.' She replied almost before he had finished asking the question.

'I'm sorry.' He dropped her hand and backed away a little. 'I didn't mean to upset you but I want you to think about it. I might not have known you long, but so far all I've heard you say about your fiańce has been rather negative. I'm sure he's a smashing bloke,' he added quickly without much conviction, 'but maybe he's not the right one for you. That's all.'

'Look, I really shouldn't have brought you into this. I'm sorry.' Jo got off the stool and stepped backwards away from him.

Damn! he thought. *Now I've really buggered things up.* He also stood up, but had the sense not to make a move towards her and began putting the glasses in the sink instead. 'The bathroom's next door to your bedroom if you want a bath,' he said, turning on the taps. 'There's a towel in the airing cupboard in the corner and I'll pop a spare robe on the door knob for you. I'm going to potter around for another hour or so, so take your time. There's another loo so I won't be bashing at the bathroom door to get in.' He smiled over his shoulder at her. Weakly Jo smiled back before escaping.

Do I love Si? she asked herself as she undressed and ran the bath. She lay back in the hot water but the question wouldn't go away. *Do I love Si? Do I love Si? Oh, shut up!* she told herself sternly *you know damn well you love him, now get to bed.* But she didn't move. The question continued repeating itself until suddenly it changed, making her sit up, splashing water over the edge of the bath. *Does Si love me?* It was very similar to the question she used to ask herself when they first started going out with each other. Except then it had been, *Why does Si love me?* It was a good year into their relationship before she accepted his love without questioning it, and she realised that she had only stopped torturing herself with doubts when he had given up his rented flat to move in with her.

At the time she had been delighted and had even tried to share the news with Maggie but her mother had just snorted and made some comment about Simon using her. 'Just you wait,' she had warned. 'You think you've got what *you* wanted but the day he moves in will be the day it all changes because at that point, my girl, he's got you just where he wants you. Under his thumb.' Jo had protested that Simon wasn't like that, but as she remembered the conversation she began to wonder if maybe Maggie hadn't been right after all. And the thought that she might have been grated.

She got out of the bath and began drying herself. Cautiously she unlocked the door and felt round the edge. True to his word Alan had hung a towelling robe there and gratefully she pulled it on. She peeped round the door to check he wasn't there and, hearing music from what she assumed to be the living room, she scuttled next door to the bedroom, yelling out ''Night' just to let him know that the bathroom was free.

Jo curled up under the duvet but couldn't settle down. It was partly because she was overtired but mainly because she was subconsciously listening for sounds of Alan in the bathroom. She eventually dozed off about an hour later, when to the best of her knowledge he was still in the living room. Suddenly she woke up with a jolt.

No, said a voice inside her head. *I don't love him. Not any more. He's just a habit.* The thought was so startling that she sat up in bed and switched on the light next to her, as if it would help her think more clearly. She considered the voice in her head and then got out of bed, pulled the still damp robe around her and belted it firmly as she opened the door.

Music was still playing softly and a gentle light spilled into the hallway. She made her way towards it and crept into the room. Alan was sprawled on a large Chesterfield sofa, one leg raised against its back. His arm was bent over his eyes. A gas fire was flickering and his shoes lay in front of it. He had taken off his jacket and tie and these hung over the back of a dining chair. For a moment Jo thought he was asleep and, surprised at how disappointed this made her feel, she turned to go back to her room.

'I'm awake. Don't go.' Alan spoke lazily and sat up, giving her a slow smile. 'Everything OK?'

'It's fine. I've come to apologise. That's all I seem to do to you, isn't it?' She tucked her hair behind her ears and went to sit next to him. 'I'm sorry for biting your head off. I've been thinking about what you asked – about Si – and I think you're right.' She paused before her next words came out in a rush. 'I don't love him. I don't love Si any more.'

There, she thought, *I've said it.* And she felt a huge surge of relief flood through her. Alan said nothing but leaned towards her to kiss her cheek. 'Come here.' He held out his arm and willingly she snuggled up against him. Again silence descended between them but this time it was comfortable. Another CD started on the player and the sound of a lone saxophone filled the room.

Neither said or did anything.

Jo breathed deeply, allowing the smell of him that she hadn't quite been able to forget wash over her. She couldn't explain what it was. It was both sweet and sour at the same time and as she breathed it in she recognised the thrill of excitement she had felt when he first touched her hand at the restaurant. It seemed like a lifetime ago.

Alan raised his left hand and moved it to her cheek. Jo inclined her head towards the movement and he turned her face upwards to meet his. This time when he kissed her she felt no sense of guilt. She lifted her arms to wrap them round Alan and as the saxophonist played his slow husky music Jo began to softly stroke his neck. Alan swallowed; her touch was gentle but inviting and he could feel his body beginning to respond. He kissed her again, this time with increasing passion, and eagerly Jo pulled him closer. A sensation deep in her belly spread a glow through her body and when Alan ran his hands down the back of her robe she wriggled a little, encouraging it to loosening at the waist, to fall off her shoulder slightly. She could feel the heat from the fire mingling with the warmth of his hands which first flowed over her shoulders and, after what seemed like an eternity to Jo, finally began to caress her nipples. He bent his head to kiss her breasts and as he did so she stroked his head, again massaging the nape of his neck and slipping her hands inside the back of his shirt.

Suddenly he stopped and Jo wanted to scream with frustration. But it was only so he could lead her into the bedroom. The saxophone carried on playing in the living room, the sound just trickling across the hall. Alan quickly undressed before pulling Jo towards him, pushing the robe off her shoulders to lie in a heap on the floor. He ran his fingers through her hair and up and down her back as she stood on tip-toe to reach his mouth. At last they moved towards the bed and made love.

She and Simon had long ago learned how to arouse each other so even though their sex life was satisfying it had become predictable. For the first time in years Jo found herself reacting to something different. The unpredictability of another man's touch excited her as Alan's eager fingers explored her body. His touch alternated between firm and caressing. Jo luxuriated in it, riding the sensations as wave after wave washed through and over her, and her physical release matched her emotional one. Seeing and feeling her enjoyment encouraged Alan even more. Jo in turn delighted in exciting him, seeing how her fingers and mouth drew responses from him until, exhausted, they both finally collapsed in a heap. Jo curled up in the curve of his body and he put his arms protectively around her, enjoying the feel of her against his naked skin.

He woke before she did the next morning, and although they had both shifted during the night he was childishly pleased to note that they were still wrapped round each other. He lay very still, afraid of waking her. *Oh God, Jo, are you going to hate me?* he wondered, not wanting her to stir if her reaction was going to be a hostile one.

As if she could read his mind Jo shifted and opened her eyes. A puzzled looked crossed her face as she tried to work out where she was. She shut her eyes again and groaned as she remembered what had happened the night before. 'Oh God, Alan, you must think I'm the biggest slut out. I tell you I don't love Si any more and within a few minutes I've got you into bed.' Alan's worries about her reaction melted away and he laughed. Jo reopened her eyes with a snap. 'Are you laughing at me?'

'No. I was just lying here hoping you wouldn't hate me for jumping on you as soon as you told me it was all over with Simon.' Jo allowed a wide grin to creep across her face as she propped her head up on her elbow.

'It sounds as if we both pounced on each other? I guess this brings me back to where I started last night, doesn't it?' He looked puzzled. 'What do I do now, Alan?' She looked down at his face, again seeing the way his eyes creased at the corners and noticing the overnight growth on his chin.

'This,' he said and pulled her down to kiss her mouth firmly. It was another hour before they got out of bed and then they had to rush to get ready for work. Jo didn't care that she would be wearing the same clothes as yesterday, or that she and Alan would be the butt of speculation. One thing she had learned since being involved with Exhibitions International was how much everyone there loved gossip. She thought the world of television was bad, but she discovered that the exhibition world could knock it into a cocked hat. As ever with gossip some of it was true, much of it speculation but the whole company seemed to thrive on it. *Well, this will give them something to talk about,* she thought as she gave a startled Alan a passionate and lingering goodbye kiss at the foot of the stairs leading up to her Portacabin.

Sure enough the gossip was circulating by lunchtime, albeit quietly due to the large number of hangovers around the place that day. But fortunately it was intermingled with other titbits from the night before. It had obviously become quite a drunken party – so much so that one of the sales team had managed to get herself locked into a stockroom cupboard with one of the security men. Their story was that they'd no choice but to stay there all night until an exhibitor came along next morning to replenish his stand, only to find the intertwined couple asleep under his rugs. Jo and Alan became just another item of gossip, and as neither went out of their way to deny anything it was a two-day wonder. Soon the gossip-mongers had moved on to new ground, in particular the 'accidents' that were continuing.

On the third public day of the show the early-morning staff came in to discover that a number of stand names and numbers had all been swopped over, not only infuriating the exhibitors but also confusing visitors and creating more work in the organisers' office. Two days later all the light bulbs were removed from the roomset features and someone added bubble bath to the waterfall in the tropical garden. And so it went on. Jo managed to find out about all the incidents and, although her crew were now spending some time on their next project, where possible they carried on trying to be in the right place at the right time, capturing both the discovery of the 'accidents' and their aftermath on film. At work she felt confident and happy but meanwhile at home, with Simon, things went from bad to worse.

At the first opportunity on the day after the preview party Jo had insisted that she and Alan sit down together to talk things through properly. It was just after the rumours about them had begun spreading so they sat openly in the canteen and held on to each other's hands throughout the whole conversation. 'I've got to go back and talk to Si,' she explained. 'I've got to tell him the engagement is off but after four years I can't just throw him out on to the streets. I mean it's not his fault I don't love him any more is it?'

'Isn't it?' Alan sounded doubtful. 'From everything you've said it sounds as if it *was* his fault. After all, you're the one who's made all the effort while he seems to have done nothing other than moan and groan and bonk your brains out. I know, I know, I'm being unfair,' he added hastily, seeing the look on Jo's face, 'but I'm greedy. I want us to be together and I want that now. I know it's unreasonable of me to expect you just to turf him out, but I'd be lying if I didn't say it's what I want.'

Jo tucked her hair behind her ears and began to speak but it sounded as if she was just voicing her thoughts out loud. 'I've got to tell him it's over. But I don't think I'll tell him about you just yet. I mean, I know now that it was over a long time ago, even though I couldn't face up to it. Alan, you're the catalyst, not the cause, so I think for everyone's sake it would be better if I kept you out of it. Please don't look so hurt. It's not going to be easy and even though I don't love the man any more that doesn't mean I want to go out of my way to hurt him.'

'No, I suppose not,' Alan said, but he didn't sound as if he meant it. He begrudged her sentiment, jealous that Simon obviously still had some control over her feelings.

'I'll tell him tonight,' Jo promised as the radio crackled out his name, calling him back to the press office. But when she got home to Hampstead that evening Simon wasn't there. Instead, propped up next to the largest vase of red roses she had ever seen, was a note. With a sinking feeling she opened the envelope and as she read his grovelling apology she sank to the bottom step of the stairs.

At any other time his words of repentance and love would have soothed and reassured her but right now they were the last things she wanted. What she needed was the moody, difficult Simon so she could summon up enough anger to tell him it was over. His sympathetic comments about her feelings and words of regret at not being there more for her when she was going through a bad time made her want to cry.

At least, she thought as she got to her feet to answer the phone, *he's away on that sales conference*. In all the fuss she had forgotten that he was going to Jersey for four days until his note reminded her. With a sigh she picked up the receiver only to feel her heart sink even further as she heard Simon's voice.

For a split second she played with idea of being a coward and telling him that the engagement was off over the phone, but as she turned round she saw the roses again and knew she couldn't be that cruel. Forcing a bright note into her voice she thanked him for the flowers and his note.

'Darling, I'm so sorry for being such a bastard. Honestly I am. It wasn't until last night when you weren't there that I knew just how much you mean to me. I shouldn't have told you not to come home. It's your place, after all. I missed you so much, where did you stay?' She murmured something about a friend and Simon rushed on, his verbal apology even more profuse than the words written on the sheet of paper that Jo now held tightly scrunched up in her hand. 'I promise when I get home we'll sort . . . I mean *I'll* sort this whole thing out. I love you, Jo.' She made some suitable reply, hoping he wouldn't hear the lie in her voice.

Oh, Si, she though sadly as she hung up. *Why couldn't you have said that two weeks ago? Why leave it until it's too late?*

She had told Alan firmly that as much as she wanted to be with him she would be staying at her own place until Simon had gone. 'I don't want to make things any harder than they have to be,' she explained.

However, Simon had obviously meant what he said and from the moment he returned he went out of his way to be helpful and supportive. Jo tried to talk to him but somehow she couldn't find the words. By the time they went to bed on his first night back she still hadn't been able to say anything. She tried to keep to her side but he reached out and pulled her towards him.

'Oh God, I've missed you. I've been a pig, Jo, but I promise you it's going to stop.' He kissed her mouth and even though she wasn't interested in sex with him Jo did as she had done so many times in the recent past and let him make love to her. Afterwards he rolled over and fell asleep, not noticing or caring that she had been unresponsive.

'Tomorrow,' she promised herself, 'I'll tell him tomorrow.' But the next day came and went and still she couldn't say anything. She became more and more miserable, but whereas in the past Simon would have either ignored her, or been annoyed by her moods, now he went out of his way to be sensitive to her feelings, and that made her feel even worse.

Alan tried to understand, and to a certain extent he did. He remembered only too well how difficult it had been for him to tell his wife that their marriage was over, and in their case there hadn't been anyone else. It had taken him six weeks to start that particular conversation so he knew what Jo was going through. But still he was impatient.

'This isn't helping anyone, you know,' he commented one evening as the show entered its third week, when Jo had again lied to Simon about late filming so she could spend some time with him. They were sitting in a small chip-shop down the road from the Pimlico Centre, drinking coffee and picking at their chips. The front of the shop was a take-away section and there were a few tables at the back covered in red and white checked cloths. Salt and pepper pots and bottles of vinegar supported the paper napkins, and each table sported a bright red plastic tomato full of ketchup. It wasn't the most romantic place, the strip lighting was too harsh for that, but they had become regulars as it was the nearest place to the exhibition.

'I know, but how the hell do you think I feel? I hate lying to him. I'm so bad at it he must know something's wrong, but it's so difficult.' Jo picked up another chip and dipped it in her ketchup. 'Do you know what the hardest thing is?' she asked, not looking at him. Alan shook his head. 'Sharing a double bed with a man I no longer love. It must be one of the loneliest feelings in the world. Especially when I know I could be sharing it with you.'

Alan had picked up a chip but now stopped with it hovering in mid air over the pool of sauce. 'Are you telling me you're still sleeping with the guy?'

'Well where did you think I was sleeping? On the sofa?'

'I don't know. I hadn't really considered it, but I thought that after all you said about caring for me you would have at least stopped sharing a bed with him. Just tell me that you're not having sex with him any more. Are you?' Alan was looking at Jo's face as she tried to think of how to answer the question. Only last night Simon had rolled on top of her. Alan was right. It was sex, that was all it was. Just sex. Not love making, not like with Alan. But she had paused a second too long.

'Jesus Christ!' Alan erupted. 'Here's me trying to be understanding. Trying to accept that you "have to do this in your own way and time".' He mimicked her voice. 'And all the time you're screwing the arse off him. Talk about having the best of both worlds. Boy, am I an idiot. According to you you've been lying to Simon ever since we got together. How do I know you're not lying to me too? How do I know that I'm not just the fling of the production? From what you've told me about filming, very wittily I might add, there's usually one torrid affair per programme. Maybe I'm this one's? How do I know that as soon as you pack up your cameras and move on to the next programme you won't find some other benighted bloke to play with. Tell me, Jo, what's the male equivalent of a bimbo, because whatever it is that's me.'

Alan dropped his chip and went to get up but Jo moved faster and was on her feet, eyes blazing as she leaned across the table to look down at him before he had even pushed his chair back.

'Yes, Simon and I are still having sex, but not through any desire of mine. Technically you could call it rape because all I do is lie back and think of England. In fact, I don't think of England. I think of *you*. Don't you think that's the biggest kick in the balls I could give Si? That the only way I can get through sex with him is by thinking of you, which, incidentally, I do a lot because sex with you is incredible. If you don't know by now that it's you I want to be with, that it's *you* who matters, then maybe you *are* dumb enough to be a male bimbo and maybe it's better I find that out now and stay where I am. Goodnight, Mr Waterman.'

Jo snatched her coat from the back of the chair oblivious to the stunned faces of the four workmen who were the chippy's only other diners, and stomped angrily out into the night air. It was the fact that he was right that made her so very angry. That he had recognised what she hadn't, that she was trying to have the best of both worlds. The stability of the life she knew (it was safe even if it did make her miserable) with the support and excitement of the new world she was trying to create with Alan. She sat in the car and took a few deep breaths before starting the engine.

Alan sank back into his seat letting the rage flow through him, enjoying his sense of indignant fury. How dare she make him feel as if he were in the wrong? She was the one cheating on someone, not him. All he wanted was to be with her and to look after her but if she didn't want that, if she wanted to carry on being treated like a willing doormat by her fiance and mother, then sod her!

Jo calmed herself down as she drove home. She resolved, again, to tell Simon tonight that it was over. She had to prove to Alan that she meant what she said. But by the time she got home Simon was so full of concern about her late hours and so keen to reiterate how much he loved her that as before Jo was cowed into compliant acceptance and said nothing. At least that night Simon didn't show any interest in sex.

So the situation continued, with Jo trying to please everyone at once, covering up her feelings in front of the crew by maintaining her usual bright and breezy persona; lying to Simon, and hating herself a little more every time she grabbed an hour with Alan. By the time the show had been running for three weeks Jo's life had settled into a pattern, albeit a difficult one. She was spending less time at the exhibition now, and was pulling the crew away to the next part of the series, though she was planning to have the full crew there for the break-down in three weeks' time.

She was still in regular contact with Suzanne, who let her know that she was aware of what was going on between her and Alan, though she was clearly not that bothered – so long as it didn't get in the way of the exhibition. Oddly enough she seemed more concerned about Maggie than she did Alan and it was Suzanne's questions, rather than Jo's own feelings, which prompted her to keep in touch with her mother.

Then two things happened to upset the pattern. First DCI Thomas told her that they were not treating Howard's death as suspicious. He had clearly been drunk and tripped over the pipes, smashing his head on the corner of the concrete pillar. They believed he would have died instantly. The fact that he was in the basement was dismissed as irrelevant. The inquest re-opened and the coroner quickly recorded a verdict of death by misadventure.

Howard's body was released for burial.

Jo greeted the news with a frown. She knew that Maggie wouldn't arrange Howard's funeral so it would fall to her to see that, thirty years late, her father got a decent burial. She anticipated a difficult time persuading her mother to attend the service, let alone take an interest.

Secondly she realised her period was a week late.

PART TWO

Exhibition

'Plenty of room on top. Hold very tight, please.' Peg helped a passenger to her seat, took her fare and then turned back to carry on her conversation. 'Please, Rita. It won't be any fun if you're not there.'

'It's not that I don't *want* to come, it's just that Mum'll be worried sick if I'm out when there's a raid on.'

'Well, don't tell her where you're going. Say you're staying with me. Emily's not on the phone so she'll have no way of checking up and you can call her the next day to let her know you've survived anything Mr Spoilsport Rotten Hitler wants to drop on us. Come on, Rita, it's a one-off.'

'Oh, I just don't know, Peg. I've never lied to Mum before and it doesn't seem right somehow.' Rita fiddled uncomfortably with the strap of her gas mask as she looked out of the window at yet another pile of smouldering bricks and glass that had been a small row of shops the day before. She was determined that this time Peg wouldn't get her own way and talk her round.

'Honestly, you make me sick,' Peg blustered. 'It's not as if there's anything for you to stay home for, is there? All the blokes have gone away. I won't be sorry to see the back of 1940. I know we've still got a few days to go but who cares? And that's another thing, where's your Dunkirk spirit? The way things are going we'll be spending the next ten years running and hiding like scared rabbits down holes in the ground and by the time it's all over and we come out we'll be old maids. Well, if you want to spend the rest of your life sitting in a rocking chair knitting socks you can. I'm going to the Lyceum.' And she let go of the handrail above the seat to go swinging down the bus to collect the rest of the fares. She ignored Rita as she passed her on the way back and jumped on to the platform before going up top to check the passengers there.

When she came back down she tried another approach. Whatever happened she was going to the benefit that had been arranged for Sunday night at the Lyceum to help the bombed-out East End. Emily had finished altering her red dress and it looked gorgeous. She also knew from her preening in front of the mirror that she looked gorgeous in it, but that having plain, dowdy Rita with her would make her look even better. 'Rita, *everyone's* going, and anyway you won't be lying to your mum because you can come and stay with me afterwards. It's called being selective with the truth. You tell her you're staying with me but what you *don't* tell her is that we're going out. I'll let you borrow my brown dress if you come.' Peg knew Rita loved that dress. The fact that it would make her look even duller next to Peg in her red one was another reason she was prepared to let her friend wear what had, up until now, been her favourite dancing dress.

'This is my stop.' Rita stood up to get off the bus, pleased that for once she'd stood her ground. As she stepped off the platform Peg raised her hand to ring the bell.

'Freddie's going, you know.'

Rita hesitated. Last time they had all gone out she and Freddie danced together quite a lot, and she did like him. She turned to look up at Peg. 'You're sure Mum won't find out?'

'How could she? Look, if you're worried about Emily, don't be. I can take care of her.' Peg dismissed her landlady with a toss of her blonde curls.

Rita made up her mind. 'All right,' she said without much enthusiasm. 'Count me in.' Peg rang the bell a couple of times and the bus lurched slowly down the road, avoiding the odd bits of rubble that the civil defence crews had missed.

'Great!' yelled Peg. 'I'm off shift at four on Sunday so meet me at the depot with your things. It'll be fine. You'll see.'

Rita raised her hand to show she had heard Peg's words then pulled her collar up and hat down against the cold December air. She picked her way along Camden High Street to the solicitor's where she worked and as she opened the door a huge yawn split her face. 'Morning, Miss Cooper. Had a good Christmas? 'Nother heavy night, wasn't it?' he carried on, not waiting for an answer to his first question. She nodded at young Mr Greenaway and quickly scuttled past him, not wanting to hear more tales of his work as an ARP warden. It was the thought of spending yet another night cramped under the stairs with her parents and two younger brothers that made her decide she was pleased she was going out with Peg. At least if she stayed with her she knew she would have a better chance of a good night's sleep. Emily's house in Roupell Street had a large basement that they used as a shelter which not only had plenty of space in which everyone stretched out, but also blocked some of the noise from the anti-aircraft guns.

She still didn't feel comfortable about not telling her mother the truth, particularly as Mrs Cooper sucked her teeth in disapproval when she heard Rita mention Peg's name. 'She's trouble that one, you mark my words, miss. A right flibbertygibbet who'll get her come-uppance one of these days.'

'Oh Mum, Peg's all right. Really she is. She just likes to have fun, that's all. It's not her fault the boys find her attractive.'

'That's as maybe but you just remember, Rita, that you're a good girl. I don't want you bringing trouble to this house, do you hear?'

The conversation had been repeated throughout Saturday with

added grunts from her father from behind his newspaper as Mrs Cooper embellished her impressions of Peg. When Rita finally left the house at three o'clock on Sunday afternoon she was more than ready to escape and was actually looking forward to the evening ahead.

She got to the Waterloo depot at ten to four and was waiting for Peg when her bus came trundling into the garage. It stopped with a screech of brakes and Peg jumped off the back, unhooking her ticket machine from her belt as she did so. 'Thank God that's over with.' She made her way to the office to hand in the machine and punched herself off shift. The next crew was waiting and although most of the drivers and clippies were women these days, a few men were still part of the rota. Peg pulled her jacket down over her hips and ran her fingers through her hair, teasing the curls out as she did so. One of the lads gave a low wolf whistle and with a happy laugh she winked at him as she tucked her arm into Rita's. 'You're too young love, come back in a few years' time,' she yelled at him, making the pimply youth blush.

'Trouble is,' she said cosily to Rita, 'I've got a feeling that soon that's all we'll have left. Ah well, let's not worry about that. There's sure to be something interesting at the Lyceum tonight. Got your frock?'

'I thought you said I could wear your brown one?' Rita's face clouded over as she thought of her skirt and the hand-knitted sweater she was wearing under her coat.

'Of course I did, and so you shall. Tonight's going to be fun and we've got lots of time to get ready. Tonight, Rita, you and I are going to make their eyes pop out of their heads!' Not for the first time Rita found herself remembering her mother's warnings about Peg but any doubts she had were quickly pushed to one side when they got back to Roupell Street.

Peg led the way into the house, calling out for Emily as she went. Her landlady appeared from the back, wiping her hands on her apron as she came up the couple of steps to greet them. Peg planted an unceremonious kiss on her cheek as she made her way past her into the kitchen. A fire was glowing in the range and the kettle whistled gently on top of it. The room felt warm and cosy as Rita walked shyly in. Peg had only ever meant to lodge with Emily for a short time when she first moved to London from Sidcup but as her landlady had taken on the role of a kindly aunt who she could wrap round her little finger (and who didn't demand the rent on time) she had decided to stay where she was. Emily was a widow from the first war and even though she didn't always approve of her lodger's behaviour she did enjoy the company. Especially on cold nights like tonight when she brought friends home.

Despite the sugar and butter rationing that had been with them for nearly a year Emily had managed to put together a delicious tea with a real sponge cake. Greedily the two younger women sat down at the battered old table. They chattered happily about the entertainment ahead as Emily sat and listened, recalling the dances of her own youth. 'Come on,' said Peg, 'we'd better go and get ready.' Rita made a move to help clear the table but Peg pushed it to one side. 'Oh, leave it. You don't mind, do you, Emmy?' She was half way out of the kitchen door before Emily answered.

'Go on, the pair of you,' she said with a smile and without waiting to be told twice they ran upstairs to dress themselves. Rita was pleased that Peg was in such an expansive mood and sat obligingly in front of the mirror as she twisted her hair and helped her apply some make-up. Usually she only wore a bit of lipstick, secretly agreeing with her mother that only 'tarts' wore anything more, but Peg seemed to know so many clever ways of applying colour to her cheeks and eyes that she let her get on with it.

'There,' said Peg as she stepped back to admire her handiwork. 'Much better. Now out of the way so I can do mine.' With more speed than Rita would have thought possible Peg wound her already glossy curls into a full and flattering style and quickly applied make-up to her own face. 'Well, don't just stand there. Get the dress on.' Rita turned to the dress hanging outside the large wooden wardrobe and carefully stepped into it, not wanting to ruin her hairdo. Peg helped her button it up and then took her by the shoulders and turned her round to face the mirror. Rita felt wonderful. Peg really was a lovely friend to let her borrow the dress which not only showed off her brown hair to its best advantage but also managed to make her look a lot slimmer than she really was. She was about say thank you again when Peg stepped out from behind the wardrobe door where she had been putting on her own dress.

Rita's mouth fell open. Peg looked like a film star. The red woollen dress clung to her shape in just the right way and when she moved it swirled round her calves. Its ruching at the front was lower than Rita would ever have dared wear but somehow on Peg it looked good, showing off the swell of her breasts. Peg twirled and as she did so the fabric lifted to show even more of her elegantly shaped legs. Rita was a bit shocked – any more and you would see her stocking tops. 'You look wonderful,' she stammered, suddenly feeling plain and mousy beside her colourful friend.

'So do you,' replied Peg, but from the tone in her voice it was clear that the only person she was looking at was herself. She fluffed out her curls and puckered her lips at her reflection before turning back to Rita. 'Emily altered it for me. I'm not sure that it's quite right but I suppose it'll have to do.' She knew she was fishing for compliments but why not? She *did* look good and, after all, that was why she had asked Rita to come with her.

The two women went downstairs and said goodbye to Emily who sent them on their way with warnings about 'being careful'. They were lucky. It was still quite early and it looked as if the Luftwaffe might be giving them a night off. The barrage balloons glowed eerily against the night sky but they didn't linger to watch them. They did not want to be caught half way across the Thames if the sirens went off and they walked quickly across Waterloo Bridge into Wellington Street on the outskirts of Covent Garden. A few stale cabbage leaves clung to the gutter and a stack of stray apple boxes was propped against the sand bags outside the door to the Lyceum but neither of the women saw them as they made their way inside.

The bright lights and noise hit them as soon as they pushed through the heavy blackout curtain hanging across the doorway. Gold and red decorations blazed brilliantly and the sound of the music already playing in the dance hall below made them forget the cold night outside. Peg knew a number of the men were watching her as they took off their coats. Studiously she ignored them and when one plucked up the courage to ask her for a dance she imperiously grabbed Rita by the arm and led her inside, making some suitable retort. The band was playing *South of the Border* and the floor was full of dancing couples, many of the men in uniform. They stood at the top of the stairs and Rita saw the rest of their friends leaning over the balustrade at the other side of the hall. She pointed them out to Peg.

'I don't see Freddie there.' She stood on tip-toe trying to see over people's heads.

'Oh, sorry, I forgot to tell you,' Peg said nonchalantly. 'He's on fire duty tonight. He said if it's quiet he'll try to come in later.' Rita sank back on to her heels as the disappointment surged through her. Peg had done it again. She probably knew all along that Freddie wouldn't be there but had used him as the bait anyway. Ah well, now she was here she might as well enjoy herself.

She turned back to say something to Peg but a group had got between them and by the time she had pushed her way through the crowd to join her the moment had passed. Their friends were chattering away but Peg wasn't listening to a word anyone was saying. Her eyes were scanning the floor until at last she saw what she was looking for. Near to the stage was a particularly lively group of airmen. She grabbed Rita by the arm. 'Come on,' she said as she dragged her down the elegant staircase, not caring who she elbowed as she made her way to the floor.

'Where are we going?' Rita asked, rubbing her arm where Peg had gripped it too tightly.

'To have fun. Now stop asking questions and trust me.' She carried on elbowing her way round the hall, stopping a few yards short of the group she had seen from the balcony. She smoothed her dress over her curves and began to walk in an almost casual way towards the stage.

'Say baby, I was hoping I might see you tonight.' An enthusiastic pilot grabbed her round the waist and with feigned surprise Peg turned to greet him.

'Why, Chuck. What a lovely surprise. We only decided this afternoon to come and see what was going on. It's great to see so many people here on a Sunday night.' Peg looked round the hall as if she were seeing it for the first time and Rita stood awkwardly behind her being jostled by the crowd. It was now patently clear that Peg had used her so that she could 'accidentally' bump into this latest man of hers.

'Who's your friend?' Chuck bent his head in Rita's direction.

'This is Rita. Rita, say "Hi" to Chuck.' Peg put a special emphasis on the word 'Hi' which made the pilot laugh.

'We'll get you talking like a good American yet. Nice to meet you, Rita.' Just then the band finished playing amid loud applause.

'Good evening, ladies and gentleman. It's great to see so many of you here for tonight's fund raiser for the East End. We'll show Hitler that he can chuck what he likes at us but we won't be beaten!' A huge roar of support rent the smoke-filled air. The compère hushed the crowd. 'We've got a really terrific line-up for you tonight and all of our performers are giving their fees to the fund.' Another yell of approval from the crowd. 'But you haven't come here to hear me talk.'

'Too right, mate!' yelled a voice from the middle of the hall.

'So let me introduce the next band. I hope you're ready for this. It's Joe Daniels and his Hotshots!' The crowd shouted its approval as the sound of a trumpet hit the air, cutting off the last of the compère's words.

The music wasn't the sort of thing that Rita had heard much of. Peg had talked a lot lately about 'swing' and it was obvious from the way she and Chuck were dancing not only that they shared the same taste in music but also that this wasn't the first time they had danced together. Rita had heard about the 'Eagle Squadrons' – young Americans who had joined the RAF without waiting for their government to come into the war. Trust Peg to have got to know one already! The band played one up-beat number after another and as they did so Chuck and Peg danced harder and faster. Rita stood at the edge of the floor, knowing that yet again Peg had forgotten all about her. With a sigh she pushed her way back to their friends on the balcony. She stood with them and watched as the dancers closest to Chuck and Rita stopped to look at the performance they were giving. The on-lookers backed off, giving them more room until finally the couple had a sizeable patch of the shiny wooden floor to themselves.

Chuck didn't need a second invitation. He grabbed Peg and swung her this way and that, fully aware of the red wool creeping further up her legs each time he spun her round. Peg didn't care. She was having the time of her life. She loved being the centre of attention and dancing like this with Chuck she knew that virtually every male eye in the room was focused on her. From his vantage point on the stage Joe Daniels could also see them and he encouraged his musicians to play louder and faster, pushing the young couple to greater extremes until finally they came to a spinning halt, perfectly in time with the upward shriek from the trumpets. The audience cheered and yelled and Joe was about to instruct the band to play an encore when the unmistakable wail of the air-raid siren stopped him.

The compère was quickly back on stage. 'Ladies and gentlemen, please make your way to the shelters and we will resume the fun as soon as we can.' With much mumbling and groans of disappointment the crowd did as they were told. Chuck and Peg were still catching their breath as the floor cleared.

'I don't want to go,' said Peg defiantly through her gasps.

'Then don't. Have you ever been up top when there's a raid on?' Chuck asked with a glint in his eye.

''Course not. But I'd love to see it. You'll look after me, won't you, Chuck?' A tremor of excitement went through her.

To be out in a raid!

It would be something to tell the girls at the depot tomorrow. To boast about being outside while they were huddled in cramped shelters or under blankets down the smelly Underground with only a bucket to pee in and not even a bit of platform to call their own. Still exhilarated from her dancing Peg's face glowed with expectation.

'Come on, you two.' They were being hurried along towards the shelter downstairs but without looking at each other they both made the same decision at the same moment and before anyone could stop them they had ducked behind the blackout and out into the open air.

The December coldness hit them as they stood waiting for their eyes to adjust after the bright lights inside. But they didn't need much adjusting. Outside the sky was a red glow as far as they could see. The air was heavy with the smell of burning masonry, wet wood, gas and cordite, thick with centuries old dust and smoke and heat. They could hear the anti-aircraft guns rattling across the night from the City and see the search lights sweeping across the smoke-filled sky.

'This way.' Peg suddenly took control and grabbed Chuck's hand, pulling him towards the Embankment. A warden spotted them as they ran across the Aldwych. He yelled after them but amid the din they pretended not to hear and ran faster to get away from him. Peg ran as fast as she could down towards Fleet Street but the warden kept up. The sky glowed with an eerie light and the air was thick with smoke, but still the warden chased them. Laughing back over their shoulders at him, they carried on running down the street, ducking automatically as an incendiary bomb hit a building not far from them, sending shudders through the ground. Only when they had almost reached Ludgate Circus did they stop having finally shaken the man off.

'I didn't think we'd lose him,' she gasped, leaning back against a wall with her chin tilted upwards. Chuck was also resting, bent forwards with his hands on his knees as he gasped for breath. Peg turned to make a comment when something caught her eye. Straightening up she cautiously made her way to the centre of the road.

'Bloody hell!' Peg exclaimed before she could stop herself. 'Chuck, come and look at this.' He went and stood behind her, following her pointing finger up between the smouldering, flaming buildings that flanked Ludgate Hill. Her eyes were wide with amazement and streaming from the acrid smoke. She seemed to merge with the folds of her dress as her skin and hair reflected the red glow of the fires which were blazing out of control around them. The noise was deafening. The high wind and the fire's own back-draft created a blanket of heat which thundered and crackled out of control. Below it were the sounds of fire sirens and air-raid sirens, anti-aircraft guns and the noise of glass cracking in the heat as walls rumbled and crashed to the ground. But it was none of this that had wrenched the expletive from Peg. What had was the sight of St Paul's Cathedral looming out of the rolling grey-black clouds. It stood tall and majestic above the thick, impenetrable billows. Its white stone work reflected the vivid orangey red of the sky and it looked like a huge cut-out image stuck against the background.

'Jes-us!' Chuck swore as he took in the sight before of them. The air was so hot it hurt him to breathe and he could feel the smoke grinding its way into his skin. 'Baby, maybe this wasn't such a good idea. This looks like kinda serious and I'd hate anything to happen to you. Let's go down to the shelter.' Peg turned to face him, her eyes blazing almost as fiercely as the fire.

'No. I'm not missing this. If you're scared then you can go but I'm staying.' She turned back towards the City which, from what she could see, was a mass of fire.

'Well at least let's stay down by the river.' She was going to argue with him when the sound of a fire engine siren came shrieking towards them and a wall on the other side of the road crashed to the ground, sending up sparks and dust as it hit the street. She turned to follow Chuck down to the river, but no matter what she was determined to stay out in the open.

This time Chuck led the way as they ran towards the comparative shelter of Blackfriars Bridge. The tide was exceptionally low and they stood together in the shadows peering out at the skyline as it flamed overhead, watching as the fire fighters' hoses fell short of the water level. 'You know, you're quite a lady,' Chuck yelled in admiration, his voice hoarse as his throat was seared by the heat. 'There's not many dames I know who would get a kick out of seeing their home town burn to the ground.'

'It won't burn to the ground. And who cares if it does? It's only bricks and mortar.' Another bit of the wall that had fallen so close to them minutes earlier crashed down and from their position under the bridge they could feel it reverberate even more than when they had been at street level. Peg jumped and Chuck moved closer to her.

'Hey, don't worry. It'll be OK. I'll look after you. Say, it feels kinda cold after being up there. Here, put this on.' He had grabbed his flying jacket from the edge of the stage where he had left as they danced and he now took it off to put it round Peg. He swung it round her shoulders and used the lapels to position it properly. As he did so his hand brushed one of her breasts and he felt her nipple harden beneath the thin wool of her dress. He used the jacket to pull her closer to him and she lifted her arms, wrapping them round his neck. With a sudden movement he jerked her towards him and kissed her hard. He half expected her to slap him down as so many other British girls had done but Peg, it would appear, was genuinely different.

Her fingers were playing with the nape of his neck and as he moved his tongue inside her mouth she didn't push him away but responded with a similar passion. He let go of the jacket to run his hands over her body. Still she didn't stop him; if anything she turned herself towards him, making herself more available. Tentatively he let his fingers creep inside her dress, feeling her soft breast with its hardened tip. She pushed herself even closer towards him, edging him on.

Oh God! thought Peg. *Don't stop! I want this to carry on and on and on.*

She knew she should stop him but couldn't have done so even if she had wanted to. The evening had been too exciting and standing here under the bridge necking with Chuck was the best thing that had ever happened to her. His hands were now moving down her body and she could feel him groping with the skirt of her dress, slowly raising it higher, easing his fingers between her thighs.

She knew she should stop him. Automatically she found her hands wandering towards his trousers and she was amazed at how hard and big he felt under his uniform. She knew it was because of her that Chuck was like that and that knowledge excited her even further. As his fingers played with her stocking tops she found herself fumbling with his fly-buttons.

She knew she should stop him, that things had gone too far, but still she didn't, wanting instead to experience everything this strange and thrilling night had to offer. As her mind struggled to think of what to say and do the rest of her body was delighting in the strange new sensations that were beginning to chase through her. It was as if it no longer belonged to her and when he finally pinned her against the wall and thrust his way into her the loud, raw yell that burst from her amazed her.

'Oh my God!' gasped Chuck. 'I didn't mean to go that far. I meant to stop. I . . .'

'Am I complaining?' Peg interrupted his remorseful flow. 'Don't make me feel cheap by apologising. If I hadn't wanted you to do it then you wouldn't have.' Her calm voice belied the emotions rushing through her. She wanted to scream and yell and shout. After all the fuss and bother she had finally done it, and done it in style with a Canadian pilot in the middle of the biggest air raid she had ever seen. Wait until she told Rita!

'Have you got a hanky? I'm a bit messy.'

Mike turned the corner of the street, once again checking his map as he looked down the tight row of narrow terraced houses, searching for the one he wanted. As he neared it he nervously wiped the toe of his already shiny boots on the back of his trouser leg.

'Watcha, Mister!' One of the boys playing in the street had noticed his uniform and was trotting behind him, yelling questions as he got closer to the house. 'You shot any planes down? Have you, Mister? Have you?'

Mike stopped and the boy did the same, positioning himself squarely in front of his quarry. 'Well 'ave you?' He stood with his chin up as he squinted into the April sun, his hands shoved defiantly deep into the pockets of his knee-length trousers, his shirt hanging half out at the back.

'One or two, son, one or two.' Mike rubbed the boy's head but before the lad could object he also pushed half a crown into his hand. 'Go on, off you go.'

'Cor! Thanks, Mister,' and the boy ran back to show his spoils to his friends who were waiting further down the street. Mike sighed.

I wish it was that easy still to feel excited about the war, he thought as he stood on the doorstep of 15 Roupell Street. He straightened his already immaculate RAF tie and knocked on the door.

Upstairs Peg heard the noise but ignored it, knowing that Emily would bustle through from the kitchen to answer it. She had more worrying things on her mind. It had been the beginning of February when she first thought she was pregnant and by the end of March she was certain. Even if she hadn't been sure about what her body was telling her, her clothes confirmed it. Her uniform was beginning to feel tight and very soon she would begin to 'show'. Since that night under Blackfriars Bridge she and Chuck had seen a lot of each other, often finding a dark corner in which they came close to, but never actually repeated their nocturnal fumblings. She had decided to wait as long as possible before giving Chuck the news that he was going to be a father. She wanted to hide the evidence as best she could and had spent the afternoon trying on all her clothes, working out what she could wear to disguise her expanding waistline. She had got as far as trying on her black skirt with a purple jacket and was now experimenting with different ways of tying the belt to give her the best figure possible. She was looking at the results of her third attempt and had just decided that with the jacket bunched over the belt she would be able to get away with it when Emily called up to tell her she had a visitor. She took a final glance at the mirror before making her way downstairs.

She peeped over the top of the bannisters and, seeing the blue uniform with its American insignia, felt a thrill go through her. 'Chuck, what a . . . oh!' she finished as Mike turned round and she saw she had made a mistake. 'I'm sorry. I thought you were someone else.'

Mike swallowed hard. Chuck had spent a lot of time in the mess boasting about this great British lady he had found – a looker who also delivered. Like everyone else Mike had assumed he had been exaggerating but seeing Peg standing slightly above him on the stairs made him realise that, if anything, Chuck had underplayed her looks.

'I'm sorry to disappoint you.'

'No. That's quite all right.' Emily appeared from the kitchen carrying a tea tray and ushered them into the front room. She was clearly treating their visitor as a special guest as the front room was always saved for 'best'. She placed the tray on the polished table and after apologising for the lack of a cake, rather heavily said she would 'leave them to it'.

As the door shut behind her Peg looked at her visitor who, having done as he had been told by Emily and sat down, very quickly jumped to his feet again to introduce himself. 'I'm Michael – Mike to my friends – Horrocks. I know you're Peg and I er . . .' He faltered as he looked uncomfortably round the over-filled chintzy room with its cheap china ornaments and heavy blackout curtains hanging either side of the window. 'I'm sorry about this. I've never had to do anything like this before and I never thought I would. You don't think it's gonna happen to one of your own, do you?' He looked helplessly at Peg who gave him a puzzled frown.

'I'm sorry. I don't know what you're talking about. Milk?' she asked, raising the jug, pouring some in as he nodded.

'It's about Chuck.'

'Oh my God! Don't tell me he was part of the offensive against the raid on Coventry? He's hurt, isn't he? Where is he? Can I go and see him? What's happened to him?' She was facing Mike, her hands clenched and her eyes wide as she fired questions without giving him a chance to answer. Chuck had said she was sharp as well as a looker. That she had quickly, and correctly, surmised that Chuck had been part of the counter-attack against the German bombardment of the Midlands proved this.

Mike swallowed again. This was going to be even harder than he had thought it would be. 'Peg, I'm sorry but Chuck didn't make it back to base. I'm his squadron leader and when we went through his things we found this addressed to you. I thought it would be better if I brought it personally.' He held out a large package and with a surprisingly steady hand Peg took it from him. With what looked to Mike's eyes like great composure, she sat down in one of the over-stuffed armchairs, delicately crossed her legs and opened the package.

The sun shone on her bent head as she read Chuck's letter before turning to the other item that was enclosed. It was a photograph in a card mount and from where he was sitting at the other side of the room Mike guessed it was the one Chuck had had taken to send back to his parents in Illinois the day he got his posting to the air force base.

Peg's mind was racing. *Chuck can't be dead. Who the hell am I going to get to marry me now?* She had that very afternoon decided that the next time she saw Chuck she would start the campaign that would ultimately get her a now much-needed wedding ring. It was a nuisance that she would have to marry a man she didn't love but she knew that once she was married and the baby had been born and weaned she would be able to arrange things to ensure she still led an independent life. Now she would have to think again. *Damn Chuck for getting himself killed!*

She read his letter, acutely aware of Mike watching her as she did so. Chuck had archly told her how much he had enjoyed her company and how much he had appreciated her warm welcome and on-going friendship. 'It proved to me,' he had written, 'that the British are not as unfriendly or unaccommodating as we poor Americans had been led to believe.' He had then written a bit more about how if she was reading the letter he would be dead (or missing) and said that he hoped she would remember him with affection. She flipped open the cover of the card mount around the photograph and looked at Chuck's image. He was grinning cheekily at her, one arm propped on his raised leg, his head and his cap at a jaunty angle, and he had written across the photograph, 'To a Great British Lady. Yours, Chuck.' Peg thought ruefully of her widening figure and if Mike hadn't been sitting opposite her would have probably torn the photograph in two.

She carried on studying the picture as an idea began to form. Within a few moments she knew what she was going to do and surreptitiously she bit the inside of her lip until tears came to her eyes. She gave a convincing sniff and turned her now watering eyes to Mike. 'He says he's sorry that he never got to take me home to meet his parents. You see, we got married a few weeks ago but knowing your feelings about married men flying he didn't want us to tell anyone.' Peg remembered Chuck telling her once how much Horrocks was against married men being airborne and now hoped that this piece of information would add truth to what was an out-and-out lie.

Mike looked surprised. Not only had Chuck said nothing that even hinted at marriage, but his behaviour and conversation were not what he'd have expected from a newly married man. He had described how he had met Peg and what had happened on the Embankment in such lurid detail that the rest of the men in the mess had got decidedly hot under the collar as they listened to him. The men also knew that Peg was not the only woman he was seeing. They had all marvelled that he had not been caught out and it now looked as if he never would be. On the other hand the marriage would explain why he had left a letter addressed to Peg in his locker.

'I'm sorry. I didn't know.'

'As I said, Chuck knew you wouldn't approve.'

'No. No, I probably wouldn't have. What are you going to do now?'

'I'm not sure. I'll stay here with Emily until I can sort something out.' She decided not to mention the pregnancy and gazed over his shoulder out of the window criss-crossed with tape. She hoped she looked like a newly bereaved widow. From his tone of voice Mike seemed to believe her. Maybe Chuck's death wasn't such a bad thing after all. Mike was talking now so, concentrating on looking as if she were holding back tears, she faced him again.

'Look, if there's anything I can do, or if you need anything, please call me.' He scribbled a number on a piece of paper and handed it to her. The uncomfortable interview was at an end and, making his excuses, he said he would show himself out. Peg stayed where she was until the front door slammed and then let a slow smile cross her lips. It was amazing how easy it had been. All she had to do now was convince Emily. Quickly she gathered up the tea things and carried them down the steps into the kitchen.

'Your young man gone, has he?'

'He wasn't my young man. He was his squadron leader. He came to tell me that Chuck got killed. Oh Emily, what am I going to do?' With a sob she put the tray on the table and buried her face in her hands. In a flash Emily was standing over her, easing her into a seat as she refilled the kettle to make another cup of tea.

'It won't be that bad, Peg. You can go and stay with my sister in Surrey. She's got a farm there and it'll be safer there until the baby's born and then you can . . . Why, what on earth's the matter?' At the mention of a baby Peg's head had snapped up and she was now staring aghast at her landlady. Emily gave a little grin. 'In your eyes I may be an old spinster, but I still know a pregnant woman when I see one. My mother had eight and since I was the eldest I soon learned what to look out for. Oh, don't worry. You've hidden it very well but another couple of weeks and it won't be so easy.'

On hearing this Peg's tears dried up immediately. 'Oh Emmy, do you really think I could go to your sister? We could tell her that I was married and my husband got killed.' Emily looked shocked at this remark.

'But that would be a wicked thing to do. It would denigrate the memory of all those men who have been killed,' she said with pious dignity.

'Well, it is true after a fashion. I mean, who do you think put this bloody thing here? The last time it happened by itself it led to Christmas and I don't think anyone's going to believe I'm the new Virgin Mary, do you?'

'I said I would help you and I will, but not if you carry on blaspheming like that and being awful about our brave boys.'

'But that's what I'm trying to tell you. This baby is Chuck's and he got killed, so it's not exactly a lie to say that the baby's father got killed, is it? Anyway, I'm only thinking of the baby,' she lied. 'It's going to have a bad enough start in life, not having a father. What hope has it got being born a bastard into a world that's gone half mad? Let's at least give it the best start we can by allowing its parents the dignity of a marriage licence.' Peg was now holding the tops of Emily's arms as she studied her face, hoping that this plea might convince the older woman to go along with her plan.

'I'll write to my sister tonight and tell her that this young pregnant widow I know needs a billet. I'll also go through Mum's things and find her wedding ring. Silly for it to be left sitting there when it could be put to good use.'

Peg's face lit up, but Emily continued.' No, don't get all excited. I'm doing this, as you say, for the baby. Not you. You deserve everything you've got but I can't say as under the present situation, given half the chance, I wouldn't have done likewise. And I will say this much for you – at least you were loyal to that young man after you met him, so I suppose if things had continued you might have got married.'

'Oh, yes Em. I think we would have done. I really do. After all, if he didn't think he mattered to me why else would he bother to leave instructions that I was to be informed if anything happened to him?'

Peg was five months pregnant when she moved to the farm in May 1941 and when her baby girl was born in September, weighing just over six pounds, everyone accepted her as the premature daughter of Mrs Peg Timpson and Captain Charles Timpson, American citizen late of the RAF.

'Ple-ee-ase, Mummy. I promise not to say nuffink.'

'I promise not to say *anything*.' mumured Peg, automatically correcting her but not really listening as she peered in the mirror, concentrating on shaping her eyebrows. 'Go on then, but when Auntie Emily comes and tells you to go to bed you go immediately.'

The little girl nodded her head vigorously, making her curls bounce up and down. She raised her foot and hooked the heel of her slipper over the edge of the bed, using her pyjama-clad leg as leverage to heave herself on to it.

'Look out for my dress!' screeched Peg, seeing Anne reflected in the mirror, and she jumped up to hang it safely out of her daughter's way. Anne shrank back against the pillows of the unmade bed as her mother swooped down on the hanger. For a moment Peg considered sending the child out of her room but then she changed her mind and sat down again at her dressing table with a sigh.

'What's wrong?' asked Emily as she came in looking for Anne, pouncing on her when she caught sight of her among the heap of bed clothes. 'There you are, you monkey!' She swept the child up into the air making her squeal with delight before settling her against her right hip. Anne put an arm round Emily's neck and stuck the thumb of her free hand into her mouth as she rested her head against Emily's shoulder.

'Oh Em, I'm just so fed up with it all. Having to "make-do-and-mend", not having anything decent to eat, being tired all the time – I swear I look at least forty. There's no fun any more.'

'Hmm. Let me tell you, young lady, that you are having more fun than most people. And as far as shortages are concerned, thanks to that nice Major Horrocks we do a lot better than most. Do you know Mrs Liversey spent an hour and a half queuing at the butchers yesterday, and for what? Whale meat sausages, that's what. The smell was disgusting and those poor kiddies of hers were nearly sick eating them. You should have seen their faces when I gave them the end of that jar of raspberry jam.'

'You did *what*?' Peg jumped to feet and glared at her landlady as she virtually spat out the words. 'You gave the last of our jam, our *real* jam, to those brats down the road because they didn't like their dinner? Honestly, Emily, what are we supposed to eat?'

'Well, like I said, Major Horrocks is so generous I thought it would be a kindness. You know we're not meant to hoard.'

'I don't call the scrapings in the bottom of a jam jar hoarding,' Peg said through gritted teeth.

'Want bread and jam,' added Anne from her vantage point in Emily's arms.

'Oh great! Now look what you've started. Come to Mummy, darling.' Peg held out her arms and Anne eagerly reached across from the older to the younger woman. 'We haven't got any jam because nasty old Auntie Emily has given it away but Uncle Mikey will be here soon and he might have some chocolate. Won't that be nice?'

Anne's eyes lit up and she nodded her head happily. Anne liked her mummy's friend. He talked in a funny way that made her laugh and he always brought her presents. He also brought Mummy things that made her smile, and she was always in a good mood when Uncle Mikey was with them and didn't shout at Auntie Em like she had just done. Yes, Anne liked Uncle Mikey.

Emily was about to tell Peg off for encouraging the child to see Mike only as a source of treats when Peg let out a yelp. 'Oh my God! What's the time? I'll never be ready. Here, you take her.' Peg almost threw Anne back at Emily, so that Emily had to dart forward to make sure she caught her. 'Oh, damn! There he is now and I'm nowhere near dressed.' Peg ignored the look of dismay that crossed Emily's face as she swore when she heard the knocker fall against the front door. 'Be a darling, Em, and look after him for me. I'll be as quick as I can, I promise.' Her anger of a few moments ago was forgotten. Sighing, Emily resettled Anne on her hip as she made her way downstairs with a shake of her head to let Mike in.

'Hi there, Em. How's my favourite bit of Old England?' Emily blushed a little as she always did when Mike Horrocks talked to her. 'Hey, and what are you still doing up, young lady? Isn't it past your bedtime?'

Anne lifted a chubby finger to her lips. 'Tshh. Don't tell Mummy.'

'Okey-dokey. I won't. Now then, I think I might have something for you. Where did I put it?' Mike began patting his pockets absent-mindedly. 'Nope, that's not it. And it's not there.' He gave Emily a wink and Anne began to squirm in her arms. 'Hey. I guess I got it wrong.'

'No!' Anne said firmly, knowing exactly where he hid her presents. She waggled a finger at him, beckoning him forward and obligingly he moved near enough to her so she could lean across and dive into his top pocket. 'Here 'tis!' she cried, triumphantly pulling out the bar of chocolate her mother had promised.

'You know you don't have to bring her something every time you call. It'll spoil her. You can have one piece now and we'll save the rest for later. Now, what do you say to Uncle Mike?' Emily extracted the bar from the child's hands. Anne, knowing when she was beaten, turned to Mike. 'Thank you for my chocoler, Uncle Mike'. She struggled with the word chocolate, making him laugh.

'What must you think of me, keeping you talking in the hallway all this time? Peg won't be long.'

'Don't worry about it. The longer she takes the more time we have to chat and for once, Em, let's cut the conversation about me waiting in the parlour. We both know I'll end up in the kitchen so why don't we just go straight there?' Mike's implied intimacy made her blush again but she didn't argue and led the way to the back. She put Anne down and the girl immediately found her favourite rag doll, which Emily had made when she was born, and settled down to play with her.

'I don't know what you do to that mite but she's a good kid. I wish my nieces and nephews back home were half as good as Annie.'

'We don't have to do anything with her. She's always been a good child. Sometimes I think she's a bit too serious for her own good but rather that than a child prone to tantrums.' Emily busied herself with the kettle and Mike sat at the table watching Anne as she played at feeding her doll, repeating the conversations she overheard as she and Emily queued for their rations.

'I can offer you a bit of cake if you like,' said Emily. 'I mean it's called cake but what with dried eggs and fatless sponges I don't know as that's what *I* would call it. But it's the best I can do, I'm afraid.'

'That's what I love about the British. Tea and cake at all times even if you can't get the ingredients. Well, Em, I've a little something for you too.' He put a small parcel wrapped in paper in the middle of the table. Shyly Emily moved towards it and opened it with careful fingers.

'Oh, Major Horrocks.' She gave a little giggle of delight as she saw the yellow creaminess of the butter, and the white lump of loaf sugar. 'Are you sure? I mean you won't get in trouble, will you?' A frown of concern crossed her brow.

'Hey, why d'you think I was so pleased when the "Eagles" were taken under the wing of the US Army – so I could get all those goodies for my best gals. Besides, it would be worth getting into trouble just to see you enjoy yourself making a proper cake. Don't use it all at once,' he finished jokingly as the door opened and Peg came in.

'Wow! You look terrific.' He gave a whistle as he got to his feet. Knowing he was right Peg smiled at him. Emily had once again worked wonders with her needle and this time she had managed to use an old pair of chintz curtains to make Peg a new summer dress. Of course the pattern conformed to the regulations but something about the way Peg wore clothes gave it a style that belied its origin.

'I don't know. I'm five minutes late and the moment my back is turned there you go spoiling everyone. How are we meant to do our bit if you don't give us a chance?' Peg coolly smoothed her already immaculate hair.

'Hey, come on! I can't have my three favourite girls doing without, can I? And talking of which . . . this is for you.' He held out another parcel which Peg took slowly, but the moment she opened it her composure disappeared.

'Mike, you angel! You little darling. Look, Em. Nylons. Six pairs! Oh, Mike, I love you.' She flung her arms round his neck and kissed him firmly on the mouth, making Em turn away in embarrassment. 'We'd better go. Night, night, Anne.' She bent down and lightly kissed her daughter's head. 'Don't let her stay up too late, will you, Em? Oh, and don't wait up.'

''Bye, Em.' Mike saluted as he left and blew a kiss at Anne before following Peg out of the house.

'You wouldn't think it was nearly mid summer, would you?' Peg remarked, giving a little shiver in the cool June evening air as Mike shooed the children playing in the street away from the car and opened the door for her.

'I'm getting used to your British summers.'

'Where are we going?' Peg asked as she settled herself into her seat, rearranging herself to her best advantage and lifting her hem a fraction to show just a bit more of her legs.

'Well, I'm afraid it's not going to be a late night, sweetheart. There's something big going down and all leave has been cancelled. That's how I was able to pull a few strings and get the use of a car – to make sure I get back to Northolt on time. I'm due back at base by twenty-three hundred so it's gonna have to be dinner only.'

'Oh, Mike. I didn't get dressed up like this just for another lousy half portion of spam fritters. You promised me we'd go dancing.'

Mike concentrated on keeping the vehicle on the right side of the road. After nearly three years in Britain he still had to think about which side of the road he was on when he drove. 'What can I do, sweetheart? I put a call into Ike and Mr Churchill to see if they could rearrange things but even though they said they'd see what they could do Hitler decided to be difficult and say "No".'

Mike's attempt at humour didn't work and by the time he parked the car in a back street in Knightsbridge Peg was in a foul mood.

'Where the hell are we?' He was standing on the pavement holding the door open for her but Peg made no move to get out of the car.

'It's a great little place. Andrew, one of my boys, told me about it. He came here last time he was on leave. He said something about doing a great steak.'

Peg looked up at him. 'Steak?' she queried sarcastically. 'It's probably horse or something equally revolting.'

'You won't know till you try it, will you?' God, she could be so frustrating when she tried!

Begrudgingly she stepped out of the car, pulling her arm away from him as he made a move to help her. Her frostiness continued while they ordered and didn't lift until their first course of mushroom soup was served. 'My God! It really *is* mushroom soup.' It had been so long since she had tasted real mushrooms that she forgot about the fact that she was in a temper with Mike.

There was no steak on the menu that night but their waiter told them (with a nod and a wink) that the kitchen could do them a nice piece of gammon. Peg didn't quite believe him but had ordered it anyway. Now as they sat waiting for their main course she took a proper look at the restaurant. In many respects it was nothing special, being situated in the basement, but nevertheless it had an air of sophistication about it. A few discreet prints hung on the embossed-paper walls and the lights glowed with a warmth that showed the cutlery and crisp linen off to their best advantage (even if the dimness did hide the fact that some of the tablecloths were fraying a little at the edges).

By the door was a small desk with a light that bent over the reservation book and from here a very glossy-looking middle-aged woman was organising the sittings. The desk was an old wooden one that had clearly been polished many times, as it had accumulated a deep shine that revealed its age. From what Peg could see of the twenty or so tables that were carefully placed around the room they were also quite old, as were the high-backed winged chairs that she and Mike were sitting in. The atmosphere was akin to sitting in your favourite aunt's house before the war and it was clear that the restaurant was doing well as the woman at the door was turning people away, even though it was only seven-thirty. Peg noticed that more tables could have been fitted in if space hadn't been left in the middle of the room for a tiny dance floor.

'Mike, look. We might get a dance after all.'

'I doubt it, sweetheart. If I'm to be back on time we'll have to be away by nine at the latest and Andrew said the band doesn't start until ten. I'm sorry, kiddo.' It looked as if Peg was about to sulk again when their waiter reappeared.

'There you are, sir, madam, two house specials. Enjoy your meal.' And again he winked at them as he left.

Cautiously Peg took a bite of the pinkish meat on her plate. 'It's gammon. It's *gammon*! Mike, you're forgiven.' She hungrily cleared her plate, not caring whether she looked unlady like or not. To have real food at last instead of Woolton Pie or some other horrid concoction thought up by the government was a treat. It didn't occur to her to ask where the meat had come from, or what Mike was having to pay for this rare luxury.

They ordered coffee, which wasn't exactly one hundred per cent pure, but still feeling happily full of dinner Peg decided not to comment. She slipped her foot out of her shoe and ran it gently across Mike's ankle. He didn't say anything, nor did he pull his leg away. She knew the effect she was having on him and timing her question carefully asked, 'Do you really have to go back to base so early? I mean, I thought you were in charge, Major. Go on. Break the curfew and stay and dance with me a little. It *is* Saturday night and it can't be that important for you to get back, surely?'

Mike sighed and finally moved his leg. 'I'm sorry, sweetheart, but it is. No,' he continued, holding up his hand to stop her speaking as she took a breath to argue with him. 'No matter what you say I'm back on base at twenty-three hundred and that's that.'

'I hope you enjoyed your meal?' Both looked up to see who was talking to them. The glossy woman was standing over them smiling benignly down.

'Oh yes, it was delicious,' Peg said with a wide smile.

'It surely was,' added Mike. 'Tell me, where do you get your supplies?'

The woman gave a knowing laugh. 'I assure you, sir, all our supplies are legitimate and nothing you have eaten is black market goods. May I get you some more coffee?'

Embarrassed, Mike agreed and the woman beckoned the waiter over. He filled Peg's cup and then picked up Mike's to do the same. As he did so a good-looking man tried to squeeze past the table. Peg had seen him get up and was idly watching him as he made his way down the room. When the cup of coffee tipped up and into Mike's lap she could have sworn that it wasn't quite an accident, even if the man's profuse apologies assured them that it was.

'I am so sorry. There's just no space in here. Alice, can't you do something about it? This poor . . .' Here he looked at Mike who had leapt to his feet and was dabbing at his uniform trying to mop up the mess. '. . . Major,' he continued, seeing Mike's insignia.

A faint smile flickered at the corners of the older woman's mouth. 'I'm so sorry, Mr Edwardes. You're quite right, of course. I keep telling the management we need more space but they're so concerned about looking after everyone that my words mean nothing. Sir, if you would like to come with me I'm sure we can tidy you up.' Mike looked from the waiter, who had an anxious expression on his face and was still holding the coffee pot and the cup, now lying on its side in the saucer slopping with coffee, and the woman and man to Peg.

'I suppose I'd better. I can't go back like this. Peg, I'm sorry . . .'

'Don't you worry about your companion. I'll keep an eye on her until you get back. After all, we can't leave her sitting here by herself, can we?'

Mike looked concerned but Alice began fussing round him like a mother hen as she called over to one of the waitresses, indicating she should take her place at the front desk. Before he could object further Mike had been whisked away to the kitchen and the man was sitting in his place, looking at Peg with a twinkle in his eye as the waiter bought him a cup and saucer.

Peg stared back at him with a practised wintry look. Just because she was flattered that he had gone to so much trouble to remove Mike did not mean she was going to make it simple for this easy, charming man. 'Do you make a habit of getting waiters to drop coffee in strange men's laps?'

'Only when they're sitting with the best-looking woman in the room.'

'And that makes it acceptable, does it? What about the party you arrived with?' The man looked over his shoulder and Peg followed his gaze to the table he had left. There were five people round it, all laughing raucously. It was clear he was not being missed.

'I'm sorry. I shouldn't have done it. But I didn't know how else to meet you. Couldn't we start again and pretend we're being introduced? I'm Howard Edwardes.' He held out a well-manicured hand. Not knowing what else to do Peg finally laughed and held out her hand in return.

'Peg Timpson.' His hand engulfed hers and his grip was firm. She felt a small tremor go through her that excited her and not knowing what else to do she took a sip of coffee. 'Would I be right in saying that you've used this method to meet people before?' she asked as she carefully replaced her cup on its saucer.

'Now there's a question. If I said "No" would you believe me?' Peg shook her head. 'In which case I'd better be honest and say *mea culpa*.' He threw his hands up in mock surrender.

'*Mea* what?' queried Peg.

'*Mea culpa*. It's Latin and basically means you caught me fair and square. However, it literally means I am the culprit.' Howard watched for a reaction but she gave none. Obviously this was a very self-assured young woman. He looked at her over the top of his cup. 'Now that you've got the truth out of me I want to know if all my efforts have been wasted. Please put me out of my misery and tell me if you're sharing your dinner with your boyfriend, husband' (he had noticed her wedding ring) 'or just a friend?'

Peg raised an eyebrow, using the gesture to give herself a moment to think as she quickly tried to decided what answer Howard Edwardes needed to hear. 'He's not my husband.' She laughed lightly, giving the impression that the idea of being married to Mike was a ludicrous one, sending Howard what she hoped were the right signals. 'But he is a good friend. He was my husband's squadron leader before he was killed.'

'I'm sorry,' said Howard automatically.

'Don't worry. It happened three years ago.' Then realising that might sound a bit dismissive she hastily added, 'Of course I still miss him but I've learned to keep it to myself and get on with life as best as possible.'

If he doesn't get the message from that, he never will! she thought as she demurely took another sip of her coffee.

'Good girl. It's so important to keep going. And besides, it's good for morale to see a decent-looking woman out and about.' The compliment rolled smoothly off Howard's tongue. That Peg Timpson was good-looking was not in doubt, but that awful floral dress she was wearing did nothing for her. Even allowing for rationing it was the usual problem, looks but no style. Mind you, the girl was sharp. He had used the spilled coffee trick many times in the past, always with success, and this was the first time anyone had not only seen through it but had the guts to call his bluff. This was definitely a girl worth getting to know.

'Thank you, and I must admit it's equally nice from our point of view to see a man not in uniform. You know, Mr Edwardes, it may be unpatriotic but sometimes I think if I don't see another RAF blue or army green or navy uniform until the next century it will be too soon.'

Howard laughed. 'It is unpatriotic but I do know what you mean. It's a reason I'm glad I'm in a reserved occupation – no, don't ask because I'm not saying – although given the chance I would much rather be out there with the rest of them, ugly uniforms or not. And talking of uniforms, isn't that yours heading back this way?'

Peg looked in the direction he was indicating and felt a twinge of regret as she saw Mike weaving his way through the tables towards them. 'That's got the coffee out but I am still a bit wet.' He looked ruefully at the dark patch at the edge of his jacket. 'I'm sorry to have to do this to you, Peg, but we're going to have to leave now. I'll have to change before I go on duty.'

'I'm sorry, old chap, it looks as if my clumsiness has ruined your evening.' Howard was now standing next to Mike. Peg looked from one to the other, biting her lower lip, trying not to let the chuckle that was hovering at the back of her throat burst out. 'The least I can do is pay for your meal as a way of making amends.'

'There's no need,' Mike said stiffly. 'An accident's an accident.' The chuckle escaped and Peg managed to make it sound like a cross between a sneeze and a cough. 'Come on, Peg, I'll pay on the way out. Thank you for looking after her for me.' And he reached down to help Peg from her seat. Knowing that making a fuss about wanting to dance would only create problems and that the fun was over for the evening Peg meekly rose to her feet.

'Thank you for sitting with me, Mr Edwardes. I do hope we meet again.' She hoped he might ask for her address but then realised that there was no way he could do so with Mike standing there. It was clear that Mike wasn't going to move towards the door without her. With a sigh she picked up her bag and gloves and held out her hand to say goodbye. It wasn't really necessary but she wanted to feel his hand grip hers again, and as before when his fingers closed round hers she felt a thrill go through her.

Mike stepped aside to let her go first, placing a guiding palm in the small of her back, clearly marking her as his. At the door she stood back from the desk, where Alice was once again firmly ensconced, allowing Mike to pay the bill and thank her for helping to mop him up. As they pulled the first blackout curtain to one side Peg glanced over her shoulder to the table in the corner where Howard Edwardes was sitting. It was as if he was expecting her to look at him and he glanced up, caught her eye and slightly inclined his head towards her, lifting his glass a little higher as if to salute her.

Peg knew that he had gone to a lot of effort to meet her. That in itself was nothing new, men had been doing that for years, but there was something different about this man, not least the fact that his small final gesture in her direction made her blush, which she didn't do often. It was a sensation she did not enjoy and she covered her confusion by fiddling in her bag for a handkerchief. By the time she was sitting in the car she had regained her composure. However, she was very quiet as Mike made his way back through the now darkening London streets. He automatically looked at the sky, which was heavy with cloud. 'Good, no moon tonight. That will help.'

'Sorry, I was miles away. Did you say something?'

'Only that it's a cloudy night. Not a good flying night but if it's bad for us it's equally bad for the Luftwaffe. I suppose that makes it a good thing, doesn't it?'

'Yes, I suppose it does.' Peg wasn't really listening. She was more concerned with working out how to meet Howard Edwardes again. It was a very long time since anyone had made her redden, and it was years since anyone had done it with a mere look. Somehow she had to meet him again. But how? Although it was obvious that he was a regular at the small restaurant she couldn't just go bowling in and ask about him. Asking about a fellow round the depot at Waterloo might work but it certainly wouldn't have the desired effect up West. No, she would clearly have to think of a different way.

'You're very quiet. Didn't you enjoy your dinner?'

Peg buried her thoughts to turn her full attention to Mike. 'Oh, Mike, it was lovely. It's been so long since I had a real meal like that. It was . . . delicious. It must have cost a fortune.' Mike dismissed the comment with a wave of his hand, secretly pleased that she had acknowledged he had pushed the boat out by finding a place that not only had good food but was willing to find ways round the five-shilling rule. Knowing he had already said too much earlier that evening when he had made reference to 'something big' he didn't want to scare her by voicing his ever-present fear of not returning from a raid. He had spent the afternoon being briefed about the assault on the Normandy beaches that was scheduled for early Tuesday morning. He knew that if this was successful it could be the end of the war, but if it failed . . . he didn't want to think about it. Any more than he wanted to think about not coming back. *If I make it back then I'm going to marry you, Peg Timpson*, he promised himself as he turned the car into Roupell Street.

'Let's just say it was a special dinner for a special gal and leave it at that, shall we?'

'Oh, Mike, you are good to me. To us,' she added as she let him take her in his arms and kiss her enthusiastically. Having been caught out with Chuck the first and only time she 'did it' she had learned her lesson. Although she enjoyed the sensations Mike stirred in her the passion she had experienced before wasn't there, so she was not prepared to let Mike go too far. If she was in a good mood a bit of fumbling inside her dress or a hand to her stocking tops (after all, he provided them so why shouldn't he enjoy them?) but that was enough. Tonight was no exception and she stopped him when she felt he had reached that point. She disentangled herself. 'Now, Mike, stop it. The neighbours might be watching and it's bad enough the way they spread gossip without us adding fuel to the fire.'

'Oh, Peg. I hope I mean more to you than just a bit of gossip. You've become very important to me. You do know that, don't you?'

Peg was smoothing her hair in her compact mirror. 'Mike, that's sweet and you know I care about you too. Truly I do.' She turned to look at him for a moment before turning back to the mirror.

'Ah, shucks! I was gonna wait until I got back to ask you this but what the hell? There's no time like the present. So, Peg, will you marry me?'

This time Peg shut her compact and swivelled in her seat. 'Say that again.'

'I said, will you marry me?'

Thoughts of Howard Edwardes disappeared as she gazed back at Mike, who was anxiously searching her face for a response. 'I thought you didn't approve of married airmen?'

'I don't . . . I didn't. Please answer the question. Is it yes or no?' Again he searched her face.

I don't love you, Peg thought as she stared at him. *I don't even fancy you, but marrying you would at least get me away from Roupell Street. I suppose I do like you and there's plenty of married people who don't even have that. It would mean I could relax a bit and . . . and what?* she asked herself. *Say no and you might not get another chance. He likes Anne, so there's no problem there, and I'm sure I can sort things out to my liking. For God's sake shut up, Peg, and say yes!*

'Oh Mike, I thought you'd never ask,' was how she finally accepted his proposal. A slow grin spread across his face and he leaned towards her, taking her face in his hands before landing a loud smacking kiss on her mouth. He flung open the car door and rushed across the pavement to the door of number fifteen where he began beating a loud tattoo with the knocker, yelling at the top of his voice for Emily as he did so.

'Em! Em! Open up. Hurry up!' Peg had by now extracted herself from the car and was leaning against the bonnet watching Mike as he danced up and down. 'Come on Emmy, come on,' he carried on yelling and Peg heard the sash window next door go up, closely followed by one over the road at number fourteen.

'What on earth's going on?'

'Search me, Doris. Can't you shut it up, mister?'

Emily opened the door, the worried look on her face clearly visible despite the darkness. Her expression changed to one of amazement as Mike lifted her clean off her feet and spun her round. 'She said "Yes", Em. Peg and I are getting married!'

'Der you mean to tell me that all this noise is 'cos Peg Timpson said "Yes"?'

'Be a rare day when she says "No",' yelled the woman next door in response to the woman over the way.

'Shut your face!' yelled Peg, who was the only one to hear the exchange between her neighbours as Mike and Emily were still busy hugging each other.

'Mummy, what's happened?' Anne was standing on the doorstep, holding her doll firmly by its leg so it dangled upside down. Her other hand was rolled into a fist with which she sleepily rubbed her eyes. Peg hustled the others inside as the surrounding windows shut with a loud clatter, scooping Anne up as she went.

'I'm sorry, darling, did Uncle Mike wake you up?'

'Hey, kiddo, I'm sorry. Come here and let me make it better.' Mike held out his arms but Anne was too befuddled with sleep to do what she usually did and go to him, preferring to snuggle against her mother.

'Anne, you do like Uncle Mike, don't you?' Emily asked the child.

'Mmm,' she replied sleepily, raising her head a little to reply. 'Chocoler.' She put her head down again and promptly fell asleep.

Mike laughed. 'Ah, well. At least I know how to win her round if she ever plays up.' Emily took Anne from Peg and said she would go and put her back to bed, adding pointedly that it would take her some time. She disappeared upstairs and Peg led the way to the kitchen where, once he had shut the door, Mike moved towards her and kissed her firmly. 'How does it feel to be engaged?'

'I don't know. I've never done it before.'

Mike pulled back a little, still with his arms around her neck. 'What about Chuck?' Too late she saw her mistake. Christ! This wasn't going to be as easy as she'd thought. Somewhere along the line she'd have to come up with a whole brief married history for the life she'd never had with Chuck. She would have to think about that properly tomorrow but right now she had to get out of this mess. It would be madness to blow it all now just because of a few seconds' forgetfulness.

'Oh, darling. Chuck and I got *married*. Back in '41 it was all so immediate that we never got engaged. Well, not formally. I mean we were out one night and he said how about it and I said yes and as soon as we could we got married. I suppose in the few weeks between we were engaged, but we never called it that. That's why I said I'd never done it before. I meant not *formally*.'

Mike seemed satisfied with this answer and heaving a mental sigh of relief, Peg allowed herself to kiss Mike back with equal intensity. By the time Emily decided they had had enough time on their own and joined them in the kitchen they were sitting down having a cup of tea. Mike was saying that he was keen for the wedding to take place as soon as possible, but Peg, although anxious for the security of a real wedding ring, wanted to wait. 'I know times are hard but I got cheated out of a proper church wedding the first time round so I want to do it right this time.' *There,* she thought, *that ought to put him off the scent.* She felt pleased with herself as she set the first piece of her imaginary married life with Chuck in place.

And Mike had to be happy with that. He had to leave to get back to base and try as he might he couldn't pin Peg down to a date. 'This way,' she argued, 'I know you'll come back to me.' (*I sound more and more like something out of the flicks every minute*, she said to herself.)

'You bet I will, sweetheart!' Reluctantly he left the house to head back to Northolt, but despite the ordeal that lay ahead of him he could only think about Peg. It was a surprisingly happy Major Mike Horrocks who whistled his way back into base at a minute to eleven that night.

* * *

'I still don't know why you wanted to come here,' Rita complained as yet another elbow was dug in her back.

'Because it's special. Because it's important and because I needed to get out of the house and away from Emily's nagging and Anne's whining. And now I wish I'd come by myself instead of bringing a misery like you along. In fact, if you don't buck up I'm going to undo this belt and leave you to find your own way home!'

Rita's eyes widened at the thought of being left alone among the vast, seething crowd. Even standing on tip-toe she couldn't see over everyone's heads. She'd never seen so many people in one place before in her life and it scared her. It didn't seem to bother Peg who was clearly loving every minute of it. Even now she was shoving and pushing Rita towards a lamppost, dragging her friend unwillingly behind her as they had buckled a belt through their bags to make sure they stayed together.

'Watch it, mate!' said Peg sharply as a huge man tried to turn round in the throng and nearly caught her on the chin.

'Sorry, girls. No 'arm intended. 'Ere, want a leg up?' And without waiting for a reply he cupped his hands into a stirrup and managed to clear enough space round him to bend down a little.

'Yes, please. Hang on though.' Quickly, and without reference to Rita, Peg undid the belt, leaving it hanging limply from her bag. 'Right. Ready.' Again the man made his stirrup and Peg put her foot into it, allowing him to help her clamber up the lamppost to balance on its wide base. 'Rita, it's incredible. The whole of the Mall is absolutely crammed. I've never seen anything like it.'

'There's room for you as well if you want.' The man was again forming his stirrup but Rita shook her head.

'Please come down, Peg. You'll fall.' Peg laughed at her friend's concern but, seeing how genuinely scared she was, she reluctantly let herself be helped from her vantage point.

'Isn't this fantastic!' she yelled over the din. 'Let's see if we can get closer. Come on!' Delighted by the news that the war was over but scared by the raw emotion and elation that was flowing around her, Rita unhappily grabbed hold of Peg's bag and again submitted to being dragged along in her wake. She had managed to keep sight of Peg, who was now dancing with a soldier, the pair of them in the middle of a small group singing *Roll out the Barrel* at the tops of their voices. The crowd around the Queen Victoria Memorial was as thick as ever and the rumour that Their Majesties were going to appear on the balcony at Buckingham Palace looked as if it might become reality when a small door in the boarded-up windows at the back of the central balcony suddenly opened.

Peg seemed to spring to life and somehow managed to get herself pulled up on to the Victoria Memorial. She reached down and grabbed

Rita, hauling her up next to her on the memorial steps close to the Palace gates. The crowd began to yell, 'We want the King', over and over again. Then they saw a movement in the shadows behind the gap in the boarded window and the roar from the mob, already hoarse with yelling, grew even louder. If it were possible it increased again, to thunderous proportions, as King George VI, Queen Elizabeth and the Princesses came out to share the festivities.

Rita, finally entering into the spirit of the day, was jumping up and down, cheering with the rest of them. Peg (who was higher up) held on with one arm with her head thrown back as she yelled her approval. Never mind that the balcony looked dilapidated and signs of bomb damage were clearly visible. Never mind that the drapery across its façade was shabby. To the crowd looking on it represented the fact that they had all been through the last terrible years together. As one they started to sing the National Anthem. The people outside the railings stood and waved for what seemed like ages until the Royal group finally went back inside to carry on celebrating privately the fact that London, and the country, had survived one of the worst onslaughts in its history.

In the hubbub Peg's dancing partner had somehow managed to jump up on her other side and was holding her in a familiar fashion round the waist. 'Want to go and hear Winnie make his statement then?' he shouted in her ear, loud enough for Rita to hear and worry (she'd hoped they would now go home and join in the street party going on there) and clutch at Peg's free arm, nearly knocking them all off balance.

'Who's your friend?' asked the soldier, suddenly aware that Rita was still with them.

'This is Rita, and this is . . .' Peg realised she didn't even know his name. 'Who cares who you are?' She turned to Rita and asked roughly, 'You coming down Whitehall or staying here?' She didn't sound very interested in her answer.

'I'd rather go home.'

'Fine,' said the soldier. He clearly wasn't going to waste his time with a dreary girl who seemed scared of her own shadow when so many other happy ones were available and ready to be kissed.

'You wouldn't leave me, would you, Peg?' Rita felt close to tears.

'It's up to you, Reet. I came out to have fun and we're going down Whitehall,' Peg said firmly. She could happily throttle Rita sometimes, but there was no way she was going to let her spoil her fun – not today. Not knowing what else to do Rita unhappily trailed along as they set off and somehow (Rita never did work out how) they not only made it right down the Mall and through Trafalgar Square but also managed to get into Whitehall itself. In fact it wasn't as difficult as she imagined it would be, as so many people had the same idea that they were carried along with the general flow. Peg also jumped on to the front of a lorry carrying more revellers and by the time they reached Whitehall they had been kissed and hugged by more people than Rita could keep track of. She had to admit she was beginning to enjoy herself.

As they waited for the formal announcement Peg again managed to find a good vantage point, balancing on the bonnet of a delivery van. For the first time in five years Big Ben began to strike three and a silence, all the more remarkable because of the size of the crowd, descended over Whitehall. Loudspeakers which had quickly been put up by the authorities crackled through the unusual silence and as Winston Churchill began to address the throng his was the only voice to be heard. His rumbling, ponderous tones announced the end of hostilities with Germany. 'In all our long history we have never seen a greater day than this.' It was amid cheers that he declared, 'The German War is, therefore, at an end.'

The mob erupted.

Anything else coming through the speakers was drowned by a tidal wave of sound as whistles were blown, horns honked, and anything that could be used to noisy effect was deployed. If it had been difficult to see before now it became totally impossible as people threw hats in the air and unfurled flags, waving them precariously over the crowds. Rita turned wide-eyed to Peg. 'Is that it, really over?' she asked in quiet disbelief, but in such a soft voice no one could hear a word she said. Peg had lost her soldier in the crowd but was now hugging a sailor as if she'd known him all her life. Another sailor standing next to Rita grabbed her waist and turned her round to plant a slobbering kiss on her mouth, which she indignantly wiped away with the back of her hand.

The crowd, still loud in its delight, began to thin and Peg attempted to get down from her perch. As she did so she wobbled and if it hadn't been for a steadying hand would definitely have fallen. Gratefully she accepted the offered help and once her feet were back on the ground and she had straightened herself up she turned to say thank you to her rescuer. He was a tall, good-looking man who seemed vaguely familiar, but everybody did that day (she thought she had seen her own father three times which was nonsense, since as far as she knew he was back home in Sidcup if he hadn't been killed in the war).

'You probably saved my life. Thank you.'

'My pleasure. I think the most I saved you from was a nasty fall and a trampling but glad to be of service.' He gave a mock bow and she began to blush – and suddenly she knew why he was familiar. He seemed to recognise her at the same moment and gave a huge laugh of delight. 'Don't say a word. It's Peg Tomson, isn't it? How is that young pilot friend of yours?'

Peg looked at him and then she also laughed. 'Actually it's Peg Timpson and Mike's fine, thank you, and he's managed to avoid having coffee poured over him as well as surviving this lot. I must say you've got a good memory, Mr Edwardes, remembering my name after all this time.'

'Obviously well matched, because you remembered mine. Now, this is no place for a respectable young lady so why don't I take you for a bit of proper civilised celebration. Hmm?' Peg was about to say how much she was enjoying what was clearly to Howard Edwardes the uncivilised behaviour going on around them when she caught sight of Rita. She was standing in her usual meek manner waiting for Peg. Everything was ebbing and flowing around her and all she could do was stand there like a stuffed dummy. It made Peg so angry that the uncharacteristic concern she had felt for her friend disappeared and the refusal she had been about to give turned into an acceptance.

'I'd be delighted, but I just need to talk to my friend.'

'She can come too. The more the merrier.' Howard didn't really mean it but knew he had to make the offer. He was relieved when Peg turned that part of the invitation down.

'No, that won't be possible, she's got to get home. Her mum's really ill and bedridden. She's only been able to get out for the afternoon because a neighbour said she'd keep an eye on the old lady for Rita. (At that precise moment the 'old lady' in question was dancing down the middle of the street with her sister and the pair of them were giving a loud, if tuneless, rendition of *The Lambeth Walk*.) Peg went over to Rita and told her brusquely that she would have to make her own way home after all because she, Peg, was going out with an old acquaintance. From the look on her face it was clear that Rita didn't believe her so for good measure, and to prove her point, Peg yelled over her shoulder, 'Won't be a moment, Howard.' She guessed he wouldn't be able to hear her but hoped that if he did he would forgive the informality and put it down to the high spirits of celebration.

As usual she had her way. Rita was left to go home by herself, which in the end was more fun without Peg, as she got back early enough to join her family and neighbours at the street party and boast about seeing the King and Queen and the Princesses. Peg in the meantime was allowing herself to be steered along Constitution Hill and round Hyde Park Corner towards Knightsbridge. It was a long walk, mainly due to the number of people around, but neither of them minded and by the time they arrived at their destination in the late afternoon they were laughing and joking with each other like old friends.

'Oh,' said Peg, surprised as they stopped. 'We're here.'

'Best place I know. Come on.' And he led the way into the basement where they had first met just over a year before. As she walked in Peg remembered how she had promised herself she would somehow get to meet the debonair Howard Edwardes again. She had made a few attempts at the time but they came to nothing and deciding no man, however charming he may be, deserved to be chased that hard, she had given it up as a bad job.

Although it was not yet six o'clock the small dance floor was crowded with people and as they entered the room a yell of welcome went up from a group in the corner. Howard pushed his way across the floor, lifting his chin in greeting to the band who were playing for all they were worth, sweat glistening on their faces with the effort. He ushered Peg in front of him, making a couple of the men who had greeted him move to let her sit down. Introductions were made and Howard caught Alice's eye. Although immaculately dressed as before she was not quite as glossy as she had been the first time Peg saw her. A couple of strands of hair had escaped from the neat chignon, but she was nevertheless still very much in charge despite the apparent chaos around her. So much so that the instant Howard raised his hand she was over by their table.

'Isn't it wonderful, Alice? Peace, glorious peace. Over at last. Well, at least in Europe,' he modified as an American corporal sitting on his right opened his mouth to protest. 'And I reckon that calls for a real celebration. What's everyone drinking?' He looked round the table at the assorted glasses and bottles. 'Well never mind that. Alice, tonight's a night for champagne. I know we've still got some of the '27 left so let's have it where it can be enjoyed.'

A frown crossed Alice's brow. Seeing it Howard laughed. 'Always the book-keeper. Well, don't worry. I'll pay for it so the accounts will be straight. Now go and get it.' With a smile she went to do as she was told and as she did so Howard gave her an affectionate, and not very gentle, slap on the backside. Alice gave him an even wider grin over her shoulder which surprised Peg. She would have expected such a sophisticated woman to object to such public manhandling.

Alice quickly returned with a tray, several bottles and lots of glasses. Howard helped her hand them round and then deftly wrapped a cloth round the neck of one of the bottles, easing the cork out with a hissing sigh, without losing any of the precious bubbles inside. Glasses were filled, and raised with a toast to King and Country. It was the first time Peg had had champagne but she didn't want to let Howard or his friends know that. She watched as they (especially the women) drank from their glasses, not wanting to get it wrong, and a split second after they swallowed she did the same. It was delicious. The wine fizzed round her mouth and tasted like a cross between the best lemonade she had ever had and the long-forgotten taste of fresh picked raspberries after the sun had been on them all day.

In no time the group had finished three bottles and Peg was feeling very happy. The band changed its rhythm and began to play the popular song, *Accentuate the Positive*, 'because that's what we're doing today'. The dancers yelled their agreement, albeit in a less raucous manner than the people dancing in the streets outside.

'That sounds like a cue for a dance. Peg?' Howard got up and held out his hand to her. As she stood to accept his invitation she was suddenly aware that the dress she was wearing was a bit shabby. The combination of that sense of inadequacy and the champagne on an empty stomach made her feel defiant and she took to the dance floor with even greater aplomb than usual.

The band finished its number and went straight into *Rum and Coca-Cola*. Howard made her feel important and less self-concious about her shabby dress. She was back in control as they slowed down for *A Nightingale Sang in Berkeley Square* followed by *Sentimental Journey*.

'You could say that this is a sentimental journey for us, couldn't you?' Howard asked as he held her. Peg liked the way he danced. He was a good leader and knew how to apply just the right amount of pressure so she could follow him easily. 'After all, this is where we first met, isn't it?'

'Yes. I suppose it is,' she answered nonchalantly, not wanting him to know how vividly she remembered their first meeting. 'My God, that seems like a lifetime ago, doesn't it?'

'You too, hmm? It's amazing what we can endure when we have to. I hope it hasn't been a bad war for you though, Peg. You're the sort of girl who should always have a good time. You were made to enjoy yourself.'

Peg gave a derisory snort. 'If only,' was how she summed it up. 'I tell you, Howard, it'll be great when the fun comes back. Just think, soon we'll be able to go shopping, buy what we want. Wear what we want. Eat what we want. Go where we please without worrying about queues. It'll be wonderful.'

'You haven't been going short though, have you? I'd hate to think that a girl like you had to go without.'

'I've got friends like most girls – but it's not what you think,' she added quickly, realising how cheap her words made her sound.

'No boyfriend then? I was sure that pilot chappy of yours was a permanent fixture.' Peg thought about Mike as Howard twirled her round the floor. Since he had come back in one piece from the D-Day assault, having also received recognition for his bravery in June 1944, he had done nothing but nag about when he and Peg would get married. Although she wanted to be married, the longer it had gone on the less she wanted to be married to Mike. She had come up with one reason after another to delay the actual wedding. Her main excuse was the original one she had used, about wanting a proper wedding, but to listen to her now her nuptials had taken on the proportions of a public event in Westminster Abbey. Soon she would either have to put up or shut up.

The other problem was where they were going to live. Peg had little affection for Roupell Street. In fact she ached to get out of it and had he but known it Mike nearly got his ring on her finger when he started talking about them 'going home', which to him meant back to America. Initially Peg was thrilled, envisaging herself living a rich and luxurious life like those depicted in the Hollywood movies. But then Mike had begun showing her photographs of his home town, and talked about how he knew she would be the type of wife who would fit in with the round of church socials and sewing bees. He also talked more about his family and when Peg learned that 'going home' would also entail living in his parents' house the prospect of life in a small mid-west town rapidly lost its appeal.

'He was . . . I mean he is.' The champagne and dancing were making her light-headed again. 'We're engaged. Have been for over a year. In fact he proposed that night we came here and I accepted. Trouble is he wants us to go and live in America in some small town in the middle of nowhere and from what he says it sounds just awful. Especially as we would have to live with his parents.'

'You poor girl,' said Howard, genuinely sympathetic. 'I can't imagine you living anywhere but right in the middle of a bustling big city. Besides, it would be a waste if you were buried away where no one could see you.' As he said this a look flashed at the back of Howard's eyes. Peg saw it but couldn't quite read it. It wasn't exactly lust (that was something she could spot at twenty paces), nor was it the other look she recognised, when some man or other put her on a pedestal. What she had in fact seen was the beginning of an idea which, although centered on her, had little to do with Howard wanting her physically. They carried on dancing and flirting, but all the time a plan was growing and taking form in Howard's head. By the time they sat down it was almost complete.

The rest of the evening passed quickly enough and Peg continued to enjoy Howard's elegant, generous hospitality. By the time they left it was nearly one in the morning and she had managed to find out that in the past year Howard had bought a major share in the little restaurant. Now that the war was over he had plans to develop it, although he knew it would take time.

The crowds were as thick as ever and seemed determined to carry on rejoicing all night long. While they had been celebrating inside something wonderful had happened to London. For the first time in years the floodlights had been switched on again. Peg blinked as they came out of the restaurant and then gasped as she saw the long-forgotten sight of buildings lit up against the night sky. It was this very public show that things were changing that made her finally grow tearful. She dreaded the thought that she might cry in front of Howard and imperiously sent him off to find a taxi. Usually she would have walked or got a bus home, but tonight was different, she told herself firmly.

It took Howard some time to find a cab as people were disregarding where the pavement ended and the roads began, which made getting a vehicle through a slow process. At first the cabby wasn't keen on going south of the Thames (even if it was only by a few streets) but when Howard told him there would be a big tip, and said how much, he finally agreed.

It was nearly two when he pulled over at the corner of Roupell Street. Peg had told him to stop there, not wanting to be seen coming home late and in a taxi. Too many questions would be asked, even tonight, and it was none of their business. She was glad that she had walked the last little way for although the street party was over there were still a few people hanging round doorways chatting and laughing, oblivious to the rectangles of light that, even though the blackout had not been officially lifted, could now joyfully spill out on to the pavement. The huge storm that had broken out over London earlier had left the streets shiny and wet and they reflected the light back, adding to the festive appearance.

As she drew closer to home Emily came bustling out of the house. 'Where on earth have you been? Mike's been that worried. I told him you'd gone up West. You really should have been here. After all, Peg, he is your fiancé.'

'I know and I'm sick and tired of you and everyone else trying to hustle me to the altar. Honestly, I only want do everything the right way and you lot all seem keen to rush me through like an express train. Well I won't have it, do you hear me? I'll marry Mike when I'm good and ready and not a moment sooner. Now leave me alone and let me go to bed.' She pushed past Emily and went straight up the stairs, shutting her bedroom door firmly behind her.

It had been a wonderful day. For the first time in years she felt alive. She hadn't felt this exhilarated since . . . no. She would not think about Chuck and that night under the bridge. That was then and this was now. She had to look to the future. She put her hand into her bag and pulled out a small pasteboard card. Howard had given it to her as he put her into the taxi, saying he wanted to see her at that address in two weeks' time. No, he wouldn't tell her why but she had to promise she would be there and that no matter what she would not marry Mike before then. It was an easy promise to make. She propped the card against her mirror, considering it thoughtfully.

Howard was unlike any man she had ever met. Peg had always prided herself on being fashionable and able to hold her own with anyone but even she knew when she was outflanked. There was something about Howard that came from an inbred sense of his own style and sophistication. It extended beyond the fashionable to something Peg couldn't quite identify, but whatever it was she intended not only to get it – but to get Howard too.

Poor Howard, she thought as her head sank into her pillow. *He won't know what's hit him.*

Howard sat behind his desk looking Peg up and down as she coolly returned his gaze. The meeting was not going as she had imagined. Far from wrapping Howard round her little finger, she had the feeling that he was the one doing the wrapping. It was a new experience and not one that she was totally sure she enjoyed.

'So, what's the verdict?' she asked, suppressing the note of irritation in her voice as she tried to keep the atmosphere light.

'Would you turn round again please?' It was more an order than a question and although tempted to make a retort about not being a bleeding merry go round, something made her do as she was asked.

'Are you going to tell me what this is all about or am I going to stand here like a lemon all day?' She was facing him again and stood with her hands on her hips. She adopted this pose because it enabled her surreptitiously to pull the fabric of her skirt tighter around her, accentuating her curves. She had dressed carefully that morning, putting on a pink suit which Emily had again adapted from a pre-war outfit. The jacket sat neatly over the hip-hugging skirt and a bunch of violets was pinned to her lapel. Even though it was still morning, her pale cream blouse was buttoned to reveal just a touch of décolletage. She had on cream 'Joyce' shoes and a new pair of Mike's nylons. Her hair was arranged in a 'Victory Roll' with a small hat perched at an angle on top and her mouth was lavishly drawn in red lipstick. The whistles she had received as she made her way to Howard's Bond Street office told that she really did look as good as she thought she did, which was one of the reasons she resented the way Howard was staring at her now.

'You've got a good figure, Peg. A very good figure, but there's no need to pull that skirt tighter. Cheap clothes and garish colours do nothing to help you. If you're going to work for me then you'll have to learn the difference between what a man sees as alluring and merely available.'

'That does it!' Peg turned to snatch her bag from the chair where she had left it. She was furious. How dare Howard, how dare *anyone* talk to her in that way. 'I didn't come here to be insulted. And I'll have you know that I've had no complaints yet about the way I dress. Who the hell do you think you are anyway, telling me what I can and can't wear?' By now Howard was standing in front of her. He put his hands on her shoulders but she angrily shrugged them off. 'Well?' she demanded as she pulled her gloves on.

'I'm a man who can see a lot of potential in you, Peg Timpson. Potential I hate to see wasted. I wouldn't be saying what I am now if I didn't think you were an attractive girl, a *very* attractive girl. You're also a very sexy girl and those are commodities I value in my line of business. I know,' he said, holding up his hand to stop her as she opened her mouth in protest, 'you don't even know what I do except own a small restaurant. But you can either walk out of here and go back to ringing that bell on the buses or you can take a deep breath, calm down and listen to what I'm offering you. What's it to be?' He spoke in a soft voice, not pleading with her, or even asking her to stay. His tone was very matter-of-fact but broached no argument.

'How can I answer when you treat me like a prize cow at a cattle market and throw remarks at me that I can't help but take as personal? I can't make a decision about something when I don't even know what you're going on about, can I?' Peg replied petulantly.

'Fair enough. Why don't you sit down and I'll put you in the picture, as Monty would have said to the troops.' The charm she had recognised in Howard never left him as he ushered her back to her seat opposite his desk, rearranging the chair so the sun didn't shine in her eyes, making sure she was quite settled before going to sit down again himself.

'It's like this, Peg. I own part of the restaurant, but I also have other interests in a number of similar businesses. During the war people went out to try to forget what was going on. They needed to get away from things. Now that the war is over people are still going to want all of that but I have a feeling that what's really going to succeed is something smaller than the big dance halls. Intimate restaurants and clubs. Something with a bit of style and class at reasonable prices that everyone can enjoy. But part of creating that and making it work is to have the right people working for me. You remember Alice at the restaurant?' Peg nodded as she pictured the glossy woman. 'When I first met her in '36 she was working in Woolies. Nothing wrong with that but like you she was wasted, she had a lot more to her than that and I persuaded her to come and work for me. She isn't nearly as good-looking as you but you have to admit she has a certain . . . quality, about her, don't you?' Again Peg nodded. 'She was also bright and eager to learn. It only took a couple of years to teach her to recognise what was what. To appreciate the good things in life. The restaurant opened in '38 and Alice has been in charge since then.'

Howard had been leaning back a little in his high-backed chair, his hands carefully folded in his lap as he spoke to Peg. Now he sat forward and propped his chin in his hand as he looked intently at her. 'Peg, I'm offering you the same opportunity. To make something of yourself. Money attracts money. Even if you haven't got it, making people think you have is half the battle. Play your cards right and you could earn more money than you've ever imagined. How does it sound so far?'

Peg stared at him, her head spinning as she considered what he was saying. 'I understand what you're saying, but I still don't see what it is you're offering me.' She sounded cautious and glanced at the door to check she could get out quickly if she wanted to, not that she did – yet.

Howard chuckled. 'Let's call it an apprenticeship. If it all works out the way I want it to, and I have a pretty shrewd hunch it will, then I promise you that you will be running a restaurant or club of your own in a few years. Don't worry, you'll be paid while you're learning. However, so that I know you're not just using me for a meal ticket, initially it won't be as much as you're currently getting. I need to make sure the investment of my time and knowledge is well placed. But if you're still with it in six months' time and making the grade then the pay will increase. On the plus side, as part of your apprenticeship you'll visit some of the top clubs and restaurants in London and mix with some of the richest and best-known people in town. I shall be your Pygmalion.'

'Pig . . . who?' Peg was puzzled.

'Pygmalion. Say yes to my business proposition – because that's all it is – and you'll find out. What do you say?'

'I say why don't you take me out to lunch so we can talk about it further. After all, I feel as if you brought me here under false pretences.'

Howard laughed. 'Lunch it is. But I expect an answer by the time we've finished.'

'I promise before I eat the last mouthful of dessert you'll have an answer.'

'Good, and it's pudding.' Peg looked puzzled. 'The sort of people I want as clientèle call dessert pudding.'

'Well, you'll have an answer before you've finished it whatever you call it.'

Howard knew that she would agree but just in case he took her to Claridge's for lunch. Peg was clearly impressed, if not slightly overawed by the liveried doorman who saluted as he opened the door for them. As they made their way inside she suddenly came to a complete halt outside the Causerie Restaurant. 'Howard, I'm not dressed right for here.'

'Aren't you?' he asked gently, raising a quizzical eyebrow. 'You told me you looked fine. And as I've already told you that I agree, I think you're fishing for even more compliments. Now come on, I'm ready for my lunch.' He took her firmly by the elbow and propelled her into the restaurant. Peg was right. In her bright suit she stood out like some exotic flower among the other women in the room in their sombre suits. Although she had never been able to afford couture clothes Peg was a girl who knew quality when she saw it – and these women had it. That many of the outfits were pre-war was a testimony to their enduring style and tailoring. Peg's gloves felt as if they were sticking to her hands as she nervously smoothed her skirt while the waiter held her seat for her to sit down. Another handed them the menus. Glad to have something to divert her she looked at the list in front of her. Puzzled, she turned it over to look at the back.

'What's wrong, Peg?' Howard kept his voice as flat as he could while he busied himself with his menu.

'How do I know what's what if it's not in English?' she hissed over her menu not wanting to draw attention to herself. This was not what she had expected at all. 'And another thing . . . I usually work out what I can have with what so I don't go over the five-shilling limit but there's no prices on anything.'

At this Howard could contain himself no longer and let out a loud laugh. Peg knew he was laughing at her but somehow the noise he made was such a friendly one that she didn't mind. 'In really good establishments the lady is never given a menu with the prices on it. It is considered impolite for her to know the cost of things. As far as what is on offer goes let me translate. There's *Le Filet de Turbotin Marie Stuart* – which is fish, mushrooms and shrimps in white wine sauce; *L'Agneau de Lait Richelieu* – basically roast lamb that is quite superb; *La Caille d'Egypt aux Raisins de Muscats* – quail with grapes; or *Le Buffet Froid Salade Chiffonade* – cold meat salad.' He carefully picked out the dishes he felt would have the most impact on her and read them in a neutral tone.

'Why don't they just call it cold meat salad then?' She picked on the only thing she could to quibble about. 'And another thing. You've told me it's impolite for a lady to know what things cost but that lot has got to be more than five bob. It proves what I've always thought. During the last six years, while we've been scrimping and saving and sleeping down the stinking Tube or queuing for hours for one lousy limp chop, people up West haven't had to go without anything. Look at this lot,' she sneered, taking in her fellow diners in one contemptuous sweep round the restaurant. 'I bet they don't know what it is to go without, do they?' She gripped her menu angrily, aware that her voice had risen as she was speaking. A few people at closer tables were casting curious looks in her direction. Howard reached over and put a calming hand on hers; again that tingle went through her.

'Trust me, Peg. *Everyone* has gone without. These people are the ones who have the money to get round the rules and regulations legally. Let me explain. When I eventually get the bill our food will have cost the same as it does for everyone else eating in a restaurant today, and that is five shillings. But you're right. The food on this menu costs a lot more than that so there will be other sums as well. For example, I will be charged six shillings a head as a house charge. We'll have a bottle of wine. That is not regulated and whether we have red or white it will cost over twenty shillings. So you see, a five-shilling meal will cost at least six times that amount. The food will be paid for within the limits and we will have a superb, legal lunch.'

Peg's mouth had dropped open. 'A quid for a bottle of wine! That's outrageous!'

'It is if you haven't got it. But I have and that, my girl, is what I'm trying to tell you. I will make you a promise – and whatever else you may or may not hear about me I am a man who keeps his word. If you accept my offer then in two years' time not only will *you* not think twice about ordering a two pound bottle of wine, but I will also bring you back here for dinner. Now here's Andrew for our order. Have you decided what you would like or shall I order for you?

Staggered, Peg flopped back in her seat, indicating that Howard was in charge. It was obvious from his conversation and the degree of reverence being paid to him by the head waiter that he was a regular client at the hotel. He checked his choices first with Andrew and then herself for approval, which she gave. Despite telling herself that she would not be overawed by Howard and all that he had said – and she still felt that somehow she was the unspoken part of the deal – Peg was impressed. She had noticed that they had ice cream on the dessert list ('pudding' list, she corrected in her head) and wondered why Howard hadn't asked her what she would have after. But she had learned her lesson and, not wanting to make an even bigger fool of herself, she kept quiet.

Their first course was served with a flourish. Howard had ordered oysters for himself and *Crevettes Rose Cocktail* for Peg. ('prawn cocktail', he told her.) For a moment she was bemused by the array of cutlery that seemed to spread for miles on either side of her plate but then she glanced across at Howard. Using his eyes he indicated that she should use the ones set furthest from her plate. Meekly she picked up the fork.

'Good girl,' he praised quietly under his breath, just loud enough for her to hear and feel childishly pleased. They carried on eating and as if they had made a pact both were witty and charming through the rest of the meal. Peg was glad that she hadn't remarked about the pudding because once they had finished their main course – the quail for Howard (with braised celery and mashed potatoes, the description of which as *pomme purée* had again made Peg question the use of French on the menu) and the most succulent lamb Peg had ever tasted – the head waiter returned to take their order for their final course.

'I see by virtue of the fact that the *Pêche Mikado* with Praline is on the menu that the factory is still going strong?'

'Oh yes, sir. An excellent idea of sir's to suggest we maintain our own essential supplies. I know Chef and the management are also delighted that we have been able to maintain such a good relationship through these trying times, sir. Most grateful to you, Mr Edwardes, sir.' He inclined his head as he left them to place their order. Howard skipped pudding in favour of a large cognac but Peg let him order the *Pêche Mikado* for her.

'Factory?' she queried, unable to stop herself.

'Hmm. Another area in which I dabble. Claridge's has supported its own factory throughout the war, at the top of Drury Lane. And let's say I've been a sleeping partner and leave it at that, shall we?' Again Peg opened her mouth to comment but Howard interrupted her. 'Peg, don't worry. Everything I'm involved with is legal, stretched to the limit maybe, but nevertheless legal. It has to be. It takes too much time going round the back. I have contacts and I use them. It's as simple as that. Now you said I'd have an answer by the end of this meal so you'd better start thinking what it's going to be.'

Over lunch she hadn't exactly forgotten about Howard's proposition (how could she?), just pushed it to the back of her mind as she took in all the splendour around her and concentrated on using the right cutlery. But now she reconsidered it. Her ice cream arrived and she made it last as long as she could as she turned everything over in her head. *I can't be bought for the price of a lunch. Even if it is a bleeding expensive one!* she thought determinedly to herself, certain that Howard wanted more. *It's not that I don't want to give it*, she mused as she chased an elusive piece of praline round her plate, *but I don't want it assumed.* She looked round the room at the women once more – still gossiping, hats still bobbing, clothes still immaculately cut – and noticed one of them was lunching with a RAF pilot. For the first time she thought of Mike.

Maybe this *is my escape route, even if part of the deal means I look at a few ceilings? OK, so Mike's offering me security and America, but it's a dump, not New York or Hollywood. He'll have to understand that this is a career move. Maybe I could keep Mike on the boil in case it doesn't work out? I'm sure I could.* She put down her spoon and leaned back, looking playfully at Howard from under her hat brim. He stared back at her in cool silence. He knew what she was going to say but giving that away now would ruin everything. A waiter brought them coffee but it wasn't until she'd taken her first sip and replaced her cup carefully on its saucer that she finally said, 'You've got a deal.'

Margaret sat down elegantly in one of the hotel's comfortable drawing-room chairs, spreading the fabric of her skirt round her neatly crossed ankles as she did so and letting her fur stole drop down to hang loosely from one shoulder. She knew that every woman in the place was looking at her and she loved it. So what if Dior's New Look was unpatriotic and extravagant? She had earned tonight and if Howard wanted to spend a fortune on her then why not. *Let them stare. Silly cows!* she thought, with a mental spark of her old self, making sure that her new self's expression didn't give away what she was thinking.

Howard was impressed. He had been right about her. She had worked hard and even though he could guess how smug she was feeling nothing about her gave any outward indication of her emotions. *Attagirl,* he thought to himself and took out his cigarette case, offering it to her. Delicately she rested her hand on his to steady the flame from his lighter as he lit her cigarette for her. She took a deep pull and exhaled, tilting her chin upwards, allowing a slow smile to spread across her lips.

'Be honest, there were times when you didn't think I'd make it, weren't there?' Her voice was low and well modulated.

'You only got me seriously worried once, when Mike came and told you he was moving to New York. I had the feeling that was the only moment you really came close to giving it up and going with him.'

She lifted her chin again to allow a careful, light laugh to escape and then leaned towards him, propping her arm on her thigh as she drew on her cigarette, pushing her fur clad shoulder forwards, stroking her stole with her other hand as she gazed at him. 'I came close but let's be honest, poor Mike didn't stand a chance. I mean, any girl would pick a mink stole over a diner on the lower East Side, New York or not!'

'Well. I promised we'd be back for a celebratory dinner and here we are. I hope you enjoyed it?' he added. Again she gave a restrained laughed, and nodded. The last two years hadn't been easy. Howard had seen to that. She had almost had to learn a new language – napkin not serviette, thank you not ta, powder room not lavvy. And what was to be used with what, which wines went with which food, what was French for lobster, was it masculine or feminine – the list went on and on. And the clothes; how to recognise good fabric or a designer, what made good style good and bad style common, cheap or – even worse – vulgar.

Never before had she met a man who knew so much about women's fashion and was so right. It had at times been a degrading experience. Especially when she bought a new suit and he had made her take it back, saying it made her look like a tart. She had wanted to tell him that that was how he made her feel but, even though he had paid her regularly every week, he had never once laid a finger on her. Strictly speaking that wasn't quite true, because he had often taken her dancing, but that didn't count. He had never tried to make love to her, or even kiss her, and in the early days that had bothered her. Now it made her even more determined to have him. As she told herself that evening as they ordered dinner, *Now I not only know the sort of woman he wants, but I can be that woman. I intend to succeed.*

'I told you once that I never broke a promise and I hope I have proved that by bringing you here tonight.' They both looked round Claridge's French Salon, taking in its quiet sophistication, the gentle tinkle of the piano in the corner and the smooth efficiency of the waiters; but this time she felt as much at ease there as he did. 'But I made you another promise when we started this, and that was your own place. Well, Margaret,' she couldn't quite remember when he had stopped calling her Peg, insisting that her full name was more up-market, and she had to admit that these days she felt less and less like Peg, 'Alice has decided to move on and as I now own the restaurant outright I've decided the time has come to turn it into a late-night club. They're springing up all over the place and I don't want to miss out. I'm putting you in charge of everything. And I mean *everything*. From the decor and the music to the licences and attracting clientèle. What do you say?'

She was tempted to jump up and rush round the low table between them to hug him. Two years ago she would have done just that. Now she simply stroked the burgundy satin of her voluminous skirt and gave him a satisfied smile. 'Darling, I'm thrilled and I promise not to let you down.' She took another pull on her cigarette. She still didn't enjoy smoking but it was part of what was expected of her so she did it.

'Oh, don't worry, you won't. Not now.' The implication that previously she would have done so was left unsaid. 'There's one other thing, however. As manageress of the club – we'll think of a name for it later – you'll have to move to the flat above the premises. It'll be too difficult to have you travelling across London late at night and besides, I like to know where my manageress is if I need her. I'll make sure Alice leaves it tidy, and of course you will have a small budget so you can redecorate it in your own way. I hope that won't present any problems?'

'How could it?'

Maybe he would make his move once she was living in the upstairs flat? Of course it would be difficult explaining it all to Emily. She had been less than enthusiastic from the very first day when Peg had hurried home to share the news with her. She had expected her landlady to be excited for her but she had done nothing but go on about 'Poor Mike' this and 'Poor Mike' that. As if Mike Horrocks with his small-town promises could hold a candle to all that Howard was offering. Sometimes Em could be such a wet blanket.

At last! she thought ecstatically. *I'm out of Roupell Street with its nosey neighbours and petty attitudes, Em's nagging and Anne's whining and . . . oh My GOD! Anne!*

In all the time Howard had been working on Peg, changing her into Margaret, he had never once visited her at home, nor had he asked her about her home life. Shrewdly she told him little; a few allusions to her landlady but no mention of Anne. She had a gut feeling that if Howard knew she had a child things might not work out the way she wanted them to. To tell him now that she had a six-year-old daughter would ruin everything. There was no way she could spring Anne on Howard and she definitely couldn't move her into the new flat. 'Thank you,' she replied with mechanical charm to Howard's invitation to dance.

The band was playing the popular hit *Almost Like Being in Love* and with his usual skill Howard twirled her round the dance floor, aware of the other couples (and in particular the men) watching Margaret and the way her full skirt emphasised her elegant movements. All in all Howard was feeling pleased with himself. He had taken a risk with Peg, albeit a calculated one, but it had paid off. The woman he thought he had seen beneath the tawdry topcoat had indeed been there. He'd had to chip away persistently to find her but picturing the brash blonde who had stood in his office two years ago, and comparing her with this more subtle, golden-haired, quieter, and all together sexier woman with whom he was now dancing made all the effort worthwhile. All she had to do now was turn the club into the hottest thing in London and he would feel he had a decent return on his investment. He reckoned it would take her about six months to sort it out, which would give him time to look more closely at the proposal from Great Britain Exhibitions Limited. Now could be a good time to get into that game. People still needed homes and furniture and, following the success of the Britain Can Make It Exhibition at the Victoria & Albert, it might be a good move . . .

As Howard guided them round the floor Margaret automatically followed his lead, a half smile on her immaculately made-up face disguising the thoughts chasing round in her head. *Em will look after her, I know that. I'll just have to explain it very carefully and make sure I send enough money each week to keep them going,* she reasoned to herself. *Anne will be upset but for heaven's sake, she's old enough to understand. She'll just have to stay with her Auntie Em. I know, we'll go down to Studland for the weekend and I'll tell them all about it then.*

'Thank you.' Margaret let Howard usher her back to their table.

'My pleasure. I know this evening is a celebration but I hope you won't mind if we don't have too late a night. I have an early start in the morning.'

'Of course I don't mind, darling. Anyway, I want to start thinking about the club. When can I start work on it?'

'About a month.'

'Howard, I don't suppose I could use the cottage this weekend, could I? It would be nice to get away and I think the sea air might give me a chance to think and come up with some ideas.' She pulled her gloves on as she asked the question.

Howard helped her into her stole. 'I've got to be in Paris this weekend anyway, so it's all yours.' By the time it had been agreed they were standing in Brook Street and the doorman was hailing a taxi. In fact he was hailing two taxis. The first was for Margaret, who let Howard settle her in the back and shut the door before giving the Roupell Street address, and the second for Howard, who directed the cabby towards the Knightsbridge restaurant.

When she was told that they were spending the whole weekend at the seaside Anne couldn't contain her excitement and kept checking exactly when that was. 'It's not tomorrow, then?'

'No. You know what day it is tomorrow.'

'I know it's Thursday but what I don't know is if that is the weekend or not.' She argued with the clear logic of a six-year-old just realising that the grown-ups in her world were all stupid.

'You've got two nights before we go.'

'Ta. That's what I wanted to know,' she said seriously and clumped off to her room to begin finding the things she wanted to take with her. For the next two days she bombarded Emily and Margaret with questions and by the time they boarded the train at Waterloo early on Saturday morning Emily seriously thought the child would be sick with excitement. Instead she sat in the corner of their compartment drumming her heels against the seat and looking eagerly out of the window, asking every five minutes, 'Are we there yet?'

It seemed they had taken enough with them for two weeks, not just two days, but by half past one they had not only unlocked Howard's cottage and unpacked but had also made it on to the beach and found a sand dune to themselves where they had set up camp. Anne scrambled out of her things and into her old knitted swimming costume. Around them families were playing and the beach seemed to be full of yelling children darting in and out of the waves. At the sea's edge a man was walking up and down with some tired-looking donkeys. Children jumped up and down round the animals which patiently waited for parents to position their offspring on their backs before setting off along the sand again. 'Why don't you go and play with the other children, dear?' asked Emily as she pulled her knitting out of her bag, trying yet again to encourage the child to mix with people her own age.

''Cos I'm buildin' a sand-castle and it's taking all my conser-tration,' Anne answered solemnly as she up-ended her bucket of sand and hit it firmly with her spade.

'Leave her, Em. She seems happy enough. Anyway, so long as she's busy I needed to have a word with you.' Margaret shook her hair out from the scarf she had tied round it. With Howard in Paris she didn't have to worry too much about her appearance. Besides, she would go to the hairdressers first thing Monday morning and get it set before she saw him.

She turned her face to the sun and stretched out her legs, wriggling her bare toes in the warm sand. When she opened her eyes Emily was looking at her patiently, her fingers darting back and forth with the wool. 'Things are changing again, Em. Really changing. It's going to be so exciting but I'm going to need your help like I've never needed it before.' Margaret flung herself out of her deckchair to kneel on her haunches in front of the older woman waiting for a response. Hearing nothing but a noise that sounded like 'Harumph', Margaret ploughed on.

'Howard wants to open a new club. It's going to be a late-night one and the most modern in London. He wants me to be in charge of it all. Trouble is, that also means he'll want me to live in the flat above the place. You should see it, Em,' she hurried on as Emily stopped knitting. 'It's in Knightsbridge and it's ever so posh – I mean smart. I'm going to be able to redecorate that as well. But it only has one bedroom so you can see why I need your help, can't you?'

'No, miss, I can't, and if you ask me no good will come of this. I tell you, that Mr Howard Edwardes wants just one thing and once you're living in his place and running his business – well then, he owns you, doesn't he? That'll be that. You mark my words, you'll never find a husband then. I still think you and Mike were . . .'

'Emily!' Margaret knelt forward and put her hands on her hips. 'We've discussed that before and I told you the matter is closed. Now I won't have you even mention his name, you know it upsets Anne.'

'Makes you feel guilty, more like,' retorted the older woman, picking up her knitting again. 'And never mind me. What about Anne? What's going to happen to her? I take it Mr Edwardes still knows nothing about her? Poor mite.'

Margaret sighed. 'You can be so thick sometimes, Em. Of course he doesn't. That's what I'm explaining. Howard is setting me up in the club, that's all. If he had wanted anything else he would have taken it by now.' A slight frown, not unnoticed by Emily, crossed her brow. 'I intend to learn all I can about the business and then I'll set up by myself. You see, despite what you think Howard Edwardes does not own me, nor will he ever own me. I'm still a free agent and I'm going to stay that way. I reckon I should be able to build it all up and open my own place in about . . . oh, three years' time at the most. Then when I've got it all sorted I can move you and Anne out of Roupell Street and we'll all be together again. That's what I'm asking you, Em. Please take care of Anne for me until I can become really free of everyone. I'll come and visit weekends. Oh, and don't think I want you to do it for nothing. I'll make sure I send you money every week to pay towards her keep.'

'You can keep your money,' Emily said indignantly. 'I'll do it because I love her and I think she needs someone there for her and because I want to believe you.'

'What do you mean, you *want* to believe me? I'm telling the truth. What else do you think I mean?' Margaret jumped angrily to her feet, spraying the fine sand into the air as she did so.

'Oh, I don't doubt that you *think* you mean it, but I wonder how long it will be before you stop visiting. Before you get so caught up in your new life you forget about us.'

'Oh, Em! How could you? You know I could never forget about you or Anne. You're my family. Now I'm really hurt.' Quickly she turned and ran towards Anne who was still building her sand-castle. From her deckchair Emily could see Peg ('Peg you was when you came to me and Peg you will always be in this house,' was her comment when she had announced that she was now to be called Margaret) rush towards the child and flop down in the sand beside her. She scooped up the bucket and began filling it with sand. Anne was delighted that Margaret was helping and happily ran backwards and forwards to the sea's edge, collecting water to pat their creation into shape. It was a rare sight, mother and daughter playing together.

Emily shook her head and went back to her knitting. *I wouldn't mind so much if she didn't worship the very ground you walk on. You don't deserve a daughter like that one and that's a fact.* She heard Margaret yell something up the beach towards her but the breeze whipped away her words to mingle with the other voices and the roar of the sea. Margaret pointed towards the kiosk and, understanding that she was taking Anne for an ice cream, Em raised her hand in acknowledgment. She must have dozed off because the next thing she knew Anne was thumping her knee with a sticky fist.

'Mummy says that she's not going to live with us any more, Auntie Em.' Emily looked at the child's woebegone face and put her knitting down, carefully stabbing the ball of wool with the needles to keep the stitches in place before wrapping her arms round Anne's waist.

'But it's not for ever. Just for a while, until Mummy can get us all a nice house where we can all be together again.' Anne's lower lip began to tremble and her eyes fill with tears.

It's not fair, thought Emily, *but what can I do? I know Peg means it now but what about next week and after that?* She gave Anne another hug and out loud repeated, 'It's not for ever, Annie, and Mummy will come and see you and I'll be there.' Anne looked at her and bit her lower lip thoughtfully.

'You won't go away, will you, Auntie Em?'

'Oh pet, of course I won't. I'll be there for so long you'll think I'm part of the furniture.' The thought of her Auntie Em as an old armchair made Anne smile. Soon the reassuring words, the ice cream and just being at the seaside cheered her up and she was dragging Emily by the hand down the beach towards Margaret who was sticking shells along the top of one of the sand-castle's towers. She looked up as they approached and, seeing the reproving look in Emily's eye, went back to embedding the shells in the sand.

'Look what we made. It's the best castle anywhere because my mummy and me,' ('Mummy and I,' Margaret corrected automatically to herself) 'built it together.' Another disapproving look from Emily.

'Have you got your camera with you, Em?' It was a light question.

'I'll go and get it.' She turned and walked solidly back to their things and dug around for her camera. When she got back Anne was looking sullen again and some sort of row had started about where Margaret had put the shells.

'But Mummy, I didn't want them there. I collected them to be the front path. Now you've spoiled it.'

'But darling, I thought they looked pretty there. So the princess can see them whenever she looks out to see if her prince is coming to save her. Now look at Auntie Em and smile so she can take a picture.'

Anne was standing holding her spade and squinting seriously at the camera, the look of displeasure at her mother's interference so clear on her face that it made Margaret laugh. The wind blew and Margaret held her hair off her face with one hand as Emily took the photograph. As soon as the shutter clicked Anne turned on her mother.

'I'm glad you're going away 'cos when you're not here I'm going to build even bigger sand-castles and then you'll be sorry.' Anne threw her spade down on the sand and ran quickly towards the sea, but not so fast that Emily missed seeing the puzzled tears of a hurt and bewildered six-year-old as her world fell to pieces around her.

'Of course she'll be here, Auntie Em. I mean today is special. She wouldn't not come. I mean, she promised . . .' Anne's voice trailed off as she again knelt on the over-stuffed sofa to stare as hard as she could down Roupell Street to see if there was yet any sign of her mother.

'Your Auntie Em's just being a fuss-budget. I'm sure you're right. After all, it's not every day you have a tenth birthday, is it?' Emily said, trying to hide the doubtful tone in her voice.

'No it's not, and I was right and you were wrong. Here she is. I told you so!' Anne jumped excitedly from the sofa, rushing to the front door and out along the street to meet her mother who was walking towards her, a large box tucked under her arm. As usual Margaret had got a taxi to drop her at the corner. The only thing she enjoyed about coming back was that it gave her a chance to show off in front of all those silly cows who used to make fun of her. Well, not any more!

These days she dressed in the finest clothes and was greeted by name when she visited the couture departments of Selfridge's and Harrod's – which was hardly surprising. She was the sort of customer they liked. She had good taste, an excellent figure which was a joy to clothe and she spent lavishly on her accounts which were always paid off in full by Mr Edwardes at the end of each month. Today, as the September sun cast lengthening shadows behind Roupell Street, she was wearing a new slim-cut herringbone green tweed suit. Its skirt was cut fashionably straight and tight to just below the knee, the jacket clinched in round her neat waist and a flounced pale green silk cravat filled its neck. Her hat was small and neat and sat proudly, slightly tipped forward on top of her smooth hair, its wisp of chic veil carefully positioned. Her matching green stiletto shoes tapped satisfactorily along the pavement and the ruched green calf-skin gloves met the three-quarter length sleeves of her jacket to create a look that might have stepped straight out of the pages of *Vogue*.

'Darling! Do be careful, you'll get me all grubby!' she greeted her daughter as the child flung herself at her. 'Now let me look at you. Haven't you got big? Come on, let's go inside and find Auntie Em, shall we?' Margaret was aware that curtains were twitching and she knew that if they stayed in the street any longer it would become too obvious. *That'll show 'em!* she thought with a spark of her old self, as she let Anne take her hand (after checking it wasn't sticky with anything) and they walked the rest of the way with the child skipping blissfully along besides her. *Let any of them say I don't look after my kid.*

They went indoors and Margaret shut the door with a firm hand. Emily came bustling out of the kitchen as usual and shooed them into the parlour. Margaret had made it clear that these days she was not the sort of woman who had tea in the kitchen.

'Let me take your jacket, Pe . . . Margaret,' offered Emily, holding out her hand. Margaret sat down in the armchair that was still positioned exactly where it had been on the day Mike had come to tell her of Chuck's death, and laughed condescendingly at Emily. 'Dear Em. If I take this off I'll be sitting here in my slip. There's no room for *anything* under this jacket!' She knew she was being unkind but it was still fun to make Em blush, even if it was easier to do now than it had been before. Still smiling she turned to Anne. 'Here you are, darling. Happy birthday.' Anne's eyes widened with delight as Margaret held out the parcel she was carrying towards her.

'What do you say?' asked Emily with an indulgent but warning note in her voice. Anne was effusive in her thanks and as Margaret, smiling gently to herself, took off her gloves, she settled on the floor to open her present. Unlike most children she didn't rip the paper off but carefully unwrapped it, folding the ribbon and then the paper before turning to look at what she had been given. It was a large box with a colourful picture of Batttersea Pleasure Gardens on its lid and a statement printed in bold letters: 'Five hundred real wood pieces jigsaw'.

'Oh, Mummy, you remembered! Thank you. Will we go before tea or afterwards?' Anne seemed to glow with pleasure as she searched Margaret's blank face for an answer. Suddenly Margaret remembered that she had talked about taking the child to the fun fair that had been created up-river from what was now being called the South Bank. But she was sure it had only been vaguely mentioned, nothing firmer than that.

'But, darling, I've already been. I mean, how do you think I got your birthday present if I hadn't been there? I really don't want to go back, and even if I did I couldn't go today. Not dressed like this. No, I don't think we'll go.' As far as Margaret was concerned the matter was now closed. 'Now what do you think of your present?' She leaned towards Anne who was still kneeling on the floor.

Anne looked back at her, blinking hard, trying not to let her mother see how disappointed she was. She had promised to take her, really she had, but what could she do? She swallowed the lump in her throat. 'It's lovely, Mummy. Thank you. Do you mind if I go and play with it now?'

'Of course not. I need to talk to Auntie Em anyway. Go on, off you go.'

Anne scrambled to her feet and picked up the box as well as the ribbon and wrapping paper. She walked as slowly as she could out of the room and waited until the door had shut behind her, then she couldn't bear it any longer and ran up the stairs so fast that she nearly fell. By the time she reached her bedroom and threw herself face down on her counterpane she was already crying hard. She hurled the box across the room so it hit the wall, making all the bits fall out on the rug, the bright disjointed pieces shining in the afternoon sun, then buried her face, and the sound of her sobbing, in her bedclothes. She had told everyone at school that she was going to the fun fair and now Mummy had gone without her. She always looked forward to her Mummy's visits, which weren't nearly as often as she would have liked, but this one was meant to be special because it was her birthday.

Mummy had promised, she knew she had. Mummy could be so mean sometimes but she wouldn't let her see how upset she was because that would make her cross. Besides, ten was ever so grown-up and ten-year-olds didn't cry.

While Anne was trying to be grown-up Margaret was trying to explain to Emily how busy she had been and why she had missed a few weeks' visits and who she had gone to the fair with and what fun Battersea was. Emily didn't want to know.

'I won't have it, miss. You treat that child like a pet poodle. She adores you – why I don't know – and I've heard nothing from her for weeks 'cept "Mummy's taking me to the fair for my birthday" and "We'll go on the dodgems and Big Dipper and helter-skelter", and what happens? You come sweeping in here like lady muck with bits of cut-out wood and think she'll be happy. Well you listen to me, my girl. To everyone else you might be Miss High-and-mighty Margaret Timpson, manageress of some club or other, but to me you're still plain old unmarried Peg who has a daughter and responsibilities. You know nothing about her and you never ask. She needs to be loved but when you do pay us a call it's always "Me, me, me". Well, I've had enough. Little Annie deserves more than you give her. Lord knows I do my best for her but I won't have it disrupted by anyone, not even you. If you can't treat her proper then you're not to come any more, do you hear me?'

Margaret sat with her ankles neatly crossed, a bored expression on her face as she listened to Emily who stood squarely in front of her, her hands plunged into her apron pockets, her head nodding backwards and forwards as she railed at her. When she finished speaking she glared down at Margaret, waiting for an answer. The younger woman stared coolly back and then reached into her handbag to pull out a cigarette which she screwed into a holder before flicking her lighter.

'Really, Em, you do make mountains out of molehills, darling, you really do. Quite honestly I've got better things to do with my time than come running down here to this . . . dump,' she scoffed as she tossed her head, indicating the house, '. . . every five minutes. And as for the kid, well, I can do without that as well. Frankly she bores me and so do you. You want her to yourself? You can have her.'

She stood up and smoothed down her skirt, giving the jacket a tug to realign it before she opened her bag again and took out an envelope which she threw on the table. She shut the bag with a snap. 'That, my dear Emily, is the last few weeks' money that I promised you and believe it or not, knowing I wouldn't get down here again for the next few weeks, there's extra in there as well. But that's it. I've worked hard, really hard to make sure there's enough money for her, but you just seem to think it grows on trees. Well, if you want to look after her then you can. Totally. That's the last money you'll get from me.'

'Oh Peg,' sighed Emily, all the anger flying out of her, 'do you really think that's what this is about? Money? Love, it's so much more than that. It's about being here for her, being involved with her, loving her and knowing when to give her a hug or a telling-off. Making home like it used to be. Remember the fun we all used to have? I didn't mean it, Peg, honest I didn't. Please sit down and let's pretend I never said nothing. Please?'

'Oh no you don't! You've made it very clear how you feel about me as a mother. You obviously feel you can do a better job so you can have it. It's all yours. And as for this not being about money – if you haven't worked out yet that *everything's* about money then you're a more stupid old woman than I thought. Now if you don't mind, I'm leaving.' She swept past Emily, who was standing with one hand clasped to her throat and the other spread across her open mouth as she shook her head in disbelief. She followed Margaret out of the parlour to the front door. Margaret stopped for a moment, cigarette holder clamped between her teeth as she pushed the leather of her gloves back between her fingers. Then she opened the door and without looking back said, 'Tell the kid I said so long.'

Howard stood half-hidden behind the plush red velvet curtain at the bottom of the stairs and looked round the Ruby. Business was good, very good. Giving Margaret her head with the place had really paid off. At first he hadn't been sure about her idea of using lots of reds and deep blues in satin and velvet. He feared that, combined with the pleated gold lamp shades, braid and tassels, it might make the place look like a bordello. But she had proved him wrong. Their customers loved the smoky intimacy the colours gave the place and as it was in a basement it had the advantage of helping people forget what the time was, making them linger longer and drink more. Many a customer staggered up the stairs thinking it was about midnight only to discover it was closer to three in the morning and that the odd bottle of wine had become six or seven. Yes, business was very good indeed.

Margaret was standing near the bar which had been installed at the far end of the room. The tables had been reduced in size and increased in number, while maintaining the degree of privacy that late-night drinkers demanded. The small dance floor was still there, and a samba band played alternate nights with a pianist. It was clear that Margaret was in charge but she ruled the Ruby from a position to one side of the polished mahogany counter rather than behind it, bridging the gap between staff and clientèle. She was resting her chin in her hand, her elbow propped on the bar as she listened, apparently enthralled to a man regaling her with some story or other. Her ubiquitous cigarette holder was held between her fingers as she kept her eyes fixed adoringly on the speaker's face.

To his amazement Howard felt something stir inside him and with a jolt realised that he was jealous. Jealous of some stupid little man too pissed to know that he was being used. He stepped forward a little to get a better view of her. Her hair was pulled back into its now familiar chignon and she was wearing a gold brocade dress cut to make the best of her figure. It had a low-cut back that showed off the curve of her neck and the straps lay across her shoulders, dipping to a curving at the front revealing the fullness of her bust. (*No 'falsies' there!* Howard thought to himself.) The dress carried on in a close-fitting straight line to mid-calf where it was slit up the back. Across her arms was a stole which, because she was leaning forward, draped across the swell of her golden backside. One hip was swung out in a provocative manner, revealing more of her legs as the slit up the back of her dress swung open. It had been a long time since Howard had regarded Margaret as anything other than one of his protegées. He was surprised to realise that in training her he had forgotten what it was that had first drawn him to Margaret Timpson. How could he have had such a sensual woman at his fingertips for all these years and done nothing about it? Well, maybe it was time he changed that.

He enjoyed the sensation of watching her while she was unaware of his presence, and used the cover of lighting a cigarette as an excuse to stay looking at her a little longer. As he did so he noticed with a wry smile that maybe she wasn't being quite so attentive as her speaker imagined. Without moving the top part of her body she carefully slipped off one of her high pointed shoes and flexed her obviously aching toes, rubbing them up the back of her well-turned calf. She then did the same with her other foot, finally straightening up with a gale of laughter as the story came to an end.

'That's very funny, darling. Very funny indeed. I really must try to remember it. Now look, I've been so busy listening that I've let you sit there with an empty glass.' She turned to attract the attention of one of the waiters and, as expected, when he came over to take the order her companion insisted on buying the next round, as well as a drink for herself. She accepted the proffered note, tucking it into her cleavage saying she would get it later.

She began to work her way round the room, stopping first at one table and then the next with a friendly word here and there. By the time she made it over to the door all the tables she had stopped at had ordered more drink and she had added quite a few notes to the stash down the front of her dress. 'Evening, Howard. Enjoying the floor-show?'

'What floor-show?' he asked, looking round the room to see what he had missed, steering her back towards the bar with a hand in the small of her back.

'Why, me in action, you fool! I saw you come in and hide behind the curtain. What sort of manageress do you think I am not to know exactly who comes and goes in my own club?'

'And I thought you hadn't noticed. I'm impressed, Margaret. You're doing a good job. I was looking at the books the other day and was reassured to see that profits are nicely up.'

'Of course they are, darling. Look at them. Lambs to the slaughter. Got more money than sense, this lot, but whom am I to complain? They want to spend it and I'm happy to help them. Fools!' As she spoke of her customers the smile on her face never faltered and anyone looking over would have seen Margaret Timpson talking to the boss in her usual friendly manner, never thinking for one moment that she was pouring scorn on them all.

'What time are you planning on shutting tonight?'

She gave an elegant shrug of her shoulders. 'When the last silly sod goes. Darlings, good night!' she added more loudly, waving an almost regal hand towards a drunk couple staggering up the stairs.

'Mind if I wait for you?'

Good God! she thought. *Don't tell me he's finally going to make a move?* Mentally she cast an eye round the flat upstairs, hoping that it would be tidy enough for him and, more importantly, that no signs of her previous night's visitor would be visible. Out loud she just said, 'If you like. Scotch and soda as usual?' He nodded.

Somehow, but without the customers becoming aware of being rushed, she managed to get rid of them all by two-fifteen – very early for the Ruby – and was locking up. 'That's OK, Pamela. You go. I'll finish off,' she said to the last of the waitresses who was clearing glasses from the tables. The girl didn't need telling twice. No sooner had she gone than Howard called Margaret over to the bar.

'Leave that. Let the staff do it in the morning. Come and have a drink.' He slid off the high, leather-covered stool as he spoke and moved round the bar. 'How does champagne sound?'

'Delicious as ever.' She turned off a few more lights as she made her way over to take his place on the stool and watched as he took a bottle from the refrigerator behind the bar and opened it with a firm hand. He found the glasses and slowly poured her one, handing it to her with his usual half bow. She laughed as she took it. 'Come and sit round here with me. I can't have the boss on the wrong side of the bar, can I?' It was his turn to do as he was told and as he came to join her she ran her hand up her neck, easing the tension there.

Howard didn't sit down but walked round behind her and gently removed her hand. 'Let me.' He put his hands on her almost bare back and began to massage it. She let her head drop forward, making the vertebrae stand out a little, and with practised fingers Howard ran his hands down her neck, feeling the knots and pushing against them.

Margaret wanted to yell with sheer joy and pleasure. This was what she had been working towards since he had started to transform her in 1945. Eight years since then, six since they opened the club. Six years of wanting and waiting and at last it looked as if it would pay off. His hands felt warm against her bare skin and despite her tiredness she felt alive and vibrant. Neither of them spoke. Howard used his thumbs at the base of her head and his fingers spread across her shoulders. The expectation made her feel as if she were going to suffocate and when his hands dropped forward so his fingers were almost tucked inside her dress and he finally bent to kiss the nape of her neck she couldn't stand it any longer and turned to kiss him back.

It was if he had lit a fire inside her. One minute she was sitting on the bar stool, the next they were lying half-naked across the bar itself passionately making love. Never mind the various men who had kept her company in the small flat over the years. They didn't matter. Nothing mattered except Howard.

'My God! Just think what I've been missing all this time!' he gasped a few minutes after he'd collapsed on top of her and lay panting, bathed in sweat. She said nothing but wrapped her legs round him, holding him, not wanting to let go, suddenly scared about what would happen next. Would eight years of wanting be over in a few moments? Would he get up and go or . . .

Her fears were unfounded.

'I take it you have a bed upstairs?'

'Of course. Care to join me?' Feeling slightly awkward, they climbed off the bar and gathered their discarded clothes. Margaret simply wrapped her stole round her and led the way to the tiny office behind the mirror of the bar and up the narrow staircase to the flat. Behind her all Howard could see were her stocking tops and the sway of her hips wrapped in the stole. As soon as they got upstairs he unceremoniously dumped his clothes in the living room and grabbed her again. This time they shed all their clothes and when they woke up the next morning in a tumble of sheets their progress from the living room, down the hall and into the bedroom could be traced by a trail of garments.

Margaret usually had no problem in dealing with her lovers the morning after the night before, but somehow Howard was different. She felt like a foolish virgin – wanting to ask questions; wanting to know when she would see him again; wanting to know if she had been any good. Wanting to know if he would want her again.

Common sense told her it was because he mattered to her but that didn't stop the questions. Then Howard answered all her silent queries easily and simply. 'Maybe I should start keeping a suit here? What do you think?'

'I think it's a good idea. Anyway, you don't have to ask me. It's your flat.' She made her tone sound as uninterested as possible but inside she was almost drunk with relief as she rose and headed towards the bathroom. 'Margaret, one thing.' She stopped in the doorway, tying her dressing gown sash as she did so.

'What's that?'

'Last night mustn't be allowed to happen again.' She stopped fiddling with the bow she was making and let the ends fall against the billows of satin over her thighs. She hoped her features didn't show the dismay she was now feeling. All she wanted to do was run and lock the bathroom door, sit on the floor and cry. So that was it? He would use the flat as a changing room? How could she have been such a fool?

Howard propped himself up on one elbow, and she felt faintly sick as she looked at his broad shoulders surrounded by the white of her pillow cases. 'I mean, a bit of passion is all well and good but we're both too grown-up and sensible to let an accident spoil things. Margaret, you and I could have a lot of fun but let me make one thing absolutely clear. I have no intention of becoming a father. Better women than you have tried to trap me that way and I don't want to know. I like my life the way it is. The last thing I need to worry about is a child – especially an unwanted one, which in my book they all are. Don't worry, I'll take care of it, but I thought it only fair to warn you that if you're thinking pipe, slippers and children at your feet you've got the wrong man.'

Her shoulders began to shake and eventually she was laughing so hard that she had to hold on to the door jamb to steady herself. Howard had no idea what she was laughing about but the sound was infectious and soon he was laughing with her. 'Thank God! I thought you were going to say . . . well, never mind what I thought. Just don't worry. If I wanted children I wouldn't be running a bloody night club, would I? Now come here.' She virtually leapt back into bed and when he reminded her of what he had just said she spectacularly proved to him that they could indeed have fun, and without the risk of an unwanted pregnancy.

And if, as she stroked and caressed and kissed and nibbled, the thought of Anne slipped across her mind she pushed it firmly out of the way. Anne belonged to another time and place, to a stupid girl called Peg. She had absolutely nothing to do with Margaret and Howard. Nor would she. Margaret had waited too long, and fought too hard to lose it all over a slip-up thirteen years before. This was the chance she had been waiting for and that morning as she and Howard once again tangled themselves in her sheets, she promised herself that within a year she would be Mrs Howard Edwardes. After all, Howard had made it clear that he didn't want children but he had said nothing about a wife.

In fact it took her only four months to get Howard to ask her to marry him and six weeks after that she was walking out of Chelsea

Register Office on a crisp October morning. Her new mink, just one of her wedding presents from him, swing from her shoulders as she admired the way her wedding band fitted so neatly under her diamond and ruby engagement ring. In truth she would have preferred either a diamond solitaire or sapphires, but Howard had insisted on a ruby, arguing that if it weren't for the club they wouldn't be together. Having spent so many years bowing to his better judgement she didn't argue.

Howard stood next to his new wife on the steps and looked down at the friends who had come to wish them well. Some were regulars from the club and therefore knew Margaret better than Howard, others were colleagues from Great Britain Exhibitions, the company Howard was now concentrating on building up, and therefore knew him better than her. A small group were people they both had in common while an even more select band consisted totally of glossy, smiling women who were all staring at Margaret and asking themselves, 'How did she do it?', 'What has she got that I haven't?' or, as one of their number cattily remarked as she threw a particularly large handful of confetti in the couple's general direction, 'Well, girls, she must be the best screw in London!'

Alice stood at the back of the crowd and just for a moment he caught her eye. She raised an eyebrow, half smiled and then lightly kissed her gloved fingers in his direction. Howard inclined his head slightly towards her. It was his way of thanking her for all her years of loyalty. Of course he had said a proper thank you the night before, in the privacy of her mews cottage bedroom, but he knew she was a sensible woman and wouldn't make things difficult. He had given her a final chance to become Mrs Edwardes but she had kissed him on the forehead in an almost condescending manner and laughed at him.

'Howard, don't be so bloody ridiculous. If I thought you meant it, or even loved me, I might consider it, but all you really want is a trophy. I have to say that I think you're right to get married. The "young bachelor about town" can only carry you so far in business. When a man reaches a certain age he needs to look respectable, even if he isn't. Tomorrow morning you are marrying a girl who adores you. She's perfect for the job. Underneath that seemingly fiery nature she's pliable, whereas I would want to interfere the whole time. Now stop being so silly and give me a kiss, you stupid man.' He didn't need telling twice and while the bride shared umpteen bottles of champagne at the Ruby with her friends on her hen night, the groom spent his stag night cosily tucked under the bedclothes of another woman.

'Look, here's the car!' yelled one of the crowd, pulling Howard back to the present. A large sleek Daimler festooned in ribbons and tin cans pulled up in front of the steps. As their friends moved back to let them through Howard suddenly bent down to sweep Margaret off her feet and, amid yells and screams of delight, deposited her in the back of the car before he settled down next to her. She flung her bouquet out of the window, not caring where it landed, and waved madly as the car pulled into the King's Road traffic. But before it could turn right into Sydney Street and then on to the Ruby where they were holding the reception Howard tapped on the driver's shoulder and told him to turn left into Oakley Street and on over Albert Bridge.

'But what about the reception? I mean, we can't not go to our own wedding reception,' Margaret laughed.

'Why not?' asked Howard. 'By the time they realise we're not showing we'll be well on our way to Dorset, and besides, it'll be like it is any night at the club. You'll be chatting to everyone but me, trying to get them to buy more booze, they'll expect you to run round after them and I'll be left admiring my manageress and not my wife.'

'Well, put like that I suppose you have a point. Anyway, I'd far rather be cuddled up having an early night with my husband in front of a roaring log fire than cuddled up with a roaring crowd having an early morning!'

'Oh, very witty, Mrs Edwardes.' He put an arm round her and she snuggled against his shoulder, feeling his solid body beneath her cheek.

'Call me that again.'

'What, Mrs Edwardes?' He chuckled.

'Mmm. I like the sound of it. Mrs Howard Edwardes. It makes me feel as if I belong somewhere.' She put an arm across his body and gave him a squeeze which he returned by tightening his grip round her shoulders.

'I'm glad you've mentioned that because I want to talk you about something. Sweetheart, I want you to stop running the club.'

She let go of him and sat bolt upright. 'But why?'

'It's like you said. Now you're married to me you belong somewhere and that somewhere isn't a club in Knightsbridge. It's with me. I've already found the next manageress. Obviously I want you to stay put just for a while as a sort of hand-over period, say for a month, but after that I would like it if you were at home. Anyway,' he carried on quickly, seeing a look of anger begin to spread over her face, 'if you're at the club until the small hours, and in bed getting your beauty sleep during the day I'll hardly see you. And you won't be able to decorate the flat and accompany me to all the exhibitions during the day, will you?'

The mention of their new home stopped Margaret from letting rip the torrent of abuse she was about to hurl at her new husband. It had never occurred to her that he would want her to give up the club, *her* club, the one she had created, made into one of the best in London and nurtured into a thriving business. But maybe he had a point? The mansion flat was in a large block right in the heart of Maida Vale, overlooking Little Venice. It needed totally redecorating and he had given her an open cheque book to do it. For the time being they were staying in a rented place in Finchley Road but Margaret was keen to get him settled in their own home as quickly as possible. *That way he won't have to spend so many nights at his club*, she told herself. But she wasn't letting him off the hook that easily.

By the time they arrived in Dorset she had let him talk her round to his way of thinking. It had cost him another fur coat and a diamond bracelet. Mrs Edwardes went to bed a very contented woman.

Anne stood and watched as the coffin was lowered into the grave. It had been a simple funeral with just a few people sitting at the back of the church; most of them neighbours from Roupell Street who were clearly there because they felt they should be rather than because they wanted to say goodbye to Emily.

Her death had been typical of her life, so quiet and unassuming. She had just got on with it. One minute she was 'going to spend a penny', the next she was sprawled on the floor. Anne had heard the crash and rushed upstairs to find out what had happened. Emily was sitting in the hall holding her chest with a startled look on her face. 'Sorry to be a bother, love,' she said and, with a noise that sounded a bit like the air being squeezed out of a hot-water bottle, she died.

No fuss. No drama. No Emily.

And now she was being buried with the same lack of fuss. Even the weather couldn't be bothered to do anything much, and the grey drizzle falling from an equally grey sky gradually seeped through their clothes. Mrs Liversey came over and made some remark of regret to which Anne murmured a reply. She knew she should invite them all back to number fifteen for a cup of tea but she couldn't bear it and even though they hovered, waiting for her to say something, she managed to avoid catching their collective eye long enough for them to get the message and drift back to their homes.

She stood looking at the grave for so long that eventually the men leaning quietly on their shovels came over and asked if she minded if they filled it in. 'What? Oh no. No, please carry on. Sorry to keep you waiting.'

'That's OK, miss. Sorry about your trouble,' said one with a thick

Irish accent, and he touched his cap with a respect that seemed more genuine than anything anyone had said to her all morning. She pulled her coat collar up and shoved her hands deep into her pockets as she walked away. She knew she should cry or at least feel some emotion but all she felt was the same flat nothingness that had been with her since Emily died. She wanted to cry but the tears just wouldn't come. She caught the bus home and stared out of the window as it rattled through south London, not seeing anything of the grey October day. It dropped her just outside Waterloo Station and she walked slowly back to Roupell Street.

It felt odd letting herself into the empty house. That morning at least Emily had still been there, lying in state in the parlour. There had been so much bustle when the hearse arrived and the men in their old-fashioned morning coats and shiny top hats had taken her away that Anne hadn't really noticed her going. But now she could really sense the emptiness of the house, even though bits of Emily still remained – her battered coat and hat hanging in the hall; the smell of baking and lavender that always hung in the air.

Wearily she removed the black armband from her coat sleeve and put her own hat and coat on to the stand, catching sight of her reflection in the mirror as she did so. *Now what?* she asked herself, sliding the armband back up her arm. But couldn't find an answer. The clock in the parlour struck quarter-to-something. She glanced at her watch – the one Emily had given her for her sixteenth birthday – and was surprised to see it was quarter to four. Was it really nearly five hours since they had buried Emily? She sighed and set off down the hall into the kitchen to make a cup of tea.

The inertia stayed with her for days as she vaguely drifted around the house. She made a few half-hearted attempts to start going through Emily's things but it felt such an invasion of privacy that she invariably left it after a few minutes. It wasn't until she received a letter just before Christmas asking her to go to see Emily's solicitor that her mood changed.

She sat in the office above Charing Cross Road with a cup of tea carefully on her lap, a rich tea biscuit balanced in the saucer as Mr Sutton went through the document in front of him. The only warmth came from the fire roaring in the small grate on one side of the room. The domed brass hood over the fireplace and the fireguard around it meant that it retained more heat than it gave out, and consequently one side of her felt hot and the other cold. Mr Sutton didn't seem to notice, any more than he saw the threadbare carpet or dust on the old books that were piled round the gloomy room. He just sat and pored over the papers that he must have read a number of times before. The clock ticked loudly on the shelf. He grunted to himself a couple of times before finally looking at Anne over the top of his half glasses.

'Well, me dear. Probably comes as no surprise but she left it all to you,' he said in his staccato manner. 'There's the house. Owned it freehold, y'know. Nearly seven hundred pounds. And this.' He picked up one of the envelopes on his desk and held it out to her. Seeing nowhere else to put her cup she placed it carefully on the floor and took the envelope, noting the wax seal on its flap. 'Come on, me dear. Nothing in there to bite you.' His corns were hurting and he sounded brusque as he spoke to her.

'Do I have to open it now?' His attitude made her want to escape as quickly as she could from this dismal office.

'Course not, me dear. Take it home. Look at it there. Any questions, call me. Now sign here, here and here.' Gratefully she took his pen and signed where he pointed. He blotted the ink and, bending round his voluminous belly, took a key from a bunch on his desk and opened an old-fashioned cash box. He carefully counted out just under seven hundred pounds in crisp white notes and handed them to her. 'You're a lucky gel, me dear. Very lucky. Not many gels your age who have that much money.'

'Frankly,' Anne snapped, 'I'd rather have Emily here and not a penny to my name. Good morning, Mr Sutton.' She stuffed the notes into her handbag, her tone making the man blink at her curtness and later remark to his secretary about 'the rudeness of the younger generation'.

Normally she would have walked home but knowing she had all that money in her bag made her nervous so she hailed a taxi. The driver raised a disparaging eyebrow when he heard she only wanted to go across Waterloo Bridge to Roupell Street. He made Anne feel so guilty that she gave him a larger tip than the journey warranted. Gratefully she scuttled inside. Delaying the moment for as long as she could, she took her time making yet another cup of tea she didn't want before sitting at the table, the brown envelope in front of her. Finally she reached forward and picked it up.

It was nothing special, and obviously didn't have much in it as it was almost flat. She broke the seal, watching the red wax crack and fall on to the table. Cautiously she opened it and put her fingers inside to pull out the contents. Her overriding emotion was one of nervousness but she was also curious. As she expected, there wasn't much inside. A note from Emily, what looked like a recent newspaper cutting and a couple of photographs. She could hear Emily's breathless voice in her head as she read the note.

My dear Annie,

I am sorry I'm not there to look after you any more and hope it hasn't been too much trouble, pet.' (*Only Emily could apologise for her own death,* Anne thought with a weak smile.) 'These are just a few bits I thought you might want. The little photograph was taken in Dorset just after the war and is a lovely image of Peg. The bit from the paper is from 1956 (have to tell you that, love, as I don't know when you'll get this). So you can see she still takes a nice picture. The other snap is Chuck – your father. He was a good man, Annie. Shot down in the war but I think he and Peg would have married if he had lived. Honest, love, really I do.

Well, that's all for now, pet. I hope you'll be happy. You deserve it.

Tata. Love always.

Auntie Em

She put the note down and turned her attention to the other items. First the large photograph of Chuck. She scanned the image trying to see if she could see any resemblance between the young man and herself, but there was none – any more than there had been a likeness between her mother and herself. She felt nothing. It was a picture, that was all. The newspaper cutting was the next thing that came to hand. It was a photograph with a caption. A good-looking, broad-shouldered man had clearly just introduced the sleek woman at his side to the new Queen. The woman had been caught with her gloved hand outstretched and in mid-curtsey. The caption read:

> 'Mr Howard Edwardes, Managing Director of Great Britain Exhibitions introduces Mrs Edwardes to Her Majesty The Queen and His Royal Highness the Duke of Edinburgh at the gala opening of the 1956 Home Maker Exhibition.'

For a moment Anne was puzzled as to why Emily had kept this scrap of newspaper, until she looked at the woman in the picture again. So that was what had happened to her mother. She looked at the picture and felt . . . what? She didn't know.

It was the little snap of the laughing woman on the beach, wind blowing through her hair, and the solemn child by her side that provoked the biggest reaction from her. It wasn't these two people, or the vague memories of that hot day in Dorset, that made the tears she had ached for cascade down her face, but the shadow of the third member of the group. So typical of Emily, there but not there. Only the angle of the sun had given her any presence in the photograph at all.

Anne let the tears pour down her face. Great racking sobs shook her body as at last the emptiness exploded inside her and she really felt

Emily's absence as a tangible thing. She let it wash over her, almost enjoying the pain, luxuriating in the sense of loss. But it couldn't go on for ever and eventually the tears dried and her breath stopped coming in gasps. She didn't bother to dry her eyes; just sat there in the fading autumn afternoon looking at the papers and pictures spread before her until she could no longer make them out in the gloom.

She stood up and switched on the light. *Now what?* She repeated the question she had asked herself after the funeral. It ran through her head over and over again as she tossed and turned in her bed that night, until finally she gave up trying to sleep at four the next morning. She made her way down to the kitchen to boil some milk to see if that might help. The papers were lying on the table where she had left them. She drank her milk and as she did so an idea began to form. By the time she got to the bottom of the cup she knew what she was going to do.

It was easy enough to find the address for Great Britain Exhibitions – she just looked up the telephone number. One phone call later she had the address written on a piece of paper. The fact that it only took her a total of fifteen minutes meant she had the rest of the day to get through before she could set out for the offices in Warwick Avenue. She wasn't quite sure what she was going to do but she dressed carefully, wearing a neat brown wool skirt and yellow twinset under her coat, applied a little bit of make-up and at the last minute put her hair up under her hat in the hope that it might make her look older. It was exactly four-thirty when Anne locked the front door behind her.

She had put one of Emily's fivers in her bag, and with a cool manner that belied her feelings made her way to Waterloo Tube station. The line went direct to Warwick Avenue and as she stepped out into the open it was beginning to grow dark. A fog was also forming. She checked the street numbers against her piece of paper and after a few moments' hesitation turned right out of the station, searching for the building. When she reached it she stood outside, considering her options.

Maybe she should just walk in and demand to see Mr Edwardes and tell him who she was? But he might refuse to see her and have her thrown out, then she would never get to see Peg. It might be safer just to send him a note? But if he didn't read it, or still refused to see her, she would again be stuck. Beginning to wish she had never started what she now felt was a wild goose chase she decided to go to the milk bar over the road. The fog was becoming thicker and beginning to seep into her clothing and tickle the back of her throat. At least with a cup of coffee in front of her she could pretend she was waiting for someone while she decided what to do.

She opened the door of the café, making a set of bells above it jangle.

The warm smell of hot milk and people, and the sound of the Gaggia machine as it frothed the milk, enveloped her as she walked up to the counter to order her coffee. Turning down the offer of a doughnut, cup in hand she looked for a table and found an empty one in the corner, right next to the window.

Right, she told herself firmly. *This is madness. It's not going to achieve anything so why not drink your coffee and go home? Because I can't,* answered an annoying voice in her head. She shook it a couple of times to clear her thoughts and took a sip of coffee. She glanced out of the window and as she did so a rectangle of light cut through the thickening fog. Then the silhouette of a large man blocked the light as he came out and stood on the top step. Anne could tell he was pulling his collar up round his chin and positioning his hat more firmly on his head. He walked quickly down the steps, crossing the road to stand directly on the other side of the glass from where Anne was sitting.

She was almost positive that he was Howard Edwardes. Her fingers were trembling as she quickly opened the clasp of her bag to take out the newspaper cutting. It was difficult, but just as she had persuaded herself she was wrong he turned slightly, looking up the road, and suddenly his profile in the light from the milk bar matched that in the picture. In her haste to leave she almost knocked her cup over but she grabbed her gloves and bag and propelled herself outside. The damp, cold air made her shudder after the warmth of the café and now that she was all but a few feet from him she had even less idea what she was going to do. Suddenly his arm shot up and he seemed to leap into the road. A taxi ground to a halt by the kerb, as did one behind it, both cabbies sure that this man was their fare. As the two drivers yelled at each other Howard quietly got into the first cab. Head down, and not sure what she was doing, she scuttled past him and climbed into the second one just as the other pulled away.

'Follow that cab!' she said breathlessly to the driver.

'Gawd, love, do you know 'ow many years I've wanted someone to say tha'? Couldn't you've picked a better night than this, wiv a real London particular comin' down? What's 'e done, deserted you, 'as 'e?' He gave her a gap-toothed grin over his shoulder as he signalled right and set off a few feet behind the taxi in front.

'No, I'm his niece and we were meant to meet but I was late because of the fog,' Anne lied. It was clearly the right thing to say as it set the cabby talking about the horrible weather and how in the last pea-souper it had taken him nearly two hours to drive round Regent's Park. Anne grunted in the right places, trying to work out where they were going. They came to a junction, turned right, drove a little way along and then left into a much busier road. The extra traffic meant Anne could just about see where they were going and the road signs told her they were in Maida Vale. She was also now just able to see the taxi in front. It signalled left to pull in to a large, sweeping driveway that appeared to curve in front of a very imposing block. She almost yelled at her driver to stop, so worried was she that he might actually take her at her word and literally follow the cab in front to its destination.

'All right, love. No need to take on so. I've looked after "nieces" before.' He winked as he said this, giving the word 'nieces' an odd emphasis. Puzzled, Anne carefully counted out his fare and gave him a tip. She waited a moment to watch him disappear into the thickening fog before walking as calmly as she could down towards the glow that marked the entrance. Her heart was pounding in her chest and she was sure it echoed loudly in the eerie silence that the fog was creating. She followed the path down towards the metal-grilled glass doors and anxiously searched down the rows of bells to see if she could see the name Edwardes. She was about to turn away, disappointed as none of the numbered bells had names against them, when the door opened and a man in a burgundy uniform asked if he could help her.

Oh my God! she thought with horror. *Of course a block of flats like this would have a porter*. She could see beyond the door and down the hallway towards a small booth. The hall was painted pale cream with paintings in heavy gilt frames on the walls and the thick carpet matched the colour of the man's uniform. 'I'm looking for my uncle.' She maintained the lie she had used with the taxi driver. 'I know he lives here somewhere but I've lost the actual number. I mean, I know it's Clive Court.' She glanced at the name on the brass plaque above the bells.

The porter saw the glance. 'And who exactly might your uncle be, miss?'

His tone made it plain he didn't believe her but she managed to stand her ground. Running away would really make him suspicious. She felt close to tears. 'Mr Edwardes, Mr Howard Edwardes.'

The porter's shoulders relaxed a little. 'Ah,' he said knowingly, 'another of Mr Edwardes' nieces, are you? It's number 634 but take my advice, miss, and don't pay a call today. Your auntie's home, if you know what I mean. But I can give him a message, quiet like, miss, if you get my meaning?'

And suddenly she did, understanding not just what he was saying but also what the taxi driver had meant. She felt herself blush a deep scarlet. 'No, no it's all right, really it is. I'll . . . um . . . I'll call him tomorrow. Thank you.' And without waiting to hear another word she turned and ran back towards the main road. The porter watched her until she vanished into the fog, which was now chokingly thick and yellow. He gladly shut the door but some of it oozed under the slight gap below it to swirl down the hall as he made his way back to his cubby hole.

I don't know what these girls see in him, really I don't. Mind you that one was a bit young, even for Mr Edwardes. He shrugged and settled down again with his latest Penguin, dismissing Mr Edwardes' niece from his mind.

Clinging to the railings and walls she made her way along Maida Vale, bumping into other pedestrians as they tried to get home. She didn't know this part of London and hoped she was heading towards the Tube station she'd noticed from the taxi. She used the fog as an excuse not to think about Clive Court or Howard Edwardes. Admittedly it wasn't as bad as some, at least she could see a few feet in front of her, but it was still thick enough to slow everyone down. Occasionally the gloom would be broken by an eerie glow from the lights of a tram or bus but it wasn't enough to be of any real use. She lost her bearings and eventually almost fell into the entrance of Maida Vale Tube. *Thank God!* she thought as gratefully she paid her fare for a single back to Waterloo. Although the Tube journey itself was no slower than usual it was another forty-five minutes before she tentatively felt her way out of the station to Roupell Street.

By the time she got home she had already decided what her next course of action would be.

It took her the best part of a week to write the letter to her mother. The first draft was full of anger and hurt. It ran for five pages and although she felt better having written it Anne knew she couldn't send it. Far from encouraging Peg to meet her, it would probably ensure she never saw her again. The next drafts weren't any easier but by the time she posted the envelope the letter had been cut to one page and was written in a quiet, businesslike tone. All she could do now was wait.

Margaret was bored. In fact she was more than bored, she was fed up. Christmas and New Year were over, all the parties had finished and everyone seemed to have gone into post-festive-season hibernation. Even the January sales didn't excite her any more. Howard had called her at about ten the previous night to say he was staying at his club and, though the noise in the background sounded very un-club like, she hadn't queried it.

That's the trouble, she thought as she drifted from the kitchen to the living room, leaving the breakfast things on the table for Consuelo to clear away. *The only thing I'm not bored with is Howard.* She stopped and peered at her face in the gilt-framed mirror that hung over the sideboard. She was half-dressed and had put on her dressing gown (a heavy daffodil yellow silk creation which complimented her colouring magnificently) over her underwear while she decided how she was going to spend her day, as that would dictate what she would wear. Her reflection stared back at her as she turned her head this way and that. *Not bad for a woman of thirty-seven.* She dabbed a speck of toast from the corner of her mouth and pushed her hair back off her forehead, making sure she didn't dislodge her French pleat. She frowned as the light caught a glint of grey. *I must get that retouched.* She let her hand fall to her side and went to sit on the sofa to flip idly through the latest issue of *Vogue*. She'd already seen it three times but liked having the latest issue around the place. She got up again and moved to the table in the middle of the room where a huge vase of expensive out-of-season flowers stood. She began plucking at the odd drooping leaf.

She was just thinking about calling Prunella to see if she wanted to have lunch when she heard the sound of a key in the door. She listened carefully, holding her breath. No, it was OK, Howard had gone straight into the kitchen. She quickly slipped out of the living room and across the hall into the bedroom, undoing her sash as she went. She really hadn't expected Howard home so early. He usually went straight to work if he stayed at the club, and she knew how much he would hate to see her still in her dressing gown at this time of the morning. She flung it to the floor and grabbed a fine tweed 'sack' dress, throwing it over her head. When the new, loose, unfitted shape had first been introduced in the autumn of '57 she had hated it but then, seeing how the design houses had cleverly tailored it to emphasise bust and waist, she had spent a couple of delirious months reorganising her wardrobe. Even that had eventually palled and all Margaret could think now was delight that it was so easy to get into.

Her mules hurtled across the carpet as she kicked them off and pushed her feet into her stilettos. She gave her pleat one final pat and opened the bedroom door, looking her usual immaculate self just as Howard reached for the handle from the other side. 'There you are. I was just beginning to think you'd gone out.' He leaned forward to kiss her and a vague smell of stale cigars and Schiaparelli's Shocking wafted over her. The pit of her stomach tightened as she recognised the cloying thick sweetness of a perfume that wasn't hers. Howard had introduced Margaret to Jean Patou's Joy early in their relationship so it was the only perfume she ever wore, loving it partly for its soft floral warmth and partly for its exorbitant price tag.

'I must change my shirt. Can't go to a board meeting in yesterday's, can I?' Margaret's mouth smiled at him but the expression stopped below her eyes which showed nothing but a deep stillness which Howard either didn't notice or chose to ignore. This wasn't the first time he had come home from his 'club' smelling of another woman. She wanted to fire questions at him. To shout and ask him who it was, what did this woman have that she, his wife, didn't? Where did they go, and why? Instead Margaret just gave him the mechanical smile, fearing she would lose him altogether if she dared say anything.

She opened the door to let him into their bedroom and went to the wardrobe to select a freshly laundered shirt from the drawer. She crossed to put the shirt on the bed for him and stooped to pick up her dressing gown. By the time she was upright again Howard was standing with his dirty shirt undone, loosening his cufflinks, his braces hanging down by his legs. 'Here, let me.' He held out his wrists to her as she deftly removed the studs.

'You know the best thing I ever did was marry you?' She looked at him with surprise and he put his arms around her, pulling her close to his warm body. With his shirt undone the smell of stale cigars and perfume had lessened and even though her common sense told her not to she found herself returning his kiss with her usual passion. 'Lock the door. We don't want the Spanish woman walking in on us, do we?' Margaret knew she should walk to the door, open it and leave Howard standing half dressed but fully aroused. She knew if she did that she would win before the battle lines had even been drawn. But she also knew that she would find it easier to walk on water than turn her back on Howard when he was so obviously eager to have her. She locked the door.

Losing herself in sex she found herself wondering what it was about Howard that made him behave as he did. Why was it that whenever he had spent the night with another woman he always came home and made love to her with renewed vigour? Did he really think that would persuade her she was imagining it? The trouble was that when it was over and she was lying, as she was now, wrapped round him in that lovely post-coital glow, she could believe it really was all right. *Which is why I let him get away with it. Because he always comes home and it's incredible.* She gave a satisfied sleepy smile as Howard glanced at the bedside clock and eased himself out from under the tangled covers.

'I've got to go. You stay there and doze.' He dropped a kiss on her forehead and picked up his clothes, taking them into the en suite bathroom to shower and dress. She lay in bed and listened to the little sounds he made. She stretched languidly as he came back into the bedroom straightening his tie. 'By the way, this arrived for you this morning. Don't forget we've got that reception at the Brussels Embassy tonight.' Margaret groaned at the thought of another night making small talk to yet another group of people tied up with the Brussels World Expo that was taking place later that year. Howard dropped a blue envelope on to the bed, kissed her again and went, shutting the bedroom door with a click behind him.

Margaret propped herself up on her pillows. She wriggled as a hairpin from her now collapsed French pleat dug into her and she swept it out from underneath her with one hand as she picked up the envelope. It had a London postmark and, puzzled, she turned it over, trying to find a clue to the sender before opening it. She couldn't think who she knew in that part of town and she certainly didn't recognise the handwriting. She reached for the paper knife next to the bed and inserted the tip, ripping down the triangular flap. The first two words were enough to make her feel physically sick and the rest of the contents finished the job, sending her retching towards the bathroom.

Dear Mother,

I do hope this letter won't come as too much of a shock but I thought you might want to know that Auntie Emily died in October last year. It was quite unexpected and so sudden that she would have known nothing about it which is good, don't you think? I'm sorry I couldn't let you know sooner, but I didn't know where you were until recently.

Now that I know where you live maybe I could come and visit you and your husband? I would like to renew our association and hope that after all this time you would too? Emily left me her house so you can write to me there. She never did get a phone put in so unfortunately you won't be able to call. Maybe we could get together next week and talk about things?

I look forward to hearing from you.

With kind regards from your daughter,

Anne

She sat on the floor, the letter crumpled in her hand. *My God, what am I going to do? Howard will go mad if he finds out about Anne! Christ, why the bloody hell did that stupid cow Emily have to die? In another few years Howard will have stopped sowing his wild oats and it might be possible, but not now. I'll just have to write and tell her it's not convenient. Except she knows where I live. She might just turn up on the doorstep. Then what? 'Oh Howard, I'd like you to meet my daughter.' That'll go down well and it will be all Howard needs to sue for divorce. He may screw around a bit but he's mine and I'm not letting some stupid girl take away all I've worked for.* Shakily she got up and with her mind made up was able to act decisively.

She brushed her teeth, fixed her hair and make-up, quickly dressing again before going into the study – Howard insisted on keeping a workroom at home. There she carefully smoothed out the letter as best she could and replaced it in its original envelope, gumming the flap down again. Turning it over she scrawled through the address and scribbled next to it 'Not known at this address'. Automatically she dropped it in the tray for Consuelo to post on her way home then realised her mistake and whipped it out again to hide in her bag until she went out and could do it quietly herself.

Margaret gave a sigh of relief as she put it into the post box. What could have been a huge problem had been quickly and easily solved. She immediately forgot about the letter until a week later when another arrived.

She instantly recognised the envelope and the handwriting.

Again it was Howard who dropped it in her lap. It was one of those rare occasions when they had not only shared the same bed the night before but were also eating breakfast together. He made some joke about a 'secret lover' which at any other time Margaret might have used as an excuse to have it out with him about his various dalliances, but knowing the dynamite the letter potentially held she laughed it off. She tried to put it in her pocket but Howard saw her. 'If it's not a secret lover why aren't you opening it now?'

'No reason.' She took it out and slit the paper.

Dear Mother,

I wrote to you recently and I'm not sure if you got my letter or not. I wanted to tell you Aunt Emily died and I had hoped we might meet? If it's difficult for you to get out then why don't I come round and see you? Shall we say four o'clock on Friday?

I look forward to seeing you then.

Anne

Margaret sat very still, not daring to move in case anything she said or did betrayed her. She stuffed the letter into her pocket and went to pick up her tea cup but her hand was shaking too much. Instead she reached for a piece of toast. She didn't want it but she had to do something normal. It felt like sawdust in her mouth and she thought it would choke her.

'Anything interesting?' Howard asked as he flipped through the pages of the *Daily Mail*. 'In your letter,' he explained as he saw Margaret's puzzled expression.

'What? Oh, no. It's just some information about that Spring Ball.'

'Oh, God, that bloody thing. Do we really have to go, sweetheart? It'll be full of dull people braying at us the whole time. You know how much I hate those things.'

No you don't, she thought to herself. *You only hate them if it's something* my *friends want us to do*. She gave a shrug and out loud said, 'If you don't want to go we won't. I'll send our apologies. In fact I've got a few letters to write so I might as well do it now while you finish the papers.'

Howard nodded, not really listening as he bowed his head to look at the stock reports. Margaret left him there and quickly went into the study where she pulled out a piece of their heavy ivory personal stationery. She hesitated for a moment, seeing their name and address embossed at the top, but then shook her head. *Stupid woman, she already knows where you live so you don't have to worry about* that. She thought for a moment before quickly scrawling.

Dear Anne,

Your letter came as a great shock to me. I had hoped you would realise that I did not wish to renew our acquaintance. However, if you insist on seeing me then I shall be, not here, but at the Lyons Corner House in The Strand at four o'clock next Friday. I intend to make this the only meeting we shall have when once and for all I shall clarify the situation.

Should you choose not to wait until then but turn up uninvited and unannounced at Clive Court then I shall not only throw you out but will also call the police. I hope I make myself clear.

She signed it simply, Mrs Howard Edwardes.

Despite her determination to have a good night's sleep Anne failed dismally. It wasn't that she couldn't get to sleep; rather that she spent the whole night tormented by anguished dreams that left her feeling drained and exhausted when she woke. She felt as fidgety as she had done on the day she set out to find Howard. As she prepared to go out the nervousness she had been feeling solidified into a hard, solid lump below her ribcage.

She wanted to create a good impression and look as grown-up as possible, but at the same time didn't want to look so independent that her mother would decide she wasn't needed. She vaguely remembered how fashion-conscious Peg used to be and since receiving her letter with the invitation to tea had pored over all the latest fashion magazines on the racks at W.H. Smith. In the end she had spent a bit more of Emily's money on a pair of well-cut tartan wool trousers, an oversized red sweater and a pair of flat red leather pumps. She had also decided her hair and make-up should be a bit more up-to-date so she pulled at her hair, back-combing the front to make it a bit higher, and with a shaky hand managed to apply her own version of 'the Bardot Look' (well, that was what *Woman's Own* called it). Her eyes were not as heavy as the picture she kept glancing at and although her lipstick was pale she knew it wasn't quite as pale a pink as it should be. But the time she finished she was pleased with her appearance. *Very modern*, she thought without much conviction as she put her new jacket on over the top and, with a determined nod at her reflection, set off.

Margaret had also felt nervous but as she paid the taxi driver at ten to four it didn't show. She too had dressed carefully and her stiletto heels clicked across the shiny marble floor as she made her way through the glittery entrance to find a table for tea. The numerous mirrors confirmed that at thirty-seven she still had a superb figure. The tight bodice of her full-skirted dress emphasised it beautifully beneath her fur coat. Her hat sat neatly on her head, its veil just skimming the bridge of her nose, and she was well aware that a number of men turned to look at her. The sharp slap across the fingers one received from his female companion made her smile and feel a lot better than she had done all day.

As usual Howard had asked her if she had any plans for the day and when she said she wanted to pop into Harrods to get a new scarf to go with a particular suit he had automatically reached into his wallet to give her ten pounds. She made a point of going via Knightsbridge to buy something before hailing a cab to take her to The Strand. The store's distinctive green and gold bag now sat on the empty chair next to her as she peeled off her gloves to take the menu from the nippy. Now that she was actually here she felt surprisingly calm. If Anne thought she could talk her round she was very much mistaken. No, even if she liked the child there was no way she could suddenly spring a . . . how old would Anne be now – fifteen? sixteen?—well, a teenager on Howard. She screwed a cigarette into her holder and lit it. She felt strangely cocooned among the red and gold and marble of the Corner House, as if the rest of the world couldn't touch her. She could just see the clock on Eleanor's Cross outside Charing Cross Station. It was almost four and she automatically checked the time on her wrist watch.

As Margaret looked up she caught sight of someone in one of the numerous mirrors fixed to the pillars around the room. Slowly she drew on her cigarette, watching the girl (well, woman almost) in the trousers and sweater who was standing with her hands deep in her jacket pockets. Despite the frown on her face as she explained to the waitress at the door she was looking for someone, she was very attractive. Not too tall with a shapely figure that, Margaret noted ruefully, in future years men would find interesting. The back-combed, shoulder-length brown hair was neat, unlike some of the messes teenagers (or whatever this generation was now being called) wore and even though her make-up was a bit obvious its wide-eyed effect suited the girl.

Anne took a deep breath and pushed open the double doors. She stood for a moment, horribly aware of the little girl who was jumping up and down excitedly beside her mother as she decided what she wanted her to buy from the expensive array of sweets, cakes and chocolates displayed on the counter between the various restaurants. She swallowed hard and undid her jacket, smoothing her jumper down, and walked into the tea room. Anxiously she looked around, trying to spot Peg.

'What? Oh, I'm sorry, I'm looking for someone,' she explained to the woman at the desk who asked if she could help her. She caught her lower lip between her teeth but, tasting the lipstick, let it go again. 'I think that's her over there.' She held out a nervous finger in Margaret's direction and then quickly pulled it back into her fist, not wanting to be caught pointing.

'Please could you ask her if she's Mrs Howard Edwardes and if so tell her Anne's here?' The woman gave Anne a look which clearly said this sort of errand was below her but, seeing that the woman at the table was obviously well-dressed and of a much better class than this over-painted creature in front of her, she turned and did as she was asked.

'Mrs Edwardes says please would you care to join her?' She led the way towards the table and was rewarded with one of Margaret's most beguiling smiles, the one that drew shop assistants towards her but at the same time kept them in their place. Anne stood uncomfortably, staring at her mother. She seemed more contained than she remembered her and there was a brittleness about her that she was sure hadn't been there before. *Maybe she's feeling as nervous as I am?* she thought.

'Don't just stand there. For goodness' sake sit down. I must say I thought you would have made a bit of an effort.' Margaret took the stub of her cigarette from its holder and stamped it out in the ashtray. Anne's face fell and she seemed to hunch further into her sweater and jacket.

Oh God, thought Margaret, *she looks so grown-up. Here was me thinking I looked good at thirty-seven. Compared with her I look so out-of-date.* At the same time she felt a stab of something she didn't quite recognise go through her. She wanted to reach out and hold Anne but she managed to push the urge down inside her, realising as she did so that what she had felt was a flicker of maternal love. That realisation, together with Anne's appearance, had the effect of making her even sharper.

'Now, let's get this over and done with, shall we?' Margaret's tone was businesslike but it belied her feelings. Before she could say anything more their nippy appeared to take their order. Anne reached for the menu to have a look but Margaret stopped her. 'I'll order for both of us. Toasted tea-cakes, crumpets, iced fondants and a pot of tea please.'

'Indian or China?' asked the girl automatically.

'China for me, please,' Margaret replied. 'Which would you prefer?' she asked Anne, who looked surprised.

'Just ordinary tea for me.'

'Indian,' murmured the girl, scribbling on her pad as she bustled off to place the order. They sat in silence for a while, Anne tracing the lines of the doilies beneath the glass-topped table not knowing what to say, and Margaret wanting to make things as uncomfortable and difficult for her as possible. She took her time lighting another cigarette, inhaling deeply then lifting her chin to blow a stream of smoke upwards.

'I was surprised to hear from you. Very surprised indeed. How did you track me down?'

Damn! Margaret said to herself. *I wasn't going to ask that. It sounds as if I'm actually interested . . . But you are interested, aren't you?* argued another voice inside her head, which she ignored.

'I saw something in the paper about Mr Edwardes. There was an old picture of you meeting the Queen at the Home Maker Exhibition so I got the office address and followed him to your home.' Anne dug into her pocket and pulled out the now crumpled cutting, holding it out to show Margaret who took it and studied it for a moment. She frowned and then deliberately screwed it up to drop it into the ashtray among the ash and stubs. Anne just watched her.

'Quite the detective, aren't we?' Margaret said sarcastically, leaning back to let the waitress place their tea in front of them.

'That's the China, that's the Indian.' The girl pointed at the two teapots as she left them on the table.

Anne picked up the milk jug and poured some into her cup. Margaret gave a little smug smile as she picked up her pot of China tea. Of course Anne would put the milk in first. *Howard would have a fit if I did that these days. He'd call me common.* The thought of Howard brought her back to her senses with a jolt. She had to keep Anne away from Howard at all costs. Particularly as she promised to be quite a good-looking woman. The last thing she needed to give Howard was the opportunity to meet another potential conquest.

'So what do you want?' It was a brutal question, harshly asked.

'I was hoping . . . that is . . . I mean . . .'

'Oh, for crying out loud, just spit it out.' Margaret took a sip of her tea and concentrated on buttering a tea-cake.

'Now-that-Emily's-gone-I-was-hoping-I-might-be-able-to-come-and-live-with-you.' It came out so fast it sounded like one long word.

Margaret choked on the bite she had just taken, her face dropping its mask to show her amazement. 'Are you *mad*?' she exploded, her voice losing its carefully acquired genteel tones. Conscious of people's heads turning in her direction she remodulated her tone to its usual level. 'Good God! How the hell do you think I would introduce you to Howard? Darling, I have a surprise for you. This is my bastard daughter, she's coming to live with us. Oh, didn't I mention her to you? Sorry, darling, must have slipped my mind. She was the result of a quick fuck under Blackfriars Bridge during the Blitz.'

Margaret spat the words out with such venom that Anne physically recoiled. What made it even worse was that, as Margaret was aware of the other people around them, she made sure she kept her expression as smooth and cold as possible. She knew what she was saying would hurt Anne and she hit hard and fast, noting with satisfaction the appalled look on her daughter's face. It made what she was doing easier to handle.

'I'm sorry, am I shocking you? Did you expect me to hold out my arms and press you to my beating breast? Well maybe those dreary women in that backwater south of the Thames would do that, but I won't. Listen to me and listen hard. I knew *exactly* what I was doing when I left you with Emily. I could get away with having you around during the war but afterwards the image of the poor grieving widow and fatherless child soon began to pall. You served your purpose, but if I hadn't dumped you when I did I would still be on my hands and knees scrubbing steps in Roupell Street. Howard gave me the chance to get out and nothing, *nothing*, least of all a sulky brat like you, was going to rob me of that.'

Annie don't listen to me! I don't really mean it, cried the irritating voice in her head as the hateful words carried on tumbling out of her.

'I worked hard, bloody hard to get where I am today and I'm not having some stupid girl come along and spoil it all. Oh, and don't think Howard is so naive as to think he married a sweet little virgin. He knew I had form. That's one of the reasons we're so well matched. I excited him in bed then and I still do.' Margaret enjoyed watching Anne blush as she spoke of sex.

'We're good together in and out of bed, and if you're thinking you can write to him and tell him you're my daughter then forget it. First thing he'll do is ask me and I shall tell him I've never heard of you and that you're probably some nasty little slut of a gold-digger. Besides, Howard hates kids as much as I do. The last thing he'd want is a ragamuffin like you cluttering up the place. It's not as if you need a place, is it? I mean, you said you inherited Emily's dump so what's your worry?' She took another long pull on her cigarette and picked up her tea cup.

Anne couldn't believe what she was hearing. Whatever reaction she had expected it certainly wasn't this. *What did I ever do to make her hate me so much?* She winced as Margaret swore, the words totally at odds with the way she looked. Surely no real lady would use words like that? *I'm not going to cry.* she told herself, as Margaret went on and on, finally stopping to place her cigarette holder between her still crimson lips.

'Mother . . .'

'Don't call me that. My name is Margaret,' she sneered across the table at Anne as the voice in her head carried on chattering nonsense at her. *Yes. Yes do call me that, and Mummy and Mum and . . .*

'Margaret,' Anne began again, 'I'm sorry if this is upsetting you but how did you think *I* felt? I mean, Emily was lovely, but she wasn't you. I needed *you*. No matter what you want me to call you, you will always be my mother, and it was my mother I needed and wanted.'

'Well I wasn't there and Emily was and now she's gone and as far as I'm concerned so am I. It's a bloody nuisance that she had to go and die because it means you've come to bugger it all up, but I won't let you do it.'

It was Margaret's off-hand reference to Emily that finally made Anne lose her temper. She pushed her chair back with such force that it fell over, clattering on to the marble floor. Leaning forward, she gripped the edge of the table.

'How dare you? How *dare* you? Emily was ten times more of a mother – of a person – than you could ever be. Look at you, sitting there with your fashionable sneer and fashionable clothes and your stupid husband to keep you. You talk about working hard? I'll tell you what hard work really is. It's what Emily did to keep her and me. It was working late making clothes for moronic spoiled women like you and charging a fraction of what she should because she was so grateful for the work. It was going out early to clean other people's homes and again in the evenings to clean offices.'

By now tears were pouring down Anne's face but she didn't care. She could see other people staring openly at her and the woman she first spoke to when she came in was making her way across the restaurant with a purposeful look on her face. But Anne was now in mid-flow, and determined to finish what she was saying. 'It was pawning her jewellery and her father's gold watch to make sure I could have a birthday party and presents. It was being with me in hospital and not sleeping for three days when I had scarlet fever. It was loving me, and caring for me, and I never told her I loved her because I was too stupid to know that your mother isn't the person who gives birth to you but the one who's *there* for you. You know, I hope one day you will need someone as much as I needed you and find out what it's like when they're not there. I hope with all my heart that you will know that pain the way I did.'

She turned to the woman from the desk who was now holding her in a firm grip by the top of her arm. 'Don't worry, I'm leaving.' She shook the woman off and grabbed her jacket. 'I hope you rot in hell!' she cried through her tears as, head held high, she made her way back out on to The Strand.

'Madam, I'm so sorry.' The woman was apologising profusely to Margaret who had sat ashen-faced throughout Anne's outburst.

'That's quite all right. Please don't worry about it. It was my fault.

I shouldn't have asked her to join me, should I? I'm sorry for the fuss.' Margaret stood up, glanced at the bill, gave the woman the money and pressed an extra ten-shilling note into her hand. She draped her fur across her shoulders, pulled her gloves firmly on to her hands, easing them down between her fingers, and with as much dignity as she could muster she collected her Harrods bag and left.

Outside Margaret hailed a cab, snapped her address at the driver and sank back against the leather seat, her head back and her eyes closed. She felt a prickling at the back of her nose and her eyes began to fill until the tears seeped out from beneath her lashes to trickle down her cheeks. Angrily she brushed them aside, then rummaged in her bag for a handkerchief and her compact. She dabbed at her eyes and quickly put a dusting of powder on her face to hide the marks the tears had made. *Oh Annie*, she thought, *I didn't think you'd mind so much. One day you'll understand why I had to do it. I had to leave you then and today I had to make you leave me. I couldn't risk it with Howard, I just couldn't. You are so right about needing someone. Trouble is, the person I need is Howard, not you. That's why I didn't want you then and I don't want you now.*

Margaret knew her last thought was a lie. Even to herself she had to lie, but it was the only way she could make herself believe that the feeling gnawing at the pit of her stomach was nothing to do with losing Anne. She lifted her chin defiantly and gave her make-up one last check before shutting her compact with a click to drop it into her handbag. She arrived at Maida Vale to discover Howard had called to say he would be staying at the club and for once she was glad that he wasn't going to be home. It was one of those nights when more than anything else she needed to be by herself.

Anne made it to just outside the tea-room doors before she broke into a run, propelling herself out of the main entrance so fast that she ran straight into a bowler-hatted man. 'I say . . .' he began, but with a hurried apology shouted over her shoulder she left him scrabbling around for his hat, muttering about the 'younger generation'. She didn't know where she was going but ran blindly down the road, not caring that people were staring at her as she went. In an attempt to escape the throng she darted across the road and turned right up one of the side streets off the main road. Still she kept on running until, gasping for breath, she stopped and leaned against a building as she tried to calm down.

How could she? Whatever else Emily was, she didn't deserve to be looked down on by her mother. Despised for bringing up her own child? No, it just wasn't right. If only Margaret could have heard the way Auntie Em used to speak about her long after she'd left them to fend for themselves. She would give Anne a hug and tell her how much fun Peg was. It was only recently that she had begun to realise that Emily had always ensured Anne knew that she wasn't her real mother, that she didn't forget Peg. And for what? To be called names by a woman who was no better than a – what was it Em used to call them?—guttersnipe. That was what Peg was, no more than a guttersnipe.

The sound of the word in her head made her feel a bit better. Having recovered her breath she dragged the back of her hand across her face, mopping away the last of the tears, and began to walk down the road again. She had taken so many different twists and turns that she had lost her bearings. She knew that Covent Garden fruit and veg market was behind her somewhere but she wasn't too sure where she was. Looking up, she saw the sign Great Queen Street above her on the wall, so that meant Kingsway was ahead of her. For home she would have to turn right but even though the street was filling up with people wrapped up against the January dreariness as they headed for the warmth of their own homes, she didn't want to go back to Roupell Street yet. It was getting dark. She glanced at her watch and was surprised to see it was only quarter to five. Had all of that really taken less than forty-five minutes?

She began to make her way slowly towards the British Museum, not because she really wanted to go there but because at least it gave her a direction in which to walk. The scene with her mother replayed itself over and over in her head. *But what did you expect?* she asked herself as she crossed High Holborn into Southampton Row. *Did you really think she would scoop you up, like she said? Yes, I think I did. No,* she corrected herself, *I hoped she would.* But whatever she had expected she had never thought for one moment that it would be quite so vicious or so nasty. Unpleasant and probably uncomfortable yes, but vicious, no. When she reached the Museum she was told that it was just closing so with a resigned shrug she turned and retraced her steps back to Southampton Row, taking the longer route via Russell Square.

The streets were now much more crowded and glancing up as she crossed the road she saw a clock which told her it was ten past five. She was half way across the street when she stopped dead, staring up at the clock, making other pedestrians bump into her and grumble. A car honked its horn as the lights changed and she scurried to the safety of the opposite pavement. Still gazing at the clock she made her way to the building over which it hung. Pitman's Training College stated the sign above the white stone portico. She hadn't thought beyond her meeting with Peg. She hadn't planned what she was going to do if her mother said 'no'.

Emily's money wouldn't last for ever and, even though she now owned the house outright, she would still have bills to pay and food to buy. Anne had left school as soon as she could; it hadn't occured to either her or Emily that she was bright enough to continue her education. And anyway they couldn't have afforded it. Since leaving school Anne had been helping Emily, often covering cleaning jobs for her when she wasn't up to it. But at the age of seventeen she had no real ideas about what she wanted to do. She had never thought of a time when Emily wouldn't be there to be looked after, or needed, by her. Maybe Pitman's would provide an answer?

Cautiously she pushed open the door and was about to enter when the inner double doors swung open and a stream of chattering girls burst through them, clutching books and laughing to one another about how awful classes had been or comparing typing speeds. Anne pulled back into the porch to let them pass, noticing that they were all obviously wearing skirts or dresses under their coats. Fearing she might be thrown out, or treated with the same disdain that she had experienced at the Corner House, she changed her mind and went back outside, but the idea had been planted.

That night she thought properly about her future – a future that clearly was not going to include her mother or her husband. Peg's husband . . . it was *his* fault she was by herself, not Peg's – Margaret's, she corrected herself. If Howard hadn't been around maybe she would have taken her back? *One day,* she told herself, *I'll let him know just what he's done to me.* She fell asleep with that promise echoing round in her mind.

The next morning, armed with a notepad and a pile of pennies, she made her way to the phone box on the corner and asked the operator to connect her with Pitman's College. Making her voice sound as old as possible she asked about the courses available, when she could start, how much it would cost and what sort of job it might lead to. By the time she'd finished she'd not only covered several pages of her pad with notes, but had also made an appointment to go and see a Miss Freeman.

Despite telling herself that it was Howard Edwardes who had turned her mother against her, Anne still felt the pain that Peg had inflicted on her when they met. She wanted to reject Peg as Peg had rejected her and, even though she knew her mother would never find out, she used Emily's surname when she made her appointment to see Miss Freeman.

A week later Anne walked out into the watery winter sunshine over Southampton Row. As well as using Emily's name, she had just used almost half of Emily's money as the fee for the one-year secretarial course at Pitman's that she would start in the summer term.

'I hope you don't mind, but I bumped into Paula yesterday and invited her to join us tonight.' Howard eyed Margaret's reflection as he fastened his tie in front of the wardrobe mirror. Her reflection in her dressing-table mirror stared back, and she gave a shrug.

'Why should I mind?' Margaret carried on doing her face. *Except*, she thought, *that the bumping into probably happened in bed this morning and she's the latest in a long line of tramps. Silly cow, doesn't she realise that he'll soon get bored and come home?* She sat back from the mirror, blotted her lipstick and got up to put her dress on.

Howard openly watched her in the reflection as she stepped into her Balenciaga gown and turned her back towards him. 'Do me up, darling.' He stood behind her and reached for the zip but instead of pulling it up ran his finger along her spine instead. She gave a little shudder and he bent to kiss her neck. 'We'll be late.' There was a note of laughter in her voice.

'So what?'

'But it's our party.'

'So we can be as late as we like.'

Margaret allowed herself to be seduced and hoped no one noticed she was a little flushed when they walked into the living room to greet their first guests. 'So sorry,' she apologised. 'I hope Consuelo has been looking after you? Good. Pru, darling, don't you look wonderful, and Harry, you look gorgeous too.'

Howard smiled. No question about it, Margaret was still at her best when she was hosting a party, and he had to admit she was still a very attractive woman. Maybe it was time he stopped playing the field? Depending on how tonight went this might be a good time to put his proposition to her. After all, he would have to get a move on as time certainly wasn't on their side.

'Howard, look who's here. Paula, it's lovely to see you again. It's been far too long.' Margaret stood next to Howard and slipped her arm through his. He squeezed it with his elbow. *Good*, thought Margaret, *that's another one I've seen off*. 'Please excuse me,' she said out loud, and extracted her hand, leaving Howard to talk to his guest. She noticed ten minutes later that Paula was still chattering away to him but judging by the look on Howard's face he already was bored. Margaret gave a happy smile and settled down to enjoy her own Christmas party.

The last guests left at around two the next morning and Howard stood with his arm around Margaret's waist waving them goodbye. 'Merry Christmas,' they whispered loudly down the corridor, giving a final waggle of their fingers as they disappeared into the lift. 'I thought they'd never leave,' said Howard as he shut and bolted the door. 'Fancy a nightcap?'

'Mmm . . . yes please, make mine a scotch and American, will you, darling?' She kicked off her shoes and sank on to the sofa, curling her legs up underneath her as she lolled against the arm. 'So, how do you think it went?'

Howard handed her a tumbler and she eased her body up so he could sit next to her. She leaned back against him and he kissed the top of her head gently. 'Wonderful. With you organising our parties I never have to worry, but I must say even by your standards this was pretty good.'

'Thank you, darling. I must say I thought Karen looked dreadful, and who on earth was that funny little man she had tucked under her armpit?' They started discussing their guests, not very kindly, and Margaret had to concentrate very hard not to react when Howard mentioned Paula.

'I think I made a mistake by inviting her. She's really not our sort of person, is she?'

'No, not really, so it was particularly kind of you to ask her. I mean it can't be much fun for a single woman of that age over the Christmas period, can it?' She hoped Howard wouldn't realise that Paula was only five years older than herself.

'No, I suppose not. Actually I think Christmas can be pretty dull for any grown-up, alone or not.'

'What on earth do you mean?'

'Well . . .' He took another swig of his scotch. 'It's true what they say about Christmas, isn't it? I mean about it being for children.'

Margaret sat up and twisted round to look at him. 'Howard, what are you trying to say to me?' How she kept the note of panic out of her voice she didn't know. Had Anne somehow contacted him without her knowing? She thought she had got rid of her nearly a year ago. Surely she wouldn't suddenly have decided to get in touch now? She stood up and made her way over to the bar to replenish her glass.

'Well,' Howard said slowly, 'I was thinking maybe we should try for a child.' She spun round so suddenly that the glass shot out of her hand and smashed against the marble fireplace, shattering into a thousand pieces.

'Say that again.' Had he really said what she thought or was she drunker than she realised?

'I said, how about having a baby?'

'But I thought you hated the very idea of having children.'

'Yes, I did. But why am I working my backside off if I've got no one to leave it to? Darling Margaret, not even you could spend all that I'm making these days, and maybe I'm vain enough to want my name to carry on. We can afford it, and we can easily get a nanny so you won't have to worry after you've had the baby and . . .'

'Hang on a minute. I haven't said yes yet and you're already employing a nanny. I need to think about this, get used to the idea first. You can't just say "let's have a baby" and that's it, you know.'

She knew her tone was revealing her sense of panic but she couldn't help herself. It was easy for him. All he had to do was pump away, take aim and fire. She was the one who would have to carry it and, assuming she could actually conceive, how would Howard react to her when she had a huge belly? What if she couldn't conceive? At thirty-eight it might be difficult. 'I need to think about it a little,' she repeated as she reached for a fresh glass and poured herself a neat scotch.

'Fine. But wouldn't it be wonderful if I could get you pregnant next year and we could have a baby in a new decade? I'd like that. A baby born in the sixties.'

Margaret managed to avoid giving Howard an answer until early in January 1959. She knew she didn't really have any choice in the matter. If Howard wanted a baby then that's what he would have. If she didn't consent there was always the chance he might go and get one of his girlfriends pregnant. Nothing wrong with that, it would at least save her the hassle, but it would also give him an excuse to divorce her. No, whether she liked it or not she would have to have a baby. Even before she agreed he'd stopped using condoms, but just in case she made an appointment with a discreet doctor in Harley Street for a full medical.

'Well, Mrs Edwardes, I see no reason why you shouldn't be able to conceive. You would be considered an elderly *primagravida* but it's not impossible at your age.' Doctor Haslan looked at her over the top of his glasses.

'I'm sorry, what is an elderly prim – whatever you said?'

'*Primagravida*. Elderly *primagravida* means elderly first-time mother.' He waited for her response, for her to tell him that this wouldn't be her first child, but she said nothing so he didn't pursue it. After all he might be wrong (although he doubted it) and he didn't want to offend her. She seemed healthy enough and was paying him as a private patient. 'Now,' he continued, 'as I said, there's no *medical* reason why you shouldn't conceive but let me give you a few hints, if I may, just to help.' Margaret listened carefully; she wanted all the help she could get and at this stage all advice was welcome.

It was about the same time, at the end of April, when Margaret's pregnancy was confirmed (albeit at a very early stage) and Anne finally qualified from Pitman's with a typing speed of 120 and shorthand of 50 words a minute.

Independently both mother and daughter were delighted.

'Mr Edwardes?' Howard spun round to face the nurse. It was early in the morning and he had been waiting in the hospital all night. His chin was stubbly, his tie hung loose round his neck and his top button was undone. 'Don't worry,' she laughed, and he noticed her dimples, 'everything's fine. They're both fine. You've got a daughter. A healthy seven pounds ten ounces, and she's yelling for all she's worth. Mrs Edwardes has had a chance to tidy herself up a bit and she wants to see you, so if you'll follow me.'

Howard was surprised by how nervous he felt. He made the nurse stop by the water fountain where he took a long drink and moistened his hands to smooth down his hair. They had arrived at about seven the night before and even though he had originally said he would stay with her he had realised he couldn't face it. He had spent the rest of the night either dozing on the couch or walking up and down. It was now five-thirty. The baby had been born nearly an hour earlier but Margaret had insisted that no one told Howard until the afterbirth had been delivered and she'd a chance to clean up and put on a fresh nightdress. The midwife had told her that she was sure Mr Edwardes wouldn't mind. But Margaret, despite her crushing tiredness, had pointed out with surprising frostiness for a woman who had just delivered that she knew her husband better than anyone else and even if he didn't mind, she certainly did.

When Howard walked into the room Margaret was half-sitting, half-lying in bed, her hair loosely brushed about her shoulders, wearing a touch of pale lipstick. The room smelled of Joy and as he breathed in the familiar scent rather than the sour-sweet smell of babies that seemed to permeate the very walls of the hospital, he began to relax. 'How are you, sweetheart? Sorry I wasn't there. I just couldn't take it. I feel such a rat.' It was a lie. He didn't feel a rat at all. He knew it. Margaret knew it. When he had first left her alone she had let rip, yelling every name she could think of after him (some of which almost made the nurses blush), but as the night progressed she was glad he wasn't there. She had forgotten how very undignified childbirth could be and was ultimately grateful that he hadn't seen her in such a state.

'It's OK. I'm tired but fine. Have a look at her. She should be in the nursery but I made them wait until you'd seen her.' She pointed to the cot next to the bed and, not knowing what else to do, Howard walked cautiously over and peered in. As he did so the baby woke up, yawned and stared at her father with the brightest blue eyes he had ever seen. Then she stuck a tiny fist in her mouth and went back to sleep.

It was the first communication he ever had with his daughter and it was love at first sight.

All his fear evaporated and a feeling like warm runny honey seeped through him. 'She's perfect,' he whispered. 'Those eyes. Those incredible eyes.' He looked at Margaret, who was grinning widely with happiness and relief. When she had first heard it was a girl she had wanted to scream. All that effort, that pain, that horrid lumpishness for the last nine months, and for what? A lousy girl. She was terrified that Howard would reject them both. That he would still go out and get some mistress pregnant, and keep doing it until he had a son. But she couldn't remember ever seeing such a look of pure joy on his face before, and in seeing it she knew she had finally won. That no matter what, Howard would stay with her.

It was May 1962 and Anne was trying to make her first career move. She had worked for the same company since qualifying nearly three years earlier. Starting in the typing pool at Hesketh, Dinglefield & Company, a large legal firm in the City, she had worked her way up. She was now second senior secretary to Mr Hesketh and was in line to take over the senior position in two years' time when Miss Holdgate retired.

Coincidentally, among the firm's big clients was Great Britain Exhibitions and it was when she was taking the coffee in for Mr Hesketh one day that she had heard Mr Edwardes say, 'Oh, by the way, Arthur, I'm in the market for a good personal assistant so if you hear of anyone let me know.' As usual her presence was not acknowledge by the two men beyond a perfunctory 'Thank you' from Mr Hesketh. Her hands were trembling as she put down the tray and left the inner office as quickly as she could.

Anne had sat down at her desk feeling slightly stunned. She knew she was ready to move jobs but did she dare try to get the job with Howard Edwardes? It was too good an opportunity to miss, but did she have the courage to apply? Surely it couldn't be that easy? One overheard comment and that was it – a new job that would put her within reach of . . . No, she *mustn't* think like that. It was a good job in its own right. This was about her, about Anne, not Margaret. Nevertheless it was because of the link with Margaret that, irrationally, she knew she would have to apply. What she hoped to achieve by working that close to Margaret's husband she didn't know, but at least she would be in the right place . . .

Miss Holdgate reprimanded her for daydreaming and she had quickly put her earphones on again to carry on with Mr Hesketh's dictation. It took her two days to pluck up the courage to phone the personnel department at Great Britain Exhibitions and ask about the job. The woman seemed surprised and asked how she knew about it.

'I'm currently with Hesketh, Dinglefield & Company,' she had explained, hoping that the woman wouldn't ask any more questions. She didn't.

'I'd better see you then. Could you come next week, say Tuesday, at three?' Anne was about to say it might be difficult to get out of the office but realised that if she did so it would be clear that Mr Hesketh knew nothing about her applying for the job.

'That'll be fine.' The next day she began to develop toothache (or so she implied to Miss Holdgate, whose badly fitting dentures guaranteed Anne a sympathetic ear) which led to a mythical appointment with the dentist. So here she sat, being interviewed for the position of personal assistant to Mr Edwardes, managing director of Great Britain Exhibitions. Mrs Helen Johnson was looking over her papers carefully.

'You do seem very young to be seeking such an appointment, and it will be quite a leap from the post you currently hold.' She sounded doubtful.

'I know I can do the work you have described. Also my legal secretarial experience would mean I understand any such documentation. My speeds have improved since I qualified. My shorthand is now 130 and my typing 60. Both are accurate and I am also quick at audio work.' Did she sound as desperate as she felt? 'I'm quite happy to take a test.'

Mrs Johnson put the papers down and looked at the girl through half-closed eyes. She might only be twenty-one but she certainly seemed a lot older. She presented herself well, not too much make-up, her hair was nicely done and she was pleased to see it hadn't been over-teased into one of those 'beehives' people were talking about. It was also nice to see a young woman in a suit for a change, still, she felt, the best attire for an office, instead of these sleeveless dresses that some were wearing. And it wasn't too short. 'Yes, that would be a good idea.' She gave Anne a notepad and pencil and noted with approval the clean white gloves she removed before sitting, pencil poised, ready to start her test.

Mrs Johnson spoke clearly but quickly, on occasion speeding up a little to see if Anne asked her to repeat anything. She didn't, even though Helen was sure she must have missed some of what she said. Ah well, the transcription would prove that. She showed her to the typewriter and with a sense of relief Anne saw it was the same model as the one she used at Hesketh, Dinglefield. Mrs Johnson asked for four copies. Anne put the top page together with the carbon papers and copy sheets and turned to her shorthand. She began typing under Mrs Johnson's watchful eye. She didn't falter once and the older woman was impressed to see that not only did she check the top copy, but also those underneath. She removed the carbons and handed the work across the desk, sitting neatly with her legs crossed as it was checked.

'I must say that you are certainly accurate in your work.' Mrs Johnson looked at it again thoughtfully. *She's easily the best I've seen so far and at the rate Mr Edwardes gets through his PAs I could save myself a lot of bother by giving her the job and keeping all the rest of the applicants' details on file for the next time he's looking.* She looked up at Anne and smiled for the first time. 'I think it might be an idea if you met Mr Edwardes. Would you mind waiting a moment?' Anne shook her head.

Does this mean I've got the job? she asked herself. She swallowed hard as Mrs Johnson left the room, taking the typing with her. The moment Anne heard the door click behind her she opened her bag and took out her mirror. She didn't know how long she had but she quickly touched up her lipstick and checked her hair, tucking a stray wisp behind her ear just as she heard voices in the other office. By the time Mrs Johnson walked back in she was sitting as calmly as she had been left with her handbag at her feet. She stood up as Mr Edwardes spoke to her. She hoped he wouldn't remember her from Mr Hesketh's office. If he did he didn't say anything.

'I understand from Mrs Johnson that you might be just the girl I'm looking for.' He smiled at her and she felt the tension in her shoulders ease.

'I hope so.'

'This is good, clean work – you should see some of the messes I had to endure with my last PA. Disaster area looking for somewhere to happen, and that wasn't going to be my office. Right, Mrs Johnson?' The older woman just smiled. In fact Melanie had been a very good PA but had lasted only six months. When she handed in her notice she had refused to give a reason for leaving, but as it was quite obvious that Mr Edwardes didn't want her there any longer there was no point in trying to find out. Mrs Johnson assumed it was the usual, and as Mr Edwardes gave the girl a glowing reference she guessed she was right.

'If you have any questions please ask Mrs Johnson, but I look forward to working with you . . . Anne.' He glanced at the notes in his hand, checking her name as he gave them back to Mrs Johnson, and shook Anne's hand before leaving the room.

The door shut with a click. 'Well, Mr Edwardes likes you so it looks as if you have the job. Subject of course to the usual references. I'll have to contact Mr Hesketh and check all that is in order but assuming it is and I see no reason why it shouldn't be, do you – when can you start?' Anne blinked at her. She hadn't thought about references. Maybe Mr Hesketh wouldn't give her one, not when he found out how she heard about the job. He was always going on about the sanctity of the office, and as for a notice period . . .

'I don't know. That is,' she hurried on, 'Mr Hesketh and I, we've never discussed it.'

'Leave that to me. I just hope it will be sooner rather than later. Mr Edwardes needs looking after,' she said with a softness in her voice. 'But I'm sure you'll get the hang of it and learn his ways very quickly. Now, I assume after all you've heard you do still want the job?' Anne nodded. 'Well in that case, welcome to Great Britain

Exhibitions. I'll be writing to you once all the formalities are in order and I look forward to you joining us as soon as possible.' She went on to outline the terms of Anne's employment, including her salary. It was significantly more than she was receiving and startled her, bringing home for the first time the seniority of the job she had just acquired.

She virtually floated out of the building and nearly hugged the newspaper vendor when she bought her copy of the *Evening Standard*. She did have the grace to feel guilty the next day when Miss Holdgate asked her how she'd got on at the dentist's. She spent the next two days on tenterhooks waiting for a reaction from Mr Hesketh which, when it came on Thursday, wasn't nearly as bad as she had expected. He was cross but also clearly pleased that one of their more important clients had chosen to take on a member of his staff. He went on to lecture Anne about how important it was that she performed well as, after all, it would reflect on Hesketh, Dinglefield & Company in general and him in particular. And because he was concerned about confidentiality he told Anne she could go the next day. Anne was relieved and the following Monday walked into the Warwick Avenue offices of Great Britain Exhibitions to start her job as personal assistant to Mr Howard Edwardes.

PART THREE

Break-Down

'Jo, I've got some great news!' Simon came crashing into the flat, slinging his briefcase down and hurtling into the living room where Jo was sitting on the floor surrounded by shooting and editing schedules. 'Will you stop scribbling and listen to me?' He stood over her as she carried on with what she was doing. He was trying hard to be nice to her, to make things like they used to be, but as far as he was concerned Jo wasn't even trying. Couldn't she at least stop scrawling and listen to him when he asked her to? He began to wonder why he was bothering if Jo wouldn't even meet him half way.

'Sorry, I just needed to write down that thought. Now, what's this great news?' She looked up at him and was surprised to see how animated he was looking.

'I've done really well this last month so I've been asked to go on the stand at the Home Maker Exhibition for all of next week. It's brilliant! The guys who attend the show always get millions of new customers signed up on the spot. That's mainly 'cos the punters aren't thinking about what they're doing and so they're easy to talk into buying extra products – silly sods! But what should I care? It just means loads of commission. Oh,' he added as an afterthought, 'It'll also mean we'll get to see a bit more of each other as well.'

Jo's heart sank. The last thing she wanted was Simon at the Pimlico Centre. He was sure to hear something about her and Alan. She didn't want Simon to find out it was over between them from someone else – that would be the coward's way out. She badly wanted to tell Simon their relationship had run its course, but she wanted to do it in her own way and in her own time. 'That's great.' She noticed he'd put his commission before her in order of importance.

'You don't sound very enthusiastic. I thought you'd be pleased.' He slumped down on to the sofa, scattering the carefully organised piles of papers Jo had put there.

'I *am* pleased. It's just that I doubt if we'll get that much time together. Don't forget I'm not always on the exhibition floors when I'm there, and I'm spending a lot of time on the other programmes now.' It sounded like a feeble excuse. Poor Simon, he was trying so hard to be nice but she just couldn't respond. Maybe now was the time to tell him about Alan?

'Fine, if you don't want to see me or can't be bothered to fit me into your busy schedule,' he scuffed a pile of her papers petulantly with his shoe, 'then I quite understand. Work, as usual, comes first.'

He pushed himself to his feet. 'I'm going to the pub. Don't worry about dinner, I'll have a curry with the lads.' He had gone before she could say anything, which made her feel even more guilty as she hadn't even thought about their evening meal.

Simon had in fact already agreed to meet some of his friends and discuss their impending game of rugby that weekend. Now he had a good reason to go out and pass the blame back on Jo. She really was being impossible these days! By the time he was staring into the bottom of his fifth pint he was sounding off in no uncertain terms about her behaviour. 'OK, so I know she has this job and I know it's important to her but I think I should still come first. I mean, I'm her bloody fiancé, aren't I? She's got to get her priorities right. If she's not careful she'll find that work has used up all her time and she'll have forgotten to have babies!'

'You telling us you're not up to it, Si?' asked Stuart lewdly.

'Listen, Stu. It's not me. I can keep it up as long as I want. It's her. She's getting frigid. You would have thought she'd be grateful for what she can get, wouldn't you?'

They nodded, publicly agreeing with him even though a couple of the lads felt he was being a bit unfair. 'Don't suppose she's found out about Lindsey, do you?' asked Clive.

'How could she? Unless one of you lot's been spouting your mouth off and its got back to her. Anyway, it's not that often and she's so busy she probably doesn't even notice. Doesn't even care, if you ask me.' He stared gloomily into his glass. He'd been playing around with Lindsey for about six months now and although it wasn't serious he knew that if she found out it would end his relationship with Jo, which, despite what he said, he didn't want to happen. 'She's only got herself to blame, hasn't she? I mean if she won't give it me I've got to get it somewhere. Only natural.'

'Come on, Si, you'll have us all blubbing into our beer if you go on much longer. How about that curry?' Their worries about Simon's sex life were brushed aside as they noisily left the pub.

Simon came home very drunk and fell into bed long after Jo had gone to sleep. He reached out for her but she only half woke up and pushed him off before rolling on to her side and going straight back to sleep. The next morning Simon had his usual hangover and mumbled an apology which Jo accepted with a shrug. She had arranged to go in late, leaving Tony to set up the day's first shot, and she was keen for Simon to leave on time. Sitting in her handbag was a home pregnancy test.

He eventually left and she stood at the window, half hidden behind the curtains making sure he had driven off down the road before picking up her bag and going into the bathroom. She had read the instructions the night before and even though they said she could do the test any time they also said she would get a better result first thing in the morning. She had felt such a fool peeing into the plastic bottle earlier that morning but now she rescued it from its hiding place and dipped the stick in. At first she sat and waited but then, telling herself she was being ridiculous, she went and turned on morning TV, glancing at the clock every few seconds. It was the longest five minutes of her life.

The test was negative.

Her first feeling was one of overwhelming relief, quickly followed by . . . what? It couldn't be a pang of disappointment, could it? She tried to examine her feelings but they were too complicated. She tidied up and left for the Pimlico Centre. Laura gave her a sharp look as she walked in. 'You OK? You look a bit peaky.'

'No, I'm fine. Bad night, that's all.' Laura handed her a cup of coffee. In her opinion Jo was overdoing it. What with the responsibility of the programme and the rest of the series and whatever was going on with Alan and her mother being a pest and . . . that reminded her.

'Stella phoned. Maggie's being difficult again.'

'So what's new?' Jo sounded tired but reached for the phone and dialled Stella's number. 'I know, she's told me about the calls but I thought they'd stopped,' she said into the phone in a weary voice. 'Tell her to put the answer machine on and not pick up until she knows who it is.' Jo listened to Stella wittering on. 'Oh for goodness' sake, Stella, I can't always drop everything and come running. I'll call her myself this afternoon. Tell her to expect my call at four o'clock, that way she'll know it's me and not whoever this sick crank is. Stella, please, I've got to go. I'll call her at four. Thanks for letting me know.' She hung up the phone.

'You know, that's the first time I've heard you tell that woman where to get off. It's about time too, if you ask me.' Laura spoke without looking up from her typewriter. Jo raised an eyebrow at her PA. 'Thank you, Grandma, here's an egg to suck on!' she said drily. It was the first glimmer of humour Laura had heard for a week.

One of the reasons Jo put off calling Maggie until later that afternoon was that she had a meeting scheduled with Alan at two o'clock. They genuinely had business to discuss but had both allowed an extra hour just to enjoy legitimately being together. Jo insisted they got their business out of the way first and they spent forty-five minutes going through her schedules, making lists of the last few areas where she felt they needed to shoot more material. They also discussed the continuing concerns of the health and safety people, who kept complaining about her cabling.

At last they shut their notebooks. Jo took a sip of water. 'I've got something to tell you. Don't worry. It's all OK, it's just that I thought

I might be pregnant. I'm not, but I thought I might be. I did a test this morning and it's clear.'

'How long have you thought that?'

'About ten days.'

'Why the hell didn't you tell me sooner? Do you mean you've been worrying about this by yourself? Christ, Jo, I know you're bloody independent sometimes but I would have thought you trusted me enough by now to at least let me hold your hand and share it with you. Maybe Simon wouldn't have wanted to know but I'm not Simon. After all, I would have been responsible . . .' His voice trailed off. 'I take it it would have been mine?'

Jo shrugged miserably. 'I don't know.' The look of distress on Alan's face made her wish she had lied but she was too weary for anything but the truth and now she'd hurt him.

'You still haven't told him then?' Alan's voice sounded flat and Jo couldn't look at him.

'I want to. I just don't know how to. Every time I think it's a good moment something happens and it's gone. He'll probably find out anyway. That was the other thing I had to tell you. You know the big Simplicity Insurance stand in Pim One?' Talking about the exhibition made her feel on safer ground and she finally looked at him.

Alan nodded; the stand had won the best-dressed award and the new policies the company had launched at this year's show had gained them a lot of attention in both the consumer and financial press. Despite Simon's cynical appraisal of the general public, thanks to that coverage the majority of their new customers knew exactly what they were buying. In turn, Simplicity Insurance had been offering such good deals to customers who signed up at the exhibition that they had attracted a lot of visitors. 'Well, that's the set-up Si works for and he's doing a stint on the stand. All next week, in fact. He's thrilled. More commission,' she explained unhappily.

'Oh great! Jo, I'm only human and enough is enough! You've got to tell him . . . or I swear I will.'

Alan's threat made her angry. 'Look, I've got enough on my plate at the moment what with arranging this funeral and keeping an eye on Maggie and trying to talk to Si, let alone bring this fucking programme in on time and in budget. The last thing I need is you adding to it.' To her intense fury she burst into tears. Alan was beside her like a shot.

'I'm sorry,' he soothed. 'It's just that I want us to be able to be together. I'm fed up with sneaking around and if Simon's going to be here next week I'd like to feel I don't have to spend the time looking out for a knife in my back if . . . or knowing this place when . . . he finds out by accident!' Jo gave him a watery smile. But as it turned out it was Simon's presence at the show that finally brought the situation to a head.

Simplicity Insurance had built a huge stand and their new, cheaper and easier insurance policies and discounted rates had visitors two and three deep each day from the moment the show opened until closing time. There were fifteen members of staff on hand to handle queries and sign people up on the spot. Needless to say the younger women visitors took one look at the staff and waited until Simon was available to answer their queries. And it wasn't only the visitors who wanted information, other exhibitors did too. By the time Simon started his stint on the stand Simplicity Insurance staff were getting in an hour before the show opened just to look after people working on other stands. Which was how Simon met Sandi.

Sandi was a tall, willowy blonde working as a model for one of the big bedding firms. She spent most of her day wearing a night shirt, a lot of make-up and not much else as she lay on her back showing potential customers the benefits of a certain flexible orthopaedic bed and pillow. Which, with the addition of a pair of very high-heeled shoes, was how she was dressed when she approached Simon for a quote on her car insurance on his second day. The moment he saw her Simon was determined he'd have her. He joked with his colleagues that he'd test her bed to its limits by the end of the week and soon they had opened a book on it, with several hundred pounds at stake. Oblivious to the fact that she was being regarded as little more than a thoroughbred filly Sandi managed to walk past Simplicity Insurance several times a day, always stopping to chat briefly with Simon.

Jo did try to spend time with Simon, especially on his first day, but it was as difficult as she had expected. By now she was spending less time at the Pimlico Centre and more time working on the other programmes in the *Women in Focus* series. Due to the pressure of the tight shooting schedules most of the crew had also been moved to other venues but as Jo felt that some of the material already in the can wasn't quite right – and she was determined that everything should be perfect on her first programme – she drafted in some freelance support. Unfortunately Doug, the freelance cameraman, not understanding the nuances of the health and safety regulations, managed to upset the inspectors by dragging cables round the exhibition during opening hours, which they said would put visitors at risk. They had threatened to stop all the filming so Jo was quickly called back to the Centre and spent nearly half a day in meetings being her most charming as she tried to persuade them to agree to alternatives. In the end they compromised. Doug could carry on shooting but only after the show closed. It wasn't ideal, as she really wanted to get footage of the show's variety of demonstrations while the visitors were there. The range was enormous, from kitchen gadgets and self-watering plants to bigger items such as sleeping bags that became tents and all the various types of furniture. In the end she had to do it their way or not at all. So it was that, for a few nights after the exhibition closed, a lone cameraman could be found wandering round the stands. Extra footage of the demonstrators and one-on-one interviews, together with people watching, was shot separately to be edited in with the existing footage later on.

Doug had finished his work and was sitting in the Portacabin's cramped editing suite viewing rushes and laughing raucously with Martin, the editor. 'I know you can't use it but I went to get the bendy bed stuff in the can and was doing a long panning shot when I saw 'em. Obviously they didn't know I was there but . . . go on, it's a bit further on, keep going . . . it's just after this – there! Can you believe it? Two people bonking their brains out in the middle of the fucking Home Maker Exhibition not giving a toss who might be watching! People get their kicks in the weirdest way.'

They both watched, amazed by the images on the screen. Doug had walked from one bedroom set into the next and stopped dead. Of course he should have just walked away or at least turned off the camera but instead he'd carried on filming. And not just filming but zooming in and out and training the telephoto lens lovingly over the sweaty bare bodies rolling around on the bed. The bed itself was adding to the excitement as they had obviously set its mechanism going and it was rearing up and down all by itself.

There was something about the people on the screen that seemed vaguely familiar to Martin but, he told himself, having spent so long at the bloody Pimlico Centre he was probably just recognising faces that had bobbed up in more than one shot, and like every other red-blooded male he had certainly noticed Sandi. He made a mental note to check it in the final edit; it always looked so amateurish if the same faces appeared in the wallpaper shots. Meantime he was enjoying the cabaret.

Both men had a hard-on as they watched and to cover their voyeuristic mixture of embarrassment and enjoyment were roaring with laughter. In fact they were making so much noise that Jo heard the din as she walked past and put her head round the door to see what was going on. The men were so intent on what they were watching that they didn't hear her until she gave a sharp intake of breath and they both turned to look at her over their shoulders. Martin went hot and cold as in a flash he realised the face wasn't wallpaper at all. It was Jo's fucking fiancé! *Shit!* he thought as he slammed his finger on the stop button. Unfortunately the image frozen on the screen was a close-up of Simon's face, shot under Sandi's bare breast at the moment he climaxed. It was an expression Jo knew well, but not one she had ever expected to share quite so publicly, or with her crew.

'Sorry, Jo,' Doug apologised, thinking it was the imagery that was embarrassing the director. 'I just came across it, so to speak. No pun intended. It seemed funny at the time.' His smile faded as he saw Jo's stony face.

'I'm sure it did,' she said tersely. 'Martin, please would you dub that footage on to VHS for me and then dump the original. I don't want anyone else to see it. If they do, not only will I find out about it, I'll also know exactly who showed it to them and I'll personally take you by the balls and sling you off this programme.' She clearly wasn't joking.

It was Simon's last day at the Pimlico Centre and he'd had a great time. Not only had he signed up enough clients to guarantee his bonus for the next six months, he had also won his bet and by pocketing Sandi's g-string as proof two nights ago he'd been able to collect the pot of £400.

He and Jo had agreed that they would travel to and from the exhibition halls separately as they were both on different schedules. Jo had left early that afternoon, telling Laura she had to do some paperwork at home. She didn't even bother to tell Simon she was leaving. Not that he would have cared; he stayed behind for a quick end-of-week drink with his colleagues. It was close to nine when, feeling very pleased with himself, he whistled his way up the steps of the maisonette and let himself in. *I won't tell her how I got the money. Just say it's a bonus.* He giggled at the thought – as far as he was concerned Sandi was very much the show's bonus. *I'll take her out for a slap-up meal. I might even suggest we go away for a real romantic weekend somewhere, four-poster beds, that sort of thing. She'd like that. Might help soften her up a bit as well.* Simon was definitely in a very good mood.

He shut the door behind him and looked at the pile of suitcases in bewilderment. 'Jo, what's all this stuff in the hall?' Jo came out of the living room, a glass of wine in her hand, and she leaned against the door frame. She was amazed at how remarkably calm and in control she felt. It was something she hadn't experienced for a long time and it was wonderful.

'Yours,' she said lightly.

'What? Why's it here?'

'There's something I want you to see.' She held out her hand invitingly, wiggling her fingers at him. Uncertainly he took them, allowing her to lead him inside. 'Sit down.'

Suddenly feeling oddly sick he did as he was told. Jo picked up the remote control and flipped it on. For a moment he wasn't sure what he was watching and then the penny dropped like a stone. He stared in disbelief as he saw himself and Sandi writhing around on a bed that was heaving itself up and down in harmony with what was going on on top of it.

'How . . . I can explain . . . I mean . . .' He looked up at her dumbly, not knowing what to say. He couldn't deny it – after all it was there for anyone to see – but how did she get hold of it? Who the hell had filmed it and why? He ground to a halt.

Jo spoke. 'You see, I used to listen to you when you talked about your work so I have a pretty good idea about the various policies you sell and what they all mean. Maybe if you'd listened more to me when I talked about *my* work, instead of dismissing it as irrelevant, you might have learned something. This is called an establishing shot. Of course it's usually used to establish a setting, not the fact that your boyfriend's been having it off with the first available woman. However, in this case it's served its purpose. I want you out of here and I want you out now!'

'Please, Jo. I'm sorry. What else can I say? It shouldn't have happened. You know it's you I love. She meant nothing. It's like you say, she was available, that's all. Please don't do this to me. It won't ever happen again. It's never happened before. Please, Jo, I need you.' He was standing up now, looking at her with those big blue eyes and a look of such pain on his face that for a moment she hesitated. He seemed so genuinely upset and so truly sorry that she nearly put her glass down and held out her arms, but he lost the ground he had gained when he said it had never happened before. Her resolve snapped back into place.

'Tell me then, who is Lindsey?' She wouldn't have thought it possible he could go any whiter but he did, and an unpleasant greyish pallor spread across his face.

Jo carried on. 'You see, we both know this was shot a couple of nights ago. It ended up in my editing suite yesterday and I had to wait till today to get it on VHS so we could watch it together.' She smiled grimly. 'You just might have got away with the big remorseful act if Katie hadn't called *last* night to see if we wanted to go round this evening. I was so hurt and angry with you that I blurted out that I'd found you'd been having it away with someone. I didn't say anything about what or where, just 'I'm so mad. Simon's been screwing around,' I think those were my exact words. 'Simon's been screwing around.' You know what she said? She said that she'd known about Lindsey for some time, Stu had told her, and she'd wanted to tell me but didn't know how. Poor love, she didn't realise she was actually telling me something I *didn't* know. I pretended I knew who Lindsey was and asked her a few questions. So don't tell me it won't happen again. You've had three of us that I know of in the last six months and God knows how many others. No doubt while I was sitting here looking at those stupid roses you left when you went to Jersey you added someone else to the bloody harem!' She paused for breath – she wanted to keep calm – then continued.

'Shall I tell you what the most painful thing is about this? It's not that you've fucked other women but that in doing so you put me at risk. I mean, did you use a condom? I couldn't see one in that.' She tossed her head at the TV screen. 'So I doubt it. Who knows what you might have exposed yourself – exposed us – to?' Simon said nothing. *Shut up!* she told herself. *Who the hell are you to take the moral high ground when you and Alan never thought about that side of things either? God, you can be such a bloody hypocrite when you want to.* She took a sip from her glass to give her the chance to pull her thoughts back on track.

'Now, your cases are in the hall. I've probably left some things out but once you've had a chance to check it all let me know what's missing and we can arrange for you to come round and collect it.'

'Jo?' Simon said helplessly. She moved towards the door and although there was nothing threatening in her behaviour he felt as if he had no choice but to do as she asked. If she'd lost her temper it would have been better, easier somehow than this unruffled approach. It was so business like. So cold. Had he really thrown away four years because he'd broken the eleventh commandment and got found out? Stupid, stupid, stupid. But it wasn't his fault, was it? He'd been careful. He would have got away with it if Stu hadn't babbled to Katie. Wait until he got hold of Stu.

He looked at the pile of luggage. 'Where shall I go?'

'That's your problem. Oh, and one last thing.' She held out her hand, wiggling her fingers at him. 'The door keys, please.' It was that request more than anything else that really stunned him. He'd thought he might be able to come back when things had quietened down a bit but if she was asking for the keys . . . He rummaged in his pocket, took them out and dropped them into her outstretched hand. Jo wrapped her fingers round them. They still felt warm and she gripped them tightly, not caring that the corner of his key-fob was digging into her hand. She stepped round him and silently opened the front door. Without another word he bent down and picked up his cases, taking two journeys to get them all outside and stacked by his car. He turned to look at her as she stood and watched him and then quietly went back inside, closing the door behind her.

She leaned with her back against the door. It hadn't been that difficult after all. The hardest bit had been packing his things, particularly his shaving kit and toiletries from the bathroom. She made her way back to the kitchen to refill her wine glass, dropping his keys on to the table as she went. It felt odd knowing that the place was her own again. Of course she'd been there many times without Simon but this was different. He wouldn't be coming back.

She walked through the house picking up the few things of his that she had missed and piled them up by the door. There wasn't much – a couple of framed photographs, a few magazines that he would probably throw out anyway. It was odd how easily his presence had been wiped away, as if his four years in the house had never happened. The bathroom looked totally feminine again, the bedroom showed no signs of a man having been there. She smiled to herself, enjoying a sense of peace she hadn't felt for a long time.

She knew she should call Alan and put him out of his misery. He really had been very patient, even allowing for their row. But something stopped her. 'Tonight's for me,' she told her reflection. It was still reasonably early but she decided to have a bath and ran the hottest one she could, for once not having to worry about whether or not her antiquated system would be able to produce enough hot water for a second one later on. She liberally poured in her lavender oil, overdoing it on purpose in the knowledge that Simon couldn't have a go at her for using so much it made his bath smell of lavender too. She picked up a book and an apple and eased her way into the water. It was heaven. About an hour later, as it was growing cold, she got out and dried herself, sprinkling talcum around without thinking about clearing it up. Then she curled up in bed, out of habit leaving half of it empty until she remembered she didn't have to share it. She rolled to the middle and stretched out, enjoying the space and not caring that her damp hair would make the pillow soggy. She'd just use another one. Her hair! She sat up in bed and then got out again to peer in the mirror. That would have to go too. She had to stop hiding, had to do what *she* wanted.

That night she slept better than she had in weeks.

'Hello, Mrs Edwardes?'

'Yes.'

'I do think it's time you 'ad a proper word with that daughter of yours and got her to tell you what 'appened to your 'usband. She knows all about it. And while yer at it, tell her to do as I ask before someone gets hurt.'

Maggie dropped the receiver back into the cradle with a clatter. It was getting worse and she had the feeling that whoever was making the calls wasn't talking about Joanne. Whoever it was *knew*. The sensible thing would be to call the police but it would mean telling Joanne and that she couldn't do.

Howard's funeral was on Monday. She didn't want to go. She didn't know who else might be there. Maybe she could have a turn? She had to think of some way to get out of it. She sighed and pushed the switch on her chair, propelling it forward. The phone rang again. This time she remembered to let the machine answer it.

'Hello, Maggie, it's Jo, so you can pick up the phone.' Maggie lifted the receiver. 'That's better,' said Jo. 'I wanted to let you know I'm planning on coming over on Saturday to talk to you about the funeral.' Maggie grunted. Jo wasn't sure if it was a response to the fact she would be visiting or the funeral. Either way she ignored it. 'I'll see you Saturday, then.' She hoped Maggie might say something but she didn't.

Jo made sure she was on time, not wanting to aggravate Maggie more than was necessary. On her way in she bumped into Edna, strolling around as usual, and gently steered her back to the security of her own flat. Today she had strings of beads round her neck and a feather in her hair and was trying to do a wobbly Charleston in the front hall. Jo returned to Maggie's front door and let herself in. Her mother was in the living room, facing the TV, and by virtue of the fact that she didn't turn her chair round when Jo came in it was obviously going to be a difficult afternoon. Jo walked to the sofa, purposefully crossing Maggie's eye line.

'Good God! What have you done to your hair?' Maggie exclaimed, turning to look full-on as she caught sight of her daughter's neat new cut. That morning Jo had gone to her hairdresser and demanded to have her hair cut off. She had told the stylist that she had no particular idea in mind so he could do whatever he thought would suit her – as long as it was short. It was the sort of invitation he liked and the result was a fabulous style which, while short, had a fullness about it that flattered the shape of her face beautifully, and made her eyes look enormous. Maggie's comment, criticism implicit in its tone, automatically made her reach up to tuck a piece of hair behind her ear but as it was no longer there she just rubbed her earlobe instead.

'I decided it was time I did something with it,' she said defensively.

'Turn round.' She did as she was told.

'About time too.' Maggie liked it but wouldn't dream of saying so even though Jo knew her comment masked her approval. She took advantage of the situation to launch into the plans for the funeral.

'Now, about Monday. I've arranged for the car to pick us up from here at ten o'clock, which I hope won't be too early for you?' Maggie gave her a withering look. 'Fine,' she carried on quickly. 'I brought along the order of service in case you wanted to see it before then.' She held it out but Maggie made no move to take it so she put it on the tray on her wheelchair. 'I hope you approve of what I've chosen. It was difficult finding the right hymns and readings after all this time.'

'How about something to do with Sodom and Gomorrah?' Maggie muttered.

Jo ignored the comment. 'By the way, it'll just be you and me in the car. Unless you can think of anyone else who should be in it with us.'

She made it sound as throwaway as possible but Maggie picked her up on it.

'What about that fiancé of yours?'

'Simon won't be there. He's gone.' She threw it into the non-existent conversation, hoping Maggie would let it pass, but of course she didn't.

'I'm not surprised. It amazed me that he stayed around for as long as he did. God knows why he didn't walk out years ago. Trust you to lose the only man who's ever shown any interest in you. You can be so stupid sometimes. How I ever raised a daughter like you I'll never know.' Was Jo imagining it or was Maggie taking some sort of malicious pleasure in the fact that she and Simon had split up? She knew they didn't like each other but had hoped Maggie might at least have said she was sorry, even though they would both have known she wasn't.

'Actually, I threw him out.' Jo sounded surprisingly casual.

'You did *what*?' Maggie looked at her incredulously. 'What on earth made you do that?'

'Because I finally discovered he was a shit and had been sleeping with other women.' Again that defensive note. *Why do I let Maggie do this to me?* she asked herself. *I was right to chuck him out, I know I was, so why do I feel I have to justify everything I do to her?*

Maggie looked at her for a moment and to Jo's surprise began to laugh. It wasn't a giggle but a proper laugh, dripping with cynicism, that made Maggie's eyes water. Jo stared at her. 'What's so funny?'

'You are. Throwing a man out because he sleeps with other women. So what? Let 'em sleep with who they like. Just be sure it's you they come home to and it's your bills they pay.'

'That's a terrible thing to say! It makes it sound as if you only value someone as a meal ticket. What about loyalty, what about commitment and love?'

'Loyalty, commitment and love?' Maggie sounded scornful. 'Is that what you got from Simon or what Howard gave me? Is that what you really think your precious father gave me?' She was leaning forward in her chair, her fists curled on the tray in front of her as her eyes narrowed behind her glasses, her face twisted with anger.

'Well, now that we're finally going to bury him I think it's time you heard the truth about your wonderful father. So Simon's been sleeping with other women. So what? Your father did nothing *but* sleep with other women. He did it when we were engaged, he did it when we were married. Do you know he was even in some tramp's bed the night before our wedding? He thought I didn't know about it but I found out. So what did I do? Make a fuss? Throw him out? Not me! I hung on for all I was worth. I'd worked hard to become his wife and I wasn't going to let some slut take him away from me. No, throwing him out would have been too easy.'

'Stop it!' shouted Jo. 'I don't believe you. I don't want to hear this.' She put her hands over her ears but Maggie's voice penetrated the barrier.

'God, you're so dense. Why do you think nobody looked for him when he disappeared? Everyone knew what he was like. Everyone knew what had happened. 'Poor Margaret, Howard's left her at last and who can blame him? Wonder which one he's run off with?' No one doubted it for a moment and the simpering pity they showed me was revolting. Your father did that to me. In one fell swoop he made me an object of pity and I won't accept being pitied by anyone, least of all those bitches your father called our friends.'

'I don't understand, Maggie. Why are you telling me this now?' It was little more than a whisper. The confident woman with her new short hair cut had become a quivering coward.

'Because I don't want to go to his bloody funeral. What little grieving I did I did years ago and I'm damned if I'll go through some charade just to have people look at me and feel sorry for me all over again. I'm so tired of hearing you go on and on about how wonderful he was. He wasn't wonderful at all. He used people, he took them and made them into what he wanted them to be and then dumped them. If he had been around when you were older he would have done the same to you. You know, when he met me I was considered a woman with spunk. Two years it took him, two lousy, rotten years to squeeze it all out of me, to mould me into what he thought a woman should be. And when he finally deigned to marry me, it wasn't because he loved me but because he thought it was about time he got hitched and I happened to be available.'

Maggie chose not to remember the fun she had had and how much she had wanted Howard.

'Then you were born. And do you know why you were born? For the same reason he married me. Because he thought it was time he was a father. No love, nothing. Just his own bloody timetable. Do you want to know why he spent so much time with you? Because that way he could control you and use you against *me*. I'd served my purpose by then. I'd made him respectable. I'd been a good wife to show off on his arm and when he commanded, I spread my legs and you appeared.' Despite herself Jo flinched at Maggie's coarseness.

'Well, maybe vanishing when you were small was a good thing. It made sure at least one person genuinely thought well of him. You were too young and stupid to be hurt by him. Howard was a bastard all his adult life and the one thing I'm getting pleasure from is the thought that he lay beneath that floor and rotted for thirty years!'

Jo stared at Maggie. Funny how they both remembered the same man so differently. Did her mother really feel about Howard the same revulsion she felt towards Simon? How could Maggie hate so passionately the man her daughter remembered as being kind and adoring? The man who had made her young life fun by whispering secrets in her ear and giggling with her? Couldn't Maggie see it was her fault that he slept with other women? That the constant nagging and shouting which was so much a part of her childhood memories was what had forced him away from home? Couldn't Maggie see that she had only herself to blame for driving Howard away? Or was it that she chose to forget the fights, finding it easier to blame something other than her own jealousy?

'My God!' Jo exclaimed suddenly, a look of amazement on her face as realisation swept through her. 'This has nothing to do with who Howard did or didn't sleep with.' She stood up and walked closer to her mother. 'In fact it's got nothing to do with Howard at all, has it? It's *me!* You're jealous. You're jealous of the relationship I had with my own father. You were so scared of losing him that you saw every female as a threat, even your own six-year-old daughter.' She shook her head in disbelief, her mouth slightly open.

'Christ, I've been such a fucking idiot!' She addressed herself to the space between them, running her hands through her short hair. 'All these years I've been trying to be the person you wanted me to be but you've always let me know I've never got it right. I don't dress properly, I don't use the right words, I don't have the right friends. I'm not confident enough for you. You go on and on about how everything I do is wrong but that's not the problem, is it? It's simpler than that. You just can't stand the thought that I loved my father and he loved me – because he did. He really loved me. Even if you won't say it out loud, deep inside you know it And you can't stand it, can you? You don't see your daughter when you look at me. You see a rival.'

Jo didn't know whether to laugh or cry at the sense of relief her discovery had given her. She understood why people talked about a huge weight being taken off their shoulders.

'You make me sick, you really do.' She sounded calm and in control. 'I don't care if you're at the funeral or not. The car will be here at ten. It's up to you.' Jo picked up her things and walked to the door. She swung her wrap over her shoulders, concentrating on setting its folds as she spoke, not looking at Maggie as she did so.

'Maybe if just once you had said you cared about me, instead of always seeing everything from your own selfish point of view, it wouldn't have been so bad.' It was a statement rather than an accusation.

It was very late. Jo knew that because the light in the hall had been switched off and Mummy only did that when she went to bed. She had tried very hard to stay awake because she had a plan. Inge-lis at school had told them all about Christmas in Sweden. She had told them about the sprites of the trees. How if you made a wish on a Christmas tree on Christmas Eve and the sprites caught it they would make it come true. She knew that if Mummy found her she would be cross and if Mummy was cross it would mean she'd been a naughty girl and then Father Christmas wouldn't come. So she had to be very quiet.

Carefully she climbed out of bed and put on her slippers. It was very dark indeed. She picked up Loopy Lapin, her big yellow bunny rabbit with the chewed ear. Daddy had given it to her just before he left and now it kept her company instead of Daddy. She crept out into the hall. Even though the lights weren't on she could still see the shape of the Christmas tree against the window. Maybe their Christmas tree didn't have a sprite? No, it must have, Inge-lis said all the trees had sprites. She looked at the tree, seeing the different baubles and tinsel take shape as her eyes grew used to the dark. The occasional light from a car outside made it sparkle a bit but not as much as when all the fairy lights were on. Sprites were like fairies, weren't they? Maybe they would help her more if the lights were on? She knew how to turn the lights on, because one day when Mummy was out Consuelo had let her do it. She flicked the switch.

In the dark the bright reds, yellows, greens and pinks looked even brighter than they did in the daytime. The colour seemed to fill the room while the tinsel shimmered and glittered and the star at the top twinkled at her. She screwed up her eyes tightly and squeezed Loopy Lapin as she made her wish. Please bring my daddy home. She said it inside her head so no one would hear. But if no one could hear how would the sprites catch her wish? She swallowed and whispered it just loud enough for them to hear. Please bring my daddy home. A sound erupted from behind her and, terrified, she spun round just as the overhead lights snapped on.

Mummy was standing there. 'And what do you think you're doing? Asking Father Christmas to bring Daddy home?' She was about to explain about the tree sprites but Mummy didn't want to hear. 'It's not going to help and the sooner you get that into your stupid little head the better. He's gone and for all I care he can stay that way. And another thing – you're nearly seven years old. It's time you grew up. There is no Father Christmas. Never was and never will be. You can stand here making your silly wishes until the small hours of the morning if you like, but Father Christmas won't appear and neither will your precious father. I'm going back to bed. Turn off the lights when you go.' And she walked out, leaving Jo feeling as if someone had punched her in the stomach. She crept back to bed and, gripping her rabbit tightly, cried herself to sleep. When she woke up the next morning she cautiously opened her eyes. The sock at the bottom of her bed still hung as limp and as empty as it had been the night before. There were no lovely, lumpy bits and she knew Mummy had been telling the truth.

Jo woke up with a start, tears pouring down her face. What on earth had made her dream about that first Christmas without Howard? She had forgotten about the incident years ago but obviously it had survived somewhere buried inside her. She switched on the light and reached for a tissue. It was four a.m. For the first time she missed having Simon beside her. No, she corrected herself, it wasn't Simon she was missing but someone.

When Jo had told Alan on Sunday morning that Simon had finally gone he had been delighted. She also told him everything that had happened with Maggie but, although he wanted to be with her and share her new-found freedom, he was on duty at the Pimlico Centre and couldn't rearrange his schedule.

Things had quietened down at the exhibition as far as incidents were concerned. Attendance, however was way up and with a fortnight to go they had already ushered far more people through the doors than they had done during the entire six weeks of the previous year's show. Everyone involved was thrilled. An increased number of visitors meant more people buying and therefore some very happy exhibitors. Off the back of that the sales team had already booked several large stands for the following year. Club secretaries had virtually queued up to add their names to the advance mailing lists for organised group visits and despite the usual detractors the show had generally been well received by the media.

The only person who wasn't enjoying herself was Suzanne. The attacks on the show itself had stopped but instead they had become more personal and were now directly aimed at her. She discovered the first when she came out of the building late one evening to find the tyres on her car had been let down. A few nights later a pot of paint had been splashed across its bonnet.

Cyril was one of the two security guards on duty in the traffic office when she signed herself out and saw the mess on the car. 'Oh deary me, madam. That is a nasty mess, innit?'

'You'll never shift that. That's gloss, that is. Absolute bugger,' said Barry his colleague knowledgeably. ''Course, it'll need a respray.' Suzanne gave them both a tight smile but chose to say nothing. She knew that if she did then the culprit would have the satisfaction of knowing he had got to her – and she wasn't going to give in that easily.

However, as a result of her lack of response things took a different turn. Cyril waved her through with a smart salute the day she came in early for a meeting, only to discover that someone had broken into her office. Roger Dudley was called immediately and as they stood in the corridor outside the office she confirmed rather tersely that yes, she had locked the door and yes, she had taken the key with her. By now Gordon had arrived and Roger was addressing himself to him – preferring to talk to another man who shared his loathing of Suzanne rather than speak directly to her.

'Look, Gordon, you've seen the rota, you know we've 'ad full security up here. I don't deny there's a problem and I'm doin' all I can to sort it, OK?' Roger's attitude was one of total boredom.

Gordon had been about to give a sharp reply in the hope that any blame would be shifted from his area of concern to Roger's when the lift door opened and Suzanne interrupted him. 'I think this conversation should continue inside, don't you?' She ushered the men into her office and indicated they should sit down. The mess was appalling.

Roger looked round, trying to hide his satisfaction that at last that stuck-up cow had been dealt a blow. 'Well, I've got to call the police and I don't want to disturb nothing.' He gave Suzanne a pointed look implying she had made a mistake in suggesting they sit down. Gordon also hesitated.

'Oh, for goodness' sake, I doubt if the culprit has left bum marks on the seats. Just sit down, the pair of you. All the police would do is dust the place and I guarantee you they wouldn't find any prints. I see no point in bringing them in.' Roger was about to argue but, seeing the look on Suzanne's face, he thought better of it and did as he was told. 'Look, a couple of things have happened to my car so I think we can safely assume that all of this –' she indicated the chaos by a lift of her chin – 'is personally directed at me. Going to the police makes it public and smacks of giving in; of admitting I can't cope, which is utter rubbish. I can cope perfectly well indeed and I won't be brow-beaten. Do I make myself clear?'

'Well, yeah, but as 'ead of security I can't just ignore it, can I? I mean, I've got to go through the motions.' Roger attempted to argue while Gordon picked a piece of fluff off his trouser leg.

She was standing by the window and the early morning sunlight was streaming in so Roger couldn't quite see her face. 'You may be head of security but while I'm here this is my office and my responsibility. The key is in my name, not yours. My name is on the contract and what I say goes. And right now what I am saying is *leave it alone*. I'm in charge and no petty-minded would-be thief or bully is going to get the better of me. I won't give *anyone* the satisfaction of knowing that this,' she swept her hand round the room, 'has created so much as a ripple in the way I run things.'

She fixed her gaze on the two men. 'If either of you say so much as a word to anyone, and I mean anyone, about this then I swear you'll regret it. I'm sure you understand what I'm saying?' They nodded. She was making herself very clear. Silly bitch! But there, that was women for you. 'Roger, you may go. Gordon, please stay. There's something else I wish to discuss with you.'

As Roger left the room Gordon resettled himself in his chair. 'Do you know how much I dislike that man?' he asked her as she picked her way over the scattered contents of her drawers and files to sit behind her desk.

'You too, hmm? Maybe it goes with the territory. The sooner he retires the better.' She felt slightly mollified that someone else disliked Roger Dudley. That Gordon disliked her just as much was something that over the years he had managed to keep hidden, mainly by making sure he had as little contact with her as possible. He had never liked her. Who did she think she was, taking over like she did when the boss had gone? It wasn't right, a woman telling them all what to do. Silly stuck-up bitch. One of these days Suzanne Prescott would get what was coming to her and if he could do anything to make that happen sooner he wouldn't hold back.

'Gordon, I meant what I said. No one must know about this. It really is a personal vendetta but I can handle it. Please let me know if you hear anyone talking about it, will you?'

Gordon was puzzled but if she didn't want it known someone had it in for her then who was he to argue? It was one less thing for him to worry about. 'Fine.' He shrugged. 'If you want I could have a word higher up and ask for Roger to be assigned elsewhere, like the Auditorium for the last two weeks.'

'No. I'd rather keep him where I can see him, and besides, moving him off the show, especially with an edict from on high, would get everybody gossiping again. We've had enough of that already this year and I think it's fairly common knowledge how we all feel about our Mr Dudley as it is.' She gave a wry smile which Gordon felt he should return before leaving her to get on with her work. In fact after he left she did nothing but sit staring at the muddle. She could tell it was pure vandalism, done, like everything else, to create as much disruption as possible. Despite what she said it infuriated her to think that she was letting him get away with it, but what else could she do? She would *not* give in. She had come too far and unfortunately he was right – she did have too much lose if the truth came out. The question was who really had the upper hand? He with his knowledge or she controlling his cashflow? In the long term she decided she did, but only just.

* * *

The Monday of the funeral was a glorious balmy spring day and though of course Jo felt sad that they were burying Howard, part of her felt happier than she had for a long time. After all the years of missing her father, she was pleased that at last she would have somewhere to go, a grave to visit and to remember. She was determined not to think about the picture Maggie had painted of him. The more she reflected on what Maggie had said a couple of days before the more she came to understand just how accurate her accusation of jealousy had been.

The morning traffic seemed lighter than usual and she arrived at The Warren well ahead of schedule at nine-thirty. The first thing she saw was Stella hovering anxiously. She had barely parked the car before the warden was there, holding the door open for her and blocking the way. 'Oh, Jo, I don't know what to do. I mean she's got to go, hasn't she? I keep telling her she must but she just sits there and won't budge.'

'I assume you mean Maggie doesn't want to go to the funeral?' Jo looked up at Stella from behind the steering wheel.

'Yes, what else would I mean? She says she won't even join everyone for a sandwich afterwards. She must go, mustn't she? What would people think? I've got everything ready for later like you asked, but every time I try to check she's happy with what I've done she turns her back and won't talk to me. Your flowers are here but she hasn't even ordered any, unless she asked you to do it because she didn't ask me and . . .' Jo reached up and put a soothing hand on hers.

'Stella, it's not important. If she doesn't want to go then that's fine.' Stella was amazed by Jo's lack of concern.

'But she's his widow!' she exclaimed, as if Jo didn't know.

'Yes, and I'm his daughter. I'm tired of playing games with her, Stella. If she wants to behave like some cantankerous old woman then I'm not going to argue. If that shocks you then I'm sorry, but I won't let her manipulate me any more. In fact I'm not even going in to see her. It's such a lovely day I'll wait outside for the car. If she changes her mind it'll be here at ten. Now excuse me please.' Stella finally stepped out of the way and Jo shut the door, locking it before she strolled off round the gardens, humming to herself.

At five to ten the hearse and cortège pulled into the grounds. Jo took a deep breath. Now the time had come she wasn't feeling quite so cheerful. Maybe Stella was right and she should have gone in to see Maggie, to persuade her to come to her own husband's burial. She glanced at her watch – if she was quick she could still do it. She didn't have to. As she came round the corner of the building she saw Maggie steering herself with silent dignity down the ramp. Carefully one of the ushers lifted her into the car, (it was clear she was no weight) and helped another to heave her chair in beside her. Jo pulled her shoulders back and walked over. She nodded good morning to the men and stepped in to sit beside her mother.

Neither woman said a word as they followed the hearse to the church.

When they arrived Jo was pleased to see Alan's car in the car park. There had never been any question that he wouldn't attend. They had talked about whether or not he should go to The Warren with her but had agreed it wouldn't be a good idea. Jo got out of the car and left the ushers to help Maggie. As Stella had said, there were no flowers from Maggie, and despite Jo's resolve to be firm she did feel Howard's widow should be represented. She quickly added Maggie's name to the card on her own magnificent arrangement of spring flowers even though she knew her mother would not share the sentiment she had originally written: 'Remembered with constant love and affection, always in my heart.'

A few people from Boadicea Productions were there to give Jo moral support, as were members of the Home Maker Exhibition team. Jo was touched to see Suzanne was among them. However, she couldn't help noticing that apart from a handful of The Warren's residents there was no one else she would consider as Maggie's friends. She felt a twinge of compassion for her mother. Had she really come to this? Had her years of accrued anger and bitterness left her a lonely old woman? Jo felt guilty about her recent determination not to be so available for her. As they sat down at the front of the church she tried to take Maggie's twisted hand but was shrugged away.

The service and interment went smoothly but as the first clod of earth went into the grave and hit the coffin lid Jo found herself becoming tearful. Alan gave her a tissue and took her hand to give it a squeeze which she gratefully returned. She bowed her head, automatically looking sideways at Maggie as she did so, trying to gauge her feelings, but her mother's face was a mask. Maggie sat as steadily as she could in her wheelchair, head upright, staring straight ahead with no trace of emotion. To anyone who didn't know her her expression could have been mistaken for dignity and extreme grief, but Jo knew better.

Because of the way in which people were gathered at the graveside Suzanne was standing opposite Maggie. Her head was bowed and the only time Maggie showed any reaction was when Suzanne looked up and caught her eye. For a moment the two women stared at each other and then Suzanne pulled her gaze away.

Although a general invitation had been issued Jo made a point of asking Suzanne to come back to The Warren, and so she was there when Maggie finally condescended to join everyone in the public lounge.

People sympathised politely with Jo and tried to do likewise with

Maggie but she refused to respond. She sat sullenly pushing a sandwich round her tray as she tried to pick it up with her knotted fingers. 'Here, let me help.' Suzanne bent down and picked it up, placing it between her twisted finger and thumb.

'What are you doing here?' Maggie hissed, not wanting to draw attention to herself.

'Your daughter invited me.' She emphasised the word daughter.

'You shouldn't have come.'

'Why not? He was found under my floorboards and, besides, I wanted to see you again.' Maggie nearly choked on her sandwich, bringing Stella scuttling across the room to thump her on the back. Maggie got rid of her and made eye contact again with Suzanne, who had gone back to the centre of the room when Stella came over, pulling her back to her side.

'My daughter might have invited you to the funeral but I didn't invite you to my home, such as it is. So make your excuses and leave. *Now!*' For a split second the spark that many years ago had been Margaret crossed her face. Suzanne, much to her surprise, found herself doing as she was told, experiencing again the same sense of deep hurt that she had felt nearly thirty years ago, the last time she had been rejected.

With as much dignity as she could muster she made her excuses to Jo, who, aware that Maggie was being difficult, tried to apologise for her mother. 'Suzanne, I'm sorry about Maggie – I think the funeral has upset more than she likes to admit. She's also been getting nasty phone calls which have unsettled her, so please forgive her.'

'Oh, don't worry. I quite understand. Now I really must be going. Look after yourself Jo, won't you?' Something about Suzanne's tone made her last comment sound so genuine that Jo just stared after her as she hurriedly left the room. Maggie also watched her go, a look of defiance on her face.

As Suzanne left she found herself questioning Maggie's control over her. Who was Maggie Edwardes after all? Just an old woman stuck in a wheelchair because of crippling arthritis. But as she got into her car a thought suddenly struck her about Maggie's nasty phone calls. Jo hadn't said how they were nasty but what if . . . She felt herself go pale. *Surely Maggie didn't know?* She thought *He wouldn't have told her would he? Not Maggie. My God, if Maggie knew who else knew? Had Maggie told Jo? No, of course not. Maybe he had finally found a way of getting back at her properly. Oh Christ!*

No sooner had Suzanne gone than Maggie turned her chair round and, without a word to anyone, propelled herself out of the room. Jo saw her go and for a moment considered running after her but Alan saw the way she was looking and whispered 'No' firmly in her ear.

He was right. The only way she was going to win this battle once and for all was by being strong.

It was the last time she would see her mother alive.

The door opened quietly but even though Suzanne's head was bent over her work she was aware the moment the knob began to turn. She'd been listening out for him for the last quarter of an hour. She knew they were playing a very high-powered game. He'd played his first card by being late so she played hers by letting him stand there watching her, thinking she was oblivious to his presence until she suddenly flicked the switch behind her desk, flooding the room with light. It had the desired effect, giving her the upper hand as he jumped like a startled rabbit. Round one to her.

'Pity you weren't that observant back then, innit?' He tried to regain the ground he'd lost. 'Interestin', you wanting to see me. I take it you've come to your senses and want to discuss terms then, do you?' He sat down without being asked.

'Of course I don't. Whatever gave you that idea? I've already said I won't change the arrangement and I mean it. No, the reason I wanted to see you, my friend, was to tell you to lay off Mrs Edwardes. You're barking up the wrong tree. She knew nothing then and she knows even less now. She's going a bit gaga anyway.' She lied, hoping he wouldn't know that nothing could be further from the truth. 'This is between you and me. Why you're even bothering her I don't know . . .'

He began to laugh. A harsh, rasping sound that turned into a cough which interrupted her. 'Maybe no one else round 'ere knows exactly who you are, but I do.' He sounded smug.

Suzanne began to feel that she no longer had the situation under control. 'What are you talking about?' She tried to sound puzzled but her voice lacked conviction and the moment she asked the question she regretted it.

'Let's just say the law don't look kindly on relationships between men and their wives' kids from a previous encounter, shall we?'

Suzanne felt numb as she stared at him in disbelief. No one knew about that. How could they? Her eyes flicked sideways to the bottom drawer of the desk. It was the slightest of movements but it was all the confirmation he needed. He saw the glance and barked his laugh again, hugging himself with glee.

'You really are a silly cow!' he said contemptuously, loving her discomfort. ''Mazing how they give it to you on a plate. You keep the stuff in the first place and leave it where anyone can get at it. That note from your Auntie Em don't say much, do it, but it says enough. I'm not so stupid as you think, see. I read that little note. Bit vague but interestin'. I had a feelin' I was right and you lookin' down there tells me I was. And you an intelligent woman an' all!' He lit another cigarette, taking his time as he relished taking the lead in this most peculiar of battles.

'You're nothing but a sneak thief and a nasty little blackmailer.'

'Names, names. Don't flatter me, love. Blackmail is a nasty word. Couldn't we just say you pays me for information? Or lack of it?' He chuckled at his own joke. 'And as for being a thief . . . That's you, not me. You're the one who took everything from Mrs Edwardes, not me. Those letters prove it. I'm hurt you could think such a thing of me. There's nothing missin', is there, so technically I ain't a thief. So, back to business. As we was saying, I'm comin' up to retirement and I don't want you to think I ain't grateful to you for lookin' after me all these years, 'cos I is, but I feel I'm going to need a bit more.'

Suzanne said nothing so he continued. 'Now, *you* know there was a witness and *I* know there was a witness but the law, well, I think they also has a right to know, don't they? A right to the truth. Be a pity if you lost all this 'cos you couldn't see sense, wouldn't it?'

She was feeling brave again. 'You won't go to the police. You're too scared of the law to do that.'

'Did I say *I* would go to the cops? I don't think so. No, I'll keep talkin' to that old mum of yours and when she's so terrified she's shittin' herself then I'll tell her the truth and *she'll* go to the law.'

'Maggie may be old but she's not stupid. She'll want to know how you know.' Suzanne spoke in a quiet, flat tone. He leaned back in his chair – he was enjoying this more than he'd imagined.

'Not stupid, your old ma? I thought you said she was losin' it?' Too late Suzanne saw her mistake. 'Don't you worry yourself 'bout that. Got it all worked out, I have. I'll tell her how I know. Tell her I was there and when the police ask I'll tell 'em it was your idea to pay me. Hush money. That's what it was. Didn't want it, I'll tell 'em, but what could I do? Needed the job and you was in charge. What with my history I couldn't afford to lose it could I? I *had* to take the money. Oh, I'll tell 'em you made me. I'll admit it came in handy all right but funds I should've reported will become insignificant compared with what you did. So you see, it'll be you they clobber not me.'

He pushed himself to his feet. 'Oh, and don't think that letter'll help I'll just tell 'em you made me sign that an' all. Come on, love, I'm a reasonable man.' The look she gave him clearly indicated she thought otherwise. 'You've got 'til the end of the show. If I 'aven't had your answer by then you'd better get ready to say goodbye to all this.' He stubbed his cigarette out on the door jamb and tossed it into the bin. Someone was walking by as he opened the door so he quickly pulled himself up smartly and said loudly, 'Good night.'

After he left Suzanne didn't move for a good five minutes. Then she buried her face in her hands before eventually getting up to go over to the bar where she shakily poured herself a neat gin. She knocked it back in one gulp, then poured second to which she added tonic. Tumbler in hand, she turned off the lights before sitting on one of the sofas that gave a view out across the balcony and over the Thames.

Kicking off her shoes she curled her feet up under her and gazed out of the huge plate-glass corner windows. Up-river were the long fingers of the deserted Battersea Power Station. Down-river she could see the Houses of Parliament and Big Ben. It was close to ten o'clock. Beyond that the sign outside the Hayward Gallery twinkled on the opposite bank, while on her side of the river St Paul's stood proudly above the city as did the NatWest Tower. She sighed. For thirty odd years she had watched this view change without being aware of it. When she had first arrived signs of the damage done during the war could still be seen, but new buildings had appeared as old ones finally came down. She had seen Canary Wharf grow until its illuminated peak was so much a part of the London night sky it seemed impossible to think of a time when it hadn't been there.

But such a time had existed. So too did a time when she would have laughed if anyone had told her that one day she would be sitting *in* this office, not outside. That she would be the one running the Home Maker Exhibition and making a fortune from it instead of just a salary for taking messages and serving tea and coffee. Oh God, she was tired!

No, she corrected herself. *weary, that's what I am, weary. If I was tired I could have a good night's sleep and feel better, but this goes deeper. Maybe he's right and I should give in? There used to be a purpose to this, I had a reason, but now . . . ?*

An image of Maggie sitting in her wheelchair as tall and proud as her arthritic body allowed sprang to mind. She took a long sip from her glass and nursed it between her hands. *I wonder if Howard hadn't appeared in her life things would have been different between us? If maybe we would at least have been friends?* A brightly lit cruiser made its way up river and she watched it idly. Suddenly a long forgotten picture of other boats flashed into her mind. A string of three large barges carrying models of the Eiffel Tower, the Taj Mahal and the Pyramids on their decks tying up opposite the Pimlico Centre ready for Celebration of the World, which was the theme of the 1966 Home Maker Exhibition.

'Look, here they come!' Howard's excitement was infectious and everyone turned to look towards the City. The sun was setting and its orangey rays reflected down the river making the whole horizon glow. The water shimmered and in the distance the string of barges could be just be made out. Howard had brought his binoculars and gladly shared them with his staff as they clustered on to the balcony to witness the majestic arrival of the models as they travelled from the Isle of Dogs where they had been created.

Below them on the pavement the press waited and some of the exhibitors had broken away from adding the finishing touches to their stands to watch. Members of the public were standing along Millbank and further down-river people were leaning over the Embankment wall yelling and waving at the barges. The Pathé News team was doing its best to capture the mounting excitement. 'It's going to be the best year yet!' Howard enthused. 'Anne, please would you go and get the champagne from the fridge?' She stepped back into his office, taking Tricia with her to help carry the second tray. Howard glanced over his shoulder. God, she was a looker. Not in an obvious way but he still fancied her. The fact that she was a damn good secretary helped.

PA, he corrected himself. *Why they had to get airs and graces and become PAs I'll never know*. He turned back towards the river. For four years she'd been his right-hand and in all that time the most he had been able to do was give her a kiss on the cheek at Christmas. Howard knew that even though he was now in his mid-fifties he didn't look it. He didn't fool himself by thinking he had the same good-looks as when he was younger but he did know he carried himself well, and had a distinguished air about him. He had kept his figure and it wasn't only Margaret's response that told him he still knew how to please a woman. But it wasn't Margaret he was interested in any more. He wanted Anne, and she knew it. The longer she held out the more he wanted her. *Maybe this year*, he told himself as he released the first cork, making sure it arced across the road followed by a plume of champagne. He still knew a good press picture when he saw it and sure enough, next morning many of the popular papers carried shots of both the models and that first flying cork.

But he wasn't there to see them.

Margaret was feeling peeved. In fact she was downright angry. How dare Howard treat her like this? Bad enough that he had chosen euphemistically 'to sleep at his club' the night before the Home Maker Exhibition opened, but she'd thought he would be home by now. After all, it was getting on for eight-fifteen and if they had to be at the Pimlico Centre in an hour's time he was cutting it a bit fine. She smoothed her hair again and checked her appearance. She knew she was looking good and was relieved that it was a cool day as it meant she could wear her mink without it being perceived as showing off. The bedroom door flew open and Joanne burst in.

'I've told you before about knocking before you come in here. What do you want?' Joanne pulled back a little. Mummy sounded so cross with her she wondered what she had done wrong this time. She held out a red ribbon.

'Please would you put my ribbon in for me?' She went and stood in front of her mother with her back turned so she could attach the ribbon to her hair. 'Where's Daddy?' she asked, trying not to wince when Margaret pulled a little too hard as she finished teasing the bow into shape.

'I don't know, but he's going to be in such trouble when he gets home.' She looked at her watch – it was nearly ten. For the first time she felt worried. Maybe he had gone straight there, in which case he could have at least called and told her, or sent the car for them. He knew how much she looked forward to being with him on preview day, being presented and being seen as his wife. She also knew how important it was to Howard to have her and Joanne there, looking just right. Understated but expensive. She frowned and looked at her daughter, who was still gazing up at her. 'Oh, go and get your coat on, and ask Consuelo to get out your white hat and muff.' Jo didn't need telling twice and willingly shot off. Mummy was so horrible today but she was going to see Daddy's work and she liked that. It was exciting.

Margaret swung her mink over her shoulders; she loved the way it moved and the luxurious feel of it. She picked up her gloves and bag and went into the hall to the phone table. Quickly she dialled Howard's direct number at the centre, strumming her fingers on the table top as she waited for him to answer, but it was his secretary who picked it up. 'Good morning, it's Mrs Edwardes. I know he must be very busy but I need to speak to my husband, please.'

Anne hesitated. 'I'm sorry, Mrs Edwardes, but he's not here.'

Although they had yet to meet Margaret hated the coolness of Howard's secretary's voice. She was polite enough but she didn't show the right amount of reverence to Margaret when she talked to her on the phone. She always sounded so damned superior. 'Well, when he gets back tell him we're getting a cab and will be there as soon as we can.' Displeasure dripped from her voice.

At her end of the phone Anne heard the tone and swallowed hard. 'I'm sorry, when I say he's not here I mean he hasn't come in this morning.'

Margaret felt a sinking sensation in her stomach. 'Hasn't come in?' she repeated dumbly. She thought for a moment. 'He must at least have phoned?' It wouldn't be like Howard to be out of touch with the show on the very day it opened.

'No. No one's heard anything from him. In fact we're all at sixes and sevens, what with the show due to open in half an hour. Isn't he with you?'

'If he were here I wouldn't be calling, would I?' Margaret replied icily. 'I think I'd better stay here until he calls, then. If you hear from him before I do please let me know.'

'Of course, Mrs Edwardes. Goodbye.' Anne dropped the receiver into the cradle with a sigh of relief. Why hadn't she heard about them finding Howard? She knew the men had gone in as agreed at midnight the night before and should have been out by now. So why hadn't anyone told her about him? *Of course*, she argued to herself, *being shut away in the offices doesn't help. Maybe I should go out on to the floor?* But she knew she couldn't leave the office unattended. A loud knock on the door made her jump and before she could say anything the Colonel came blustering in. He was a bluff man who had been working for Great Britain Exhibitions when Howard first bought his way in. Howard had quickly come to appreciate his worth and was prepared to put up with his airs and graces (such as his insistence that he was referred to by his old army rank) because of the way in which he oversaw the build-up. He ran it like a military operation and his attention to detail meant Howard could leave the job safely in the man's hands. He could also be trusted to train up the new apprentice, Gordon Mayfield, who had started working with them in 1965.

'Where's Edwardes?' he barked at Anne.

She shrugged. 'No one's heard from him,' she said miserably. She tried to persuade herself that Howard was all right but the day dragged on and the only murmurs she heard about Howard was everyone's surprise that he wasn't there. She grew more and more worried.

It was the worst day at work she had ever had. The show opened on time as usual with the Colonel standing in for Howard and Gordon standing in for the Colonel. Even though the staff were fidgety the Princess and Lord Mayor didn't notice anything was amiss. The post-opening reception followed its usual pattern and the exhibitors started trading as soon as they could. The day was punctuated by phone calls from Margaret, who rang regularly to see if they had heard from Howard. Anne continued to field the calls, feeling worse with each one.

In Maida Vale Margaret was frantic.

She had swallowed her pride and not only done the unheard of and called Howard's club but had also called a number of friends to see if they had heard from him. This was particularly galling as she knew he'd had affairs, with several of the women she spoke to and she hated creating the impression that she was a desperate wife who couldn't keep her husband under control.

When, by five o'clock, neither she, the office nor his club had heard anything she finally picked up the phone and dialled 999. Initially the sergeant told her they couldn't do anything if a grown man chose to disappear, but eventually she convinced them that something must have happened. It was the photographs in the morning papers showing

Howard the night before as he released champagne corks over the Thames that finally persuaded them to send someone round to take down the details.

Margaret paced up and down the living-room carpet, one arm folded tightly across her waist as it supported the elbow of the other. Her cigarette holder was clamped between her fingers and she bit on it firmly when she put it to her lips. The worry that had been with her all day had once again become a simmering anger. *How dare Howard do this to me?* she stormed to herself. *How dare he make me a laughing stock? I bet those bitches are all on the phone to each other now, giggling away to each other.* 'What did you say?'

The policeman sighed. He had dealt with some difficult customers in his time but this woman was something else. He had expected to see some sign of worry or concern, especially after the way she had insisted they send him round, but all she seemed to be was angry, very angry indeed, yet contained at the same time. He repeated his question. It was all pretty basic stuff. When had she last seen him? Any reason why he would want to . . . he had been going to say leave home but changed his mind and said disappear instead. Any financial problems? At this Mrs Edwardes had snorted and said, 'Does it look as if there are?' He could have said she wouldn't be the first wife to be taken in by a bankrupt husband but again thought better of it. He just wanted to ask his questions and leave as soon as possible. He finally shut his notebook and promised that someone would be in touch once the notes had been written up. He told her most people who vanished like this usually turned up within a few days and that he was sure that Mr Edwardes would walk through the door very soon. Margaret just grunted and indicated he could show himself out. He almost felt like bowing as he shut the door behind him.

He stopped half way down the long hall to put on his coat. As he did so a door on the left opened and a child, who couldn't have been more than about six, cautiously peeped out. He could see over her head into a bedroom that was clearly hers. It was decorated in a style that any little girl would have adored and was full of obviously expensive toys. Despite this it was a saggy, large yellow rabbit that the child held to her chest, probably as some sort of comforter. He could see that she had been crying, and crying hard. He knelt down and formally held out his hand. 'Hello, my name's George. What's yours?' She gave a sniff and a jerky sigh came from her throat. She ignored his question. He tried again. 'Haven't you got a pretty bedroom?' She looked over her shoulder and then back at him, biting her lower lip as she nodded her head.

'Daddy did it for me. Do you know where my daddy is?' She searched his face anxiously, willing him to tell her Daddy would be home soon. That everything would be all right and Mummy would stop being in such a temper.

George, who had three children of his own, believed in telling them the truth at all times and, much as it troubled him to see this little girl so upset, he gave her the best answer he could. 'We're going to see if we can find him,' he said soothingly, but this wasn't enough and her eyes filled with tears again. The living-room door began to open behind him and as he turned to glance over his shoulder the little girl disappeared back inside her room.

'I thought you'd left,' Margaret said curtly as he straightened up.

'Just going, madam.' This time he did leave. He filed his report when he got back to the station and although he observed that 'any man who valued his balls' wouldn't put up with Mrs Edwardes he also said that it was clear the daughter adored her father and that by the look of her bedroom her father loved her. 'Maybe this time we haven't got a bloke who's just done a runner. Maybe we've stumbled across a real disappearance.' The desk sergeant laughed at him.

'Come on, George, you and I both know real mysteries don't happen to coppers like us. You've been watching too much of that *Dixon of Dock Green* on the telly. This is real life and he probably has done a runner, lovely little girl or not.' Reluctantly George had agreed.

Once the Celebration of the World barges had moored Howard went down to the river to inspect the models properly and have more publicity photographs taken. They were lucky it was such a glorious evening and he was whistling happily to himself when he returned to his office. Anne was still clearing away the glasses and bottles when he walked in. Her hair glowed in the evening sun making the lacquer on her beehive sparkle. As she bent over the top of her mini skirt crept up her legs and Howard watched appreciatively.

Prick tease, that's me, Anne thought to herself, acutely aware of Howard watching her as she bent just that bit further to give him a better view. She knew that men found her attractive. But even though she had made friends at work and through them had had plenty of opportunities to find herself a boyfriend, she had always preferred to maintain her independence. She'd had her fair share of sexual advances, some of which she had accepted, so she certainly knew what Howard wanted, but up until now the time hadn't been right. Within a few days of starting to work for Howard she had been told by several people about his reputation. She didn't want to be just another number in his personnel files, another secretary who came and went in six months.

No, to get her own back she had to make him want her so badly it affected his home life and his relationship with Peg. So far she had managed to avoid officially meeting his wife. The last thing Anne wanted to do was bring her identity to Peg's attention. Anonymity was the best way. So even though Howard always made a point of asking her to join the official line-up being introduced to the member of the Royal Family who opened the show, she always used the excuse of having to get everything ready for the post-opening reception to get out of it. That also meant she avoided his wife who traditionally was the first person Howard introduced.

Last year she had almost bumped into her.

Anne had been helping in the en-suite kitchen, making sure the waitresses kept circulating with bottles and plates of canapés as she usually did (keeping an eye on the staff was another excuse she used to stay behind the scenes) when she felt a tug on her skirt. Looking down she saw a child of about five. She was wearing a dark brown velvet dress with a heavy cream lace collar and cuffs. Half her shoulder-length hair had been pulled into a tight ponytail tied with a matching brown velvet ribbon that sat on top of her head. She had on thick cream lace tights and brown T-bar sandals. She smiled shyly at Anne and as she did so revealed the gap where her two front teeth should have been. She made an enchanting picture and Anne crouched down to talk to her on her own level.

'Hello, and who are you?'

The child's missing front teeth made her lisp slightly. 'I'm Joanne and please could you tell me if the seams on my tights are straight? She turned round and stood still while Anne looked at the back of her chubby little legs.

'Perfectly straight. Why?' she asked, bemused.

'Because Daddy says they should be and I've been to do a pee-pee by myself. My daddy's very important. This is his work,' she explained, as she grabbed a handful of her dress on either side and heaved at her tights.

Anne smiled to herself. She had seen pictures of Howard's daughter on his desk. Typical that he would dress his child like this and insist the poor kid kept her seams straight. *Honestly, men and the demands they put on females!* she thought to herself. 'Would you like me to help pull those up properly?' she offered with a smile.

'Yes please,' Joanne replied with obvious relief. Anne took her hand and led her out of sight behind the screen that hid the jumble of coats and jackets to help her sort herself out. 'Is that better?' she asked as she smoothed the velvet skirt down again.

'Yes. Thank you. I'm a big girl really but I couldn't ask Daddy 'cos he's busy and Mummy would just get cross. I had to promise not to bother her if I came and I've always wanted to come to Daddy's work.' Her expression was serious, obviously not wanting Anne to think she was being babyish.

'Well, I think you look ever so grown-up and important.'

'Joanne, Joanne?' Even after all this time Anne recognised the voice calling to the child. She froze where she was, hidden behind the screen desperately hoping Peg wouldn't put her head round it as she looked for Joanne.

'It's Mummy!' Her eyes grew bigger; the poor kid looked almost scared.

'Well, you run along and tell her you went to have a pee-pee all by yourself so she wouldn't be bothered and I'm sure it will be fine.' She gave the child a gentle push with her hand but stayed where she was. She heard the child's mother cross-examine her then reprimand her when she said she had gone for a pee-pee.

'Not pee-pee, Joanne, lavatory, you went to the lavatory.' She heard the child repeat, 'I went to the lavatory,' very solemnly and then added proudly, 'But I did go by myself! Well, almost. A nice lady helped me a little bit.'

'Yes, well, I suppose you didn't bother me with it. Good girl,' her mother said begrudgingly. 'Now come along, we've got to go home.' And the two of them had left the room. Anne peeped through the gap in the screen to check they had gone before she emerged.

She had avoided meeting Howard's wife last year and she certainly had no intention of meeting her this. 'What do you think of the models, Anne?' Howard was standing just that little bit too close to her.

'They're impressive, Mr Edwardes. I think visitors will love them.'

'But do you think they'll bring more people through the doors?' She considered the question carefully, knowing that when he made this sort of query he genuinely wanted her opinion. Just because he couldn't get her into bed didn't mean that he didn't value her work. She had proved to be an efficient secretary who not only stayed one step ahead of him and pre-empted his business needs but also had some very valid ideas and suggestions. As a result he often asked her to sit in on meetings, not just to take notes but so she could give her opinions. Many of her suggestions were taken up and, unusually for a man in his position, he always made sure she was given full credit for them, and often a bonus. It was because of this level of involvement that she had a greater awareness of the plans for the Home Maker Exhibition than many of Howard's staff who probably had more of a right to know than she did.

She looked at the models, flood-lit now that it was dark. 'By default,' she answered honestly. 'I mean, a lot of people will come to have a look and I expect they'll say "well, now we're here we might as well go and see the rest of it'. So yes, I think it will work in part.'

Howard nodded, accepting her comments as shrewd. 'Well, we'll know after it's all over. Has that bottle still got something in it?' Anne looked at the bottle in her hand.

‘It’s almost full, and so is that one. I was going to put them on one side and if they were OK use them in the office after we open tomorrow.’

‘Oh, come on, let’s finish them between us.’ He picked up a clean glass from the tray and took the bottle from her, deftly pouring its contents. He gave it to her and filled a second glass, clinking it against hers before he drank, almost emptying the glass in one gulp. ‘Cheers. Here’s to a great show and, if I haven’t said it yet, Anne, thank you for all your help and support. I really do appreciate it. Especially this year with all that chaos going on in the basement.’

Anne pulled a face. More than anyone else she was aware of the problems that had been caused when the management of the Pimlico Centre had announced their plans to add a third exhibition hall to the centre. Reactions to the news had been mixed. Howard, and therefore Anne, spent hours in meetings renegotiating their contract with the management until they finally got the deal they wanted. As from 1967 the Home Maker Exhibition would spread across all three halls. It would provide more space to put in eye-catching features and, even if the sales team groaned as they saw their targets move upwards again, everyone was actually pleased with the new tenancy agreement.

It was the day before the contract was due to be signed when the management had revealed that work would begin the very next day. The first job was to seal the cavernous basement area beneath the exhibition halls and the work would be done during the build-up period for the 1966 Home Maker Exhibition. Howard was furious and argued against it but with just twenty-four hours to go there was little he could do. He knew he was beaten when they threatened not to ratify the new terms if he continued objecting. The work began, and the mess was worse than anyone had imagined.

Dust seemed to find its way up through every nook and cranny to hang in the air like fine mist, bringing complaints from exhibitors as it settled on stock already positioned on stands. The noise was another problem, as the old pool mechanism was raised several times to just below floor level and then dropped again. The graunching of the iron props rumbled round the halls and tempers were even more frayed than usual. Then as suddenly as it had all started it stopped. The peace was wonderful and the last few days of the build-up period had been smoother than ever before, probably because everyone was so grateful for the comparative quiet.

Howard poured himself another glass of champagne and made to refill Anne’s glass but she shook her head, putting her hand over it. ‘Oh, come on, another won’t hurt.’

‘No, I know, but let me finish this one first.’ She took another sip to show willing and Howard emptied his glass again. *That’s his fourth*, she thought as she smiled at him over the rim of her glass.

The fact that she was now doing little more than raising it to her lips and lowering it again without drinking was something Howard didn't notice.

'You know, I sometimes think this is the most exciting time of the show. Build-up almost done, we can see how it's all going to look and the punters aren't in yet. The calm before the storm.' Another empty glass. Trouble was he didn't hold it quite as well as he used to. Including what he had drunk when the barges arrived he had finished almost two bottles by himself. He was looking a bit glazed and, slightly unsteady on his feet, he lowered himself on to his chair and leaned back.

Anne picked up the almost empty bottle and topped up his glass, a half smile on her lips. He didn't stop her. God, he wanted her. Maybe this was his chance to make a move But not here. Not in the office. It had to be somewhere different. She was probably a – what did they call it now a days?—a raver . . . yes, that was it, she was probably a real little raver when she got going. He let the effect of the champagne wash over him as he imagined Anne beneath him, wriggling with pleasure. His eyes snapped open. 'Sorry, I wasn't listening.'

'It's OK, I was just saying how surprised I was that the work in the basement has taken so long and made such a mess. I mean, I thought all they would have had to do was brick up the doors or whatever it is they have down there.' She kept her tone neutral but, perching on the edge of his desk, she crossed her legs so her hem rose higher.

As she saw Howard's eyes follow her rising skirt a sense of amazement washed over her. My God. This was it! After three years of watching and waiting for an opportunity to get her own back the moment had finally arrived. In all that time Anne had had no idea quite what she would do. All she had known for certain was that she would spot the time when it came . . . and now it had!

Oh, this is too easy! she thought as she smiled innocently at Howard. *I'll go with him tonight and tomorrow I'll let him persuade me to join the line-up. If I can tell when he's had sex then I'm sure his wife can as well. It'll give her such a shock to see me and then when she realises that I'm Howard's latest . . . I'll make sure she knows. A little glance, flicking a bit of fluff off his collar, that's all it'll take.* She gave him a wider smile and he leaned forward. For a moment she thought he might put his hand on her knee but then reprimanded herself. He was far too experienced a player for a clumsy gesture like that. The tension crackled between them. What was he going to do?

'You've never seen the basement, have you?' She shook her head. 'Come on, I'll take you down and show you.'

'What, now?' She was immediately cross with herself for letting her surprise show, but as her genuine amazement made Howard chuckle she saw it wasn't such a bad thing after all.

'Of course now. Once the show's opened we'll be too busy, and besides, the crew are coming in from midnight to finish the work so it'll all be closed by ten tomorrow morning. You see, it's now or never.' He pushed himself to his feet and wobbled a little. She pretended not to notice. 'Come on.' He held out his hand to her and she took it, feeling a tremor of something go through her as she jumped off his desk. 'Don't forget this.' He scooped up the other almost full bottle of champagne and their glasses as they left the office. As soon as they got outside the door he let go of her hand and she followed him to the lift. In silence they descended to the ground floor. From there Howard led the way to the side staircase and pushed open the double doors. The sound of their feet hitting the concrete steps echoed up the stairwell and when he pushed his way through another set of doors, letting them slam behind him, that noise also disappeared upwards.

He took her hand again and walked purposefully along the twisting corridors of the basement. The further away from the stairs they got the more spartan it became until the strip lighting overhead stopped all together, to be replaced by occasional hanging lights with metal shades that lit only part of their route as they walked underneath them. Somewhere a door slammed and a breeze wafted along, setting the lights swinging and making the shadows dance. There was a smell of newly disturbed dust and an even older, musty smell that seemed to pervade everything. They carried on and the floor sloped gently downwards until Howard turned left into a much narrower passage. It seemed lower than it was as all along the ceiling and down one side ran pipes of different sizes. Finally Howard stopped by a small wooden step-ladder. It was propped against a wall and about three feet above the floor was a dark, doorless opening.

Anne's heart was thumping as Howard climbed the steps and put the champagne and glasses down carefully on the top one. He reached round the corner into the darkness and fiddled around for a moment. A pale light appeared. 'Mind how you go.' His voice was low and thick. He carried on up the ladder and stepped into the gap. The steps creaked as they took his weight. There was another ladder dropping down on the other side, this time a metal-runged one set into the wall. It was longer than the wooden one as, much to Anne's surprise, the inside of the cavern was deeper than the outside. She let him help her down, feeling the warmth of his hands round her waist as he lifted her to the ground. Anne pretended to stumble and steadied herself by putting an arm across Howard's shoulders. He held her tighter.

Anne blinked in the gloom. What had seemed quite a bright light outside now appeared very dim indeed. She peered upwards and saw that the light came from three single uncovered bulbs, hanging on heavy cords and chains at regular intervals across the ceiling. Beneath them were a series of tall, broad concrete pillars with angular corners supporting an iron prop that disappeared upwards. They were linked by a circuit of more large pipes that left an eight-inch gap between them and the floor. Solid metal clamps and plates bolted to the floor held them in position. The levers and cogs of a huge wrought iron hoist also loomed out of the shadows. She tried to make out more but the size of the basement and the inadequate light meant she could see nothing beyond deepening tones of murky grey, blue and black.

'There are three more of those,' Howard said softly in her ear, making her jump as he followed her gaze to the hoist. 'One in each corner to support the water tanks when they're full. The pipes are linked to the hydraulic mains circuit round London and it's that pressure that fills the tanks. They used to raise and fill the tanks all the time until a few years ago. It's actually a superb example of inter-war engineering. Remember the Pimlico Regatta?' Anne nodded; it used to be the biggest event in London and she had often wondered how they got all that water inside the Pimlico Centre. Howard took her hand again. 'Be careful you don't catch your foot on anything.' He walked towards the middle of the basement and came to a stop. 'This would be the deep end, twenty feet if needed.' She squinted into the dark nothingness below her.

This is madness! she thought. *Please don't tell me he wants to have me down here? I can't go through with this. Will he fire me if I leave him? Is it worth it?* The thoughts tumbled over each other. *You've come too far to go back now*, said a voice inside her head. *Go on, you can do it.* She turned to face Howard again. 'It's interesting. I'm glad I've seen it.' She made the words sound as sexy and full of innuendo as possible. 'It's surprisingly warm, isn't it? I thought it would be cold and damp.'

'Warm as toast. Here, have a drink.' He had rescued the bottle and glasses from the top step as she adjusted her eyesight. She could see the glasses twinkle as they caught what little light there was and even though the last thing she wanted was more champagne she accepted the glass he held out to her. Again she pretended to drink as Howard emptied first one and then another glass. 'You're right, it is warm, isn't it?' He looked around. 'Let's sit down.' He led the way to one of the concrete pillars and took off his jacket, making a long pad of it which he placed on top of the large pipe at its base. Anne sat down and leaned back against the flat side of the pillar, closing her eyes as Howard sat next to her. The stone was hard and cold under her shoulder blades. She hadn't been joking when she had said it was warm and she could feel patches of dampness beginning to form between her breasts. Howard gently ran his finger up and down her bare forearm. When she didn't move or react in any way he twisted round and in so doing moved so far that he fell off the pipe, landing on his knees in front of her. The champagne slopped out of the top of his glass and splashed against her thigh, making her start and open her eyes. 'What are you doing down there?' she asked in a low voice.

He shifted his position so he was crouching in front of her. 'Hoping you might join me.' She laughed and leaned forward, making sure she angled herself so he could look down her dress, which he did willingly. *It's too easy, show him a bit of cleavage and he's all yours*, she thought as she took his face in her hands and very slowly lifted his chin so she could reach his lips and kiss him. He knelt so he could reach her, putting his hands on her knees as he did so, inching his splayed fingers further up her thighs as they kissed. *Damn, bloody tights!* he swore to himself, but she obliged by parting her legs a little so he could push his hands closer to her crotch, making her wriggle as he did so. Her dress had been pushed almost to her waist but as he got closer Howard moved his hands to reach up behind her, holding her in a firm embrace while his fingers fiddled with her zip and his tongue eagerly searched her mouth.

'God, this is a ridiculous way for two adults to behave!' she gasped, pulling away as she felt him undo the zip.

'But it is fun.' Howard maintained his hold on her. 'Of course,' he continued, 'it could be even more fun.' Anne gave him a knowing smile which he took as her understanding of the situation. Confident that he had established the game plan he let go of her and stood up, dusting his trousers down. Anne stayed where she was watching him, her lower lip caught between her teeth.

'You are enjoying yourself, aren't you?' she said pointedly, looking at his groin. Howard's eyes followed hers.

'And you're not?' he retorted, helping her to her feet. 'The workmen aren't due for another four hours yet so we've got plenty of time and still half a bottle of bubbly. Where are the glasses?' She bent down to pick them up, tipping what was left of hers out behind the pillar, hoping he wouldn't notice. Howard was too drunk to notice anything so mundane and he filled them both up again, concentrating hard so he didn't spill any. 'Here's to a working relationship!' He drank heavily as Anne watched him.

'Those trousers are going to get even dustier if you're not careful,' she told him. He looked ruefully at his knees and the trails of dust that still clung there despite his earlier attempts to clean them off.

'Won't do my shirt any good either, will it?' She shook her head. Howard looked round and in the half light spotted a pile of tarpaulins heaped against one of the iron struts. 'That looks cosy.' Anne followed his gaze and then slowly reached up behind her to finish undoing her zip and step out of her dress. She hoped she would have the courage to see it through and the voice in her head tried to talk sense to her, helping her maintain whatever dignity she could in what she knew was a ludicrous situation. *I feel such a fool, behaving like some common tart, but tomorrow morning when she shakes my hand she'll know and that one moment will make this worthwhile.* She laid her dress next to his jacket which was now half hanging off the pipe and when she turned round he had already removed his tie and shirt and was now fumbling with his fly.

'Here, let me.' His hands fell to his sides as she released the tension on the fabric by undoing his zip. She let her hand gently brush against him and was startled by the strength of the response she felt. She wanted to run away but stood her ground as he stepped out of his trousers and, much to her amusement, carefully folded them along the creases. 'This isn't the Ritz, you know.' She held out her hand to take them and the rest of his clothes but as she went to add them to the pile on the pipe a few feet away she began to laugh. She couldn't help herself. 'I'm so sorry, but you look so silly standing there in your underpants and socks.' He hooked his thumbs round the waistband and she felt a surge of panic well up inside her. 'It's the socks,' she said quickly and to her relief he raised first one foot and then the other and peeled them off, tossing them to her one by one to be placed with the rest of their clothes.

There was a sudden gust of air and the overhead lamps swung a little, making the shadows even longer as the light shifted around the basement. Anne and Howard stood looking at each other until he bent down to pick up the bottle and his glass which he filled once more, leaving about an inch of champagne in the bottle. He drained his in one final gulp and as he threw his head back Anne couldn't help but admire his body. *He may be on getting on a bit*, she thought, *but he's not in bad shape.* His arms were still muscular, as was his torso, and in the orangey light his skin glowed and the hairs on his chest had a golden gleam. He lowered his glass and looked straight at her.

'Funny how men look stupid in just their underwear but women look so alluring.' He ran his eyes over her body, savouring everything he saw from her full breasts, still contained in her bra, to her shapely legs. *At least she's got a bit of meat on her*, he thought as the gently swinging light revealed her slightly rounded stomach. He'd waited long enough for this moment and was determined to enjoy what was to follow – and doing it down in the basement made it even more interesting. 'Come here,' he said out loud.

The secretary in Anne responded automatically and she took a step towards him before changing her mind. 'No,' she said with a giggle in her voice. 'You come and get me.' *Might as well make him work for it*, she thought as she darted round the corner of the pillar with a shriek. Howard followed, pausing to put his glass down next to hers by their clothes, but holding on to the champagne bottle. There might only be a bit left in it but she wouldn't be the first woman off whom he had licked champagne.

Anne waited until he almost caught her and then darted off in another direction, towards an identical pillar. Howard followed. She decided to let him chase her around four or five of the squat columns before allowing him to catch her. She headed towards yet another pillar with Howard still in pursuit. Anne danced round it, squealing as she dodged first left and then right, with Howard mirroring her movements. She turned towards one of the big iron hoists in the corner and then changed her mind, swerving instead to her right. Part of the pipe that ran round the basement was closer than she'd realised but she spotted it in time and leaped over it, aiming slightly to her right, missing another pillar that seemed to loom up out of a patch of darkness which the pale lights overhead couldn't quite reach. *Next time I'll let him catch me*, she decided as she glanced over her shoulder to check how close he was.

Everything seemed to happen so quickly.

One minute Howard, still clutching the champagne bottle, was behind her, the next he was sprawling face down in the dust while the bottle rolled away into the shadows. Like her he had seen the pipe at the last minute, and he too had taken a flying leap at it. But unlike Anne he misjudged it, catching his foot as the rest of him sailed over. Sober it wouldn't have mattered, but with the best part of three bottles of champagne inside him he wasn't able to break his fall and he hit the sharp corner of the pillar closest to the pipe with a sickening thud before ending up on the concrete floor.

Anne stopped. She stood and stared.

Surely he was mucking about? It was the oldest trick in the book, wasn't it, pretend you're hurt and as soon as they get close . . . tag and you're it. But there was something about his stillness that bothered her. And the crunch when he'd hit the pillar . . . Cautiously she stepped towards him. 'Howard.' Why was she whispering? 'Howard,' she repeated a bit louder. 'HOWARD.' She yelled his name as she bent over him and crouched down, shaking his shoulder. Did he move or not? She wasn't sure.

He was lying on his front with his right hand raised above his head as if he had put it out to stop himself falling. His left arm was bent at an unusual angle pointing to his feet and his legs were also in an unnatural position. The words 'He's dead' flashed through her mind, but he couldn't be. Could he? He mustn't be! But the confirmation she needed came when she put her hand to his forehead and felt something warm and slimy. She jumped back and looked at her hand. In the bad light she could tell it had something on it, a dark smear that glistened. Horrified, she backed away. Help, she had to get help. But where to go and how to explain it? That was when she heard the noise. Already terrified she spun round, frantically peering into the darkness, but in the half light she could see nothing.

Maybe it was one of the workmen? Maybe they had seen what happened? They would say it was her fault. That she had killed him. They would find her half naked with blood on her hands. Howard's blood. That was why she was undressed, so his blood wouldn't leave any marks on her clothes. They would find out who she was, work out the connection, say she was jealous of Howard. Say it was revenge. There it was again. 'Hello!' she called cautiously into the darkness, but heard little more than a scuffling sound. Rats! That's what it was, rats. The blood, the smell of Howard's blood had brought them out of their hiding place and there were probably thousands of them in an old place like this.

The gloom seemed to thicken and the air grew hotter. Her heart was hammering. What time was it? The workmen would be there soon to seal up the basement. They'd help her. She would have to make them understand. The scuffling started again, sounding closer. She couldn't stay here, she couldn't. The workmen would find him and think it was an accident, just an accident. She would dress him and then leave. She turned round to get her clothes but in the murkiness she wasn't sure which pillar they had been left by.

In a frenzy she began searching the basement until she was almost running round each of the square concrete blocks. By the time she found the right pillar tears were streaming down her face. She felt suffocated and couldn't breathe. She went to put her dress on but, realising she'd get it covered in Howard's blood, she grabbed instead at his shirt and wiped her hands as best she could, clawing at the fabric in her determination to remove every trace. When she was sure her hands were as clean as possible she quickly put on her dress again. As she zipped it up she saw the two champagne glasses and felt herself go cold. She'd forgotten about the glasses. If the workmen found them they would know he hadn't been alone. For a split second she wondered what had happened to the bottle itself and was about to look for it when the noise started again. It sounded closer.

Hardly knowing what she was doing she frantically wrapped the now blood-stained shirt inside the rest of Howard's clothes and scooped up the glasses, bundling them into the middle of the cloth so they wouldn't bounce around and shatter. As quickly as she could she stumbled back to the doorway, hurling her armful out of the gap ahead of her before she propelled herself after it. She ran as fast as she could along the twisting corridor until she reached the section where the overhead lights were replaced by fluorescent strips. She stopped and took a deep breath.

She realised she was still clutching his clothes. What on earth had made her bring them with her? Why hadn't she left them where they were? Now she had to hope no one would see her with them. Slowly Anne made her way back to the office, checking first round every corner that no one was there. She was lucky and when she reached the fire-exit doors at the bottom of the stone stairs she remembered that there were rubbish skips outside them. The safety people had been moaning about them all week but right now they were just what she needed. She pushed open the double bars and shoved the clothes down the side of a skip, heaving some cardboard boxes and bits of wood and other waste from the build-up on top of them. She shut the doors firmly behind her and with a calmness she wasn't feeling managed not only to go back to her office and finish tidying up as she would have done under normal circumstances; but also to make a point of leaving by the manned lift so she could wish the night watchman good night.

She still hadn't worked out how she would react next day when she was told the news about Howard's accident but she hoped that by then she would have thought of something.

Meanwhile, in the basement, a uniformed figure had eased his way out of his hiding place between the heavy pipes round the walls. His boots made a scuffling noise on the pipes, which carried the sound round the cavern. Shame they were sealing it up. He would miss creeping down here for forty winks in the warmth. 'Specially as no one else ever came down. That was, until tonight. Given him a jolt when he had first heard them voices but it had been fun seeing the boss and his secretary rompin' around starkers. Given him a nice bit of relief, it had, seeing her tits bounce around like that. Pity they hadn't gone any further really. He'd enjoyed watching them. Silly of the gaffer to go and slip like that.

He pulled the back of his hand across his mouth and gave a laconic stretch. Ah well, better go and see if he could help the silly old sod. Might get a few bob out of him, or even a few quid. The thought of money spurred him on. He paused for a moment to straighten his tie and put his cap on properly. Didn't want to give the game away, did he? Could tell the boss he was just doing his rounds as usual and found him, like. Being diligent, that's what it was. He pulled his torch out of his pocket and made his way over to the corner where Howard was still lying.

'Cor lummy,' he said for effect, trying to make it sound as if he had just happened across Howard by accident. 'What have you gone and done to yerself, sir?' He bent down, shining his torch on Howard's face. 'Well, well, well. Now this is interestin'.' In the pool of white light Howard's open eye stared up at him. His right cheek was pressed to the ground and a trickle of bloody saliva dribbled from the corner of his mouth, hanging in a long strand, trailing in the dust beneath it. If his appearance hadn't been enough to tell him Howard was dead then the deep gash across his forehead would have proved it. It ran diagonally from his left temple to above what could be seen of his right eye. A pool of blood had collected below Howard's head and glistening shards of skull edged the cut. It wasn't a pretty sight. He stood up slowly.

Question was, what to do now? Raise the alarm, or . . . or do what she'd done and leg it? Wouldn't help if they found him now, would it? He was already dead. But it might be useful in the future. You never knew what might come in handy, did you? He felt the old tingle go through him as he realised that once again he'd got some information that might be worth something. OK, so he'd promised his parole officer that he'd be a good boy, but they were all so fucking stupid. Doing time was the best thing that had ever happened to him. Got fed regular and a good education to boot – what he'd learned about the blackmail game! No wonder they'd caught up with him. The way he operated before was amateur to what some of the blokes had been up to. The best lesson he'd learned was to value your information. The bigger the information, the higher the price. And this was information all right. This could be the big time. But he had to be careful. Not waste it. That was lesson number two: timing. Bide his time and see what happened. Let her feel secure before he put in an offer. But how much was it worth?

He grimaced as he pondered on it. Ah well, give him something to think about in the small hours of the morning, that would.

Jo was feeling guilty about Maggie. Admittedly she had said some terrible things the weekend before the funeral, but was that justification for ignoring her?

'From what you told me and from what little I saw of her, yes it is.' Alan sat across the desk from her, holding her hands in his, gently stroking them with his thumbs. They were in his office in the press centre but as usual the conversation had drifted from the professional to the personal.

'But she hasn't got anyone else. There's only her and me. I can't just leave her in the Warren without going to see her.'

'I give up with you.' Alan released her hands and sat back. 'So what are you going to do? Pop in one day to see her as if nothing has happened, as if nothing has been said? Do that and you're right back at square one. The next time she's feeling bored she'll kick up a fuss and you'll go scuttling down there like you always did. Do that, Jo, and every bit of independence you've fought for will be brushed aside in an instant. In fact it'll be worse than before because you won't have stood your ground. Don't be a fool. Come on, Jo, finish what you've started.'

She looked at him unhappily. Of course he was right, so why did she feel so wretched? 'Oh, Alan, I don't want to let you down, but maybe I could just phone?'

'Jesus Christ! It's not about letting me down but about letting *your-self* down.' He could feel himself growing angry with her wimpishness. 'Don't ask my permission. I'm not the important one here, you are, and your relationship with your mother. Look what happened with Simon. You were so proud of yourself for sticking to your guns and not letting him back. This is exactly the same thing.'

The scene the previous weekend, when Simon had turned up on the doorstep unannounced, sprang to her mind. It was one of those rare evenings when her time away from work coincided with Alan's day off. She had invited him round and they had been sitting over a pizza and a bottle of wine when the doorbell rang. When Jo answered it she was amazed to see not only Simon standing there, but also his suitcases stacked in front of him.

'Hi there,' he said breezily, as if nothing had happened. 'Be a love and give me a hand with the cases, will you?' and he began heaving them through the front door. For a moment Jo just stood and watched him, open mouthed.

'What do you think you're doing?' she finally asked.

'What does it look like? Moving back in. Come on, Jo, let's kiss and make up. I can see you didn't mean it – after all you're still wearing the ring.' She looked down at her hand. Sure enough the diamond winked back at her. Funny really, she'd forgotten it was there. After so long it felt such a part of her that she had stopped seeing or sensing it. She grabbed at her left hand with her right and began pulling at the ring but it didn't want to budge. Angrily she licked the finger and tried again. It took a bit of effort but finally the ring moved, leaving her finger red and sore.

'It was a mistake.' She held it out to him but he refused to take it. 'I told you, it's over, Simon. When I said I wanted you out I meant it. Maybe when we first met I might have changed my mind but not now. I don't love you or want you, and I don't need you either.' Her arm fell back by her side, her hand still holding the ring.

'No, I can see that,' Simon said pointedly, looking over her shoulder. Alan had come out of the living room to see what was keeping Jo and was standing in the hall. 'So, it's all right for you to have a fling but not me?' Jo tried hard but couldn't stop herself from blushing.

'Alan is a friend. Something you never were.' As she said it she realised how true that was. Over and above the love and affection she felt towards Alan was the greater feeling of friendship. That, she now knew, was what had been missing all those years with Simon. She had felt such an overwhelming gratitude towards him for wanting to go out with her, for wanting to go to bed with her, that that emotion had totally drowned anything else. She now understood that her gratitude had enabled him to manipulate her, to use it against her in some sort of emotional blackmail. It was too one-sided, and no basis for a relationship. The blush vanished as quickly as it had appeared.

'Simon, I threw you out because I didn't want you here. I still don't, nor will I in the future. I'm giving you one last chance to take the ring.' She held it out again between her forefinger and thumb. He hesitated for a moment and Alan took a step forward. Simon looked from one to the other and then snatched the ring from her fingers.

'Don't think I'm going to give *you* another chance,' he snapped at her as he began shoving the cases back outside again. Jo watched him in silence and shut the door firmly behind her as soon as he was back on the pavement. She leaned against it, hands behind her back.

'Whew. I didn't think I had it in me.'

'I did.'

Jo remembered how they had gone back inside and the comfortable cosiness of the rest of the evening. No tension, no worries about what each other might want or do, just their relaxed friendship. She remembered the release she'd felt as she finally understood Simon's control over her. And as she did so she was suddenly able to apply it to how Maggie had controlled her all these years. Of course she had always known her mother managed to manoeuvre her whichever way she wanted, but she had never really understood why.

Now she knew. Now it made sense. Maggie had felt a similar gratitude towards Howard for giving her status. When he went that went with him, leaving Maggie emotionally destitute. The only way she could hit back was by taking it out on the one other person close to her – her daughter.

'Out with it,' said Alan, seeing her expression change.

'It's difficult to explain . . .' And it was. Jo knew what she was feeling but couldn't quite put it into words that would make sense. 'But you're right. I'm not going to see her.'

'Now,' she continued, suddenly businesslike again, 'about dates for you and Suzanne to view the rough cut.'

Despite Sergeant George Wilmot's assertion that Howard would probably show up in a few days there was no word from him. Not so much as a phone call to the office or a hastily scribbled postcard to Maida Vale. Nothing. Margaret became increasingly ratty and Joanne more and more miserable. It was three weeks after his disappearance when an embarrassed Consuelo presented herself at the living-room door. She held a tea towel in her hands which she was winding round and round her fingers. Margaret had told her she didn't want to talk to her but the woman insisted, finally getting her attention when she blurted out, 'But Meesis Edwardees. I 'ave no monies to pay ze bills.' Margaret stared at her. 'What do you mean you've got no money?'

'Meester Edwardees, he gives me ze 'ousekeeping every week but for three weekes no Meester Edwardees so no monies.'

'Shit!' Margaret felt as if someone had dumped a bucket of cold water over her. She reached for her handbag and took out her purse. 'How much do you need?' She handed a few notes to Consuelo, who gratefully escaped back to the kitchen.

Margaret hadn't thought about money. It had always been there. If she wanted something she either charged it or asked Howard and he gave her whatever she needed. As far as bills were concerned she didn't get involved. She had made it clear to Howard when they married that if he didn't want her running the club, for which she was paid, she certainly wasn't going to run his home for him as an unpaid skivvy. Howard had laughed and agreed he would take care of everything. It actually suited him very nicely that his wife didn't know how much things cost or what went in and out of the house.

But now it was a problem.

All their accounts at the bank were in his name only and she didn't even know how much was in them. Every week Howard paid an allowance into her own account which more than covered her needs, and that was all that had mattered to her. Margaret made her way into the hall and picked up the pile of mail addressed to Mr Edwardes that had accrued since Howard had gone. Most of it was official-looking, which was why she had left it. They were usually nothing to do with her. Now she took the pile, which was quite substantial, and went to sit down in the study. She used a paper knife to start slitting the envelopes before pulling out the contents one by one. Almost all bills. Telephone, gas, electricity, the charge accounts at Harrods and Selfridges, which included all the groceries. There was a huge florist's bill (*and those weren't all for me by any means*, Margaret thought drily) and one from the wine merchant, as well as other bills to do with the flat itself. There was also a note from the bank, dated the previous week, with which they had returned a number of her personal cheques.

She had no idea her cheques hadn't been honoured. With a sense of dread she reached for a piece of paper and began adding it all up. My God! Was that really what they spent? She thought about her clothes and the way in which they lived, but then shrugged. They could afford it. She'd call the bank and get them to handle it all.

She rang the number on the top of the bank's letter and asked to speak to the manager, Mr Higgins. She waited while they connected her. A quick word would do it, then maybe she should go out? She had barely been out since Howard had vanished and she could do with cheering up. She had just decided to treat herself to tea at Fortnum & Mason's when she was connected to Mr Higgins.

'Ah, Mr Edwardes . . . Oh, I'm so sorry, *Mrs* Edwardes, forgive the mistake, but as you know it's usually your husband I deal with.'

'Quite,' said Margaret crisply. He may be their bank manager but he was still her inferior. 'A slight problem appears to have arisen which my husband is unable to take care of at the moment so I needed to talk to you about covering those cheques. Sorry I didn't get back to you sooner but they've only just been brought to my attention.'

'Of course, Mrs Edwardes. I must admit I was a little surprised when one of my clerks brought them to *my* attention but I'm sure we can sort it out. For the last couple of weeks we've had no instruction from Mr Edwardes about the usual transfer of funds from his account to yours which would explain the problem. If you ask him to give that instruction then we will reissue the cheques immediately.' On the same day that the clerk had told Mr Higgins about the cheques he'd had a visit from the police. Routine, they had assured him, but they were looking into the disappearance of Mr Howard Edwardes and wanted some information about his affairs.

Normally if Mrs Edwardes wrote out one cheque too many (which she did from time to time) he would let it through knowing that Mr Edwardes could, and would, cover it. But the police saying he had disappeared . . . well, that made a difference. As soon as they had left he had requested all details on Mr Edwardes' accounts and, seeing no movement on it over the last few days, he had taken the decision to bounce Mrs Edwardes' cheques. He hoped by the end of the conversation to find out what had happened to the man.

'That's a bit difficult, you see.' She didn't like the way this conversation was going. 'I mean, he's away at the moment and I don't know how to get hold of him.'

There was a pause at the other end of the phone. Mr Higgins sucked on his dentures and swivelled his seat to look out of the window. 'That's going to make things rather awkward. You see, without his authorisation I can't do anything.'

'But I'm his wife!'

'Yes, Mrs Edwardes, but apart from your own personal account you aren't a recognised signatory on the rest,' he explained patiently, and while this sank in carried on quickly. 'Mrs Edwardes, this is as embarrassing for me as it is for you, I do assure you, and I hate dealing with this sort of business on the telephone. Why don't you come in to see me? How does Thursday at three sound?'

'Fine,' she said feebly and hung up. Howard going had been bad enough, but Howard leaving her without any money was worse. Surely she could sort something out, make Mr Higgins understand?

She could not.

The interview on Thursday, although perfectly polite and charming, was easily one of the most unpleasant she had ever had to endure. Not only did she have to admit that Howard had done more than gone away, he had disappeared; she also had to admit that without him she was broke. Mr Higgins called the accountant for Great Britain Exhibitions who explained that since Howard had been gone for over two weeks, a period which could realistically be termed a holiday, a decision had been taken that they couldn't keep paying his salary indefinitely so it had been put on hold until his return.

Margaret had been dumbfounded when this was relayed back to her. 'Can they do that? Have they got the authority?'

'Unfortunately, yes they have. Which doesn't solve our little problem.'

'It might be a little problem to you but to me it's a huge problem. What am I going to do? What about my daughter?'

'Ah, yes, little Joanne. We might be able to come to some arrangement whereby she is given a small allowance from her father's estate.'

'What did you call it?' Her eyes flashed at him. 'An estate is something dead people have. Howard's not dead. Just missing.' She screwed a cigarette into her holder, a thoughtful expression on her face. 'Of course, if he were dead then there'd be no problem, would there? Honestly, why didn't I think of this sooner? I mean, I know he's written a will that looks after me and Joanne so surely we just, what's the word . . . invoke the terms of that and everything can go back to normal, can't it, Mr Higgins? Can't it?' She demanded as he didn't answer.

'Not exactly . . .' He ran a finger round his collar. Margaret got up and began pacing the room.

'Now what?'

'Well, you see, I'm no solicitor but I believe – now I may be wrong – but I do believe that the law stipulates that if someone, such as Mr Edwardes, disappears then a set time has to elapse before he can, in law, be deemed dead and therefore his will read and the estate released. I may be quite wrong but let's explore that avenue first. If there is still a problem we can talk about an allowance for Joanne.'

He wasn't wrong. By the summer of 1967, over a year after he had disappeared, they still hadn't heard from Howard. Margaret was in the horrific position of not only being denied access to Howard's funds but having to rely on the meagre allowance the bank was granting her for Joanne as a minor. And to make matters worse she had to sign an agreement saying the money would be repaid to the estate when Joanne came of age. Unless of course Howard came home or gave instructions before then, which everyone now doubted. She had fully expected him to turn up in time for Christmas and when he didn't felt an even bigger fool. Clearly he had left her – and without so much as a backward glance.

Life at Clive Court became more and more untenable. Margaret got rid of both Consuelo and the extra daily and began looking after the flat herself, which she hated, taking it out on Joanne. The child became withdrawn and increasingly solemn, which in turn made Margaret snap at her more. Joanne tried to understand what had happened but her unhappiness and confusion grew until she finally stopped trying to communicate with her mother at all.

And then, just as Margaret was thinking she might actually have to go back to work, the lifeline arrived.

Margaret had long dreaded the arrival of the post as every day no matter how hard she tried, bills kept on coming. Admittedly they were far lower than they used to be, but they were still bills. So when the long brown envelope landed on their mat she looked at it with her usual distaste before opening it. Joanne sat opposite, drinking her milk as quietly as she could. She was trying to gauge her mother's mood to see if she dared give her the note from school that said they were all going to see a pantomime at the end of term and could she send the money for the ticket by the end of the week? Demands for money were guaranteed to make her mother cross. Margaret read the brown envelope's contents and then reread them. Slowly a smile spread across her face. 'Do you know what this is, Joanne?'

Amazed at the change in her mother's mood she nervously shook her head. 'This, my darling, is salvation. Thank you!' she yelled at the ceiling as she began to dance round the kitchen. Joanne felt even more uncertain than usual and never did find out what it was all about, but at least it meant she could give her mother the note before going to school.

Margaret shoved everything into the sink and picked up the paper, but she couldn't concentrate. The clock hands crawled round until they finally said nine o'clock. Taking the letter with her she went into the study and called the solicitors, Hesketh, Dinglefield & Company, asking for Mr Hesketh. He took her call immediately, reassuring her that far from being too early for him he had been at his desk for an hour already. Niceties out of the way, Margaret referred to his letter.

He explained that basically what was being offered was a sort of power of attorney that would ensure Great Britain Exhibitions would be able to continue trading. He said that the company had managed quite nicely until now but as Howard had been its driving force something would have to be done if it were to continue. The offer to take on this work in return for a percentage of the profits, while at the same time giving Margaret a modest income, would ensure that things kept going if she were willing to agree. In fact, he said pointedly, it was only out of politeness that he had informed her as the board were perfectly happy with the suggestion.

She heard what he wasn't saying and accepted readily. She then did as she was asked and formally replied to his letter, giving her approval for the papers to be drawn up.

Thank God, she thought as she put it in the post, *real money at last*. She didn't bother to find out the exact sums involved, she was too caught up in picturing herself as she had been over a year ago when Howard was still there and she still had money. The papers were drawn up and Margaret signed them unread, with a flourish. It wasn't until her first cheque arrived that she discovered exactly how much was meant by 'modest'. Admittedly it was more than the bank had given her but it was nowhere near as much as she had been used to, nor what she had expected from what she understood to be Howard's not inconsiderable shareholding in the company. Margaret felt as if she had been conned, but when she tried to object was told there was nothing she could do.

She had agreed and the papers were signed.

It took Anne two days to realise that no one had found Howard. It was much longer than that before she stopped seeing his half-naked form lying in the dust with one eye staring up at her, but eventually the nightmares receded and finally they stopped altogether.

There had been one odd incident a week after the exhibition opened when she was returning from the print room and tripped over a loose carpet edge. As she felt herself tumble and put her hands out to catch herself she felt someone's arms stopping her. Straightening up, the man who caught her smiled. 'Careful, miss. Don't want yer fallin' over and catchin' yer head, do we?' He had winked at her cheekily before carrying on down the corridor. His words had made her go cold. But it was surely no more than an innocent comment anyone would make. Wasn't it?

Howard's disappearance had thrown everything into turmoil but she had done her best to hold it together. When the news first broke they covered it up as best they could, and everyone recognised how important a part Anne had played in that. She still sat in board meetings taking notes but without Howard there to prompt her she didn't join in so much. The meetings became exercises in damage limitation but the more she listened the more she discovered how little the other people round the table knew about Howard's plans, and how little they actually wanted to know. Her own knowledge became obvious when on one occasion she couldn't help herself and corrected the Colonel, who asked her how she knew. 'Because Mr Edwardes told me,' she stammered, blushing to the roots of her hair. After that they included her more, listening to her comments and the calm way she was able to see the implications of a situation. So when, late one night, the idea popped into her head she didn't automatically dismiss it as nonsense.

She knew that the board members, with the exception of the Colonel who really only wanted to know about what happened when they were at the Pimlico Centre, weren't that interested in the day-to-day running of the company. All they wanted to know was how big and how safe were their individual dividends. Each board meeting was more like a get-together at a well-established men's club, and using this lack of real concern Anne began to develop her plan. She knew that if she wasn't careful it would all go wrong. She had to make sure it was water-tight, with no room for argument.

She began spending her free time at the library researching into company and estate law. Hours were spent poring over what financial information she could find and once she had done that she began quietly to solicit support from the board. So when, at the September quarterly meeting, her presentation appeared on the agenda it took no one by surprise. In fact they all welcomed it and felt that they had somehow been involved in putting the plan together.

It was agreed that with immediate effect she would take over the day-to-day running of the business. She said she didn't want a pay rise, which at first surprised them, but she asked them to grant her a percentage of the shares dividend that would accrue to Howard Edwardes' account. This had been the one potential stumbling block but when they realised that such a deal would mean they were effectively getting her services for nothing, as she would be paid out of money already allocated (albeit frozen) elsewhere, they willingly agreed. To sweeten the pill she had also said she wanted to make an allowance to Mr Edwardes' wife. (She had almost said widow but stopped herself in time.) That, more than anything else, won her the total support she needed. Agreeing to her proposal with that condition helped ease their consciences, as they had all felt guilty when they voted to stop paying Edwardes' salary. They had agreed then that they had nothing against Edwardes but, family or no family, business was business and it didn't make sense to pay a man who wasn't there. Especially if it was going to come out of their own pockets.

It took six months to get the papers drawn up and agreed. Mr Hesketh had suggested the papers be signed by all the relevant people in his office, which he said would give Mrs Edwardes the chance to thank Anne personally. Anne refused, saying she would be too embarrassed to meet her (which Mr Hesketh accepted as a sign of her kind nature) and so security packages sped backwards and forwards across London acquiring the necessary signatures.

Anne made only one other stipulation. The documents were not to be drawn up in the name by which everyone called her, Anne Prescott, but (she lied) her full name. She also let it be known that from now on this was how she wanted to be addressed and when Mr Hesketh queried her reasons she explained that the new name sounded more businesslike. As there was no legal reason why the paperwork shouldn't go through in this way, all the documents were finally signed by Suzanne Prescott.

Maggie was too much, really she was. Stella had settled down to watch *Now Voyager* on TV. She had been looking forward to it all week; she loved a good weepy, and as usual Maggie was going to spoil it. Trust her to use her emergency call button now. Strictly speaking the intercom alarms should only be used by the residents in an emergency, if they fell over in the bathroom or couldn't get out of bed, but Maggie being Maggie she was probably just feeling bloody-minded. She had been even worse than usual since Howard's funeral and Stella could understand why Jo hadn't been in touch. She waited to see if she rang again. If she did then she would have to go over. The film was due to start in five minutes. Mentally she crossed her fingers and when Maggie didn't call again Stella decided she was probably crying wolf and settled down with a box of tissues.

She had a lovely snivelly afternoon and when the movie was over and she'd had a cup of tea she began to feel a bit guilty about Maggie. 'Poor thing, can't be much fun for her. Suppose I should go and look in on her.' She popped a cardigan over her shoulders and picked up the keys. *That's odd*, she thought, when she saw Maggie's door was open. Automatically she tapped on it and called out 'It's Stella, Maggie,' as she let herself in. The flat was in silence and none of the lights had been switched on. Stella walked into the living room, saw Maggie slumped in her chair, gasped and burst into tears.

The next few hours were a nightmare. First the doctor came. He took one look, declared the death 'suspicious' and called the police, who agreed with him.

'She's been strangled, but it's an unusual angle and it must have been someone quite strong to result in death.'

Maggie's own doctor interrupted the police. 'Not really. She's had rheumatoid arthritis for years, and osteoporosis, so one quick yank on her neck and the bones would crumble and . . . well,' he finished lamely, 'it would have been pretty instantaneous.' Stella hung back. She felt awful. If only she had answered Maggie's bell properly and come across as she was meant to instead of sitting and watching TV. If she had done that she might have been able to save her. She gave a loud sniff.

'Get SOCO down here and see if anyone saw or heard anything.' Stella began to cry again, great greasy tears sliding down her cheeks. Of course she should tell them about the alarm call but if the board found out she hadn't responded she could lose her job. Dereliction of duty, that's what they'd call it, and she couldn't risk that. Telling the police about the call wouldn't do any good, would it? It wouldn't bring Maggie back. She decided to keep quiet. After all, she would only hurt herself by saying something and as it was she would be punished for the rest of her life by knowing that if she had been doing her job properly she might have been able to save the old woman.

'I'd better go and call her daughter,' she said to no one in particular. She made a move towards Maggie's phone but one of the policemen stopped her.

'Sorry, love. Better not touch anything.'

'Oh, yes, of course. I'll go and call Joanne from my own place.' She let herself out and walked towards the main door, shoulders hunched into her cardigan. As it was growing dark she automatically stopped in the main public lounge to turn on the lights. Because it was in darkness she didn't think anyone was in there and gave a start when she saw Edna. 'Good grief, you gave me a scare. Come on, Edna, back to your own flat. This is no place for you, not today, too much going on.' She put an arm round her shoulder but to her surprise Edna shook her off.

'No,' she said defiantly. 'Maggie . . .'

'Yes, Edna, Maggie's not well, which is why I think you should go back home. Now, come on and be a good girl.'

'Maggie, Maggie, Maggie,' she said, making her hands into fists to shake them angrily at Stella.

'Please, Edna, I don't know what's got into you but I really can't cope with this, not now. Come on.' She used her hand on Edna's shoulder and finally succeeded in steering her towards her own front door, but it took a surprising amount of effort. As they went past Maggie's flat Edna turned round and tried to go inside but Stella stopped her. 'Nothing to bother you in there,' she said firmly. Edna gave a gulp and began to sing over and over again in a jerky voice under her breath, 'Oh Suzanna, don't you cry for me.'

By the time Stella had got her safely back inside her own flat she had sung the song three times and was clearly going to repeat it to herself all night Stella sighed and shook her head and, full of bustling importance, made her way to her flat to ring Jo.

The crew were in the organisers' office filming the team as exhibitors and visitors trooped in and out. It was the usual mixture – from retailers who had problems with the electrics on their stands to members of the public who had lost one another, or had left something on a stand or wanted to know where they could buy an electric cheese grater. Members of the press were directed to the press office and the sales team dashed in and out, filling in the floor plan with next year's sales as they secured another exhibitor. The office manager jumped up and down to put out tannoy announcements and messages crackled from the radios that everyone working for Exhibitions International had in front of them on their desks.

Jo stood behind Tony hissing instructions in his ear. She monitored everything when one irate lady complaining (unfairly) about the attitude of the staff made such a fuss that she was escorted from the building. Jo had another camera ready outside to capture her ignominious departure. It was business as usual for everyone.

Alan hovered in the background watching all that was going on. It was not that he was concerned about the office, far from it. He knew that the chaos was under total control and that now they were nearing the end of the exhibition everyone had settled into their own work routine. They were punchy with tiredness and existing on a combination of adrenaline and chocolate bars donated by one of that year's sponsors. They were all looking forward to the end of the show. No, it wasn't his team that he was concerned about, but Jo.

Jo had spent the day before working with the film editor at Boadicea Productions in Bayswater. He had been on duty in the press office all day but when Jo called him at about seven to say Maggie had been found dead he had insisted that she stop by the Pimlico Centre to pick him up on her way to Blackheath. Her voice had sounded totally flat, devoid of any emotion, and he couldn't help comparing her reaction with how she had behaved when she heard about Howard.

She reached Pimlico just before they closed and gave an automatic response to Cyril when he told her she could park in bay three. She felt as if she had become disconnected from herself, almost as if she were floating. She seemed so vague, her eyes so big in an unsurprisingly white face that Alan refused to let her drive. He also made sure that he stayed with her overnight, fully expecting an outburst of tears to hit hard later on, but there had been nothing. Even when she had seen Maggie sitting in her chair, her head twisted at that unnatural angle, she had just said quietly, 'Poor Maggie. She would have thought it so undignified.' The police questions had been answered with quiet efficiency. She told them about the threatening phone calls and didn't even flinched when they carefully asked her if she could think why anyone would want to murder her mother. Alan was determined to keep as close an eye on her as possible.

God, he thought, *It's so bloody unfair that this should all happen at once. She doesn't deserve it. Nobody does.* He leaned against the desk by the door pretending to be busy, an unnecessary radio held to his ear. Automatically he half listened to the conversation. Something to do with closing down a stand by padlocking the security night sheets round it because the exhibitor had defaulted in making the last payment of his stand fee. It was nothing that Alan need worry about. His thoughts returned to Jo. She was too much in control, it was all too stamped down. Something had to give – and then all of a sudden it did.

Jo had no idea what it was that set her off. It might have been the little girl who was found walking round by herself and was brought into the organisers' office looking terrified because she had lost her mother. Or maybe it was the tannoy announcement asking Kylie's mother to come to the organisers' office where her little girl was waiting. She never did work it out. One moment she was feeling a little vague but still able to control a film crew; the next she felt as if she had been hit in the stomach. A surge of emotion rushed through her and she found herself howling her eyes out.

'Thank God,' muttered Alan under his breath as he moved towards her, wrapping his arms round her to steer her out of the hubbub of the main office. They sat on the sofa in his office and she curled into a ball, her face pressed into his jacket as she sobbed. For the second time he found himself holding her and crooning over her bent head, wishing he could take some of her pain away. 'It's all right, it's all right,' he repeated as slowly her sobs subsided into gulps until she raised a tear-stained face to look at him.

'Why, Alan? I know she was difficult but why would anyone want to kill her?'

Alan shrugged, feeling totally useless. He couldn't give her the reassurance or answers she so desperately needed. 'I don't know, but if the police can track down who made those calls maybe you'll find out.' Jo blew her nose loudly and began pulling at the edge of the handkerchief he had given her.

'You know, I was really looking forward to this job. It was going to be my big break, the one that would get me all the plum directing jobs. And now I just want to get it over and done with. It's become the biggest nightmare out. Except for you,' she added quickly.

Alan held her hand. 'Stop saying sorry,' he chided her gently. 'Even though you're glad I'm here I feel guilty because if I hadn't been you and Simon might still be together.'

Damn! he said to himself. *Why did I have to bring his name up now? Go on, Waterman, rub her nose in it, you bastard.*

'No.' Jo shook her head. 'It's not your fault. We should have split up years ago. In fact we should never have got together in the first place. It's just that on top of Howard and now this . . .' She trailed off as the tears welled up again and the lump at the back of her throat got too big for her to swallow. Alan gave her hand a squeeze and was about to try to say something helpful, although what he didn't know, when an announcement over the tannoy cut through the noise filtering in from outside.

'This is a staff announcement. I repeat this is a staff announcement.

Would staff please note that Mr Eastlight is in the building. That is, Mr Eastlight is in the building.'

'OH, FUCK!' exclaimed Alan.

'What's up?' Jo was startled by the alteration in his mood as he jumped to his feet. He seized his radio and switched it to security channel three, holding it to his ear so he could hear properly the rapid exchange going on between Gordon in the organisers' office and Roger Dudley in security.

'Bomb alert,' he said over his shoulder as he dashed out of the room. Jo gave her nose and eyes one last scrub and shoved the handkerchief up her sleeve. If a major crisis was going on in the exhibition it was her job to film it. No time for personal feelings now. Those would have to come later.

She took one final deep breath and followed Alan into the main office, grateful that the alert meant no one was giving her sideways glances. Gordon was barking out orders to the team and down the radio simultaneously. Jo gave Tony his instructions and sent the second unit down on to the exhibition floor telling them: 'use your initiative and if they evacuate the building go with it'. Tony focused his camera on Gordon who was talking urgently into his radio.

'Gordon to Roger, do we have an evacuation situation or not? Over.'

'Roger to Gordon. Affirmative. Get your lot to ask exhibitors to check their stands for anything dodgy. If they find something don't touch it, just call us on channel two. Get the stands shut down and we'll get the punters out. Anyone asks, it's a council fire drill. Over.'

'Understood.'

'You know the procedure. Just don't do anything to panic no one, OK?'

'OK.' Gordon released the button on his radio and looked round the room. 'Right. In case you didn't get that, security have confirmed that the alert is being taken seriously. So to remind you of the drill – each of you go round your own section. Get exhibitors to check for anything suspicious. If they find anything put a call to me with the instruction to go to channel two. Then tell me the location. Do not give me that detail on an open channel. I'll want stand number, hall, section and exhibitor name. Leave security to get the visitors out but what ever you do don't do anything to create panic out there. Once your section is clear report to me and then vacate. Now GO.'

Jo captured the whole briefing and the look of genuine fear on everyone's faces. The evacuation took exactly nine minutes but it was an hour and a half before the sniffer dogs had finished going round the exhibition and the all clear had been given. The police later confirmed that it had been a very carefully researched hoax, using the language, code words and voice patterns they had to take seriously. They tried to trace the call but the fact that it had been made from inside the building meant that at the time it was logged any one of twenty-five thousand people could have been responsible. It was like looking for a needle in a haystack.

When Suzanne heard the news she was not surprised. He had done the one thing, short of actually blowing the place up, that would hurt the show the most. He had hit the numbers through the doors, which would have a knock-on effect for everyone, never mind how much it would unsettle them all. The evacuation meant many people didn't want to hang around and wait an unspecified time before going back inside so she had had to agree (reluctantly) to offer a refund on tickets sent in, or promise free entry later on to anyone who presented a ticket with that day's date on it. In the end the hoax cost them ten thousand tickets which, although it rankled, was not too bad considering how well they were doing on attendance figures. What worried Suzanne more was how far he would go to get his own way.

'Come in.' It still sounded odd saying it even though she'd had Margaret's power of attorney for almost a year now. In that time she had begun to introduce ideas for expansion that had already paid off. The show had been redesigned to help people find their way around with greater ease and make it what the new marketing men were calling 'more user-friendly'. She had also insisted that they create an area dedicated to the bedsits that were springing up all over London, to attract the hordes of young people who were now living by themselves or in what the Establishment called 'open sin'. London was the city that 'swung' and Suzanne made sure that the Home Maker Exhibition swung with it.

The board had been uncertain at first but when they saw how many more people came and how much bigger their bonuses were they relaxed. Gradually they stopped mumbling about her being 'too young to know what she was doing' and gave her greater freedom to do as she wanted. She was feeling more secure as each day went by. Howard's disappearance had become part of the office's folklore and if she was ever haunted by images of him she chose to ignore them, almost persuading herself that he had done what everyone believed and simply vanished. But it still seemed odd to have someone knock at her office door. Especially, she thought glancing at her watch, at this hour.

It was barely six in the morning and she had come into the Pimlico Centre early to get paperwork out of the way so she could go down on to the floor and see for herself how the build-up for that year's show was coming on. She was particularly keen to check the new gardens she'd added in front of and behind the show homes, pointing out that as most houses had gardens theirs should too. She was still thinking about the changes that had been made to the floor plan and wasn't really aware of who had come into the room until he was standing in front of her.

'Mornin', miss.'

'Oh, good morning. Um . . . I think you've got the wrong office. Security is two doors down,' she said helpfully, seeing his uniform.

'You're Suzanne Prescott, aren't you?'

Suzanne nodded, a puzzled furrow on her forehead as she tried to work out if she knew the man and where she might have met him. The trouble was all she ever saw was the uniform, not the men behind it, so even if they had met before chances were she wouldn't remember him. 'Yes, that's right. Is there a problem?'

'With the show? No, that's all fine. No problems there, well, not exactly, but you could say there's a problem if you want.'

'I know it's early but I am busy.' He was clearly a time-waster and even this early in the day the minutes were precious to her. She didn't have time to play twenty questions. Best thing would be to get rid of him as quickly as possible. 'If there is something wrong then you probably need to tell the security office and they'll let me know what's happening when I get their report, OK?' She got up and walked to the door, holding it open for him so he would get the hint. He didn't move.

'Nah. This isn't what you'd call a security problem. It's to do with the basement.' He paused, letting his words sink in. She stood by the door looking irritated. Silly cow, he'd show her. 'Well maybe I should say there's a problem in the *body* of the basement.' Suzanne stared at him for a moment as she began to sense what he was talking about. That was better. This time she understood him. She shut the door and made her way back to her desk.

'You'd better sit down.' She sounded a lot calmer than she felt. Maybe there was a problem in the storage rooms below the exhibition floors and he was calling that the basement, so the panic that was threatening to choke her was unnecessary. Maybe he had just used an unfortunate turn of phrase? He leaned back in his seat and stretched his legs out in front of him, crossing his ankles and clasping his hands behind his head nonchalantly. The dawning light outside gave him an odd pallor.

'What do you mean, in the body of the basement?' She repeated his words carefully, wanting to make sure that they were talking about the same thing. But if he did know, how had he found out? She felt a line of sweat prickle her top lip and the back of her neck beneath her hair. Her fingers were intertwined and her hands lay lightly on the top of her desk but she could also feel them begin to get damp. In contrast her mouth was dry and she was having problems swallowing.

He began to speak slowly, enjoying the game he was playing with her and drawing it out for as long as he could.

'Well, it's like this. I've been here a few years now since I came out after doing time. Don't matter what I went down for but I'd been a good boy, I 'ad, so me parole officer got me a job here as night watchman. Bloody borin' if you ask me. Nothin' to watch, so I got meself into the habit of grabbin' a quick forty winks. No one checked up on you and if they did I'd tell 'em I was out on me rounds or in the bog. You see, I had a nice little place to sleep. Well I had till they bunged up me hidey-hole. Nice and warm it used to be down in that basement. Made meself a little den I did, behind the 'ot water heatin' pipes. Me, a packet of fags, a blanket and a beer. Then they shut it up. Pity really 'cos I'd got quite fond of the place. It was cosy-like. Which was why you sort of take note when you hears someone else down there.' He stopped to make and light a roll-up and stared at her over his hands as he cupped them round his cigarette, sucking on it to get it to light.

Suzanne returned his look with a steadiness she was far from feeling. He inhaled and blew a plume of smoke into the air before continuing. 'So where was I? Oh yeah, I hears this noise, woke me up it did, so I looks out of me den and what do you think I sees?'

'I've no idea.'

'Well I'll tell you then. It was the old boss. 'Oward Edwardes and his secretary. They was, now 'ow can I put this delicate-like.' He paused and pretended to think, struggling for the right word as he chewed on his cigarette, picking a stray strand of tobacco out from between his teeth. 'Frolickin', that's a good way to put it, innit? They was frolickin'. Then the frolickin' stopped, didn't it? He tripped over and hit his head. Accident, it was. Any fool could see that, OK, but she got stupid. Panicked and left him there when she should 'ave told someone. That night they finished sealin' it up and blocked him in wiv' it. Two years later he's still down there. Must be pretty grim by now. Wouldn't be much fun if they went down and got him out, would it? 'Course if I was to tell 'em he was down there they'd want to know 'ow I know. Difficult, that. I'd have to tell 'em I wasn't doing me job proper, wouldn't I, and that would bugger me parole. Don't want that so I had a think and decided to come to you and see if we can come to an arrangement.'

Again he stopped, waiting for Suzanne to say something. She lifted her hands and propped her elbows on the desk to rest her chin on them. 'And why would I want to do that?' She hoped he couldn't see how much she was shaking, and that her voice wouldn't give away the fear she was feeling.

''Cos I could make things difficult for you otherwise. I mean, it would be my word 'gainst yours. If I was to tell 'em he was there then they'd know I must've seen somethin'.' He moved in his seat and was now leaning forward, his forearms resting on his thighs as his eyes searched her face for a response, a sign of fear, something to show how she was feeling. She was a cool one, he'd grant her that. He ploughed on. 'If I was to tell 'em you pushed him I could make 'em believe it.'

'What about your parole?'

'Well, that's why I thought we could do a deal.'

'Go on.'

'I like workin' here. It's all right. Cushy number, no trouble. First I want you to make sure I can keep me job. Bit of promotion as I get older might be nice, but the important thing is it's mine for as long as I wants it. Second, even though it's easy money it ain't what you would call *good* money. I reckon you could supplement me pay each week. What do you think?'

'And what do I get out of this "deal"?'

'Well, I keep quiet. I tell no one what happened that night so you also gets to keep your job and the perks what goes wiv it.'

'Blackmail. That's what this is, isn't it?'

'I prefer to look on it as a business agreement.' He got up and walked to the window to look out at the river. The sun was rising and the windows of the Houses of Parliament glimmered as the first light hit them. He stood with his hands behind his back, the stub of his cigarette dangling between his fingers.

Suzanne's mind was racing. Did she dare take the risk and stand up to him, tell him to get out? Maybe she could pre-empt the problem by going to the police herself. Tell them all that had happened? Even as the thought came into her mind she dismissed it. She hadn't worked so hard for the last two years or lived with the fear of discovery for all that time to throw it away now. She had five more years to work before Peg would be able to claim all that had been Howard's. Already she had begun to turn his holding in the company round, chipping away at it as more blocks of shares were released. She had kept a close eye on which of the shareholders had bought what volume and had seen with relief that even though she'd had the same choice as the other shareholders Peg hadn't bothered to buy any. Over the next five years she would release more shares, increasing everyone else's holdings until Peg claimed hers, when it would be so small it would give her enough to live on but no more. Five more years was all she needed. By then she would have expanded the company, made it bigger, spread into Europe. No, she couldn't let him get in the way of her plans.

'I need to think about it. How much did you have in mind?'

He smiled at the Thames before turning to face her. He'd won. That last question proved it. She had indicated she wanted to play ball. All he had to do now was wait, apply a bit of pressure and he was home and dry. *Thank you, Tommy*, he thought to himself, remembering with gratitude his cell mate and all he had learned from the older man who had taken him under his wing those early days in the Scrubs. He walked over to the desk and scribbled a sum on her notepad. She looked at it but made no comment. He took this as her acceptance and held out his hand. 'Pleasure doin' business wiv you, Miss Prescott.'

'I haven't agreed yet.' Suzanne also stood up, not wanting him to have the advantage of height over her.

'True, very true. But you will, 'cos you've got too much to lose. Why don't I pop back later to finalise it all? Let's see, it's Wednesday today so how about sometime Friday mornin'?' His hand was still held out in front of him. Not knowing what else to do Suzanne took it.

'Friday then.' For the second time that morning she opened the door for him. This time he left, giving her a broad grin as he did so. She shut it firmly behind him and on legs that felt as if they were made of cotton wool walked back to her desk to bury her head in her hands.

'My God! What am I going to do?' she muttered to herself, even though she already knew the answer. But could she trust him to take the money and not say anything? She would have to think carefully about how to handle him, about how to maintain control and ensure he would keep quiet.

For the rest of that day one question after another chased itself round her head. As she inspected the gardens she was asking herself, *Is he asking too much?* The question as she looked across from the balcony in Pim One was, *Will it stop here or will he want more?* Suzanne barely saw the final adjustments to the entry awnings as she did the sums, working out how much he would cost her a year. By the end of the day she was mentally and physically drained but she had at least worked out how she could stay in charge.

On Friday morning she pulled into the car park at eight-thirty. He was chatting to a colleague outside the traffic office and both greeted her politely when she walked in giving a perfunctory 'Good morning.' She had cleared her diary of all appointments that morning and shut herself in her office saying she was looking at budgets. In fact she couldn't concentrate on anything as she waited for him to arrive. Her ears almost hurt with listening out for him but his gentle tap on her door still made her jump. 'Come in.' The door opened quickly and he slid into the room, sitting down without waiting to be asked.

'Well, I said I'd be back Friday so here I is. What do you reckon?' He came straight to the point.

Suzanne pushed her seat back and stood up to begin pacing the room. It was a deliberate movement and one designed to unsettle him but it had no effect. He just sat, watching as she slowly walked backwards and forwards.

'I've considered your proposition very carefully and although it is, shall we say, a bit unorthodox, I think I will accept. However,' she added quickly, seeing the slow smile spread across his face, 'I have a few conditions of my own.' He raised his eyebrows as he looked at her, waiting to hear what she would say.

'First, I don't want anyone ever to be able to associate us with each other in any way whatsoever. With that in mind I will send you an envelope containing the money in cash each week. There will be nothing else in it, no letter, nothing but the money.

'Secondly, the sum we agree today is *it*. That figure is five pounds less than the one you have suggested. There will be no coming back for more at any time in the future. To make sure I will increase it annually by two and a half per cent. There will be no discussion over this amount and if there is payments will cease immediately and I will go to the police myself. I will tell them you have been blackmailing me, and because of your record they'll believe me. Don't look so surprised. You don't think I'm stupid enough not to have checked up on you, do you?'

He scowled at her. She might be a looker standing there in her trouser suit, tits making interesting bulges, but she was smart too. God, he hated clever women.

'Thirdly, I have drawn up this document. Once we have agreed terms you and I will sign it. There is one copy only which I will keep to use as proof if you push me too far.'

'So, you want to stack the deck in your favour, do you?'

'Of course. I need to have some insurance, don't I? You get the money and somehow I'll guarantee you keep your job. That bit suits me nicely. I'll be able to keep an eye on you, though how a man with a record ever got a job as a night watchman I'll never know.'

He winked at her. 'I fooled some of the people all of the time. Persuaded the silly sods I'd gone straight, didn't I? Besides, I ain't got form for thieving have I?'

Suzanne ignored his question. 'Finally if you break this agreement then I swear to God you'll wish you had never been born. I'll make sure that you get done not just for blackmail but also murder and I'll probably add rape for good measure.'

'But I never went near you!' he protested. 'Never laid a finger on you!'

She stopped pacing the room to stand in front of him. 'I know that, and you know that, but no one else does – so watch it.' She went back to her seat. 'Those are my terms. They are non-negotiable. Take them or leave them. You have five minutes to make your mind up.'

'Hang on, hang on. I gave you three days.' He didn't like the way she was taking over his deal, twisting it round so she was in charge.

'More fool you. You've now got four and a half minutes.'

'OK, OK. I agree. But you start payin' next week.'

Suzanne reached into her drawer and pulled out an envelope, taking out a sheet of paper and pushing it across the desk at him. 'This is the document. Sign it and date it here and here.'

'Without readin' it first? You must be doolally!' He reached out and pulled it towards him. It covered one side and clearly laid out the facts. That there had been a fatal accident involving herself and Howard Edwardes. That as he had been avoiding his duties he had witnessed it but said nothing. He was now insisting she paid him for his silence. It specified the amount she would pay him and that it would rise by the agreed percentage each year. He looked up at her.

'Reads like you done nothing. As if it were my fault he's down there.' He sounded indignant.

'Are you saying the facts are incorrect?'

'No, 'course I ain't. The facts is fine. It's just the way you put 'em. It looks a bit, well, all written in your favour. That's all.'

'Blackmail is a tough business. It's each for his or her own. You started this, not me. Of course if you're now saying you've changed your mind?' Suzanne reached out to take the paper back from him. He snatched it away from her.

'Oh no you don't. Where's a pen?' She handed him one and he quickly scrawled his name and the date underneath it. He then passed the paper and pen back across the desk and watched, holding his breath, as Suzanne did likewise. She then sealed the envelope and went to put it in her bottom drawer. His eyes followed her movements and, aware of how closely he was watching her, she changed her mind, folding it into her handbag instead.

'Much safer there, I think. Oh, and don't bother trying to find it. I'm going to keep it with my personal papers elsewhere.' Suzanne got up to show him out, wanting the interview to be at an end as she knew she couldn't keep the cool front up much longer. It had been hell trying to stay in charge, to act as if he didn't scare her when in truth she was terrified. That morning the very thought of the meeting had made her retch and she could still taste the foul bile in her mouth even though she had brushed her teeth twice since.

Determined to have the last word he turned at the door and handed her a piece of paper. 'You'll need this.'

'What is it?'

'Me address. After all, you need to know where to send the cash, don't you.'

'I'm not going to let you do it alone.' Alan was leaning against the filing cabinet in the corner of her office as he drank an early Monday morning cup of coffee.

'Oh, for crying out loud, Alan. I'm not a baby. I'm quite capable of clearing out her flat by myself.' Jo looked up at him with angry eyes. There were dark smudges underneath them and she looked pale and drawn.

'I'm not saying you're not. Just that it's a shitty job and you don't *have* to do it by yourself.' He put his mug down on top of the cabinet and went to sit on the edge of her desk. He ran his fingers gently down her cheek, saying quietly, 'Jo, I'm Alan, not Simon. I want to be involved. Please don't shut me out.' It was a heartfelt plea.

Jo made the old movement to tuck her hair behind her ears and ended up running her fingers through it instead. 'Maybe I want to do it alone. Maybe I *need* to do it by myself.' She sounded petulant. *Stop fighting him you bloody idiot,* said a small voice inside her head. *You know you want him with you, why fight when you don't have to?* Having Alan with her as she began the horrid job of sorting Maggie's things was something she desperately wanted, but after fending for herself for so long she didn't know either how to ask for that support, or take it when offered.

'OK. That's different. But don't feel you have to. Jo, I care about you. I care a lot and I hate seeing you like this. It makes me feel so fucking useless.' He straightened up and went to the door. 'Call me if you change your mind,' he said as he opened it, but before he could head back to the halls Jo had blocked his exit. 'I'm sorry, Alan. I'm just so tired and confused. Ignore me, I'm being stupid. You're right. I'm only having a go at you to protect myself. I feel so guilty about it. As if it's my fault . . .'

'We've been through all of that.' Alan shut the door again and put his arms round her, encouraging her to rest her head against him as he interrupted her. 'It had nothing to do with you, sweetheart. You didn't live with her so it could have happened at any time.' She inhaled deeply. There it was again, that scent that was so much a part of him, that made her feel so safe.

'I know, but I still feel responsible.'

She looked up at him, exhaustion written all over her face. Hardly surprising really – what with burying both her parents within the space of a few weeks, seeing solicitors and coping with her job as well as breaking up with Simon. He kissed the top of her head. She felt so right with him, and the more time they spent together the more Jo realised just how bad things had become with Simon over the years. Even when they first met she had never felt like this about him. It was as if she had been with Alan for years, not just a few weeks. She gave him a lopsided smile. 'Come on. There's work to do.'

Reluctantly he let go of her and went back to his office. Now the show was in its final week the press office wasn't so busy. Since opening, nearly one and a half million people had trooped through the gates of the Pimlico Centre, almost four hundred and fifty thousand more than the previous year. That the discovery of an old body had helped the attendance figures nobody doubted, but as an event it had already been consigned to the show's long history as plans got underway for the next year's exhibition.

Once Alan had left the office Jo helped herself to another cup of coffee, drinking it slowly as she gazed out over the Thames. *Just one more week, then I can get the hell out of here*, she thought with relief. It was sad, really. She had looked forward to it so much, but such a lot had got in the way to confuse it. At least Suzanne had come through. She smiled to herself as she thought of the reason why she was there. If anyone had told her that she and Suzanne would have become so close she would have laughed at them. Now it didn't seem so silly. She felt an empathy with the older woman that was a totally new experience for her. That, and her feelings for Alan, she decided, were the two things that had got her through it all.

Coffee finished, she made her way over to the main halls. She went in by the side traffic door where Cyril gave her a cheerful 'Good morning.' She waved back to him. *Nice old boy*, she thought. *In fact most of them are OK*. She went into the briefing room, where the rest of the crew were waiting for her. She switched to her usual upbeat style, hiding the personal problems behind bright professionalism, and for the final time gave out her weekly schedule sheets. Some of her comments made them laugh. As ever, with her crew Jo Edwardes was totally in charge. This week the full crew was back, to focus on the closing days and the break-down. They were all looking forward to the end of the filming at the Pimlico Centre and even though many of them had worked on shoots which, on paper, were much tougher, this one had surprised them. The combination of spending up to twelve hours a day in a large, un-airconditioned building, jostling through the crowds and walking surprisingly long distances as they traipsed through first one and then another exhibition hall, had proved exhausting. Like everyone connected with the show they felt as if they had missed the spring. That, combined with the various coughs and colds they had all caught, meant they'd had enough of the place.

'Look on the bright side,' Jo said in response to their groans as they checked their still punishing schedules. 'Seven more days and we're out of here.'

'Halle-bleeding-lujah!' muttered Tony's assistant, much to the amusement of the rest of them. They had been a good team and probably wouldn't come together again until the final edited version was screened at a preview. Just one more week of manoeuvring between the stands and then everything they had shot and recorded would be handed on to the editors. They would finally pull all the footage together under Jo's direction, making sense of the hundreds of disjointed scenes and interviews, piecing it together to create a programme that would entertain and inform.

That Monday night she drove home on automatic pilot and fell into bed aching for sleep. But lately sleep, when it came, hadn't helped. She was either sleeping so deeply that she woke up with a thudding headache or else she had such violent and angry dreams that she felt as if she hadn't slept at all.

Maggie's funeral had been awful. Suzanne was there, which Jo found touching, but it saddened her that even fewer people attended Maggie's funeral than Howard's. She knew her mother had been a proud and difficult woman, but until she saw the empty church at her funeral she hadn't realised just how alone she was. Like so many other people with relatives living at The Warren she had assumed that because there were communal rooms and outings planned for the residents they had an active life. It wasn't until Maggie was dead that she appreciated how lonely an existence it must have been. Her sense of guilt was enormous.

Jo had been fine throughout the service, but broke down at the interment. It was seeing the newness of Howard's grave next to Maggie's that brought back all her feelings about her father, making her even more aware of how badly she had let her mother down. She had cried openly at the graveside, holding on to Alan not caring who saw her as she mourned the mother she had never been able to reach. Yet at the same time she despised her for shattering the image of Howard she had nurtured over the years. Jo knew that what Maggie had told her about her father was true. She had spent many hours since the last time they met thinking about all that her mother had said and now, with the benefit of hindsight, could see how Howard had united himself with his young daughter against Maggie. She could imagine how hard it must have been for her.

Suzanne hung back a little, standing beyond another gravestone. Jo's tears made her feel wretched, and angry. She shut her eyes. *Why couldn't she feel like that? After all, Maggie was her mother too. In the end had Maggie deprived her of even that? The ability to grieve, and to miss the woman who had given birth to her?* She opened her eyes again. Coming here had been a horrible mistake. She could have made an excuse and not attended but even as she had considered that option she knew she would be there. Dear God, she had only intended to hurt Maggie emotionally; to deprive her of the things she loved in the same way that her mother had done to her.

Suzanne knew Jo had seen her so she was forced to go over to her, to mumble her sympathies before escaping. She wanted to go back to the Pimlico Centre where things were safe, where she could hide behind the carefully manufactured image of Suzanne Prescott.

But it hadn't turned out like that. Jo had been so pleased to see her that she had insisted she went back to The Warren with them. The usual sandwiches and cakes had been laid out in the communal lounge and even though all the residents would attend as a matter of course Jo wanted to feel that there were at least a couple of people there who were on her side. When they got back the lounge was already full, but despite that it was more subdued than usual. Everyone who lived at The Warren accepted death as their final departure from the place but the death they anticipated was a natural one, not violent like Maggie's. Her murder had made them all jumpy so it was a quiet, and quick, gathering, with the residents staying as short a time as possible before scurrying back to the relative safety of their own flats.

Even Edna, who usually enjoyed a chance to show off, had skulked in the corners of the room avoiding people. At one point Jo had taken Suzanne over to her to remind her that they had met before but Edna had given a little whimper and fiddled nervously with the necklaces round her neck, twisting them until one broke, scattering bright blue beads across the floor. Suzanne used the ensuing muddle to slip quietly away. It was once they had collected all the beads that Edna seemed to brighten up and started singing about Suzanna again.

'That's the only thing she sings these days,' Stella complained to Jo. 'It was bad enough when we used to get a different repertoire but this is driving me mad. Poor love. I think she'll be the next to go. Totally losing it, she is. You're dancing with the fairies these days aren't you, Edna?' She asked in a loud voice as the old woman curtseyed to them. Edna stopped and put a finger to her lips, shaking her head slowly from side to side.

'Suzanna,' she said firmly, repeating it again as if they were the stupid ones.

'Yes, dear. We know all about that Suzanna of yours. Now off you go.' Stella gave her a pat on the arm and turned to help Mrs Carlton get another cup of tea and a sandwich.

Suzanne swung the car into The Warren. She wasn't sure what she intended to do now she'd arrived in Blackheath. One thing was clear, however; it was not knowing that was driving her slowly mad. Playing mind games with Maggie meant she was losing her edge. All the control she had carefully acquired over the years was slowly unravelling, not because of what was going on around her at work but because Maggie was hovering in the background like the spectre at the feast. That he had told Maggie something was obvious, but she had to find out exactly how much, which of the details she knew were the truth and which were lies. Once she knew that she could decide what she was going to do about it. Like it or not, facing Maggie was the only way to get those questions answered.

She slammed the car shut and made her way across to the door. Taking a deep breath she pulled her shoulders back, resettled her bag on her shoulder and pressed the bell, answering, 'It's Suzanne,' when Maggie's voice asked who was there. For a moment Suzanne thought Maggie wasn't going to let her in, just leave her standing on the doorstep, but then she heard the click as the door catch released. Suzanne walked down the hall to the flat. The door was slightly ajar so she went straight in, not bothering to shut it properly behind her. Maggie was sitting in her wheelchair in the living room, her back to the door as usual. Playing for time Suzanne removed her driving gloves, placing them carefully over her handbag. 'May I sit down?'

'What do you want? I have nothing to say to you.' Suzanne sat down anyway. If Maggie had hoped ignoring her would get rid of her she was wrong. With an irritated sigh she finally turned her chair round to face her. As she did so the afternoon sun fell across her face. She had aged since Howard's funeral. It was as if by burying her husband Maggie had finally faced up to the fact that he wouldn't be coming back. She was slumped further down in her chair than Suzanne expected and her already gnarled fingers seemed even more twisted. She was having problems moving her neck but despite this stiffness her head seemed to wobble a little, and her glasses shook as if she couldn't control her movements properly. Was this what had become of her? A frail old lady sitting in a wheelchair in The Warren waiting for . . . nothing?

'I need to talk to you.' Suzanne crossed one leg over the other.

'Funny how nothing changes, isn't it? Remember how you came begging to me to take you in? I was in charge then and even though I'm in this contraption I'm still in charge now, aren't I? You sit there controlling your empire, running your business, Madam Chief Executive, but you still need me, don't you?'

Suzanne swallowed, hard. To a certain extent Maggie was right and she hated the older woman for that. 'Look,' she said, standing up. 'I haven't got time for stupid games. I want to know what he told you. How much you know. Once I know that we can probably reach some sort of agreement about how to proceed.'

Maggie gave her a puzzled look. 'I don't know what you're talking about. Who do you think has told me what exactly?'

'Oh, for God's sake. Look, let me make myself clear. The longer you muck me about the less willing I'm going to be to negotiate with you. The only person who will suffer by your delaying tactics is you. It might work with Jo but it won't with me.'

A slow look of understanding spread over Maggie's face. 'This is about those phone calls I've been getting, isn't it?' Her head bobbed slightly faster as her voice rose. 'Isn't it?' she insisted. Suzanne nodded. Maggie must be playing dumb deliberately. 'In which case I want to know why I'm being threatened on your behalf.'

'What do you mean, "being threatened"?'

'The man on the phone keeps telling me to talk to you. To get you to co-operate. Co-operate with what? And why won't you do it? I don't like being threatened in my own home. I should be safe here but thanks to you I'm not. I'm a vulnerable old lady and I should have better than this. If you hadn't stolen my husband's company from under me then I wouldn't be here now.' Her voice again rose as she spoke and by the time she finished she was shouting at Suzanne.

'Is that what this is about? Is that what you think I did? What about what you took from me? You took my childhood, then you destroyed my teenage years, and as if that wasn't enough you took my love, which was the one thing I had that was truly mine. Because believe it or not when I was little I *did* love you, and Emily made sure I carried on loving you too, right up to the end. Do you know why I call myself Prescott instead of Timpson? It's because *I* chose it. I wanted to share a surname with the woman who *really* cared for me. But because I was too wrapped up with you I never told her how I felt.'

Suzanne's voice dropped and softened a little as she continued, a note of regret in her tone. 'You know, when I was little I thought you were the most fun, the most glamorous mother anyone could ever have. You had exciting friends and did wonderful things. It didn't matter that I wasn't included because I shared it all with you in my head. But you even took that away from me. So don't you dare sit there and accuse *me* of stealing. I don't think I stole anything from you. You agreed, you signed the papers. It isn't my fault that you were too stupid to bother to check what was going on.

'When that agreement was drawn up – which if I remember rightly you pounced on with great delight – I designed it to give you a chance, but you were so busy being Lady Muck that you couldn't see where it might lead. It was presented to you on a silver platter under your own bloody nose and you still couldn't see it, could you? Every time we brought out more shares, every time the company grew you were given exactly the same opportunity to be a part of it but you always turned it down. So don't you dare blame me for the fact that by the time you finally laid your hands on Howard's stuff you only got a handful of shares. A lot happened to the business in those seven years because I made damn sure it did. And we moved on while you sat and rotted and waited and wondered about your precious husband. Well, maybe it's time you heard the truth about him. About what really happened.'

'God, you make me sick!' Maggie spat back, interrupting Suzanne's vehement flow. 'Don't you think I didn't *know* he had affairs left, right and centre? But it was me he came home to and that's what mattered.' She tried to hold her head up proudly but her arthritis wouldn't allow her the dignity of the gesture and she succeeded only in looking pathetic.

Suzanne stood up and in two strides was across the room. She stood in front of Maggie who had bent her stiff neck back as far as it would go to look up at her. She seemed to cower as Suzanne carried on talking.

'No it wasn't. All that ever mattered to Howard was the chase. Once he got what he was after he got bored. Whether it was women or a business deal. Why do you think he went through so many secretaries before I came along? Because they let themselves be caught too soon and then he discarded them. Threw them out like rubbish and that, my darling mother, is exactly what he did with you. I did it differently, I made sure I was worth more to him than just sex. Any slut could give him that, and he had you on tap waiting for him at home, didn't he? No, I waited until he was panting for it. I'm sure you had more sense than to let him catch *you* too soon but letting him catch you at all was a mistake. You let him catch you and then he got bored. Bored, *bored,* BORED!'

Suzanne had been pacing the room as she spoke but was now standing behind Maggie. She grabbed hold of the handles of the wheelchair. As she finished talking she leaned forward and yelled her final comments in Maggie's ear. She was pressing down on the handles with such force that her knuckles were white. The front wheels lifted off the floor and Maggie tried to raise her hands to her ears, to block out the raised voice and the words of scorn it was throwing at her, but failed, getting only half way.

Suzanne's last words had finally got to her. That Howard played around she could accept. That he treated her as no better than one of his petty little business deals, or worse, the other women he slept with, using and dumping them as he went along, was something she didn't want to hear. She deflated like a balloon.

'Annie,' she cried. 'Please don't.'

It was hearing herself called Annie, that long forgotten nickname of her childhood, that made something snap inside the woman who had created Suzanne Prescott thirty odd years ago. A haze swam over her vision until she felt as if she were looking through a red mist. Her heart began to beat faster. She could feel it pounding in her chest, in her throat and thundering in her ears as an incredible sense of outrage surged through her. Not knowing what she was doing she let go of the handles so the front of the wheelchair bounced back to hit the floor. Maggie was tossed forward and then backwards.

Still standing behind her Suzanne raised her hands alongside Maggie's face, dashing her mother's frail fingers out of the way with a sweep of her own arms before placing one hand on the back of her head and the other under her chin. Using all the force she could she jerked Maggie's head round violently to face her as she screamed at her, '*No one, but no one calls me Annie. Do you hear me*?'

There was a sickening crack as she twisted Maggie's neck. For a split second Suzanne could see terror in the old woman's eyes, instantly followed by the same staring look of death she had seen on Howard's face all those years before.

The crack wasn't a loud noise but, combined with Maggie's staring eyes, slightly open mouth and the sighing rattle at the back of her throat as the last her breath was exhaled, it was enough.

The mist in front of Suzanne's eyes began to evaporate until everything was back in focus again. The only sound was the ticking of the clock as she looked down at the now limp figure she was still supporting in her hands. She let go of Maggie and her body slumped in the wheelchair, head dangling at an odd angle on its broken arthritic neck. Suzanne stepped back. She hadn't realised how forceful she had been. All she had wanted to do was shut Maggie up, to stop her bringing back the images from the past.

Frantically she looked round the room. Apart from her bag and gloves on the sofa there was no sign she had been there. She grabbed them and ran towards the front door, stopping to compose herself before opening it. She made sure she left Maggie's door as she'd found it, slightly ajar behind her, and called out loudly, 'Bye, Maggie,' before walking down the hall and into the car park.

She felt an odd mixture of exhilaration and disbelief as she turned on the engine and steered the car out on to the main road. The further away she got the calmer she felt. It was if someone had taken a huge weight off her shoulders. For the first time that she could remember she felt free. It wasn't until much later that the full impact of what she had done hit her.

As she drove away a small figure peeped out from a corner in the hallway. Suzanne had been so determined to get to her car and escape that she gave only a cursory glance to check no one had seen her. Edna's usual smiling face wore a worried expression as she watched the younger woman stride down the hall and out of the front door. The old woman was wearing her usual assortment of clothes, necklaces and bracelets which jangled a little as she stepped into the open. Holding up her skirts she half tip-toed and half danced towards Maggie's door. She nudged it with her fingertips as she had done a few minutes before when she heard the sound of raised voices coming from the flat. It hadn't been shut last time and this time it also responded when she pushed it. She glanced round cautiously before going inside.

'Maggie, Maggie, Maggie,' she sang quietly to herself. Edna knew

Maggie was in the living room because that was where she had been when that nasty lady was shouting at her but nevertheless she made her way down towards the bedroom. She had seen Maggie's make-up laid out neatly on her dressing table on previous occasions when she had strolled into the flat. A slap across her fingers always stopped her from touching it but now she had the chance to see what was there she wasn't going to waste it. Enthralled she carefully helped herself to a red lipstick and wound it up to apply it to her mouth. She pouted at her reflection and then wound it up a bit further to use it to paint two round circles on her cheeks. She giggled happily at her image and danced back down the hall until she saw Maggie's wheelchair through the gap in the living-room door. Now she remembered.

The nasty lady had shouted at Maggie. Poor Maggie. It wasn't nice to be shouted at. She had held her head and that wasn't nice either. Poor Maggie.

'Maggie, Maggie, Maggie,' she sang again as she danced into the room, holding her skirts up and swishing them round in time with her song. She stopped by the chair but Maggie didn't say anything. Not even 'Go away' as she usually did. Edna dropped her skirts and put her head on one side as she considered Maggie, who was sitting in a funny way. She tried to prop her up by putting both her hands under her shoulders to shove her upright. She didn't respond. She put her hand under her chin and with the flat of her palm clumsily raised her head. 'Mag-gie,' she sang in a long drawn-out note. Maggie stared at her, wide-eyed and unblinking. Edna didn't like it and let go of Maggie's head which fell forwards on to her chest. That was what it had done when the lady had stood up. That was when she had run away to hide. She didn't want to go back to her flat. Not yet. Not if Maggie wasn't well. Poor Maggie. She looked round the living room to find Maggie's alarm bell. Edna knew Maggie must have one as all the flats at The Warren were fitted with them.

It usually hung over the arm of Maggie's wheelchair but in the scuffle with Suzanne it had been dislodged and the cable now snaked its way across the carpet. Edna bent down and picked it up, pushing the button hard. She waited a moment, but there was no reply. She was about to push the button again when the phone rang, making her jump. She dropped the cable and went to stand over the phone, looking at it as it rang. The answer machine cut in, and she heard a man's voice. Feeling confused, she decide that maybe it would be best to leave before she was found there and got in trouble. She danced her way out of Maggie's flat.

Jo rolled over in bed and rearranged the pillows trying to get comfortable. The clock radio said it was 3.42. She wanted Alan but it would be too easy to rely on him. This was *her* problem. Alan had tried to make her see she wasn't responsible but no matter what he said she couldn't help feeling that things might have been different if she and Maggie hadn't had the argument. A part of her knew she was being silly, but somehow Jo found it easier to cope with Maggie's death if she blamed herself. The image of her mother sitting in her own living room, helpless in a wheelchair while someone strangled her was too much to think about. *Oh, Maggie*, she thought, *There was so much about you I didn't know. Didn't understand. I wonder if Howard hadn't died when he did whether we might at least have been friends?*

The question was still running through her head when she and Alan arrived to start clearing the flat. Jo paused for a moment before going inside, putting down the cardboard boxes ready to fill them up as they went through Maggie's possessions. It felt odd not hearing her mother's querulous voice drifting out from the living room, or the whirr of her chair's engine. The wheelchair now sat forlornly in the hallway, a blanket chucked over it. Alan put a gentle hand on her shoulder, giving it a squeeze. 'Where do you want to start?'

'I don't know.' She looked around, feeling lost. 'Maybe the living room? It's less personal somehow.'

It still took a bit of time to get going but by mid afternoon most of the two old heavy sideboards had been cleared and they had a better idea of what was around in the way of ornaments and books. To Jo's amazement, not only had Maggie made a will, but she had left everything to to her. However, Maggie's solicitor had warned Jo that she might be surprised at how much her mother's estate was worth and had suggested she made a list of everything, in case it had to go to probate. Jo dictated the list to Alan, keeping a record for the solicitors so it could be sorted out.

'Ready to call it a day?' Alan stretched, arching his back. He felt grimy and hot.

'Let's just do the chest of drawers and then that's all the big stuff in here done.' She walked over to a low chest which stood against the wall. 'That's odd.' She seemed puzzled. 'There are a couple of messages on the answer machine.' Automatically she reached out and pressed replay. The machine hissed a little and then a man's voice spoke.

'Look, this is gettin' silly. You know you can stop this before it goes further. All you have to do is get her to play ball. You're her mother. She'll listen to you.'

'What's all that about?' Alan asked. Jo shrugged. Alan had walked across the room and they both stood looking at the machine, as if by staring at it they would get an answer.

'Play it again.'

Jo did so but still it meant nothing. She looked at Alan, biting her lower lip, unable to ask the question that had formed itself in her mind. The clock ticked, filling the silence. Finally Jo spoke. 'Do you think that's who killed her?'

It was Alan's turn to shrug. 'Don't know. Try using last number ID.'

She dialled the number but wasn't surprised when the tinny voice said, 'You were called today at 10.23. The caller withheld their number.' She replaced the receiver. 'I don't like this, Alan. I don't know what it means, but I don't like it. Why on earth would anyone be threatening Maggie because of something I'm doing?'

'I don't know. Play it again.'

'Why?'

'There's something about that voice . . .' They listened to the tape for the third time. Alan shook his head, 'I feel I know the voice but I can't place it. It's . . . No, it's almost there but I'm not sure.'

'For God's sake, Alan, *think*. It's important, whoever it is. Here, listen to it one more time.' For the fourth time the man's voice played back to them but still Alan couldn't identify it, although the nagging feeling that he knew it persisted.

'Maybe it'll come to me.' They couldn't face clearing anything more. Feeling very subdued they left. Alan put the tape in his jacket pocket so they could hand it over to the police but even though they talked about it on the way back to Hampstead they somehow both forgot they had it with them and it stayed there for another week.

Jo and her crew weren't the only ones counting the days till the end of the exhibition. This year Suzanne was also pleased to be leaving the Pimlico Centre. She felt that once she was no longer on site he wouldn't be able to get at her so easily. The further away they all got from the discovery of Howard's body the easier it would be to stand up to him. Thirty years she had been paying him and that, she had decided, was enough. With Howard safely buried she would make sure it finally stopped. What he did after they had all packed up and gone back to their own office she didn't care. Of course, with Maggie dead and buried the problem had also stopped being an issue and his hold on her had loosened dramatically. Thirty years was a long time to be paying for an accident.

But what about Maggie? Was that an accident too? She could still feel the papery skin beneath her fingertips. Hear the sounds as her neck broke and the last breath gurgled out of her. She put her hands over her ears trying to block out the noises that echoed inside her.

Howard had been one thing, but this . . . this was different. This was something she had actually done, not just witnessed. Suzanne jumped as her phone rang and she answered it quickly. It was Julia, reminding her that she was due to record her final interview with Jo. She had completely forgotten about it.

Before they had started filming, and long before Howard's body had been discovered, they had agreed that when the show was over she would talk about it – her perceptions of how that year's show had gone and her plans for next year's Home Maker Exhibition. But that had been then. Before finding Howard. Before Maggie died. Before he had started turning up the heat, making trouble at the show.

Suzanne hesitated for a moment, playing with the idea of telling Julia she couldn't do it, but she dismissed it almost immediately. Realistically she knew she would just be putting it off. It would have to be done at some time.

My God! What's happening to me? I never used to be a coward. In the past I could face things. I would have made things work out no matter what happened. And I coped. I wouldn't be here now if I couldn't have coped, would I? Suzanne took a deep breath as she gathered her thoughts, suddenly feeling not just tired but bone-achingly weary. 'Give me five minutes,' she called to Julia. Out came the make-up bag and she repaired her face, hoping she would be able to hide her feelings. Her eyes stared back at her from her compact. *I can't lose it now, I can't!* she warned herself before fixing her face into the expected smile to greet the now familiar crew.

As usual, it wasn't as bad as she had expected. What did shake her, though, was how jaded Jo looked. She wanted to reach out and give her a hug. To tell her she had nothing to be afraid of, that the horrors were over. But she couldn't. To do that she would have to explain more. Tell Jo how she knew it was at an end, which was impossible.

As the camera rolled Jo felt something was missing in the way she was interviewing Suzanne. She hoped it wouldn't show. Before when she and Suzanne had talked on film there had been a warmth, a rapport. Now she felt as if she were removed from her. The coolness that everyone said was so much a part of Suzanne Prescott had reappeared. Maybe it was just that they were coming to the end of their time together and that Suzanne didn't want to encourage friendship beyond the confines of the film? Jo was too drained to think about it properly, but she ached for the woman she had sat with at Ragdale Hall, cosy in their dressing gowns as they talked about their feelings. It all seemed so long ago.

When the rest of the crew had packed up and left the office Suzanne finally seemed to relax a little. 'Well, Jo, almost done. I'm sorry things turned out the way they have. I'm going to miss having you around.'

Suzanne had let the gentler version of herself resurface and she seemed genuinely sorry about all that had happened. But Jo just shrugged, too tired and wrapped up in her own problems to bother with Suzanne's change of mood. 'The show's been fine. It's other things that have been so . . .' she trailed off, unable to find the right word.

'I know.' Suzanne sounded odd. 'I wish it hadn't happened, *any* of it.' Jo glanced up from where she was kneeling on the floor putting away the last bits of equipment. Admittedly it wasn't her job to tidy up but she knew that as usual Suzanne would want them out of her office as quickly as possible. Was she imagining it or was Suzanne apologising for something?

Suzanne stood and walked over to the huge windows. There was something reassuring about the river view. God, she was tired. *Thirty years,* she said to herself, *and for what? To hurt a sister who doesn't know I'm even related and kill a mother who despised us both. Oh, Jo, I am sorry, truly I am.*

'Well, Suzanne, that's it as far as you're concerned. Alan's pencilled a couple of dates for you to view the rough cut, so I'll let you know nearer the time which one we're going for but . . . er . . . thank you for . . . well, for everything.' She held out her hand, hoping Suzanne would understand that by everything she included the friendship. Suzanne took it and much to her amazement she reached forward and kissed her cheek with a real warmth that made Jo feel suddenly shy.

'You're welcome. Please stay in touch if you can bear it?' She searched Jo's face eagerly and the tone of her voice made her sounded as if she were begging.

'Of course I can.' Jo held the older woman's hand between hers and then, suddenly embarrassed by Suzanne's uncharacteristic show of emotion, changed the subject. 'Anyway, we'll be around for a while yet, to film the break-down.' Suzanne caught her discomfort and withdrew her hand, turning it over to look at her watch. Jo was grateful for the hint and escaped back on to the exhibition floor.

The show might be in its final week but it was still busy and Jo discovered at four on the last day that it got even busier as the bargain hunters arrived. They knew that some exhibitors reduced the prices of the stock on their stands, preferring to sell it cheap rather than take it back to their warehouses. Visitors staggered out into the evening light weighed down by boxes and bags and parcels.

At a quarter to six Gordon went to the tannoy. 'Ladies and gentlemen, the exhibition will be closing in fifteen minutes. I repeat, the exhibition will be closing in fifteen minutes.' There was a last-minute flurry in the exhibition halls and even though they were meant to wait until the show had closed some of the smaller stands in the Gadget Gallery began boxing up stock, wanting to get out as quickly as possible.

At six o'clock on the dot Gordon's voice again rang out across the exhibition halls. 'Ladies and gentlemen, it is now six o'clock and the Home Maker Exhibition is closed.' The rest of his announcement was lost in the cheers and applause that burst from the exhibitors. It may have been one of the best shows ever but six weeks at the Pimlico Centre was a long time in anyone's book. They had had enough.

It was only once the doors had closed for the final time that Jo understood why the smaller stands had begun packing up early. If she thought the build-up, which had been gradual, was chaotic, the break-down was worse because all the activity happened at once.

Large articulated lorries had queued with small vans along Millbank and Horseferry Road waiting to go in and collect stock. By five past six the first of the floor tiles had been lifted ready for the small vans to drive on-site to be loaded up. Small lorries were driven into the halls and filled, stands dismantled, electric supplies unplugged, cabling recoiled on to large reels and everywhere people were folding, packing and shoving things into crates. Once again the radios crackled. This time they linked Gordon with not only the sales team (all of whom were on the floor herding up the last visitors and getting them out of the building as quickly as possible), but also the traffic office and security staff.

It was going to be a long night.

The press office had also been packed up but that task was one of the easiest ones. Some exhibitors claimed back their press leaflets and material, and what was left was just dumped in the recycling bins. By nine it was empty and even Alan had gone home, knowing he would be in the way. However, the office was still in use. The film crew needed a base in the building as the chaos of break-down spilled outside, making getting in and out of their Portacabin nigh on impossible. Coffee bubbled away and a steady supply of bacon sandwiches was brought in by the location caterers. There had been enough problems getting the crew to work overnight for the same money without risking trouble because they hadn't been fed.

By one the next morning the halls were already comparatively bare. Most of the stands had been stripped and all that was left were the upright support posts and fascia boards of the shell scheme that had created the exhibitors' stands. They would stay where they were until the PimEx Services crew came to finish dismantling them once the largest of the trucks had finally rumbled out through the loading doors. Drivers sat patiently in their cabs. Some read newspapers, some put their feet up on the dashboard to get forty winks while they waited for their turn to collect their consignment.

The trouble began at about four-thirty.

A twenty-four wheeler was half way through the gates, shuffling backwards and forwards to maneouvre into the forecourt. A large wire storage cage rolled across in front of the truck, suddenly appearing from the shadows of the building on the left. Automatically the driver slammed on his brakes. If the cage had got trapped underneath the wheels it would have done some serious damage. Nevertheless it still became slightly wedged under his front bumper so swearing and cursing the driver climbed down; not only to move it but to have a go at the guard in the traffic office for not doing his job. The other drivers joined in and it began to get nasty. The traffic controllers didn't wait but quickly put a call out for security to come and help sort it out.

In the hubbub it was easy for him to slip unseen between the cab and the trailer. It only took him a couple of minutes to get the knife out and cut through the brake cables. As soon as he had managed to pierce the first one the pressure changed instantly inside them. They hissed as the air came out of first one and then another. He sliced away at the inch-thick cables, at the same time listening keenly to the row going on in front of the cab.

'All right, all right!' yelled the driver, his voice coming closer as he went back to his cab. The door opened and the still furious man clambered back into the cabin. Timing it carefully, he ducked out from behind the cab as its door slammed shut. He didn't hang around to see what happened. It was enough to know that with punctured air brakes that truck would be going nowhere, not for several hours at least. And if that wasn't going anywhere neither was the rest of the traffic lined up round the area.

Once again Gordon was flung into the midst of it. This time he not only had to deal with tired and irate exhibitors, furious that they couldn't get their goods out because their vehicles were stuck in the ensuing traffic jam, but also with one very angry driver. 'I'm telling you them cables was cut. It's sabotage, that's what it is. It happened here, as part of this fucking circus, so it's your fault. You want it moved, you get them out to fix it. And another thing. I'll be running late on this job and I'll miss the ferry to France so I'm going to run late on the next job too. If I don't deliver on time I don't get paid, so I'm looking to you lot to compensate me.'

Here we go again! Is it really worth it just to be able to retire in comfort? Gordon wondered, adding extra hours to his time sheet as he let his tiredness spill over into a fully fledged yelling match. To hell with Suzanne's rule about treating everyone decently, including the contractors. This man was a complete arsehole if he really thought Gordon wanted to spend any longer at the Pimlico Centre than was absolutely necessary.

As that row rumbled on through what was left of the night Jo made sure her cameras were still rolling. She wasn't too pleased that the truck was stuck in the main gates, air brakes jammed on, unable to move, as it held things up for her and the rest of the crew. She needed to get the shots of the exhibition halls filled with huge trucks as everything was packed away inside them until the halls were finally empty. She knew what she wanted her last shot to be. The final truck pulling out into the early morning light leaving a great emptiness behind it. At this rate the sun would be high in the sky and the eeriness she wanted to capture would be ruined. The crew was feeling as edgy as Jo, hanging around waiting for things to happen. She went over to Tony.

'Don't say a bloody word,' she warned him as he opened his mouth to speak. 'I'm as hacked off as you are about this but what can I do? You and the lads go and put your feet up. Apparently it's going to take at least another couple of hours before they can get that thing fixed and moving. Silly to hang around. I'll give a yell when we can start again.'

Gratefully they went to curl up on the banquettes in the canteen that was still open and snatch some sleep. Jo rubbed her neck. She could do with some sleep herself and even though the stuck truck meant she could now go over to the Portacabin she decided to stay in the building. *Alan won't mind if I use his office*, she thought as wearily she made her way up there, automatically calling it his though he had officially vacated it the night before. It didn't look much like a press office any more. Boxes were stacked by the door ready to be collected and taken back to Hammersmith the next morning. The display boards covered in numerous press cuttings had been folded back into their carrying cases. Never mind, the sofa was still there. It looked comfortable and inviting. She'd at least be able to have a lie down. She was sure she wouldn't sleep, but just closing her eyes would be nice.

The radio charger unit flickered with little green lights that told her the radios sitting in it were fully charged up. They should have been returned to the organisers' office but as they were still there she took one out of the unit and turned it on, adjusting its volume so she could hear it as it sat on the table next to her. She lay down, pulling her jacket across her shoulders, listening to the hum of noise floating up the now open stairways from the halls and the disjointed voices on the radio, waiting to hear that the lorry had moved. Despite her doubts about sleep she began to drift off.

Suddenly something made her wake up with a jolt. She looked at her watch. *Bloody hell! I've been asleep for two hours.* She rubbed the grit from her eyes and shook the jacket off. What was it that had made her wake so suddenly? She looked round the room. Everything was as it should be. The sofa was not as comfortable as it seemed and even lying on it for that short space of time had made her begin to feel stiff. She rubbed her back and stretched. The radio crackled as she drew her arms back. That was it! That's what had woken her up. She grabbed the radio, looking at it like an idiot. That voice, she knew that voice, but who was it? She listened as instructions were called back and forth between security, traffic and organisers. Which one? Which one?

Her throat felt dry as she stumbled across the office to the phone, hoping it was still connected. To her relief she heard the dialling tone and with an unsteady finger punched out Alan's number, not caring that he would be asleep. 'Alan. It's me. I know I've woken you up but I need you. I need you here, now.' She felt frightened. It was partly lack of sleep but mainly genuine fear.

'What?' It was clear from Alan's tone that Jo had woken him from a very deep sleep indeed. 'What time is it?'

'I don't know, about six. But never mind that. I'm still at the Pim Centre. There's been another problem but that's not it. Alan, just get here!'

On hearing there had been more difficulties Alan managed to pull himself together. 'Jo, calm down. Take a deep breath and try again. You're not making any sense. What's going on?' He was now wide awake, terrified that something had happened to her. As she spoke in a loud whisper he was already getting dressed, pulling clothes on with one hand. Quickly Jo told him about the truck and the delay it was causing. She told him about having a sleep and how something had woken her up. 'Alan, it was the radio. A voice on the radio. I don't know who it is, there are so many conversations going on between everyone.'

'You're losing me again.'

'You're not bloody listening! I'm trying to tell you. One of the voices is the same as the one on that tape we took from Maggie's. I'm sure it is. Alan, we never took it to the police. Find it and please get down here as fast as you can. Whatever this is all about is tied up with *here*. Just hurry.'

Alan did as he was told. In the short time he had known Jo he had come to appreciate that she was basically a capable woman who could withstand an awful lot. To hear her this frightened scared him too. He drove like an idiot, not caring that the speed cameras on the A40 flashed him three times as he raced along it at over seventy. He arrived just as they finally got the large truck moving and came running into the office where Jo was pacing up and down, radio in her hand.

'Sorry, it took me a while to find the tape,' Alan gasped, having run up the stairs. 'Put it on the Walkman and you listen to that. Let me have the radio.' As Jo handed him the radio, their hands brushed. Hers felt like ice. He held an arm out and gratefully Jo crawled into it, holding on to him as he concentrated on the exchanges on the radio while she put on the headphones and listened to the hiss of the answer machine and the voice they had heard at Maggie's.

Together in the growing light of the office they listened first to the answer-machine tape and then the radio as the trucks outside gradually started moving again. Messages crackled back and forth on the radio as security passes and consignment notes were checked, loading dockets and collection notes approved. The traffic office directed the trucks to the various loading doors and then called ahead to security to let them know who was coming in. Slowly but surely they eliminated the voices, finally calling the police at eight-thirty.

The break-down continued.

PART FOUR

Epilogue

Dinah Deadman was in her element. She loved press parties. They gave her a chance to network and it was a rare event when she didn't leave without promising to call someone the next day to discuss a project. A project that usually went into production. That was how *Women in Focus* had started, at a press launch. It was meeting Helena Kennedy that had started that one and if anyone had told her that the best in the series would be the programme on Suzanne Prescott she would have laughed in their face. It had only ever been intended as a filler – the one to make the series up to the half-dozen that the network demanded.

She looked round the room, checking not only who was there but also that everyone's glasses were full and people were enjoying themselves. The secret of a good press launch was to make people feel as if they were at a party. That way they would remember it and would come to the next one. Of course, this preview was different. There was a feeling of expectation as the press knew they would be seeing something special. Not everyone got to film a woman whose story ended up being as enthralling as Suzanne Prescott's. At that moment the toastmaster raised his voice and invited everyone to go through into the BAFTA viewing theatre.

The lights darkened and for the next hour they sat engrossed as the story of Suzanne Prescott and the previous year's Home Maker Exhibition was told. The women's page editors related to the elegant woman they saw at the beginning of the film, responding to her obvious power, but squirmed uncomfortably by the end when they saw how that had been stripped away.

Suzanne had become a shell of herself; the tough, controlled exterior had disintegrated. Through a series of carefully selected still photographs taken from the footage Tony had shot on that final morning at the Pimlico Centre they watched her crumble in front of their eyes. They saw all too clearly how both her hatred and love for her mother had kept her going. They saw how without it Suzanne Prescott had nothing – not even the security of being the chief executive of the biggest consumer exhibition company in Europe. It made them feel uncomfortable, made them consider their own motives and ambitions. A lot of mothers and siblings received unexpected phone calls that night as the programme prompted the preview audience to examine their own family relationships too – especially when it was revealed that the film's director was Suzanne's half sister.

Watching herself on the screen Jo felt uncomfortable, but Alan's hand holding hers reassured her. She had argued long and hard with Dinah when her boss had first said she wanted to interview her, to include her in the documentary. Jo had resisted, but as a film-maker she knew it was what the revised storyboard needed. Reluctantly she had agreed, on the understanding that she would still have final control. In the end it had been the best thing that could have happened to her. The experience of talking about her parents, about all that had happened, had a soothing effect on her and as a result the finished documentary had a surprising finesse and delicacy.

A few people nearby turned to look at her in what they thought was a surreptitious way. They wanted to see her reaction as she watched herself on the screen but Jo had expected that and, knowing what was coming, was easily able to keep her eyes firmly forward. 'Chin up!' whispered Alan in her ear and she smiled in the dark, giving his hand a squeeze. She knew the audience weren't sure how to react to the powerful businesswoman on the screen and she couldn't help feeling amused when she felt the mood shift as the film pulled them back into safe territory.

They knew they were allowed to dislike the old man who, in their eyes, had magnified Suzanne's unhappiness. If Cyril had been a nicer man, none of it would have happened. He wouldn't have blackmailed her for all those years. There was something particularly nasty about blackmail. No one had felt anything but loathing for Cyril as he sat there, picking tobacco out of his teeth and talking about 'being in the right place at the right time'. If he had shown one bit of regret it might have been different.

'Pity about that tape, though. Careless that was. Mind you, it helped doin' what I did. You see,' he explained to the camera, 'no one actually sees you. They sees the uniform but not you. It's handy. As far as that lot was concerned I was just old Cyril. Silly old codger sitting out his working years in the traffic office, waitin' for his pension. Shows you can't trust appearances, don't it? Still, took 'em over thirty years to catch up with me, didn't it?' The lingering shot of his face clearly showed his pride in what he thought of as a job well done. That he didn't care about the people involved was obvious. The audience's feeling of revulsion grew as they watched him and if, by the end of the hour, they weren't exactly feeling sympathy for Suzanne, unable as they were to condone Maggie's manslaughter, they at least felt remorse at the waste of her talents.

After the screening people went up to Jo, wanting to congratulate her on an excellent directorial debut but uncertain as what to say about the subject matter, knowing how close to her it was. It was a difficult situation but one that Jo handled well, especially when someone had the wit to ask her what she would be working on next. Jo looked at Dinah who was standing next to her. She gave her a slight nod.

'Well,' she began, still going for her non-existent strand of hair, 'we're going to look at the invisible people. The people we see all the time but, for whatever reason, don't actually look at. I'm not talking about down-and-outs but people like little old Edna.' She looked round the group to check they knew who she meant. They smiled as they remembered the old dear who had happily danced and sang about Suzanna for them on the screen. 'Well, just because she was old and a bit senile we all ignored her. Oh, I don't mean we were unkind,' she added hurriedly. 'It's just that we now know she saw what happened to . . .' Jo swallowed. '. . . to my mother. She actually saw Suzanne but because we had put her on the mental rubbish tip we didn't listen. Edna knew exactly what had happened but just couldn't tell us normally. When I think of the number of times she sang about Suzanna to me. It makes me . . . she didn't deserve to be ignored like that.' Jo fell quiet, remembering briefly what had happened when they had visited The Warren. How Edna had been so very afraid of Suzanne.

It was listening to the messages being called from the traffic office during break-down that had given them Cyril's identity. The police had been called and, although doubtful at first, and angry not to have been given the tape earlier had finally agreed that, yes, there was a similarity between the voice on the tape and the one on the radio. As Cyril was about to go off duty the police confronted him and he crumbled, telling them everything he knew about Suzanne and Howard. By now DCI Thomas had again been called in and, in a chase that made him think of a TV cop show, he dashed through the Pimlico Centre (which now resembled a building site), catching up with Suzanne as, for the last time that year, she handed in her car park pass. As she turned to go she saw Cyril, handcuffed, being led away by two other policemen.

Tony, who had been outside the building recording the mayhem that the broken-down lorry had caused was, yet again, on hand with his camera. Realising that something major was going on he focused on Suzanne as she was leaving and caught the look on her face as she saw Cyril. He let the camera pan over her as her legs gave way and she stumbled, to be caught by DCI Thomas before she hit the ground. For a split second they looked at each other. DCI Thomas had a glint in his eye that came from catching a suspect. In contrast Suzanne's eyes were dark with fear. It was as if she knew she had finally reached the end. Ashen white, she let herself be led away.

Hard as she tried Jo could not get a copy of the tape that contained

Suzanne's confession. The police refused to release it. Instead, after the trial and conviction and using her new-found status as a relative, Jo was allowed to interview Suzanne one last time. A photographer went with her to Holloway and it was his photographs that made so many of the preview audience feel uncomfortable. Without make-up and her expensive suits Suzanne looked little more than any other world-weary middle-aged woman.

At first Jo thought she had made a mistake, that Suzanne would refuse to speak to her, but she was wrong. After thirty years of lying Suzanne almost gratefully talked to Jo. She seemed to forget that the tape recorder was there and, despite their austere surroundings, the tone of the conversation made Jo feel as if she were back at Ragdale with Suzanne sharing the comfortable cosiness that had grown between them during those few days.

Learning that Suzanne was her half sister had made Jo understand why she had felt such a closeness to the older woman. Comments she had made also began to make sense and, although initially nervous about how she would feel when she met Suzanne again, she needn't have worried. When Suzanne was escorted in by the warden the two women looked in silence at each other and then moved across the small, stark interview room to meet in a hug. Jo knew she should hate Suzanne for all the misery she had caused in her life but all she felt was an incredible sadness for the loneliness that had made her sister do all that she had. She understood only too well how Maggie had pushed Suzanne into behaving the way she did and felt that if anyone was to blame for what had happened it was Maggie herself. If she had been a less selfish person, or a better mother, then maybe, just maybe she would still be alive. And who knew where Howard might have been?

Suzanne obviously felt the same warmth towards this newly discovered younger sister and, in the hope of making Jo understand, she willingly spoke of what had happened that night back in 1966 between herself and Howard, and more recently between herself and Maggie. The powerful mixture of love and hate that had spurred her on over the years poured from her until she finally stopped and slumped at the shabby table. The determination that had kept her going for all those years had been squeezed out of her. The last words Jo got on tape became the last words of the programme.

'Jo, I'm sorry. I'm so very sorry'.

All that Jo had to do was add the final caption over the photographs. '*Cyril Hillman is currently serving five years for blackmail*' FREEZE-FRAME. PICTURE OF SUZANNE. CAPTION BOARD. '*Suzanne Prescott is serving twenty-five years on charges of manslaughter and being an accessory after the crime.*' It was as she sat in the editing suite applying these finishing touches that, with a feeling like cold water being thrown over her, Jo had realised what it was that Edna had been trying to say to them.

Later that same day Jo had made a point of going to The Warren, not to finish clearing Maggie's things but to see Edna. The old woman had been surprised when Jo knocked on her door but was delighted by the bag of ribbons and necklaces Jo took with her as an apology. She asked Edna questions and slowly she pieced together the events surrounding Maggie's death. As she listened, Jo felt that the least she could do would be to give Edna the chance to tell everyone what had happened. Quickly she had set up an interview and edited it into the finished programme. Edna loved it. She wore even more bright beads, shawls, feathers and lace than usual as she seemed to appreciate something special was happening. In her own mixture of mime and song she told the audience what she had seen.

Mentally Jo shook herself and continued speaking. 'So that's our next project, publicly invisible people.' They scribbled away in their notebooks, asked a few more questions, ate a few more canapés and drank one more glass of champagne before eventually the last one left. Their press packs were clutched under their arms but the packs' contents were academic – they were all ready to write glowing reviews when the programme was finally screened two days later on television in a prime-time slot.

The viewing public's appetite for the documentary had been whetted by the highly publicised court case, and by the grainy pictures of Howard's body released to the press by the police and eagerly seized upon by the tabloids. When the viewing figures for that week were released they showed that the programme had made it to the number four slot, being beaten only by the soaps.

Dinah grinned at Jo as she went to call the office to report on how it had all gone. 'Well done.' Jo grinned back – that was praise indeed from Dinah. She sank into one of the armchairs by the window and looked out at the traffic crawling up Piccadilly. A waiter came over and offered her a large glass of orange juice, which she took gratefully, making sure she looked at the waiter to thank him properly.

'I'm so proud of you.' Alan sat down beside her. 'But you promised me an answer when the screening was over. So how about it?' He searched her face eagerly. The worried look had gone, to be replaced by an open, contented expression. If he had his way he would have grabbed her there and then and made love to her in the middle of the BAFTA lounge. Over the last year Alan had got to know Jo much better and although not yet inseparable they had spent a lot of time together. Jo put her glass down on the table between them and leaned over to take his hands gently in hers.

Alan watched her as she gathered her thoughts together. He stopped himself from saying anything more, hoping Jo would understand how much she meant to him. And how much he understood what she wanted in terms of her own space and independence. But he also knew she had to understand that for herself. After all those years of seeing herself through the eyes of other people instead of deciding who *she* thought she was, he knew that this decision had to come from her, and her alone.

Still Jo struggled with her answer. She could see the hope written all over Alan's face but she appreciated the fact that the choice was being left to her. She respected him for his restraint. Ever since he had first suggested they moved in together he had allowed her to set the timetable, and apart from his question now he hadn't nagged at her for a response. To feel part of a relationship where she was an equal whose feelings were considered important was unlike anything she had ever known before. Jo lowered her eyes from his to gaze at their intertwined fingers. It was so difficult to know how to answer him, to say the right thing.

After four years with Simon it had taken her a bit of time to get used to having Alan as her partner. He was so different. The way he wasn't afraid to show or voice his feelings for her while at the same time knowing just when to pull back, when to give her a shove to get her to stand on her own two feet. He knew when to tell her off but how to do it in such a way that she didn't feel belittled. He had taught her so much about self-esteem that they were even able to have the odd row without her feeling threatened by it. Through Alan she had learned to value herself and to be her own person. Introductions to his parents and sisters had shown her what life with a real family could be like, and she knew it was something she wanted.

But would moving in with Alan take all that away from her again? Wouldn't she just be repeating her old pattern, going from Howard's wonderful daughter, to Maggie's disappointing daughter to Simon's doormat fiancée before finally becoming Alan's partner? Wouldn't she just be going back to being someone who only had identity through belonging to someone else? Would she stop being this new person she had discovered in herself, the person she had struggled for so long to find?

Jo looked at Alan again as the thoughts ran round her head *Living with someone doesn't stop you being you, does it?* she told herself, trying to pull her doubts together. *After all, Alan would also be referred to as my partner, wouldn't he? It had happened that day – 'This is Alan Waterman, he's Jo Edwardes' other half'. Poor Alan, they didn't care that he was the new managing director of Exhibitions International. He was just 'Jo Edwardes' other half' . . . Is that what is important?*' she wondered. '*Being half of something, a half that becomes a whole when put with its counterpart? . . . Maybe that's what we are, two bits of the same thing. But whatever it is I can't deny I do feel whole with you, Alan. And I still feel like me.*

Suddenly she knew her answer. She let go of Alan's hands and leaned back in her chair, clasping her hands behind her head. Alan looked at her warily, not sure what her answer was going to be.

'You know what I'm going to say, don't you?' Jo said, flirting with him. Alan raised an eyebrow at her, a little uncertainly. A huge grin split Jo's face and she laughed. Being with Alan was so good.

'That's all right then,' he replied as he leaned across the table to kiss Jo soundly.